Golden Boughs
& Poisoned Roots

Golden Boughs & Poisoned Roots by Sandra Patterson-Slaydon ©2024

First Edition.

Highland Artisan Press LLC

Cover art: Sandra Patterson-Slaydon

 What if... PUBLISHING | What If? Publishing:
Managing Editor: Robin Shukle
Design: Liz Mrofka

Printed by: Kindle Direct Publishing

ISBN: 979-8-218-48611-2

Golden Boughs & Poisoned Roots

Sandra Patterson-Slaydon

Dedication

to my family—related or not

Off to Scotland

The first thing that looks suspicious is this guy wrestling his briefcase from the stewardess. "I keep. I put under seat," he insists.

Well, I think the man's got something he's not supposed to. Really I do. I'm not just a dumpy old lady in tweeds, you know. I've had military training and I teach a self-defense class.

When he clutches his briefcase against his chest on the way to the restroom, I know something's up. I'm telling you, there's resolve in those black eyes. Besides, as he passes my aisle seat the outside seam running down his trouser leg looks unusually rigid.

As cool as James Bond, I lower my food tray, pull out paper and pen and scribble a line to my dead husband, Angus MacLaren. Nonchalantly, I place my compass with a mirrored lid so I can reflect the back of the plane. There's no trace of the shifty man, just two stewardesses and a steward. And yes, I still refer to flight attendants by gender.

Minutes sweep by, interrupted only by my asking the stewardesses for a soda. "Don't open the can. I'll drink it later." They acquiesce then push their cart toward first class just as the dark-eyed man slips out of the restroom—minus his briefcase. With one sharp motion the guy smacks the steward unconscious, shoves him in the rear seat then rushes up the aisle.

There's no time to think. Just like that he's along side me, so I stab him in the thigh with my pen. As he yelps, twists to grab his leg, I ram the heel of my hand into his nose. Despite watering eyes, the guy strikes my shoulder—hard. I block his blows with my forearm and stomp his insole with my Mother Hubbard shoe. Slamming my tray into the upright, locked position, I jump to my full five-foot-three inches using the momentum to slam the soda can into his temple. Dazed, the man drops into a crouch.

Several passengers scream. The young couple across the aisle press against the side of the plane. Everyone starts talking at once. A stewardess dashes toward me just as I yell, "Get Security." A plain-clothes sky marshal scooches past the drinks cart, but I don't wait. Taking advantage of the stunned man, I plant my knee on the terrorist's back, pull the belt from my jacket then tie his hands to his ankles in rodeo-record time.

Over the mayhem, I yell, "Your steward needs medical attention." A stewardess squeezes past the sky marshal who examines my half-hitch topped with a square knot. Grabbing the marshal's shirtsleeve, I point. "This guy left his briefcase in that first restroom."

He dashes down the aisle then whirls round to address the passengers. "Those of you from here back, move to the front of the plane." He throws open the restroom door, hesitates then plunges in.

I suck in breath as if expanded lungs will hold the plane up while mentally I'm pleading with the angels to spare my sorry soul. Hysterical passengers push up the aisle skirting my complaining captive. A wheezing man fumbles for his inhaler. A child repeats, "What's happening, Mummy? What's happening?"

The co-pilot white-knuckles the doorframe into first class allowing women and children through. Regulations aside I rescue my Scottie pup from her carrier under the seat. Hugging her close I step over my prisoner. Transfixed on the restroom door, I move away from the claustrophobic mash of humanity. If we're going down, I don't mean to do it posing as a sardine.

Tenderly, I kiss Raven on the top of her head flashing on my safe Colorado mountain cabin. What might be our last moments tick wantonly away. What happens to *used* time, is it stored somewhere? And doesn't the very definition of Eternity dismiss the existence of time altogether?

If that's the case, why do a thousand earth-years pass before the sky marshal reappears holding a molded plastic mechanism with snarly copper wires? The crowd up front gasps as the marshal raises a warning hand for them to stay put. "Everything's under control. I've disarmed the explosive device." His voice means to reassure, but his expression reveals he's pushed way past his limit. "Give me a minute to secure it."

His false confidence doesn't fool me. No sir, I'm scared spitless. I mean, what if that box has a secondary bomb? The skies certainly aren't as friendly as they were when I left Scotland eighteen years ago. This mess makes me wonder why I got such a bug up my backside to return. But then my premonition to study the curative properties of the Celtic trees and plants were so vivid I didn't really have a choice, now did I?

After scanning the floorboards, the sky marshal sets the mechanism on the plane's little-known designated explosion spot. Just in case, he yanks overhead luggage down to build a fortress around it. That done, he turns. "We're safe now. You may return to your seats."

Someone starts a slow firm clapping that grows until it fills the plane. Embarrassed, the marshal gestures toward me, and the applause turns riotous. Well, that's all I need. I grin, and cry and wave off the adoration. Fortunately, Raven raises her head and howls a *thank you* that elicits a gush of relieved laughter. And you know, my little black terrier's delight boosts our morale better than anything.

Visions

Stumbling back to my seat, I mutter, "Dang blood sugar, one little stress and it crashes." I swoon and twenty people manage to drop me on my patootie, but grab the pup. The good news is it's afforded me first-class accommodations. Of course, having saved the day might have swayed them a bit.

Not to brag, but while the bad guy sits in the back without so much as a bag of peanuts, I'm offered everything from roast duck to champagne. Of course, I have to refuse. Don't get me wrong, I'm not difficult on purpose. It's just that I've been a vegetarian and teetotaler since . . . well forever. Raven, on the other hand, tackles the duck without an inkling of guilt.

To be honest, after eating my hazelnut stash and their meager salad, I've begun to eye the dog's dish. Thankfully, someone digs up a vegan soup cup and an energy bar—what people call food these days. I could go on, but frankly I want to fill you in on the vision I had when I passed out.

You see, I keel over when I have a particularly strong premonition. I have the second sight, the *fey*, as the Celts call it. Get it from my Scottish grandmother who insisted I was *marked*. If you've ever wished for the second sight, be advised clairvoyance can be as much a curse as a blessing. However, it rarely goes well to announce you've seen a vision.

There are times the *fey* foretells the future—an inkling of an upcoming event. Occasionally I see an instant replay of something that's just occurred. But not on demand, so any given clairvoyant need not fear for their livelihood. On the other hand, what I saw confounded me.

I experienced a fast-forward of withering trees and plants. A diabolical mixture of evil and greed swirled out of a dark center that willed the trees to fall one right after the next. That's when I caught a glimpse of a long dead nemesis whose corpse I left in Scotland ages ago. The devastation spread wider, and a whole slew of forests spun into a kind of murky vortex. A sound like loud droning music played faster and faster. Pure unadulterated malevolence permeated the atmosphere. Just like that, there was nothing left but a dust-blown wasteland. It took an enormous effort to drag myself up out of that quicksand eddy. The music slowed like someone touched a finger to an old vinyl record. The spinning stopped, and I'm back on flight 713.

This episode might not sound particularly frightening to you, but it scared the bejabbers out of me. Witnessing those forests dying shook my foundation. It's just that I love trees the way a lot of old ladies love cats—passionately, and to the core of my being.

So as the newly crowned Queen of Exceptional Deeds, I perch on my throne—well slump in my seat—taking snorts off an oxygen tank.

It's a short, but glorious reign.

Interrogation

On land, my status diminishes considerably. I'm met by Heathrow Airport Security, then unceremoniously ushered to their office where I'm detained. After explaining two hundred and ninety-seven times what occurred—not to mention why this *elderly* lady took on a would-be terrorist—my bruised ego snaps.

"Not another word until you order some vegan Chinese food." Having recognized the word associated with grub, Raven lunges to the end of her leash. She's had enough of this confinement, too. After all, we are the good guys.

As I speak, a stately grey-templed gentleman strides through the door then in a distinctive Scottish burr, demands, "For goodness sake Samuel, get the woman some food."

I yell after Sam. "Brown rice, not white. And green tea."

The Scotsman shakes my hand. "I'm Detective Chief Inspector Ian Armstrong, New Scotland Yard." He occupies Sam's desk like he owns the place then scrutinizes my passports as if they'll reveal some hidden agenda. "Mrs. Merle Lynn MacLaren, I see you have dual citizenship, the United Kingdom and the United States."

I want to stay mad, but I kind of like the guy, so say, "My parents were Scottish. Well, also Irish and Welsh. I'm kind of a Celtic mutt." I go on like he gives a hoot. "Dad moved us to Colorado right before I was born. I've retained my U.K. passport out of loyalty."

"Which I understand you utilized while employed by one of Scotland's prestigious families many years ago. Now you live in the Rocky Mountains."

"As a flat-plains farm kid, I gazed up at those peaks like some mythical Brigadoon and swore I'd live there someday. Finally moved to a quaint village with Angus, my late Scottish-American husband. Before that, I was . . . well, all over the place." It's a good ploy to talk a lot, reveal little, and try to suss out your interrogator. But this guy's a pro.

"Do you plan to revive your Scottish friendships?"

He would go on about that. "I came to do botanical research. Becoming reacquainted is not on my agenda. It's just that I didn't leave on good . . . " Okay, I let him rattle me.

He tries to stare me down, but I don't blink. "All right, Mrs. MacLaren, I'd like to hear your version of this terrorist situation."

Teaching these guys how to nab radicals is wearing on me, so I hedge, "To summarize I spotted a terrorist and thought you young folk could use a hand."

Not taking the bait, he inquires, "Exactly how did you recognize a would-be terrorist?"

His eyebrow twitches when I tell him I had some secret-op experience while in the service. "Look it up," I say, "I was Capt. Merle *Bruce*, U.S. Army."

"It's not mentioned in your file."

I have a file? And it doesn't include my spy ventures? Now I am injured, so I add a zinger to prove my merit. "Did you find copper wiring in the seam of that terrorist's trousers?"

You notice I didn't say *pants* since over here that's what they call men's underwear. I learned a thing or two living in Scotland for twenty-one years after my discharge. Honorable, in case you had any doubt.

"We did find a fragment," Armstrong says with the tiniest quirk of admiration. "Astute of you to notice something he got through the metal detector. What else gave him up?"

I lean forward to speak in confidence. "One must be careful about having the second sight, so let's just say I sensed his every action was calculated. And those eyes, I could tell he'd accepted death."

"That's not going to satisfy the Yard, or Interpol, Mrs. MacLaren."

"Come on Ian, Sam took my statement in triplicate. I've been here forever." I look at my watch and nearly die. "Holy stars, I've forgotten about Gwynn, my late husband's seventeen-year-old granddaughter. It hasn't exactly been a normal day."

"Indeed not. You're to meet her plane?"

"Yes, I mean no. It should have already landed. You see, my stepson, Leo MacLaren, synchronized the schedules so I'd meet his daughter shortly after mine landed. She's been . . . ahem . . . in private school in L.A. We took different flights. Something about saving Leo money. Gwynn and I haven't seen each other for years, but I have her picture." As I dig it out, an additional photo of a young man slips to the floor. I grab it along with Raven then stash it right quick. It's conceivably improper that I arranged for Gwynnie and me to share a cottage with a male grad student.

Dashing back, Sam thrusts my meal at me and Armstrong hands him Gwynn's photo. "Could you find Mrs. MacLaren's granddaughter? Landed on another flight. Only seventeen and probably scared to death."

I don't tell him he's likely wrong. But before Sam runs Gwynn down, I send him back for chopsticks. I don't care, a civilized person simply does not eat Chinese food with a spork.

Reunion

4

It didn't take me long to recap the terrorist incident—having gotten pretty good at it. Anyway, by now I'm practically old chums with DCI Armstrong. He even scratches Raven under the chin then laughs when her hind leg thumps.

As Stanley finally escorts an unscathed Gwynn in, she yanks her arm away. Whatever I thought our reunion would be, it isn't. Not that black nail polish with matching accessories influences my opinion, but at the very least I expect a hug. Not the gracious greeting, "Where the hell were you?"

Gwynn's belligerence aside, I see my escape. "Gentlemen, if we're done here, I'd like to take my granddaughter to our hotel."

Convinced I'm not an international spy, Armstrong releases me after recording the itinerary for the remainder of my life. Shoot, I'm just relieved he returned my passports.

"What was that about?" Gwynn slings her backpack and starts off.

"Hey," I protest, "could you give me a hand?" Gywnn's a tall skinny thing, the reverse of my short stout teapot impersonation. She looks strong enough, so I shove my hefty suitcase at her then balance three boxes, Raven's crate, and my purse on a trolley. After all, my shoulder aches from a terrorist punch.

"You going to tell me why they detained you?"

"Just a little ruckus on the plane."

"Got into trouble, didn't you? Dad said you were a character."

"I'll bet he did. Let's see what flea-trap Leo reserved for us. Bet you're tired." With the focus on her creature comforts Gwynn dismisses the plane incident, or realizes I'm not so easy to crack.

As we settle into a taxi headed for London, I say, "We've got a whole day before we head up to Scotland to work on my Celtic tree project. I'm endeavoring to recreate what I perceive is a lost healing formula using the foliage that makes up the ancient calendar. You remember the thirteen trees that designate the months of the Celtic calendar, don't you?"

"Of course."

I flash on those delightful days before Gwynnie's mama died. Angus and I moved near Leo, Avera and Gwynn then hosted dinners to celebrate Celtic holidays and teach our granddaughter the Old Ways. It can't be the same, but I'd like her to share my enthusiasm for discovering a lost curative formula.

"There's an arboretum right here in London," I say. "We could check out some of the huge old-growth trees before meeting our housemate, forestry grad-student, Galahad Sinclair. Seems he's a wiz at locating wild foliage."

"Hey, Tree Lady, give it a rest. I'm planning on heading back to L.A. Gonna sell my drawings and share an apartment with a friend. Heather gets released in a week." Yes, juvenile detention—a whole other story.

"Leo didn't explain I'll be your legal guardian until you turn eighteen next spring?"

"What? Well, that's messed up. Should've known he'd stash me somewhere out of his reach." She sulks a few seconds then flashes an unexpected smile. "What city we gonna live in?"

"We'll be near Camelon Village, not too awfully far from Edinburgh."

"Good. I can drive there."

"Excuse me, Gwynn, what part of the word *guardian* don't you understand?"

"So that's how it's gonna be. You get into all kinds of trouble, but I can't have any fun." She's goes quiet, but it doesn't last. "Can't this Galahad guy get his own place?"

"Actually, he's letting us live with him. The cottage belongs to his employer, Laird Rex Arthur Stewart."

"What's he laird of, the local castle?" I nod then assure her he's also in the timber trade, but she crosses her arms. "Well, I'm not going to curtsey. I'm nobody's retainer." Retainer? Gwynn may be wayward, but she's not illiterate.

We speed through London while rain-streaked lights morph into unworldly shapes on the car windows. After paying the extortionist cabbie we check into our even-shabbier-than-expected hotel. Mostly, in total silence. Dang, this isn't how I want it to be. Did I ask about her artwork for heavens sake? Sorry Angus.

While we shower and pull on comfies, Raven sniffs every nook then finds her spot. I flip on the BBC after Gwynn and I snuggle into twin beds with the gaudiest spreads you've ever laid eyes on. Who chooses these colors anyway?

The TV announcer informs the entire world an elderly woman apprehended a terrorist on flight 713, but prefers to remain anonymous —then proceeds to show a phone pic of my bottom stooped over the bad guy. The twit.

"Hey, that's your flight." Gwynn exclaims. "Why didn't you tell me there was a terrorist?"

"He got taken care of right away."

"Well, you could of said."

I start to turn off the tellie so my granddaughter doesn't recognize my derriere, but hesitate as a news reporter interviews people from my flight. "She was an amazing old lady," a man brags. "A Miss Marple on steroids."

I like that one.

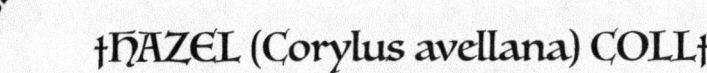

†ḣAZEL (Corylus avellana) COLL†
August 5–September 1

Okay, this is going to get deep, so pay attention here. If you aren't familiar with the Celtic calendar, you need to know it's months are different from our modern calendar. You see, way back in ancient times the *thirteen* months in the Celtic calendar (based on a 28-day moon phase) were named after letters in the *Ogham* alphabet. And this is the part I love . . . each letter is named after an important tree or plant. For example, we're in the month of Hazel, or Coll, which to us is early August through early September. Highly revered by the Celts, the Hazel tree was known for much more than its tasty nuts. Back then Scotland had so many Hazel groves the country was called Caledonia, or Hill of Hazel. The trees often grew near what were considered sacred wells, and it's believed Druid priests used hazelwood wands for shape-shifting. The Hazel tree symbolizes spiritual enlightenment, intuitive wisdom, and negotiation skills. I eat my daily handful of hazelnuts with the hope they'll keep my wits sharp. But wouldn't it be grand to resolve differences and spread peace in the world like some wise old counselor?

Gwynn's Escape

5

Well, Gwynn's gone missing. Silly me, figuring we'd spend quality time sightseeing. So when she's not on the return bus, I'm in a panic.

It's just that over the years Leo fed me his version of her exploits, using them as an excuse to keep her out of his life. I mean if you lose your mother, you need your remaining parent, not prep school. Of course, I could have tried harder, but we didn't exactly bond the last two times I saw her—at the funerals. During her mama's memorial, Leo's doctor kept the thirteen-year-old Gwynn drugged least she become hysterical. Appearances, you know. When Angus died, I was so torn up I scarcely noticed the teen mourning her grandfather. Anyway, the years have left the headstrong teen with an apparent disregard for time.

Better back up. This morning I bought tour bus tickets for Gwynn and me, but then two impeccably dresses men knocked on our hotel door. "Please come with us, Mrs. MacLarlen. It's regarding yesterday's incident. And a bit more."

Anyway, Gwynn rolled her eyes. "Thought you weren't in trouble. No way I'm waiting for you at the police station." See? I let her bully me.

So I take the Scottie pup and send Gwynn out alone figuring a seventeen-year-old can handle a guided tour of London. Truth is, I envy the kid. You know, the Changing of the Guard, Big Ben, the Tower of London with all those clever ravens. Come to find out the juvenile refunded her ticket along with mine then took her own excursion. Without a serious intervention this kid has a definite future in crime. And I haven't even mentioned her senior year loan-shark scheme. Not from lack of money—just lack of love.

But I'm the one who abandoned her in one of the largest cities in the world—in the cold and rain. Plus Gwynn might not care to be found. On the other hand, Scotland Yard owes me the mega-favor for the old 'above-and-beyond'. I dig out DCI Armstrong's card he pressed on me in case anything at all pops into my ancient mind I haven't enumerated sixteen zillion times and ring him up. "She just disappeared, Ian." He makes a lot of accusations, but promises to send out the posse.

I get especially devout when I'm in a heap of trouble. Makes me wonder why I don't pray all the time. Then again, Spirit gave us free will of which I take full advantage. So miraculously, young Galahad Sinclair, the forestry field guide and soon-to-be-housemate I engaged, knocks. I pull him inside and explain the situation.

"Don't upset yourself, Mrs. MacLaren. And please call me Had." He's too dusty blond and handsome for his own good, takes notes on his cell phone—called *mobile* phones over here—and is exactly what I need.

Another knock proves to be a burly Scotland Yard guy. After introductions the detective asks, "How often does your girl perform her little vanishing act?"

"Never before with me." Which isn't a full out lie.

Had intervenes. "Might you possess a recent photograph of Miss MacLaren?"

"Yes." I turn to the detective. "The one security used to recognize her in the airport." I'm reminding him who I am, but don't see the lights turn on.

He glances at the picture. "I'll find her in a Goth hang out. Is she on drugs?"

"No," I snap. "I assure you Gwynn is clean." I don't tell him Gwynn won't even take prescribed medicine since Leo pressed it on her after Avera died.

Galahad quietly takes over. With the desk clerk's help, Had creates a flyer outlining Gwynn's pertinent information. He assures me he'll scout the teen hangouts then excuses himself. The detective follows suit after strict instructions to ring him if Gwynn shows up. Do you think?

I'd be grateful for a bit of peace if the silence weren't so dang numbing. My body's every cell longs to hear my granddaughter's voice, whine and all. So I take action. None of the TV stations utter a word about Gwynnie. Scotland Yard insists I stop ringing them in case someone who actually knows Gwynn's whereabouts attempts to call. They aren't pacing the carpet with thirty-six Celtic designs lengthwise and twenty-four crosswise. Even my puppy yawns when I inform her that letting others take charge drives me bug-flapping bonkers.

After all, my gorgeous gangly redhaired granddaughter is essentially the extent of my kin. I tried to fit into other families. Thought I'd found one with the clan I worked for in Scotland those many years ago. I didn't get it right until I married Angus MacLaren—Gwynnie's grandfather and my fifth husband. Yes, fifth.

"Angus," I say out loud, "Gwynnie reminds me of Avera, her beautiful mama—model tall with all that blazing hair curling out in all directions grabbing up every stitch of life." Avera didn't linger after her diagnoses. Hospice came. We took turns sitting with her through the worst of it. Except Gwynnie who felt abandoned. Oh, the thirteen-year-old attended school, but at home never really came out of her dark purple room. Her dark purple mood.

Afterwards, Leo's vision of a new life didn't include Gwynn—claimed she reminded him of Avera and took the coward's route. He bundled her off to an out-of-state boarding school without so much as a farewell dinner. We were devastated. Leo amassed fast money, slick cars and Cyndi as cold and blond as the chrome sculptures she creates. I think we were relieved when Leo said they were busy networking and 'knew we'd understand.'

Angus and I moved to a cozy mountain village, bought a cabin by a river and nursed our wounds. Gwynn rarely accepted our calls and Angus never recovered. He died of a massive broken heart a year later. Guess we should have followed Gwynnie, but then a body can 'should' themselves into despair, can't they?

With Angus and his generous pension gone, I immersed myself in academia. Lived on a meager stipend for the classes I taught, and received another degree. No time or money to visit Gwynn. I assumed she'd forgotten the step-grandmother she'd known for such a short time—until last April. Out of the California smog I received an invite to her high school graduation way out in Los Angeles. Called Leo to see if they'd take me with them only to hear a litany of excuses for not going, and disgust over Gwynn's refusing to choose a university.

Seems she'd thwarted his plan to ship her off to yet another institution. If only Avera had been allotted more days on this earth—what an altered destiny for us. However, I knew I wanted Gwynn with me and Leo gladly paid me to take her to 'go find our Scottish roots, or whatever.'

Cosmology

6

Ever try not thinking about something traumatic without losing your mind? Trick is to immerse said 'mind' in another subject. I open my box marked Celtic mythology books. The text falls open to the page that prompted the visions leading to this whole excursion—the Celtic Cosmological Tree of Life. That's essentially an illustration of a big ol' tree divided into four levels if you include the exposed roots. Of course, this tree diagram is an analogy—a map, if you will, of the human inner-consciousness. It pictures those tangled roots all the way up to the sublime Creator.

I had a powerful cognition last year when I laid eyes on this ancient illustration. There was something about those roots buried in the dark *Underworld*. The tree trunk representing the dualistic *Earthly Realm* of good and evil. Its branches penetrating a *Heaven* of pure goodness and light. On top, the golden boughs extending into the *Highest Realm* where creation is overseen and sustained by the *Ancient and Unoriginated One*. Isn't that the most delightful name for the Almighty?

I wonder if Angus saw my vision? *I was in a foggy oak grove collecting tree samples. An owl hooted and two intertwined serpents slithered up a tree . . . you know, like the medical symbol—or Druidic herbal wisdom.* Naturally that inspired me to delve into the healing properties of the trees and plants that make up the Celtic calendar.

"Angus, these thirteen trees and plants might hold healing properties, lost when Druids with all their unwritten knowledge were forced underground. Is it such a stretch to think Celtic botanical medicine might yet reveal an important cure?"

I knew I had to work in the old country and involve Gwynn and Galahad when they showed up in another vision. I recognized our red-haired Gwynnie right off. It took my only remaining Scottish friend, an old monk named Father Joseph Arimathea, to identify Galahad—a forestry student willing to share housing. Nonetheless, it felt like wandering-in-the-desert until Leo's money came through. So there you have it.

Instead of having faith, I too frequently second-guess the Almighty. Like now. With the hope of discovering Gwynn's whereabouts, I envision heavenly branch-arms wrapping round her, golden boughs illuminating her path. The girl hasn't led the most spiritual life, but that can't be held against her. In case the visualization got filed on some remote cloud, I chant fervently to break through Heaven's sound barrier. "Bring Gwynn back."

Infernal silence resounds, so I formulate a sermon with severe scolding and ultimate consequences for my young protégés. Which, if you think about it, *is* positive thinking considering where she might be. I mean, a teen that looks twenty-five, alone in London. After dark. No, I draw the line not allowing thoughts of her mangled body. Being rained on. Thunder echoing.

Not thunder. Knocking on the door. I fling it open to Galahad with Gwynn. I grab her, mouth 'thank you' to Had and he slips out. Gently I lead Gwynn to the end of the bed then hug the breath out of her. Gwynn's arms hang limp, but I've never let a little thing like that keep me from loving anyone. Unconditional love requires no reciprocation. You've got to be the bigger person to fill an aching heart.

Raven's heart, on the other hand, runneth over. She's up here pushing her long snout between us. She kisses Gwynn's face then flies off the bed and tears around the room. All right, so she does care.

"Gwynnie, I've never been so worried."

"Didn't think you'd even care."

I look into her hazel-green eyes. "Of course I care. I love you, you're family. But you will *never* do that again."

She drops her head. "Grandma Merle, please don't tell my dad."

It takes me about a nanosecond to realize 'what Leo doesn't know' can't stymie Gwynnie's and my destiny. Plus, she hadn't called me Grandma since our reunion, and that counts for something. "Alright," I say, "but don't take me for a soft touch."

The poison tearing this family apart stops here.

Galahad Sinclair

I

t's checkout time, but the more I prod Gwynn the more she dawdles. Had pulls his spotless white Land Rover into the loading zone. He opens the rear hatch and Miss Pouty Pants throws her backpack at him. He stows it without complaint.

"Perhaps a word of thanks?" I suggest.

Gwynn gives me that dark look a body gets from kids who've had a tough time. She crawls inside, curls her lanky limbs around our supplies and appears to fall asleep. Following her lead, Raven sacks out, one paw over her eyes. Sleep, let alone instantaneous sleep, amazes me. Problem solving consumes my slumber. I take it as a sign of genius.

Galahad maneuvers us out of the London mayhem, onto the M1 headed toward dear old Scotland. I relax and take a 'Galahad Sinclair' inventory. He's got to be a foot taller than me, so six foot three, with sun-sandy hair and well-outfitted in a hand-knit sweater, all-weather coat, corduroy trousers and rugged boots. I strongly approve.

When I offer to help him drive, he looks surprised. "You wouldn't mind driving on the left side of the road?"

"No, I lived in Scotland, and India years ago. It'll come back to me." I don't particularly want this line of inquiry pursued, so I say, "Tell me about your work with Laird Stewart's, Logres Lumber. What's your job description?"

He hesitates then says, "I was hired to trace the attributing factors associated with the demise of Holly trees in the Logres Lumber courtyard, as well as ancient Oaks on the laird's castle grounds."

The 'tree devastation vision' jumps to mind and my voice raises fourteen octaves. "Trees dying? From something abnormal?"

"That is a correct assumption, ma'am." He answers as if we're discussing the weather instead of the living sap running through trees.

"Had, we've just met, but don't minimize, to this Tree Lady, facts concerning my best friends dying. What's going on?"

Galahad claims he shouldn't say more. I flash him a 'don't feed me that' and he throws me a bone. "Since Laird R.A. Stewart is my mum's cousin, he not only desires to introduce me to the timber trade, but needs a trusted clansman to insinuate themselves into every aspect of the firm."

"To spy on his employees?"

His raised eyebrows acknowledge my perception. "R.A. fears eco-terrorists may also attempt to poison the cultivated timber."

"Poisoned trees? Well, I didn't see that in my vision. How bad is it?"

"You have visions?" You'd think I admitted to practicing the dark arts.

"I had a precognition of forests being destroyed. Trees are in peril, aren't they?"

"We've no idea how widespread this vandalism is. I'm to watch for disgruntled or suspicious behavior. Now I have said too much."

It's just my luck to get a guide with scruples, but I take another stab at it. "Surely Father Joseph told you I'll be studying the botanical properties of the trees and plants that make up the Celtic calendar. I hope they're not in danger."

"I couldn't say, ma'am." And that's that.

We've escaped the urban sprawl. There are cottages with a bit of acreage, a *coo* and ewe or two, the occasional hedgerow, and soothing shades of green stretching for miles. My muscles relax, but my gut rumbles. I slap my belly. "Down girl."

Had stifles a laugh. I dig in the food basket, hand him a thick cheese on wheat then pass one back to Gwynn. She nibbles a bit then offers tiny pieces to my pup. Raven snuggles close. My dog sold out for a deli sandwich.

Turning back to Had, I ask, "Where do you live when you're not working a field-study job? At the monastery?"

"At times."

Conversing with this twenty-four-year-old tuckers me out, but I'm tenacious. "Does our cottage the laird lent you, have a name?"

"*Koad,* meaning sacred grove. And *Croft,* as in a farm plot with a cottage—this one located in a wooded area as specified."

Alert now, Gwynn squeals, "Whata you mean by farm?"

"Well," I say, "we're going to be able to walk and talk among the trees. Linking the various Celtic trees and plants with Ogham names is how I learned their language."

Gwynn groans, "Oh great, now she talks to trees."

"This month's tree, the Hazel or *Coll*," I add, "is when we experience innate wisdom."

"Like astrology, they tell you what to expect?"

To my surprise Had explains. "The Celtic calendar months, named for Ogham characters, don't foretell the future. Their symbolism is for guidance."

"Pretty deep. Hey, I don't have to milk a cow do I?" Her thoughts do leap about.

"It's a forest croft," Had says. "Former residents harvested firewood for the estate."

"The night-life must be awesome." I turn toward Gwynn and laugh, but she flounces back dramatically. At least our makeshift family had our first conversation.

Amazingly the country air makes me nappish. When my eyes open it appears we've passed through some kind of time warp. We're surrounded by a thick Scottish haze. I love fog, every variety from pea to consommé. In Scotland the mist creeps up from the soggy soil, or rolls in off the sea—unlike the Rocky Mountains where angel clouds sink to our mortal level. Each equally enchanting. The undulating landscape peeks through vapor on the hilltops, but it lies thick in the crevices.

Whether it's the fog, or the calming lavender scent, I sigh. "Lovely. I'd nearly forgotten Scotland's mysterious charm. It's like an unfolding poem."

"Indeed it is Mrs. MacLaren."

Like mine, Had's spirit seems at rest in these hills and woods. The outdoors suiting this rather dignified forestry student, a guy whose monkish propriety allows him to socialize, but prefer nature's solitude. Here sits a body with depth to his soul.

I cozy into his reticence. We speak when there's something worth mentioning, but the silence is as dense and consoling as the fog. Hints of ancient Druidic eras surface as we float through misty wooded dales, tiny villages and rolling expanses that fade at dusk. It's pitch black when our headlamps light the drive to our ivy-covered stone cottage.

It strikes me we've come home to the next segment of our lives. I for one, have the audacity to believe an old woman can influence history. The least a body can do is leave our heirs something worth remembering.

Koad Croft

8

Galahad pulls up so the headlights shine on Koad Croft's entrance. I lean forward to get a better look at the quaint grey-stone thatched rectangle—the emphases on quaint. I'm going to love this place.

He pulls a flashlight from beneath the seat and sweeps the beam. "The woods are this dense on three sides, then there's the hill in back."

"A sylvan sanctuary," I say. "Without trees where would a body walk among friends?"

Had nods. "My sentiments."

"Could we get any more isolated?" We've heard from the backseat.

"Oh, Gwynnie, you're awake. Make sure Raven's leash is on. She'll want to explore. I hear a *burn*, a stream."

We pile out and Had sticks a skeleton key—the kind you pick up at any flea market—into the heavy wooden door. I sigh. "So this is Koad Croft, our sacred grove."

"It's a romantic name, but this croft doesn't have a happy history," Had explains. "A woodsman, his wife and boy lived here. When Camelon Castle asked them to leave, the fellow drank himself to death."

"In that case, we best enter with a blessing on our hearts."

"Oh, spare me," my granddaughter moans.

I point to the door lintel. "Look, Gwynn, that's Ogham for, Koad Croft—an X with a vertical line through it. It signifies we'll receive knowledge of past, present and future events."

Gwynn fingers the carved letter. "It's like secret writing?"

"An ancient form of communicating."

Had turns. "The Ogham alphabet consists of various configurations of lines."

"I'll teach you the twenty-five-symbol alphabet if you want."

"Sure, okay. Are we going inside, or what?"

As Had shoves the door open, I'm transported back a couple eons.

Dark low weathered beams stretch across a nice-sized room divided into kitchenette, dining, and fireside seating. The walls look newly white-washed, the plank floors scrubbed, the furniture well, serviceable.

Gwynnie throws her backpack on the little square dining table. She dashes to the bathroom, a facility crammed in what was likely a pantry before indoor luxuries existed—sandwiched between two bedrooms at the back. Had sets his duffle on the sofa then without much effort has a blaze going in the fireplace. Soon Gwynn and Raven are on the move. They peer into the small, and yet smaller, bedrooms. "I get the biggest one," she announces, grabs her pack and disappears. I look at Had and shrug.

After calling dibs on a long table in the back, I check my room with adequate linens on a narrow bed and newspaper lining the dresser drawers. "Had, would you bring my suitcase and Raven's crate?" With her doggie home in place, Raven circles then lies down with an exagger-ated sigh. I unpack keeping vigil on the setting room.

Gwynn plops onto the sofa that makes into a bed. Had tells her he'll sleep there then meticulously places clothes in the box that serves as an end table. "I'm not used to space, or privacy," he says.

Gwynn walks around holding her phone up. "Were your parents poor?"

"We're far from indigent," he states. "We chose to live frugally."

"That's kinda dumb when you can have more." How did destiny bring such mismatched housemates together? Gwynn wraps an afghan around her warm-climate blouse. "Why no privacy?" She removes her necklace, touches the locket to her lips then lays it on the coffee table. After a decided pause Had continues. "I grew up near here at Holy Vessel monastery. My mum lives at St. Clair's convent, on the same grounds."

"Your mom's a nun?"

"Mum never took vows, she simply lives as a holy sister."

"That's unusual. Where's your dad?"

"I barely know my biological father, but since he's Logres' vice president, I imagine our paths will cross."

"Did that laird guy give you this job so you'd get to know your dad?" Gwynn's nothing if not direct.

"Father Joseph possibly conspired with the laird to force the issue. He feels I should forgive Lance for abandoning Mum and me before I was born. My parents are not legally divorced. I feel Lance La Lac is disrespectful toward Mum with his public womanizing."

"My dad's no prize either. After Mama died, he sent me away to school then started a new family. I have a baby brother I've never met." Poor Gwynn. What a slap in the face. She however, sums up the situation. "It sounds like both our dads are missing in action. That why you don't use Lance's last name?"

"Yes, Sinclair is Mum's family name."

"I get it. I keep MacLaren because I loved Grandpa Angus so much . . . and Grandma."

"Your gran's a nice lady."

"I guess, we hardly know each other."

She must think I'm deaf, but I'm not offended. Gwynn always speaks her truth. I'm just sad the kids are bonding over daddy discontent, so join the two and venture a question. "Had, have you ever recognized a place even if it's the first time you've been there?"

He thinks a bit then allows us into his private world. "Yes, the first time I visited Roslin Chapel as a child. Since then I've felt a strange belonging." He's quiet then asks, "Mrs. MacLaren, do you believe it possible geographical memories are imprinted in one's DNA?" I've hit on a subject Had's pondered.

"Without a doubt," I say. "Some philosophies call them impressions from past lives. Is that what you're asking?"

"In a manner of speaking. It's just that some of my Sinclair, or *St. Clair of Roslin*, ancestors went to the Crusades as Knights Templars then later served as Scotland's Grand Master Masons."

Like a school girl Gwynn declares, "I know this one. The Templars were the dudes with the big red cross on their chests. They protected the pilgrims on the road to the Holy Land during the second Crusade."

Amazed, I shout, "And the redhead wins the prize."

Gwynn almost grins then says, "Had, it's pretty cool your ancestors were Freemason Knights Templars." The young man's approval rating just skyrocketed.

"Galahad," I say skeptically, "Roslin Chapel contains both Knights Templar and Masonic symbols. You may have been influenced by suggestion."

"But I somehow felt the presence of a previous age—rather as if I were communing with my ancestors that built the chapel in the fourteen hundreds."

"But no visions?"

"No visions," he laughs. "Just a feeling they were present."

"They didn't tell you where they buried the Holy Grail, did they?

Some say it is hidden at Roslin Chapel."

He smiles and says, "Seriously, have you experienced anything similar?"

"Yes, when I first laid eyes on Scotland's purple heather fields. Thought at first the flashes were impressions described by my Scottish immigrant parents, but it kept happening. Call it what you will, but the feelings were stronger than *déjà vu*."

"Did you know what you would see around the next corner?" Had asks.

"Yes, and now it's all flooding back."

"You guys are weird," Gwynn states. We don't respond, so she leaps to another topic. "This castle that Laird Stewart actually lives in . . . can I see it?"

"I may be able to attain invitations for you and Mrs. MacLaren to the annual Halloween ball."

I start to nix the idea, but Gwynn's ecstatic. "That would be sooo cool."

She holds her phone up. "How come I can't get any bars in here? And where's the television? Don't *even* tell me there's no TV."

Without a drop of remorse, Had says, "We're fortunate to have local telephone service in this hollow."

"Do you use some ancient dial-up for internet?"

"No, I'll drive you to the Camelon Village Library for internet use."

Gwynn jumps up. "Nobody told me I'd be camping in the wilderness."

"It might be good to be unplugged for a while," I say.

"Grandma, how'd you get so . . . old?"

"Easy. I didn't even try."

She runs to her bedroom, slams the door so hard dust filters from the thatch then yells. "I'm not happy." To Gwynn's credit, she doesn't stay mad. Before long she returns, keeps eyeing Galahad then asks, "You gonna be a monk?"

"Maybe."

"Oh great. An old lady and a monk. This is going to be really fun."

"You have to forgive Gwynn," I say. "She was born without manners. Some kind of genetic malfunction."

Had laughs out loud and Gwynn sticks her tongue out. We're going to get along just fine.

Lessons

9

After a week we've settled into our conquered territories. After shelving books ranging from plant identification, to Celtic history, to the more esoteric Tree of Life and Ogham alphabet, I plop into what can only be described as an understuffed chair.

Gwynn places her necklace on the coffee table then hands me a book from my shelves. "Is this about that secret language?"

"Yes, the Ogham alphabet. See, each of the letters is named for a tree, plant or other natural element." I point to the page. "And that's how you write it."

"Assuming you could use them in your research, I brought my forestry textbooks from my cell at the monastery," Had says.

"A cell?" Gwynn's incensed. "I hated those bars, but good ol' Dad sprung me."

"No. Cell—as in a small humble room," he explains then fetches an armload of books from a backpack. "This text describes ancient times when all of Great Britain was densely forested. Deforestation began in the Bronze age with the invention of the axe. Hence, the disruption of the Celtic lifestyle intricately connected to nature."

"Which made me wonder if the Celts chose the set of plants and trees, marking the months, for their healing properties," I say.

"Hence your chemistry set," Gwynn says, but adds. "So what if a few get poisoned?"

"Surely you cannot be serious." Had looks at me accusingly.

In my defense I say, "I wasn't in charge of her education."

"I read about the rape of the rain forests—how that lowers Earth's oxygen level," Gwynn snaps. "I'm not brain dead,"

"But your attitude shocks me," Had exclaims. "I assume you know that trees are carbon storehouses. Humans and trees have a symbiotic relationship that . . . "

Gwynn interrupts. "We exhale carbon dioxide, CO_2, which the trees store in exchange for the oxygen they release. We need their oxygen to survive."

"They also filter particulate pollution helping to mitigate the effects of climate change. They purify our water and look here." He shoves an open text into Gwynn's hands. "From their foliage to their roots, trees provide an astonishing variety of products."

"Okay, so we need trees for stuff and so we can breathe, but why lose it over some mental case poisoning a couple? That's not going to stop the sawmills."

"It just may shut down Logres Lumber if its stock plummets," Had admits.

I interrupt. "Had, we'll discuss corporate espionage later. Gwynn wants to know why we love trees."

He shakes his head. "One only needs to walk in a forest to see, to sense the aliveness of it all. The diverse ferns, fungi, the birds, and wildlife, the rich smell of the soil—can only be experienced to be understood."

"Our ancestors lived in the magic of nature," I add. "Perceiving the sacredness."

"That was before it was destroyed, chopped down and set ablaze. Now, Great Britain is merely ten percent wooded," Had says passionately.

"Yeah, that sucks," Gwynn agrees.

"It's our duty to protect not only the forests, but the magic of the Old Ways," I say.

"I remember some of what Grandpa Angus taught me." There's a far-away look in her eyes. "Bet if I stick around, you'll jog my memory."

A bit later, Gwynn scurries to the coffee table. "Where's my locket?" In a panic she searches under the sofa. "Help me find it, you guys. It's the only thing I have of Mama's."

"Look in Raven's crate," I say. Gwynn shakes the dog's blanket and her pretty engraved locket falls to the floor. She puts it on. "You kids need to stash your stuff above Scottie level, almost anything's at risk." Raven gives us her Miss Purity look.

Gwynn kneels. "You can get help for that, you little klepto."

Had studies my little dog. "Did you name it Raven before or after you discovered its proclivity to steal small items?"

"She lived up to her name."

Shifting focus Had asks, "Gwynn, help me carry supplies in from the Rover?"

She acquiesces, and ducks through the door lintel, obviously built

38

when people were normal size. Returning, Gwynn smacks her crown on what was once a mighty oak then spits out a string of profanities the likes of which I haven't heard since my military days.

I heave my backside out of the understuffed. "Okay, there's to be no swearing."

"It's because of him, isn't it? Mr. Holier than Thou?"

"No, he doesn't get to swear either."

"Very funny."

"We'll work on better ways to express ourselves. A person needs to be their best."

With an edge to his voice, Galahad says, "Nothing wrong with that."

"Okay, but before we go to the castle, you have to teach me how to talk like a lady."

To my amazement, Had says, "Gladly."

With that round over, we retire to our corners.

Raven

10

Galahad must need to prove himself because he's led us deep into the forest to find late summer specimens. Leaving Raven in the Land Rover with plenty of air and water, Had immerses himself in his woodland work, I head toward old growth trees and Gwynn dawdles aimlessly then asks, "You checking for poison, Had?"

He answers dismissively. "I'm recording normal pH levels."

I'd hoped we'd be working as a unit by now, but the fruit of our uniqueness has yet to congeal. Am I thinking loud enough for the kids to hear?

Telling myself to give it time, I concentrate on the plants and trees. Everywhere a body turns there's a zillion more plant species. Might just run smack into the Celtic Tree of Life. I'm snagging bark, roots, and stems left and right. "Hey Gwynn, want to help me gather samples?"

She stands akimbo. "I don't have to get all dirty picking leaves for you, Dad already paid you to take me off his hands." She plops onto a stump and stares at me.

Without a bit of reprimand, I explain. "Just so we get our facts straight, when *I* asked your dad if you could accompany me to Scotland, *he* volunteered the monthly stipend."

Gwynn's silent, but I hear the gears grinding. "Why bother after all these years?"

I don't figure sharing my vision featuring this redhead would be the smartest move. Instead I simplify. "I was planning this trip when I got your graduation announcement and realized you were finally free."

"Why didn't you come see me?"

I meet her sad eyes. "Gwynn, your Grandpa Angus was a wonderful man, but he obviously didn't realize his pension stopped, should he die. We spent our joint savings on the cabin. I had no travel money until now."

Gwynn chews on that. "Well, that had to suck—I mean that was outrageously unfortunate." Behind her, Had grins at her word modification, but doesn't hand out kudos.

She looks at my array of plant materials. "I'd rather be drawing these."

"What a fabulous idea. Chose a few specimens. I'll find a way to pay you for your illustrations." That's sort of working together.

Gwynn helps with renewed intent then time does one of those relativity leaps. It's dusk before we discover Raven missing. Has someone stolen her—way out here in the wilderness? In terror mode, I whistle, but she doesn't show.

Had and Gwynn stare at me like I know what the heck to do. I can't get beyond my sick heart, so Had jumps into action. "We've a wee bit of light. We'll spread out. Break a twig every few feet, so you can make your way back. If you find the dog, call out."

"What if we can't?" Gwynn chokes back a sob.

"Concentrate on the hunt," Had says. "And pray," he adds.

Gwynn yanks on jeans and disappears. Blurred vision slows my flight, I trip over a stump, neglect to mark my trail then backtrack. Branches whack my noggin then slap me from behind. Angry vines grab my ankles. A couple eons pass then Had's call pierces the air. Hope gives me fairy-feet and I nearly fly back just as Gwynn slides into home base.

"This way," Had yells. We dive into the thicket catching sight of him scooping something into a sample bag while Raven lies stoically in a wilting circle of Hazel trees. Her brown eyes roll toward us. I sink beside my limp doggie. An acrid poisonous odor fills my nostrils. I try to hold on, but pass out.

Spinning down into a dank abyss, the stench takes me back to a time . . . no, it can't be. My dead nemeses steps out of the shadows. Under her filmy mantle, Igraine's nothing but a withered corpse with straggly black hair. Nonetheless, her raspy voice is excruciatingly familiar. "You've put your life at risk by returning."

"Igraine, we buried you years ago. What do you want?"

"Leave Scotland, or suffer the consequence," the wraith warns.

"You were malicious in life. What can you do from the grave?"

I'm answered with an ungodly cackle. Her boney finger points to a black-clad figure spreading poison through the trees. "Underlings will regain what is rightfully mine."

"Evil has no rights."

With a huff of foul breath and a screech I'm sent whirling up and up.

Gwynn hovers over me with Raven in her arms. Tears stream down the teen's face. "Grandma Merle, please don't die."

With great effort, I sit up. "I won't. Too much to do."

Had appears. "Good, you've come round. They've poisoned the soil with an abundance of potassium hydroxide fertilizer like the others. This is my first find."

Annoyance snaps me fully back. "I think you'll agree Raven discovered your poisoned trees. Maybe even followed the culprit."

As stoic as Scotties are, she still whimpers. I plead to a preoccupied Had, "Raven's paws are burnt. She's likely poisoned."

"There are no veterinarians near here."

"Then drive us to town, pretty boy." Gwynn commands and he obeys.

Long story short, Dr. Brown bandages Raven's feet then survives my withering glare that permits me to commandeer his clinic.

While Had reports the poisoned Hazel trees to Laird Stewart, Gwynn whispers, "Grandma Merle, what made you pass out?"

"The poison triggered one of my visions." The threats could be a bad omen, but I don't want to frighten Gwynnie. Instead, Captain Merle jumps into action. "Galahad, Gwynn come help me gather wild herbs." I concoct a healing extract then my kids help eyedropper the botanical formula down Raven's raw throat.

After helping for hours, Had falls asleep on the linoleum floor. In the wee hours, Gwynn and I dose off. At the light of dawn, an alert Raven licks her bandaged paws—all the world as if nothing's happened. Gwynn and I cover her with kisses and Had lays his head against Raven's side.

Back home, it doesn't actually take three people to hold Raven, apply salve, and rebandage her paws for days on end. But we're a diligent clan. Sometimes it takes a tragedy to pull a family together. The good news is, Raven felt well enough to nab Had's prized gold pen today.

†VINE (Vitis vinifera) ᚋUIN†
†BRAᚋBLE (R. fruticosus) ᚋUIN†
September 2–September 29

This month's Celtic plant is a bit complex. Some scholars believe that Muin refers to the grapevine while others feel that Blackberry bushes (Brambles) are the more accurate plant. A body would have to admit that grapevines do struggle to survive in Scotland's northern climate whereas Brambles flourish. This observation led me to utilize the Bramble for my Celtic plant formula. A more esoteric sense of the word Muin means *back* as in strength, or *neck* as in vocal-passage and speaking. In fact, during this season the Celts held their Autumn Harvest Festival to celebrate the end of their *back*-breaking growing season. It was the time to speak the truth, and to coax their more psychic members to make predictions and prophecies for the coming year. I would have liked those folks a lot.

The Makeover

11

I'm telling you, my ego wants all the credit for the tremendous progress Gwynnie has shown. When Galahad is off working his many hours at Logres, Gwynn tramps around the forest with me. She appears to enjoy collecting, photographing and illustrating the Celtic plants and trees. She has MacLaren creative fortitude—a nice way of saying she's smart, but stubborn. I admire these traits in a woman. Can't abide the subservient female that manipulates her way through life. However, when she ends each argument slamming into her room, I ask Had to store her door in the shed.

Our contest of wills does strain me. On the other hand, Galahad, raised by a bevy of monks, follows mandates without any semblance of opinion. To instill more individual decision making, I institute a food preparation rotation. Had is a by-the-book-cook, while Gwynn simply dives in. Barring a few culinary disasters, the teen is chef material.

On music appreciation nights we play everything from classical to Gwynn's popular play list. Then there's our fireside chats that result in a tell-all-tempest. Gwynn details her lucrative loan sharking that landed her in juvie, Galahad confesses to a frat-hazing pub-hopping spree enabling him to locate Gwynnie in London, and I admit to blending into the crowd to avoid arrest for chanting 'Peace on Earth'.

However, bringing out the best in my kids takes more energy than this old dame bargained for. Makes me wonder if premonitions are second-guessable. I've gone out on a limb taking my wards on, and the branch is creaking.

Gwynn pushes aside her make-shift door—a beach towel featuring a huge skeleton head. "Grandma," she informs me, "I need go to Edinburgh for a makeover." Seems she desperately needs a transformation before she attends the laird's ball. "Yeah, dumb ol' Had asked what I'm hiding under my disguise."

Her dad informed me he, and counselors from five different institutions, spent hours—and time is money to Leo—coercing and demanding she change her death-inspired get-up. Now one off-handed observation from our handsome housemate influenced her entire attitude. I pride myself on knowing which side my scone is buttered on, so without a bit of shame produce Leo's 'for emergencies only' credit card.

"You ladies have an irritating habit of spontaneity," Had complains. But bless his unenthusiastic heart, he's driving us to the big city.

We aren't on the road long before Gwynn brings up yesterday's episode. I passed out again when we attended Logres Blackberry Winery Harvest Fest and discovered poisoned Bramble bushes. "Grandma, did you learn anything from your vision?"

Reluctantly, I say, "I saw that deceased lady Igraine, with her minion spreading poison on withering foliage. However, my visions revealed the Celtic trees are being poisoned in consecutive months. Oak and Holly before we arrived then Hazel and Bramble since."

Driving into heavy traffic, Galahad takes a quick look at us. "You're right. I should have recognized the systematic pattern. But I can't accept how you acquired the data."

Gwynn takes my side. "I thought all Scotsmen believed in the second sight. After all, you sensed your ancestors at Roslin Chapel." Galahad agrees to keeping an open mind while relying on hard science.

My ego pats me on the back for helping my wards expand their minds. But now I realize said ego just negated my good-deed karma. And so it goes.

Before long we drop Raven at the Edinburgh dog groomer then on to Buchan's Woolens. "Gwynn, let's honor our Scottish heritage with a bit of family tartan."

Recognizing a sure sale, the shop girl offers Gwynn a scarf for inspection. "The aqua blue in this ancient MacLaren tartan compliments your complexion, miss."

"It doesn't look ancient to me."

"Notice the muted colors? They emulate tartans, or plaids, found at archeological sites. That gives them the ancient designation. See, these other clan MacLaren tartans? The colors change, but the pattern remains the same. The MacLaren tartan gives you quite a variety to choose from."

Had holds a Sinclair blanket he's buying for his mum. "Tartans are a great way to express family pride."

Gwynn whispers. "He who uses his mother's surname."

"Shush, we need our chauffer."

So while Had polishes off complimentary tea and cakes, Gwynn is measured for a jacket, trousers, and floor-length skirt. "Here Grandma Merle." The teen plops matching tams on our noggins. "Everyone will know we're clanswomen." I couldn't be prouder and throw on a cape of deep blue modern MacLaren tartan—a definite gale sure to blow. For effect, I top it with a red plaid shawl. Gwynn says, "Hey, that's not MacLaren tartan."

"No, Gwynn, my Scottish family hails from clan Bruce."

"So you're related to that Scottish King, Robert the Bruce?" I love this incredible girl.

Completing our transactions, we hurry along to Shear Genius. After a few short hours, Had and I sport the latest haircuts. But you should see the presto-chango they've worked on Gwynn. My grand-daughter has morphed from black accents to gentle red-gold curls and subtle peachy-pink shades that enhance her green-flecked eyes.

I'm ecstatic. "Gwynnie, send a selfie to your dad."

I'm savvy enough to know Leo will fall at my feet in gratitude if he doesn't see the credit card statement first. Gwynn who normally can't wait to use her phone isn't crazy about sending the picture. Normally, she claims her one afternoon on-line to be severe and unusual punishment. She'll say, "Time to go to the library for my obligatory Daddy check-in." She texts her rather sketchy friends, then emails her dad. Like he cares—Leo the Clueless, bragging that Cyndi sold another sculpture and baby Duncan is the most amazing kid that ever crawled the earth.

Okay, off the soapbox and on to shopping. Gwynn selects a pair of spiked-heels to wear with the leaf-strewn gossamer gown she's found for the castle ball. There she goes adding height while if you must know, I remain well-grounded and pleasantly plump. But Gwynn and I laugh and give advice. We've jumped in the clotheshorse saddle and taken off at a gallop. At one point, our eyes meet with the realization we're having the time of our lives. Who'da thought? While a bored-rigid Had dozes in a chair, Gwynn transforms from Goth to Glam.

With concern over egos sidelined, our self-image got a facelift today. We strut down Princes Street with pack mule, Had, in tow. If clothes make a woman, we're made. And here's the big one—she actually thanked me.

†IVY (Ḟedera heliẋ) GORT†

September 30–October 27

The Ivy plant is simply enchanting. Look at the way it grows and what it represents. It has those evergreen spiraling tendrils that remind a body of a labyrinth circling inward toward *self* then outward after achieving spiritual enlightenment. You see, it's Ivy's association with the moon, the portal to the mystical Otherworld that leads the seeker to these inner recesses. On an earthly level, this tough little plant brings to mind ambition and a survival instinct necessary to overcome everyday trials. It's a wonderful 'energy' to tap into, as long as you use it for good.

Lady Elaine

12

After morning meditation, I kick back with the hope of relaxing in the ol' understuffed. So wouldn't you know, Had hits us with an invite. "I've arranged for you ladies to visit Father Joseph and meet Mum today. And since it's Gort season, you can collect Ivy on monastery grounds."

"Holy poop, Had," Gwynn squeals, "you have to take me to the library. Grandma, he doesn't have the right to do this."

"It is short notice." I reprimand, but my mind is on having neglected Father Joseph since my arrival. Then there's Had's mother. Gwynn huffs off to her room when I say, "I'll walk Raven before we go." In my forest sanctuary, I try to conjure excuses to beg out, but the infernal rain drives me in, chilled to the ever-loving bone.

Tea's on, so I take a tray to Gwynn's room. "Sweetie, this is Had's attempt to include us in his family. Don't you think our excuses look pretty rude compared to that?"

"Guess so," she pouts. "He's inconsiderate for doing it today."

"Explain that. Say you're honored he wants you to meet his mum, but you'd appreciate him not making plans on Saturdays."

"Do I have to wear some kind of robe?"

"Yes, my pink flannel." She laughs and I stand. "Would you like to walk the labyrinth while we're there?"

"What's a labyrinth?"

"Oh, you are in for a treat. At Holy Vessel monastery there's a big chamber with an intricate winding path laid out on the floor. How about I show you when we get there?"

Before long, we're waiting for Gwynn outside Camelon Village Library where the parting clouds reveal blue-sky puzzle pieces. She slips back into the Rover. "I texted Leo I'm going to a convent. Let him wonder." When I laugh, Had frowns. His disciplinarian threads are woven much too tight.

Gwynn diverts my attention. "How do you know Father Joseph, Grandma?"

"I met him when I lived in Scotland eons ago. He taught me meditation."

"What is this meditation you and Had do?"

"A select few of us practice Golden Bowl meditation," Had answers. "It's connected to the Tree of Life philosophy."

I add a zinger. "For my Philosophy Master's thesis at Colorado State, I used the Celtic Tree of Life to compare similar patterns for reaching higher regions in various doctrines."

Galahad's eyebrows raise. "You have a philosophy degree?" My ratings gained another star.

"Yes, have you kids studied comparative religions?"

"Only briefly." Had brakes for a flock of black-faced sheep meandering across the muddy road—bless the little critters. And bless Raven giving them what-for.

"I studied the Bible at one of my schools." Three stars for Gwynn.

A bit speechless, I gaze at the damp autumn landscape before adding, "Studying the basic world religions is a great way to understand the heart and soul of other cultures."

"So what's the point of meditation? And how is it different from prayer?" When she grabs a subject, Gwynn's a relentless terrier.

Had turns the windshield wipers off and answers, "In prayer, a person speaks to Spirit. But in meditation they listen."

Impressed by his wisdom, I say, "The aim is to reach the inner regions and experience *Oneness* with Spirit."

Excited, Gwynn exclaims, "Hey, that picture of the Celtic Tree of Life has four regions, right up to the Golden Boughs." Look at her making esoteric connections. "It's always about the trees isn't it?"

"Since trees are some of Earth's oldest inhabitants," Had responds, "they're great symbols of life's many layers. It's believed the Celts felt the presence of Spirit in their forest temples."

"Union with a Higher Power through meditation is Universal," I add.

"How's that working out for you, Grandma?" Leave it to Gwynn to lighten the mood as we drive through the monastery's huge iron gates. Green knolls dotted with sheep stretch before us. "Holy layout. This place is huge. Let me guess, the big building is Holy Vessel monastery for the monks, and the smaller big building is St. Clair's convent for the nuns."

"You got it in one," Had says. "The thirteen-acre walled compound encircles these ancient structures." He parks and we pile out of the Rover.

"There's even a lake, I mean loch." Gwynn's impressed.

On the monastery path, Galahad's dialog is interrupted with bad news from a monk called Brother Ushtey. A double whammy in fact. "We took Father Joseph to hospital this morning. But it's good you came—Mother Superior discovered a circle of poisoned Ivy."

Had calmly inquires. "And my mum?" I swear the kid has whammy-deflecting shields.

"You'll find Lady Elaine weak from fasting," the snooty Ushtey says. "Something related to a ceremony Father held for her. *I* wasn't allowed in."

A whole lot less calmly, I ask, "Is Father Joseph's condition serious?"

Ushtey addresses Galahad as if he had asked the question. I understand why the monk doesn't want to look at the miniskirted Gwynnie, but why not me? "Father was having trouble breathing, so they put him on a ventilator."

"Is he allowed visitors?"

"I wouldn't know, now would I?"

"I suppose you wouldn't." Gwynn replies.

Why did I wait so long to see Father Joseph? Some people walk on spiritual water while the rest of us wait for them to toss a lifesaver. The great man did just that for me.

We follow Ushtey up timeworn steps through ancient oak doors into the monastery. Huge weaving looms fill a lanoline-scented entryway as monks rhythmically clatter shuttles back and forth. From the motley crew we encounter, I see I'm not the only human Father Joseph rescued. Unlike Ushtey, clean shaven to the tip of his head, a good many have beards and long hair. All wear white wool robes in varying states of repair.

Turning, Ushtey the Rude snaps, "Galahad, Mother Superior is quite concerned about the Ivy. I'll show you once you've completed your . . . tour." He frowns at Raven in Gwynn's arms. "Don't let the dog loose." Gwynn gives him her best annoyed look and he scurries off.

As we walk down a marble hallway, Gwynn asks, "What's Ushtey's problem?"

"He compensates for having served time for Common Assault," Had says dismissively. Is Had discerning enough to recognize a body's ill intentions here, or at Logres? Despite Father Joseph's illness, his mom's weakness and poisoned Ivy, Had remains as cool as a mountain stream.

We enter the room with an in-laid labyrinth path on the granite floor. "Gwynn," I instruct, "stay focused on a prayer or concern as you walk the labyrinth path. Your second sense takes over. You may receive an insight, or a sense of wellbeing."

She sets Raven down. "Stay girl." The pup minds. Gwynn steps tentatively onto the pathway, a network so convoluted it winds around and around, and back and forth to a center point then back again. With an attitude of respect, Had follows after Gwynn then I move slowly through the laps. The kids and I skim past one another several times mindful of each step we take. When I reach the exit, I feel a peace regarding the dead menacing Igraine.

As I rejoin the kids, Gwynn whispers, "Holy wow, that was profound. My cells are kind of like vibrating." Divine intervention?

With Raven on a leash, we meet up with Ushtey—odd to be named after an evil water-horse beastie. He obviously hasn't taken final vows and a saint's name. He leads us across steep rolling lawns toward St. Claire's convent. As we follow the monk wannabe up the slippery cobblestones I ask, "Had, did anyone know we'd be here today?"

Brother Ushtey falls in beside us. Is he listening to our conversation? He points to the Ivy. It grows across the lawn and up the walls around jewel-colored panes in St. Clair's main stone structure. To my relief, Ushtey walks away without a by-your-leave.

Had squats to take soil and withered Ivy samples. "Gwynn, might you photograph the find?"

She nods then also bags healthy leaves for my research. The toxic circle makes me woozy and Raven doesn't argue when I pull her close. A gust blows fumes toward me and I plop down.

The underworld pulls me toward my nemesis. Before she speaks, I cry, "Igraine, you cannot torment me on sacred ground."

"Nothing will save a meddling hag," she cackles. "It's my turn to have power over you." Igraine swirls around, but I fight back hard.

I resurface having lost any sense of peace. Gwynnie holds me upright. "What did you see?"

I whisper, "I escaped. Thought the nuns might question my sanity. It's not like I asked for the second sight."

"Never mind," Gwynn says. "It's an honor to be clairvoyant which means clear-seeing. And this place is called St. Clair's. Hey Had, your name, Sinclair, means you have intuitive insight." He shrugs although Gwynn continues to astound.

With Ivy samples collected, we ramble across the leaf-strewn lawn toward Had's mother's loch-side hut. Off leash, Raven's antics kick up a robust autumn scent that strengthens my soul.

At the one-room stone hut, Had says, "Mind waiting a wee moment?" He ducks inside.

Gwynn assesses the place. "Cool little hobbit house."

"Yes, right beside a fresh-water loch. Look how the thatched roof goes all the way to the ground on both sides."

"What's this, Grandma Merle?" She photographs a lacy plant with flowering white clusters.

"That's poison hemlock. Wonder why it's growing outside her door?"

A thousand wee moments later, Had invites us in. His mother lies in a narrow bed weak from fasting. "Mrs. MacLaren, Gwynn, I'd like you to meet Lady Elaine Sinclair. Mum, my housemates—my friends." You catch that?

I say, "Nice to finally see you in person."

"And you." Elaine's pale face, framed in a white wimple against white linens, accentuates blue eyes that bore through me. Her stare lasts ten eternal seconds. When I'm sure she's going to strike me down, she looks past me to the beautiful ginger-haired Gwynn in her skimpy black mini-dress and purple leggings—every reclusive mother's nightmare.

Gwynn gushes, "Lady Elaine? You didn't tell me your mother had a title. Am I suppose to curtsey?"

"Of course not, my dear." Elaine smiles like a saint and offers a trembling hand.

Before the girl foolishly kisses it, Had speaks. "Mum thinks she could walk a little. Would you ladies like to join us down to the loch?"

As he helps Lady Elaine to a shore-side bench, Gwynn remarks, "Excuse me, Lady, but the poisoner's been right here at the convent. Had could put a lock on your door."

"Thank you for your concern, but I'm under Divine Protection."

"Well, I'll buy you some Divine Pepper Spray, just in case." My Gwynnie's an ice breaking pro like her grandfather.

Galahad admonishes. "Gwynn, pepper spray is illegal in Scotland."

Looking toward his mom, Gwynn laughs. "He's a real stickler, isn't he?" She follows that with a thought. "If Laird R.A. Stewart is your cousin, he must be about your age. For some reason I pictured him an old man."

"R.A. is a bit younger than me, but looks no more than thirty. You're sure to meet him at Camelon Castle."

Gwynn's still fervent. "I wouldn't know what to say to a laird."

"You talk to Galahad, don't you? He's laird of my clan's St. Clair-Sinclair estate."

Gywnn punches Had in the arm. "How come you didn't say?"

He shrugs and Lady Elaine looks to her only child. "Your position matters, Galahad. The Sinclair's will depend on you to manage our holdings when I'm gone. For now, could we have a private moment concerning finances."

I never get between the wealthy and their money, yet there's nothing wrong with this old gal's hearing. Lady Elaine leans toward Had. "Invest another million pounds." He agrees, no questions asked—I mean that'd keep us in shortbread a good long time. She continues. "Are these poisonings affecting R.A.'s business?"

"Mum," he warns, "I cannot reveal that information." She falls silent, he whispers something in her ear then they sit straight-backed and regal-aired on the new tartan blanket. Finally he breaks the silence. "Will you soon break your fast, Mum?" If self-deprivation cleanses the soul, Lady Elaine's must be immaculate. I believe in moderation—moderately so.

Before long merely sitting exhausts the woman and we head back. From the hut door, I ask, "Lady Elaine, where did you get your pretty plant?"

"Most likely one of the sisters."

"Be careful," I warn, "it's poison hemlock, often confused with Queen Anne's Lace—an honest mistake." She nods a thank you.

Gwynn takes Lady Elaine's hand. "I'm so happy to have met you. Galahad grew up in a beautiful place. Is it yours? I just thought Sinclair...St. Clair's..."

"The templar St. Clair's built the entire compound. It's privately owned, held in a trust that includes R.A., Galahad and me."

"So," Gwynn muses, "Laird R.A. Stewart's mother was a Sinclair?"

"Yes," Lady Elaine sighs. "My Aunt Igraine. She . . . died when we were young."

Somehow, I remain upright.

†REED (Phragmites communis) NgETAL†
†BROOM (Cytisus scoparius) NgETAL†
October 28–November 24

The similar Reed and Broom plants were used in ancient times as a floor covering, and to fashion baskets and brooms. However, choosing Broom over Reed for my healing formula became evident when I learned the word NgETAL meant *sustenance of a healer*. Back when mankind's medicine was mainly plant-based, Broom, with its narcotic properties, was administered to the wounded to induce a healing sleep. As an aside, this month begins near All Hallows Eve, which is also the Celtic New Year. For the Celts, it was a time for action, for sweeping and cleaning both one's body and home. A person has to wonder if this month of Broom brought about the legend of healers, or witches, flying on broomsticks.

Camelon Castle 13

It seemed the Halloween Ball would never arrive, but here we are at Camelon. Having parked at a distance, Had, Gwynn and I admire Laird Rex Arthur Stewart's greystone castle built on tradition and enough acreage to house a small city. Rounded towers flank both sides, and fly ancestral dragon pendants. The enormous structure sits atop a landscaped knoll, delightfully surrounded by thick old growth forest.

"Nice set up," Gwynn decrees.

Raven's indignant barking draws our attention to the caged pup in the Land Rover. It's a chilly evening, so she'll be fine for a couple hours. No escaping this time.

Enthused, Gwynn spreads her arms. "Had, your boss must be worth millions."

"A lady does not discuss another's financial status," he scolds. "However, do consider the astronomical upkeep on such an estate."

"Good point. Oh, nobody told me there'd be paparazzi. How do I look?"

About twenty photographers dot the landscape. I adjust the autumn foliage in her golden-red hair. Gwynn appears to have stepped off a Paris runway in her swirly leaf-print gown, and after a lot of practice, as graceful as a willow in spiky heels. "Your Grandpa Angus would love seeing you tonight." She beams and I turn to Galahad, "Isn't our Gwynnie the most beautiful young woman on earth?"

He assesses the gorgeous teen. "Definitely in the top one hundred."

Gwynn's delight fills the air. "Oh Had, no wonder you don't have a girlfriend."

Me? I'm dressed as a Crone swathed in dark tweed, minus the suggested witch's hat and wart, thank you very much.

Had, appearing stately for his twenty-four years and dressed as what else, a Knight's Templar, escorts us onward. Gwynn whispers, "It's a real-life fairy tale." She smiles at the cameramen planted in manicured gardens on either side of the path.

We glide toward the castle's bank of stairs that lead to Camelon's entrance and the kilted laird welcoming guests. Well, the kids glide. It's darn difficult to look graceful with my escort double-stepping me along. I do my best as the camera strobes flash and imagine tomorrow's headlines. Halloween Party Phenomena—who can identify the mysterious Autumn Goddess, six foot in heels, Pure-Hearted Knight, six-three in boots, and Samhain Crone, barely over five foot, obviously no fool in comfortable shoes.

Life sure has changed from my solitary Colorado cabin days. Now I'm involved in solving the Celtic tree poisonings, and trot past the press with two of the most attractive young people on the face of the earth. My wards—getting our family portrait taken for the whole world to ogle. Big decision. Huge.

As we reach Camelon my Gwynnie exclaims, "Holy nobility, that castle's gigantic." You may have noticed everything's holy this and holy that since I nixed her swearing.

"If my Sinclair ancestors hadn't given these lands to the Stewarts in some outrageous dowry," Had says, "this would belong to me." Surely our saintly Galahad isn't bitter.

Running in front of us, a photographer dashes up and clicks off a couple. He holds a techie device toward Gwynn. "Give me your address. I'll send you a copy."

Gwynn shifts from worldly to clueless in the bat of a glittered eye, so I intervene by saying, "Nice try." When he doesn't move, I steer him away with a painful wrist manipulation that leaves him flexing his hand. I'd better watch my step, and Gwynn's.

Having arrived in more ways than you can imagine, we climb the fourteen zillion stairs. At the top, Laird Rex Arthur greets guests, so striking in his royal red Stewart kilt. The crowd thins and the laird watches us appreciatively. Well, mostly, Gwynn.

R.A. shakes Had's hand. "Good to see you, Galahad. We'll discuss the tree poisonings later this evening." Had begins to speak, but R.A. turns to Gwynn. "And who might this lovely lass be?"

"Gwynn Avera MacLaren, sir." Sweet as honey. "Pleased to make your acquaintance." Locking eyes with the beauty, the laird actually kisses her hand. Gwynn lowers her eyelids slightly then curtsies. He holds on until Gwynn breaks the connection by turning. "May I introduce my grandmother, Mrs. Merle MacLaren."

Laird Rex Arthur pulls his gaze from Gwynn and looks down at me. I grab his hand and inquire, "Artie, how's my little warrior?"

He blinks, begins to shake my hand, changes his mind then hugs me like a son. "Nana. Dr. Bruce . . . ah, MacLaren is it?" He looks to the kids for an explanation. Had and Gwynn remain as dumbfounded as I'd anticipated.

Gwynn says, "You know each other?" Had reddens and clinches his jaw.

Hugging me again, R.A. asks, "Nana, how did you? What a birthday gift." He looks at Had then laughs. "Och, Father Joseph's fingerprints are all over this."

"Have it figured out?" I tease. You see, I raised this prestigious man from an infant, right here in this castle.

The Unveiling

As the kids and I follow Gavin, our laird-appointed escort, into the foyer my ears go musically schizophrenic. The south hall reels with Scottish folk ballads while the north hall blasts Celtic rock.

"No way. It's Talisen," Gwynn squeals, "I can't believe this."

My mind's eye envisions the old wizard-bard, Talisen, flopping around in his grave. Not that I wouldn't jig to the beat—just to keep an eye on Gwynn, you understand.

Gavin, a gorgeous mixed-race fellow in green and pink harlequin tights, skillfully parts the costumed revelers. The probable reason for the scar running down Gavin's cheek became clear when R.A. introduced him as one of the lads that served with him in the middle east. Oh, and he's a Sinclair cousin. But it's when he inadvertently reveals a Taser tucked in his Prince Charlie jacket that I realize he's a bodyguard. I'm impressed.

Not that I need protecting, but when you're vertically challenged you need help dodging as many wayward fairy wands and other fancy dress protrudins as possible. Above danger, tall slender Gwynn, grins like a kid at Disneyland forgetting her old gran. No matter, Had propels me forcefully ahead.

The throng thins as we enter the Great Hall with its three-story vaulted ceiling and double-tier wrap-around balcony that leads to apartments, the nursery and that dreaded North Tower. Matching staircases rise to those chambers I called home for nearly eighteen years. Memories of little Artie clutching the polished oak banister drown me in nostalgia.

"This way." Gavin hurries us up a raised platform to the table of honor. "Mrs. Rose will rearrange the seating to accommodate your party." He's being quite snarky. "The Laird will join you at twenty hundred hours." That's eight p.m. to civilians, but I'll bet Gavin doesn't know I'm familiar with military time.

He hurries off as Mrs. Rose bustles up. I say, "Sorry for the trouble, Miss Pris." She sets the tray down so hard the china and crystal clang. "Dr. Bruce, they didna' tell me it was you, now did they? Why you near stopped me ticker. Then you always was one for the grand surprise." She shakes her head in mock disgust then smothers me in pillow arms.

"Priscilla Rose, meet my late husband's granddaughter, Gwynn MacLaren, and you probably know our escort, Galahad Sinclair." The kids nod their greeting as they wrap their minds around me knowing these folks. We sit where the housekeeper-cook indicates, lapping up her jolly attentions.

"I didn't expect to see you, Pris. You still running the place for Artie?"

"And who else would be taken' that on?" Without bothering to lower her voice, Pris says, "Here, move them place cards to the other side of the table. They'll be haven' their backs to the admiren' crowd. Real shame."

I catch the sarcasm, but don't get her meaning until I see the names. It's Artie's half-sister, Morgan Sinclair-Stewart and her plus-one. "Pris, you sure this is all right?"

"I never was one to question the laird. Now here, I gotta' get me back to the kitchen afore one of them featherbrains burn the place down. You ain't leaven' till we have a sit down over a cuppa. Sneaken' back ta' Camelon like that." She shakes her head.

Lowering my voice, I draw her closer. "When we have that tea, I need the lowdown on Artie's acquaintances. You willing?"

"Gracious, I'd do anything for you, Dr. Bruce. You saven' my Robbie —and him the best of the three *bairns*, too. Lives here with his Bridget since he lost his leg. Not that the laird don't keep him busy. We'll talk. You ain't leaven' till we do." Pris scuttles off calling orders to a couple boys who fall in behind her.

I've always admired that formidable woman who left an abusive husband then raised her kids here at the castle, proving herself indispensable. Seeing the old dear warms me like gingerbread, but Gwynn interrupts my thoughts. "You got some 'splaining to do, Granny."

Had leans across Gwynn. "Mrs. MacLaren? Nana? Doctor Bruce? Who are you anyway?" He acts betrayed.

I reach over Gwynn's plate to touch his arm. "Sorry Had, I wanted us to get acquainted—without the influence of my past."

I wave my hand around the marble and oak hall as Mrs. Rose's crew transforms the tabletops into cornucopias erupting with every dish known to man. The decadence overwhelms. I mean, the main table groans under the weight of a monstrous roast pig that obviously met its demise trying to down a whole apple. That'll teach him.

"This is quite a shock," Galahad say, "Mrs., that is, Dr.—you're a physician? You knew my parents?" I begin to understand Had's attitude.

I lower my voice and take a breath. "Okay, shortly after R.A.'s birth I took on the position of nanny, governess and medical doctor to the Stewart family. Laird General Stewart recruited me to raise Artie, look after his half-sister, Morgan, and their mother Igraine." I turn to Galahad. "To a lesser degree I knew your parents, Lance and Elaine. Had, I meant this to be an unveiling, not an affront."

"Yeah, lighten up, Had," Gwynn says. "She got us good. Hey, does this mean we get to be friends with these people?"

Had frowns. "You're too easily impressed, Gwynn."

I force Had to make eye contact. "Please don't be upset with me."

"Why not mention who you were when we visited Mum last month?"

"We had our differences. I felt it best not to upset her if she didn't recognize me."

Determined to support me, Gwynn says, "Besides it would have ruined the surprise."

Gwynn's relentless gears grind. She whispers. "Lady Elaine said Igraine died. Is she the ghost you see in your visions? Is she threatening you . . . and the trees?"

I nod an affirmative just as Laird R.A. Stewart—Artie, appears beside me, grins and the sun rises in his face. He signals for Gavin to ring a gong that shakes a body's eyeteeth. The bands go quiet and a bagpiper descends the stairs playing 'Amazing Grace'. Silenced guests pack the hall to hear the skirling of the pipes. There's not a dry eye—my tears reflect the reunion with my boy. And me thinking I shouldn't reappear after what happened those many years ago.

As the music ends, Gavin hands R.A. a microphone. All eyes turn toward the laird. "Welcome to Camelon Castle." His admirers applaud and he continues. "As many of you know, my ancestors were given the name, Stewart, for being good stewards to the crown. Now the taxman makes sure we fulfill that role." Laughter erupts, but he goes on. "To continue that stewardship, I enjoy rewarding my employees and friends especially at Celtic New Year . . . All Hallows Eve, which just happens to be my birthday."

That elicits a round of 'For He's a Jolly Good Fellow', during which the laird appears oblivious to any disgruntled tree-poisoners in the crowd. He says, "Thank you for that, and for another successful year at Logres Lumber where we all profit from good ol' Scottish brains and hard work." Again there's applause. He raises his hand for silence, looks down at me and shakes his head. "What I didn't expect," R.A.'s voice cracks. "What I didn't expect, was to be given the best birthday gift ever. Lairds and Ladies and Gentlemen, allow me to introduce my long-lost nanny and mentor, Dr. Bruce-MacLaren." The outburst is riotous.

I stand and smile as best I can, for truth be known the spotlight scares the holy poop out of me. And then it happens.

Some guy yells, "Och, you're the lady that saved our lives on flight 713. It's her. The lady that took down the terrorist." Chatter runs through the crowd and photos are snapped.

What can I do? I pry the microphone from Artie's frozen hand and say, "Well, I guess that shot my anonymity all to heck." I raise my glass, glance at my disconcerted wards then say, "Here's to my Halloween unmasking." The admission simultaneously brings the house down, and ends my sheltered life.

Laird Rex Arthur Stewart 15

Without so much as a breather, the Halloween party moves from table to dance floor. To my surprise R.A. dashes to the Celtic rock band, picks up a fiddle and begins to accompany them. When did my boy, with his unremarkable looks but perfect demeanor, become such a charismatic talent? The Laird in his castle—it does seem like a fairy tale. So where's the sinister ogre to challenge the flawless laird? Out poisoning trees?

After a few songs, Artie joins me saying, "Just follow, Nana." He maneuvers me across the ballroom where Gwynn and Had stand.

With every young man vying for her attention my lovely girl has hardly missed a dance. Using her new socialite voice, she oozes, "I'm having the most wonderful time." As if to prove her point a Logres lumberjack pulls her onto the ballroom floor.

Galahad, on the other hand, stands around like deadwood. Doesn't he know how to dance? It's a good bet they didn't hold many balls at the monastery, but you'd think he'd have learned to boogie at university.

"R.A.," Galahad says, "Mrs., that is, Dr. Bruce-MacLaren recognized your foliage is being poisoned in consecutive Celtic months."

Artie raises an eyebrow. "So Broom was to be poisoned next. Aidan Hunter will show it to you down at the lakes. But for now, we'll enjoy ourselves."

Galahad simply crosses his arms across his chest and watches Gwynn dance. No telling his thoughts—envy, protectiveness, revulsion? Whatever the case, he needs something to do. "Had," I say, "would you mind walking and feeding Raven?"

"You have your dog with you?" Artie asks.

"My Scottish Terrier pup."

"Wonderful, bring it inside." He signals his bodyguard, Gavin, with the facial scar, to accompany Had, possibly so the Sinclair cousins become acquainted.

Gwynn returns all aglow. "What a perfect evening."

A swarthy kid in a white tux, half a head shorter than Gwynn, appears at her side. "Hi," he says, obviously enamored of her. "I'm Mort Hamilton from San Francisco."

R.A. swoops in and twirls a blushing Gwynn gracefully away from Mort. To the crowd's delight the couple swirls around the instantly vacated dance floor almost as if they've rehearsed for weeks. Once again, Artie impresses me. No telling where he, and Gywnn for that matter, learned to perform like that, but I'm proud as a swelled-up toad.

Not only is Gwynnie acting like a lady, but I've spent the entire evening in awed admiration for the man my Artie has become. He seems to effortlessly run his estate and timber company. Before eating he graciously handed bonus checks to everyone in his employ—all as if there were no tree poisonings threatening Logres Lumber. So why do I have this niggling of dread?

After wowing everyone, R.A. and Gwynn bow to a round of applause. They grab me and head to the veranda that spans the back of the castle. The crowd follows Artie who seats Gwynn and me, runs down to receive a torch from Gavin then ignites a gimongous bonfire with a whoosh. The laird's guests cheer so loud you'd think he invented fire. Everyone appears to love my Artie, but I worry that one of this lot may threaten his Celtic trees. Unaware of any peril, R.A. dashes back and bellows into a microphone. "Let the games begin."

Enormous spotlights illuminate piping, archery, highland dance and all manner of Scottish games on the castle's massive grounds. The burliest of the burlies tosses the caber. That's like a big telephone pole. A lot of these games were invented long ago when their weapons were outlawed. Being canny Scotsmen, if an adversary came along, they threw a tree and knocked the poop out of him. I exaggerate, but you get the picture.

I've missed the old place. I'm talking acreage here, with winding paths through the bordering woods, and three football field lengths of landscaped lawns and gardens featuring a huge fountain of frolicking mermaids. "Look at that, and that and that," Gwynn exclaims. Angus would be delighted.

When a tour of the games leaves me ready for a chaise lounge, Gwynn complains, "Grandma, I haven't seen everything." We've watched enough rivalries to keep any enthusiast reminiscing for a decade—and me totally, well mostly, noncompetitive. My Artie doesn't seem to have a competitive nature either. Can a businessman be too charitable? Can all this extravagance exist without inviting risk?

A somber Had returns with Raven tucked under his arm—her legs churning air. He allows her to escape into my arms and I'm glad for the doggie smooch. I wonder if Galahad also senses a menace, but ask, "Do you want to compete in the games, Had?"

"Perhaps the archery competition." Without another word he heads for the target range. What other hidden talents does Had possess?

Gwynn switches from sophisticated to seven in a wink. "I wanna' try for an apple." The red orbs dangle on strings from, you guessed it, a huge apple tree. My charmed Gwynnie bites into hers on the third try, but the game doesn't end there. If the laird draws your numbered apple you win a prize and a kiss. Gwynn returns clutching her lucky ticket like a twenty-dollar gold piece. "I do hope I'll win." However, when the number is called, she groans along with the other disappointed women.

As R.A. announces the number a second time, a vamped-up witch struts to the podium black hair flying. My perceptive pup growls. "You got that right," I state.

"Who's that?" Gwynn whispers.

"Morgan le Fey—R.A.'s half-sister. They share a mother—Igraine of all people. Artie's dad, Laird General Stewart, married Igraine when Morgan was three years old. She never got to know her real father and Igraine wasn't much of a parent. That's where I came in, or tried to."

"I'll bet witchy Morgan scammed us." Gwynn moans. "The other women deserved a chance at the prize, and the laird's kiss." Gwynn wants a kiss from a man her father's age? Then Artie's exceptional personality does make up for his unremarkable features.

Flushing brightly, the laird faces the grumbling crowd that now believes the prize is laced with nepotism. After fastening the pearl necklace around Morgan's graceful neck, he skims her cheek with a brotherly buzz. Yet, some of the rowdy mob demand a *proper snog*. A chill blows evil omens our way as Morgan grabs R.A.'s lapels and lays a lip-lock on him that leaves him scarlet.

The Séance

Animated by the limelight, Morgan grabs the microphone. "As you know this is Samhain, the night the veil between the realm of the living and the dead is thinnest. So if anyone fancies a séance, join me in the library." R.A. shakes his head having not anticipated this antic. Morgan adds, "There's room for thirty, including the press."

The stampede commences. I plunge Raven into Had's arms, grab Gwynn, and hoof it. Remembering Camelon's floor plan from my nanny days, I shove Gwynn down a dark corridor and out a panel hidden behind a heavy tapestry. We find ourselves in a library outfitted with twelve-foot-high oak shelves crammed full of nothing but musty old books—my favorite room.

"Grandma Merle, was that a secret passage?" Gwynn is fast coming to admire her old gran.

The shortcut afforded us seats at the séance table, but I know something's up when Morgan acts pleased. "I heard you had resurfaced, Dr. Bruce." She spits out my name like a dirty word, but it's too late to renege. I can be as dense as an anvil.

The room fills to overflowing, but only five of us sit at a table inlayed with Celtic astrological symbols. Flanking Morgan and Gwynn is that smarmy smiling, Mort Hamilton. A beefy monster with angular features and carrot-orange hair, sits to my left.

"Hold hands," Morgan instructs. "Don't break the link no matter what." My giant grabs my hand in his huge calloused mitt. "I . . . I'm Aidan Hunter," he stutters.

"Oh yes, Logres Lumber's forestry manager."

"Aidan is my plus one," tawny-skinned Morgan informs the crowd.

The lights dim except for the one strategically illuminating Morgan the Magnificent. We're instructed to open our minds to universal energy. She carries on about aspects of certain planets in certain houses at certain times. She's making it up—you can't memorize the entire ephemeris—but her devotees fall for it.

Standing near Gwynn, R.A. catches my attention and rolls his eyes. Just when we think her performance benign, Morgan stops mid-sentence. She throws her neck all the way back. As her head raises only the whites of her eyes show. When the coffee brown irises reappear, they're glazed. It's actually pretty impressive.

Gwynn's hand tightens on mine, so I give it a reassuring squeeze. Carrot-top Aidan Hunter nearly releases his sweaty palm, but I hang on. I want to see this out.

Gradually, Morgan's gaze locks on R.A. then lingers until all heads turn toward the laird. I mean, call an agent, this dame is good, but as she speaks the contents of my stomach curdle. No longer does Morgan le Fey's deep voice scratch our eardrums. Instead, we hear the high-pitched whine of the long-dead Igraine—Artie and Morgan's insane mother. My nemesis.

Igraine's head swings toward Artie. "Your trees haven't a hope in hell." Holy stars, does anyone else recognize Igraine?

"Enough," R.A. demands, but the crowd's moan keeps him from stopping the farce.

"Never could take the truth you bloody brat." It's Igraine alright—sweet-talk and all. Artie remains awkwardly silent.

Igraine turns toward me. "Came for your revenge, did you Doctor Bruce?"

Playing along, I say, "Oh, is there reason to seek revenge?"

Igraine turns on Gwynn. "You won't have Camelon." With impeccable timing, she lets the accusation hang then yells so loud Gwynn and I both jump. "Not my castle." Dramatically, Igraine leans forward and screams into Gwynn's pale face, "You're cursed. Cursed to eternity, Gwynn Avera MacLaren."

Okay, now the press knows her name, and I'm seriously ticked. I can't tell you what keeps me from lunging across the table. Maybe some part of me believes Igraine has returned from her well-deserved grave. Truth is, Morgan has us mesmerized.

With a quivering voice belying her bravado, Gwynn says, "What a nut case."

Ignoring the affront, Igraine's eyes drift toward the forestry manager. "You're no better, Aidan Hunter. Bedding my Morgan to raise your social standing." Aidan's complexion brightens and his jaw clamps. Igraine laughs the same crazed laugh I heard so many times in the past.

She plunges against the of back her chair before turning toward Mort. "Yes, I know you." A devious smile crinkles her face. "You think a bastard can claim Camelon?" We suffer another pregnant pause. Igraine's demeanor changes and she smiles. "Unless you avenge me. Yes, you'll need a home since your own father wanted you aborted." In a rare moment of outrage, Artie's nostrils flare and his eyelids are but slits.

Visibly shaken, Mort breaks the circle. Morgan sags before looking up fully revived. He exclaims, "How could she know who I am? I haven't told anyone."

"Know what?" Gwynn is as lost as the rest of us.

Mort stands and announces, "Countess Morgan is my birth mother. I came here to find her—now that my adoptive parents are dead."

"My baby," Morgan exclaims. "My own little boy. I've found you at last." It's enough to gag a whole swarm of maggots.

Gwynnie gasps. "He's your son?" We're to believe these two haven't met until now, but I know they're full of it—until I glance at a pale green Artie. Without a word, he stares at Mort and Morgan. They do look awfully similar—same dark hair, skin and eyes.

Willing up a faint smile, Morgan looks to R.A. "He's my son, your nephew." Mort embraces her. They could take this on the road, but no need, the paparazzi are getting it all on camera.

Artie takes on a gracious tone. "Welcome to the Stewart family, my boy."

"You're too kind, ahh Uncle." Mort sounds grateful, but his eyes gleam as if he's swindled his way into a gold-plated existence. R.A., acting the bigger man, but digging a deeper grave, shakes Mort's hand. Camera strobes freeze the moment in indelible digitization. I'm sure Morgan planned this public acceptance of Mort into the clan—with the cunning precision I remember her possessing as a child. Igraine's child.

Now the laird has no choice but to stand by his decision with all of Scotland as witness. Questions fly around the room, but one in particular sparks Morgan's interest. "Who is the father?"

"Well . . . " she begins.

"I think that should remain confidential," R.A. answers a bit too quickly. His face and neck have gone red and splotchy.

"Well, there's no real reason to keep my love-child secret, but for the father's sake, I'll not reveal his name. At least not at the moment," Morgan adds.

Artie looks pleadingly toward me and my mind does a high-speed rerun of the last years I spent at Camelon. The only timeframe where Morgan took a nearly nine-month holiday, to visit cousins in California, occurred right after she and Artie spent their school break at the castle. I'd thought it a wonder the way teenage half-brother and sister had gotten on so famously . . . too famously if I have her gestation period right. And, I'd been responsible for them.

So overjoyed by Morgan shipping off to America, I hadn't questioned the General's acquiescence. He never said a word to me, which meant he didn't blame me for her pregnancy, nor did he trust me enough to reveal the truth.

No wonder the General took to drinking. His son and step-daughter —half-brother and sister—were lovers? Was the affair premeditated, so Morgan could hold this over the otherwise perfect son? These years later, I understand the extent of her manipulative power. Here are Mort and Morgan on the Camelon chessboard cornering the white king with their blackmail moves.

Bailing Artie out of a sticky spot, I swoon. He grabs me and says, "It was simply too much for the old dear."

As expected, Morgan twists my collapse to further her ends. "It's a shock for me, too. To be reunited with my only child, I'm the happiest woman in the world." She hugs Mort, and gives me a top-that-one look.

I hadn't known it was a competition, but I no longer worry about my terrorist takedown being tomorrow's headline news.

Lance La Lac

S ince the Halloween party refuses to wind down, I'm resting in the darkened library. When Morgan slips in with Mort, I sink deeper into my wingback chair—wouldn't want to distract them. Morgan lights three hefty black candles situated in front of a smoky mirror. I can see their reflected faces and even the silver buckles on Morgan's shoes. Mort admires his longish black hair and asks rather testily, "What's this about?"

Morgan pulls a lethally sharp dirk from her witch's cape. "It's an old Samhain ritual for conjuring one's future husband—my intended's face will appear in the mirror."

"I figured since Lance turned you down, you'd be through with marriage. Do we want to bring anyone else into our plan?" They've had time to hatch a plan?

"Just watch," she admonishes. "I'll entice my suitor's essence from the ethers."

Morgan begins humming an eerie tune, but I'm not impressed until I see movement over by the suit of armor. That's the trouble with All Hollow's Eve—the veil between this reality and the Underworld diminishes. Or is someone that knows the castle's secret passages as well as I do, entering the library? With purposeful concentration, Morgan cuts an apple into nine, spears a slice and holds it over her left shoulder. Her eyes narrow as if she's seeing beyond the mirror's surface. Nothing happens until a man creeps from behind the metal knight. I scoot to the edge of my chair—in case I have to save someone in a hurry.

The supposed apparition dashes toward Morgan, grabs the apple slice and lets out a baritone chuckle. Morgan stares at the mirror then whirls around. The man is Lance La Lac, Galahad's birth-father. "Lancelot, so you are meant to be my husband after all. Now, you will have to divorce Lady Elaine and marry me."

Caught in her web, he counters, "Aren't you and Aidan Hunter playing house?"

"Oh, he's just a bit of rough. Why did you miss the party, naughty boy?"

"Detained. Listen, I have news concerning the Broom poisoning down by the lakes. Don't know if I should break it to R.A. tonight."

Mort steps up. "R.A. has had all the shocking news he can take for one evening."

Lance stares at Mort's offered hand with distaste then turns on Morgan. "You didn't hit R.A. with this on his big night? Morgan le Fey, you little b . . . "

I step into the light. "Yes, she did, Fancy Lancy. She introduced her son in front of everyone including the press."

It takes three ticks for Lance to recall his childhood name and recognize me. "Dr. Bruce, you found your way home." Holding true to his French Celtic nature he kisses my cheeks and laughs in delight. "I would know your beautiful face anywhere." Lance, the epitome of tall, dark and sinfully handsome, could convert the staunchest celibate. No wonder he has half of Scotland's ladies tapping on his bedroom door. "Still the charmer, hey Lance? It was good to be back until Morgan proclaimed Mort to be Artie's nephew. And what? Heir to the estate?"

"Shut up, you nosey old hag." Morgan steps toward me wielding her dirk. In a flash I grab her hand pressing the fleshy spot between her finger and thumb. Morgan winces and the knife drops. She smiles at my audacity.

"Morgan le Fey, mind your manners," Lance scolds.

"Still taking sides with Dr. Bruce are we, Lance?"

Morgan pulls at his jacket just as an enormous crash erupts. Startled, we turn round. For no earthly reason the suit of armor dropped the Stewart family shield.

"So Morgan, it appears you've disturbed your ancestors," I chide.

"Alive, or dead they never approve of me, do they Dr. Bruce?" She turns toward Lance. "I want to see you privately."

"Wait your turn, Morgan." Lance links his arm with mine and escorts me toward the double doors.

Before we reach them, the redhaired giant, Aidan Hunter, enters and walks straight to Morgan saying, "My lady, there's warm milk in your room. Run on now." I figure she'll refuse, but Morgan motions for Mort to follow and heads off.

Impressed, Lance says, "What is your secret, Aidan? I never thought I'd witness Morgan le Fey acquiescing to any living soul."

"No secret. I treat her with the care and respect she deserves. She's my Madonna." Aidan sets his square jaw and leaves.

"I do hope he heard Morgan call him her bit of rough," I say.

"Yes, his devotion seems terribly misplaced," Lance adds.

As much as I don't want to for Had's sake, I like his dad. Even though I love a suave man, I slide my arm from Lance's. The snub doesn't escape him. "Sorry, but I'm here with my granddaughter and your son. I'd best find them. Nice to see you, Lancy."

"Quite right, Madame. Your loyalties lie in the correct arena."

See what I mean? How do you condemn the Duke of Debonair?

(Morning Theatrics  18

I'm weary from last night's party, yet here I sit in Camelon's sunlit breakfast room with Had, Gwynn and the castle clan. The family dines in a different room each meal as if they get bored with the same setting. The comparatively small morning table only seats twelve and a body is expected to serve themselves from covered dishes on the sideboard.

Seated across the table, Morgan addresses me. "You too drunk to drive home?"

I smirk, but a thrilled Gwynn turns to say, "Thank you, Laird Stewart, for inviting us to stay over. I've never slept in a castle before."

"I'm glad you enjoyed it, Gwynn. And call me R.A." He grins that sideways grin that always grabbed my heart. "Nana, you made the papers." He holds up the *Times*.

Dang, I'm headline news after all, but smile at the accompanying picture—me and the kids photographed by the guy whose wrist I twisted. "My stars, a body becomes public domain for nothing more than protecting a few citizens."

Artie turns to Morgan. "Our Nana is famous."

"Your Nana, not mine."

"She did save a plane full of passengers on her flight over." He holds a newspaper section toward Morgan as if it's only incidental. "Of course, you and Mort made the society pages."

Morgan lunges for the sheets just as Mort bursts through the double doors knocking young Bridget Rose with her tea tray aside. "Doesn't it ever stop raining around here?" That's our cue to commiserate, but no one obliges.

"Rain is good for the trees," R.A. points out.

Dishing up animal products, Mort turns. "I can't take this gloom. I'm from San Francisco where the sun shines three hundred days a year."

Why is he flat out lying? San Francisco is foggy and rainy much of the year.

"This is Scotland. You best get used to it," Morgan advises.

Seemingly irritated, R.A. snaps his newspaper in front of his face then holds out his cup. Bridget scurries to fill it without a word. Gorgeous dark-skinned, cheek-scarred Gavin fills a plate of food then sits beside Artie.

Making me feel I've moved to the Land of Giants, carrot-top Aidan ambles in dressed like a Paul Bunyan clone. But then, everyone here dwarfs me. I need to go back to India where a good deal of the population is normal size. I mean, our male cook in the Punjab came up to my shoulder—only time in my life I felt tall.

Morgan glances at Aidan's hands. "Och, your nails—working on a truck all night?"

Aidan smiles. "I'll show you my surprise soon." A man with a secret.

"Not interested," she snaps. Aidan lets the insult slide. She should marry this guy.

"You should appreciate your boyfriend's initiative," Gavin chides.

Morgan rises and walks to Artie. "I need money. Gavin let me sit next to R.A."

She pushes Gavin's shoulder and his patience.

"Another demonstration like that, Morgan, and I'll escort you to your chambers."

"That might be fun, Gav, but everyone knows who you really love."

Gavin smolders as Artie empties his wallet into her hand. Morgan looks at the cash and R.A. snaps, "No credit cards for you ever again. Now be gone with you." Mollified, Morgan returns to her chair.

Changing the atmosphere, Gwynn says, "Aidan, I saw you at the archery competition last evening. You're a regular Robin Hood."

The lumberjack fills his mouth, looks up and studies Gwynn's curly golden-red hair while he swallows. "You're Irish then, miss?"

"My mother, Avera Collins, was from Ireland," she announces proudly.

Without one bit of pride, Aidan says, "Me mum, too." A body must understand the racial prejudice against the Irish to appreciate this attitude. Even in Scotland, Aidan's Irish lilt marks him—the reason for his reticence?

Pinching Aidan's chin, Morgan turns his face away from Gwynn, so my granddaughter asks, "Do you have any Irish blood, Lady Morgan?"

"Of course not. And it's Countess Morgan. Unlike Dr. Bruce, I married up."

"So Countess," Gwynn snipes, "where's your Count Dracula?" R.A. chuckles.

Morgan glares at the teen. "In his coffin with the lid nailed down. I'm looking for a replacement." Morgan stares at me. "You bring her here to marry her off, Dr. Bruce?"

"MacLaren," Gwynn corrects. "Our name is MacLaren."

"You related to the sportscar McLarens?" Morgan inquires.

Despite her father's wealth, Gwynn says, "No, we're the poor American branch." She turns to Mort. "Get that? We wouldn't want you to marry down." Artie guffaws.

Having kept up with this clan, I know Morgan outstrips my record of ex-husbands. Incidentally, my second husband was her first husband, and the reason I left Camelon. It's a nasty story of seduction and deceit. I'll spare the telling for now.

Galahad, hasn't uttered a word all morning, so Gwynn asks, "Which one of those guys at the party was your dad?"

"He was detained."

"Maybe he didn't know you were coming."

"He knew." Galahad deserves better. The unfortunate fact is, one of our missions in life is to overcome our childhood traumas. A body needs to have a heart big enough to forgive their parents or guardians. You do that gracefully and St. Peter will let you through the Pearlies, hands down.

"Galahad, would you mind finding something for Raven to eat?" I ask.

The laird interjects, "Bring the wee lass to me, would ye now? She'll be needing to meet my Sandy Lad. He's looking for a lassie." Had takes off, as does Gavin.

"Artie, your brogue is showing," I tease. "You sampling the scotch this early?"

"Nay, just a wee dram every year on me birthday and one at Christmas." He accentuates his accent then adds more seriously, "Don't worry, I'm not like the General." Artie's father drank himself to death, so you understand my concern.

Gwynn addresses R.A. "Your party was fantastic. Wait'll I send pictures to my dad and his wife. They didn't want me, so Grandma Merle brought me to Scotland which I've completely fallen in love with." News to me.

R.A. shakes his head. "I love you unpretentious Americans." He's really taken to the kid.

Galahad returns with Raven and hands her to R.A. who pronounces, "A fine Scottie even if you are from across the pond." Raven licks his cheek and settles on his lap like she's known him all her nine months. She eyes his scone, slathered with clotted cream and paws his hand. He laughs and offers her tiny pieces. Two seconds in the joint and the little beggar has the head honcho feeding her.

Gavin returns holding a dog leash with an alert wheaten-colored Scottie making a determined rolling gait toward R.A. He holds Raven up. "Sandy Lad, look what I have." Upstaged, Sandy growls and Artie croons, "Is that any way to treat a lady?"

Gavin sits then heaves the well-fed Wheaten Scottie onto his lap. Sandy Lad eyes my black doggie in his master's arms with distrust. Raven, ever the diplomat, touches her nose to his. He licks her face and we decide he's in love—of course it could be the clotted cream he adores. "Nana, can you part with your pup while Gavin takes them through the gardens? Galahad, why don't you go with your cousin?" The Sinclair cousins leave and R.A. turns to Aidan. "Time to head for Logres."

Aidan shovels in eggs, bangers and toast at an impressive rate, but manages to speak to Gwynn. "Must make the lads give the laird an honest day's work."

R.A. looks toward Morgan. "Some of us have to work for a living."

"I'll go with you," Mort says. "I could get to the bottom of these tree poisonings." Unlike Gwynn who loves every minute of castle life, Mort seems about to combust.

Morgan gives Mort a shriveling look. "Not this time, poppet." She turns. "But, brother dear, we should decide where Mort will fit at Logres."

R.A. stares at Mort long enough to make the boy squirm, then answers. "If you're actually staying, I'll give it some consideration." Morgan throws her napkin in her plate and storms out. These Camelon scenes will make for great discussions with the kids—purely for research.

Aidan mutters, "That Morgan's something isn't she?"

"Always has been," I say.

"Yes, you knew herself as a wee one."

"Since she was three years old. Of course, I've followed her through the tabloids these past years."

Eagerly Aidan asks, "You see me escort her to the British Academy Awards?"

"Oh, yeah," I lie, "that was you."

"Your fifteen minutes of fame?" Mort asks.

Aidan turns red. "No."

"Come on, you've got six copies stashed away, haven't you?" Mort chides.

"Leave him alone, Mort," Gwynn insists. "I'll keep clippings from today's *Times*."

"That's different."

"No, it isn't." She sticks her tongue out much to Artie's delight.

Aidan scrapes his chair on the granite floor and leaves with, "Okay, well then...."

"What does Morgan see in him?" Mort asks.

"Never question your mother's taste in men," R.A. scolds.

"You should know."

"That's enough of that, Mort Hamilton," I snarl.

"Who do you think you are, granny?"

"Your elder, sonny." I stare him down.

Mort looks to the laird for support, gets none and stomps out leaving Gwynn and me with Artie.

He sighs. "Now that the morning farce is over, I can reclaim my role as ruler of this castle."

Trying not to laugh with tea in her mouth, Gwynnie snorts really loud.

We all split a gut.

Memories

With Galahad on Gwynn patrol, I ride the service elevator to the top floor to visit the old nursery, at least that's where I mean to go. However, Igraine's north tower chamber sucks me in like a psychic vacuum. A groundswell of palpable memories hangs over her former rooms. And the stench—a body can almost smell her presence.

"Come on, old girl." I urge myself. "Deranged Igraine is very dead. That séance unnerved you more than you thought." Speaking out loud bolsters my courage, but it's also meant for Igraine's spirit, just in case. As I turn, my breath stops at the sight of disemboweled blackbirds on a blood-spattered dressing table.

Reeling into a long trek of reminiscence, I flash on Igraine's lucid moments instructing young Morgan in the dark arts. It's not a leap to assume these bloody crow's wings framing a picture of me with baby Artie, to be Morgan's artistry. Merle, in French, means blackbird, so what better charm to use? How did Morgan know to create this elaborate magot-infested blood and guts display? She supposedly didn't know I was coming to Scotland, let alone Camelon. Well, Morgan just shot straight to my top-ten toxic-tree suspect list. The plot sickens.

Was it fate, or the old General's plan that brought me to Camelon originally? You see, the Bruce and Stewart destinies have intertwined since the thirteen hundreds. When Robert the Bruce's son died childless, the Stewart's—the Bruce's stewards—advanced all the way to the throne. So in our military days the Laird General Stewart saw our shared Scottish ancestral heritage as a sign.

The Laird General and I met on a covert mission when I served as a U.S. Army doctor and he as advisor to the U.K.'s special forces. But the old devil had already gone through channels to obtain my early discharge before he bothered to offer me the nanny position. "It'll get you out of this hell hole and into the lovely Scottish hills," he argued.

When I balked because of his underhanded tactics, he let me write my own terms. The truth was, the wily gent omitted I'd be trading one hell for another.

He claimed I'd care for his newborn son, Rex Arthur, a sick wife, Igraine as well as Morgan, her three-year-old daughter from a former marriage. I wagered a staggeringly high salary, figuring in the loss of a military pension, and thought the general incompetent when he agreed. He wasn't.

You see, Igraine wasn't simply ill, she was bug-flipping nuts. But I believe if you're meant to pay your dues with someone, you end up doing it regardless. After twenty-one years at Camelon, I had paid enough dues for a life membership in the Stewart clan. But I'm jumping ahead of my story.

Before the military stent, my marriage ended from a combination of Joe's drug dealing and our baby boy dying shortly after birth. All that loss convinced me to use my medical degree to enlist and save lives. After a couple of gruesome years patching wounded warriors, the Laird General redirected my talents.

There were plenty of times I kicked my backside for jumping into the Stewart's boiling caldron. However, once I'd signed on, I couldn't escape Igraine's maniac ward—not that she hadn't had a rough time. Igraine's husband, Morgan's father, died in the war. The story goes, their family friend, Laird General Stewart, became insanely obsessed with the tawny-skinned, dark-eyed Igraine, so he sought an overseas post to forget her. When Morgan's father showed up in the General's unit, the laird took it as an omen and ordered Morgan's dad into a deadly firefight. The General scurried home to propose marriage to Igraine. Although her refusal surprised him, he believed in the portent and slipped her a date drug. That's how Artie got here. Igraine wed out of desperation then unable to reconcile marrying her husband's apparent murderer, lost her mind.

When I arrived at Camelon, a much younger cook-housekeeper, Priscilla Rose, armed me with this tale. She then covered her nose and ushered me into Igraine's chambers. I deftly dodged a teacup, but Igraine's screams scratched my spine. I stood in a wealthy man's castle, yet his wife and her children lay in their own filth—the squalor cascading all the way to the rounded north tower walls.

"She won't let us enter excepten to bring food," Pris reported. "The laird gave me the strict orders to do as she says. I canna go against him." My attention turned to the nearly lifeless infant lying naked in a wad of soiled diapers. "We feed the *bairn* when we can, but she doesn't want him to live," Pris alleged.

As I snatched Artie from Igraine's reach, she screeched, "That's mine."

"That, dear lady, is a human baby," I snapped. "Until you recognize that fact, he is not yours." I placed the limp baby in Priscilla's arms. "Clean him and see if he'll take milk." Cuddling the stinking babe, Pris left me standing in the gagging abyss.

Igraine spit obscenities as I stripped her bedding and ordered it be to be burned. She squawked and clawed at me, but for no apparent reason quieted down as if she'd been miraculously rendered sane. "My husband, laird of this castle, will put a stop to you."

"As it happens, Laird General Stewart ordered me to take charge of you and your kids. And I always follow your husband's orders."

With Morgan, thrashing and screaming like a banshee, I headed to the bath. There was no soothing the child until I'd cleaned her and her mother then allowed the three-year-old back into Igraine's arms. I know leaving Morgan with that nut-case was a mistake, but I desperately needed to save tiny Artie.

"Igraine, when you're well enough you may visit your baby in the nursery. We'll be back to muck out your room. Meantime, I suggest you start acting like a sane person, so I'm not forced to have you committed."

"The almighty laird would never let his name be so sallied." She was right. No matter how I pleaded, the Laird General wouldn't allow his wife to receive professional treatment. Consequently, the Igraine Wars raged. Despite my fair, but firm tactics, Igraine responded like a lunatic.

I tried over and again to extricate Morgan from Igraine, but they were inseparable. Morgan just as often registered pleasure from frustrating me as did her mother—if you can believe that of a three-year-old. I fought for the child's right to a normal life, but the General approved of the vixens remaining together, so was forced to leave the she-devils to their own undoing.

Frankly I needed to focus on saving baby Artie's life which required an enormous amount of effort. An around-the-clock job, I engaged everyone from Pris to the gardener. Unlike Morgan, my Little Warrior was surrounded by loving people and quickly became the center of castle life.

His happy demeanor endeared him to everyone except Igraine. Of course, I didn't hesitate to become Artie's surrogate mother. Watching the tyke learn and grow thrilled me to pieces. From the beginning

Artie's spirit rang as honest and tender as a saint. At age two he crawled into my lap smiling like he'd planned the moment and said, "Nana, Artie wuv ou mery much." If he didn't already own me, that clenched it. R. A. Stewart never replaced the baby boy I lost, but I loved him—love him—like my own blood.

Eventually, little Pauline Rose, Priscilla's youngest, enticed Morgan down the hall to the nursery. After that, Morgan escaped the nut ward for longer and longer periods. I set up a schoolroom and tutored the three Rose children, Morgan, and finally Artie.

Exceptionally brilliant, Morgan le Fey, was a devious manipulative child. Instead of asking straight out, she wrangled whatever she wanted out of her mother, or the servants. Except me—I had her pegged and she hated me for it. She learned to speak properly, dress and bathe herself, cipher and read. Television taught her a great deal. She'd repeat phrases, especially those spoken by royalty then put on airs that amused me until I saw how she lorded it over the other kids. It's scary to witness a child with delusions of grandeur, but it somehow made her feel secure in her unstable world.

Igraine needed to pull everyone down to her small frightened level, finding sadistic pleasure in her tyranny. One day, Morgan returned to her mother later than usual, so Igraine retaliated by shoving the child into the hall. Morgan tried appeasing her mum, but Igraine remained as unrelenting as a Scottish winter.

Resigned to her fate, Morgan approached me with a demand. "I won't live like one of the servants. I'll have my own suite." However, I'd catch her rocking back and forth gnashing at her doll until it resembled the casualty Morgan mirrored.

Camelon Castle's 'normal' differed from the village folk that kept the gossip buzzing throughout the countryside. Priscilla Rose apprized us of local affairs and gibble-gabble. Consequently, the Laird General blocked passage to outsiders through Camelon's heavy iron gates. Nonetheless, I found every excuse to escape with Artie and his introduction to Camelon Village gave the castle a false air of normalcy.

Regulations aside, for her ninth birthday, Morgan invited her sweet young cousin Lady Elaine, Artie and the three Rose children. Priscilla baked an enormous red velvet cake and iced it red with pink script reading 'Lady Morgan le Fey'. The gathering went well until Morgan decided to take a slice to Igraine. "Mother is ill and can't come down today. Don't start the games without me." Morgan slipped away as if

Igraine deserved special treatment—the mother that barely spoke except to criticize.

Morgan would never suffer her mother's insults again. She found Igraine in a tub of bloody water with her jugular slashed. On the floor below Igraine's limp hand lay the suicide weapon, a silver kilt pin in the shape of a sword—a present from Morgan. The child attempted to pull Igraine from the crimson pool then let her dead mother sink to her scarlet doom. Out of her mind with shock Morgan ran down the stairs, her long black hair dripping Igraine's blood on her white satin dress. The child appeared as if she'd stepped out of a horror film. Young Morgan saw the terror on her young guest's faces then down at the blood on her dress. She fainted out cold.

The General drained the bloodied water and covered his wife. "I'll be damned if I let strangers see her like this." When the doctor asked if he'd any inkling she would ahem...harm herself, the General admitted she'd been a bit depressed, but never guessed she'd do this. Either the man was buried under a slab of denial, or a bold-faced liar.

Of course, much to the spectator's delight at the inquest, I told a different story. They had no idea how much I left out for the children's sake, but included confiscating Igraine's china teacups and other sharp objects after she began cutting herself.

I'd insulated Artie from much of his mother's insanity, but at age six, he understood she'd killed herself. I told the little boy his mother had a sickness that made her very sad. "The General says she couldn't brave it any longer," he said then never mentioned it again.

Morgan, on the other hand, was inconsolable, and right to question her mother's motives. I spoke to her of depression when I wanted to tell her Igraine was a narcissistic loonie-toon. Not that I let the Laird General off the hook. "Your step-father should have protected Igraine by procuring appropriate medical care." Yet, I couldn't reach Morgan and feared the worse for her sanity. Against my advice, the General suggested boarding school. The ten-year-old Morgan agreed, on the grounds he'd legally adopt her. The child took the name Sinclair-Stewart and left strict instructions to tell everyone her mother died of heart failure, which wasn't exactly a lie.

The good news was, Camelon transformed into a happier place with Igraine dead and Morgan away except for the occasional holiday. Years passed, but wanting to remain part of Camelon, I stayed on as family physician much longer than necessary. I even married a local attorney. My mistake was insisting we live in a croft on castle grounds. I crumbled when Morgan seduced and married him—most likely to be rid of me.

Despairing over my second failed marriage, I felt it deeper because Morgan had managed to separate me from Artie. Granted he was away at university, but had managed to return regularly. I moved to St. Clair's convent where Mother Superior and Father Joseph counseled me, but the spiritual lifestyle of Golden Bowl meditation saved me.

Having decided to leave Scotland, I visited Artie at university where we swore we'd never lose touch. However, communicating with Artie felt like cutting my heart out, and at the time, hurt more than fading out of his life. I lost myself in travel then settled in India's Punjab until my rebound husband convinced me to return to America. Once he obtained his American citizenship, he asked for his freedom and ended my third marriage. The fourth husband lasted longer, but still didn't take. I'm not complaining. My years in Colorado with Gwynn's grandfather, Angus MacLaren, were the best of the best.

Over time, I wrote Artie dozens of letters, but never mailed them. The years and miles discouraged me from contacting him. I followed his climb to success with the pride of a mother, but my congratulations were sent through the cosmos, not the postal system.

Now, I stand in Igraine's castle asylum staring at Morgan's bloody altar that shot me back in time *ad nauseam*. Why did providence return me to Camelon? So I might congratulate myself for saving Artie? And is taking Gwynn on, a chance to redeem myself for failing so badly with Morgan? No, underneath it all, I'm just an old softie. But don't go spreading that around.

What's Done is Done  20

With me deep in recollections, the door to Lady Igraine's north tower chamber creaks open behind me. I spin around expecting what? Her ghost? "Oh Artie, it's you." I'm relieved and a bit ashamed I let Morgan's black magic taunt me.

"Nana, I didn't think you'd gravitate to this room." R.A. stops dead in his tracks as he sees the carcass-laden altar. "Morgan's work? First Mort, now this." He pulls out his phone. "Aidan, get my sister to the north tower to clean up her mess. No, you bring her." Artie rubs his hand over a weary face. "Sometimes I think Morgan is demented."

I want to ask what his first clue was, but elucidate instead. "Parental role-models affect children their entire lives. Your mother, Igraine, raised Morgan helping form her personality before you children were subjected to the suicide. My own mother walked the razor's edge of sanity. Consequently, I was pretty unhinged when I left home."

R.A. drops to the edge of the bed. "Fortunately for me, you turned out saner than anyone I know."

"Well kiddo, I sought help—counseling, self-help books and a lot of Al Anon meetings. They teach a body the tools necessary to navigate life's churning waters—back to sanity. Self-realization is a lifetime job of tenacity and courage to change. And not to excuse Morgan, who seems to enjoy her brand of insanity, but Igraine was an extreme case." Artie and I are finally alone and here I am chopping at his family tree. It's just that he isn't as perfect as I'd thought. This whole Mort, the incestual son, has thrown me. Is it my place to ask about the elephant that dumped on last evening's party?

Just like old times, Artie reads my mind. "I should have told you about Morgan's pregnancy. I was so ashamed. The General knew. He sent her to his Hamilton cousins out in San Francisco. Sorry you've returned to Camelon with everything such a tangle."

"It couldn't have been all your fault."

R.A. stares at the floor. "I'm responsible for the whole muddle. One stupid decision to take drugs that won't stop punishing me."

"Did Morgan seduce you?"

He looks me straight in the eyes. "I'm not sure. She was always the wild one. We tried some designer drug she brought from school. Next thing...it was only that once, but she got pregnant. My Lord, the guilt has eaten me like a cancer."

"You thought she'd had an abortion?"

"Yes, until last evening. Now I find I have a son I don't even know. I wonder how that older couple raised Mort. He seems so . . ."

"Cock-sure of himself," I state. "Seeing Morgan capable of yesterday's fiasco, do you think she purposely compromised you all those years ago?"

"She does have an obsessive need to control everyone and everything."

"Now that Morgan's got you where she wants you, what are you going to do?"

"I just don't know." The Laird R.A. Stewart looks at me with little boy eyes.

Melting, I do my best to hug the stuffing out of him. "We'll figure this out, Rex Arthur." He holds onto me like a lifesaver. Who else?

"I have no right to involve you, Nana."

I point to the bloodstained picture of me holding young Artie. "Afraid I'm in the thick of it, my boy."

He surveys the maggot-infested bird remains and says, "This attempt at hocus-pocus was created some time ago. How did Morgan know you were coming?"

"That's part of the puzzle, isn't it? We have more questions than answers in Morgan's situation—as well as the tree poisonings. What did your men discover?"

R.A. sighs. "I met with Galahad. Your Celtic Calendar theory is correct. Aidan found a circle of poisoned Broom down by the ponds."

"When exactly?"

"Yesterday, before the Halloween Ball. Lance drove the samples to Logres to be analyzed. That's why he arrived late. It was the same fertilizer overdose, the same *modus operandi*. Have the poisonings interfered with your Celtic tree research?"

"They've not prevented my work. But when Had, Gwynn and I are out collecting samples we frequently run into a poisoned area—as if someone knows our itinerary. How else could the Ivy circle have appeared the night before we visited Lady Elaine?"

"Or are they trying to get at me through you?" Artie asks. "The poisonings are always on my property. It would be safer if you three moved to Camelon."

"You sure? The poisoner could be living under this roof."

Artie blanches. "I can't let myself believe that."

I'm beginning to think Artie is rather naïve, but say, "Of course, we'll be looking farther afield. There are the eco-terrorists to consider."

"They concern me the most," he says. "The commercially cultivated trees haven't been attacked, but what if they're next? We supply lumber to major companies. If they incorrectly hear our timber is poisoned along with our Celtic trees, they may begin looking elsewhere."

"Are your clients that fickle?"

"I wouldn't want to find out." I take his hand and lead him out to the balcony overlooking the Great Hall. Perturbed he says, "Wonder what's keeping Aidan and Morgan?" He stops. "Any thoughts on how I should handle this Mort situation?"

Remembering how sound travels from the upper balconies, I whisper. "Acting the benevolent uncle is the right tactic. I'll nose around. We can have a DNA test done to make sure Mort is actually your son. All we need are his and your saliva, or blood samples." Artie looks concerned, so I reassure him. "I have a guy at Scotland Yard."

"Of course you do." We walk down the hall to the schoolroom-nursery familiar in its muted pastels and kiddie smells all these years later. The oak munchkin chairs remain pulled up neatly at their matching table. I walk over and sit in a big old rocker.

R.A.'s shoulders relax. "You're a wizard. You and your wards will stay and help?"

"I hate to upset our routine at Koad Croft, but we could try it for a while."

He smiles wanly. "How does one catch a radical eco-terrorist group?"

I stand and we gravitate toward the row of school desks. "Artie, I'm not so sure it's an ecological group. Why are they poisoning the Celtic trees and plants in order of month? Who would know I chose to use the Broom plant in my research instead of Reed?" I shake my head. "This feels personal."

He frowns. "The Celtic Calendar part of it doesn't make sense if they're protesting cultivated forestry." Artie walks around the dust-laden nursery touching the faded rocking horse then stares at some long-forgotten scribble on the blackboard. "Who do you suspect, Nana?"

"I can't eliminate anyone at Camelon or Logres. Morgan comes to mind, but where's the motive? Gwynn, Had and you are the only people I trust. Where does your trust lie?"

"Those I consider family—the Roses, Lance, Gavin, Aidan . . ."

As if on cue, Aidan calls out. "R.A., you need us?"

Morgan yells. "You summoned, O' Mighty Laird?"

R.A. meets them on the balcony while I stay put in the nursery. No need stepping in that pile of stink.

R.A. snaps out an order. "Aidan, see that Morgan cleans that black magic altar in the north tower."

She laughs. "Aren't you grateful I conjured your nanny back, brother dear?"

Aidan leads Morgan to Igraine's chambers saying, "There's no longer need for charms and spells, my lady."

As R.A. returns, I say, "Aidan has a way with her, doesn't he?"

"I hope it lasts, but he's not the sort she marries. He's not a social climber."

We walk over to Artie's baby crib. I hang onto the railing to keep from diving into nostalgia. It's the one-eyed teddy's fault my voice goes all gravelly. "I could discreetly question the Camelon inhabitants, but what about the Logres board of directors?"

"I'll give you some Logres stock so you can attend board meetings. Although, it may be a worthless gift if the stock plummets.

I land a soft punch to his jaw. "Hey, where's my Little Warrior? Let's outsmart the enemy—who may be angling for a Logres takeover. Would you be open to an experiment? It'd be a huge risk."

"My concern lies with my employees, all part owners of the firm. But what do you propose?"

The nursery is several rooms away from Morgan and her boyfriend, yet I speak softly. "What would you say to positioning ourselves ahead of the perpetrators by announcing the Celtic tree poisonings to the media? Shareholders might sell, but if one particular organization snaps them up, we have our saboteur. I could get DCI Armstrong at Scotland Yard involved—to document the sting and nab the crooks. But first you give the story to the press. Let them interview you."

"No Nana, you're the popular face of the moment. I'll set up the interview, but you explain how your research is being stymied by this poisoner. We'll offer an award for information." He pauses. "Wait, that could put you in danger."

"Never mind, we need to catch this man—or woman. Sure you're okay with this?" Artie hugs me. Although espionage taints our moment, I have my boy back.

Just as we step out of the nursery, Gavin charges out of the service elevator. He's no longer the strong brooding bodyguard. "Dr. Bruce MacLaren, I turned my back only a second. It's just that the laird's Sandy Lad—he's mated with your Raven."

Alarmed, I look at Artie. "She's only nine months old. I didn't know she was in season." I hesitate then hold up a hand. "It is best to breed the female when she's older, but what's done is done." Artie and I lock eyes. "Never waste time ruing the past."

"Yes," R.A. says. "We accept everything that is, and move ahead."

Of course, it doesn't necessarily follow that detangling our particular Celtic knot will go smoothly.

Fencing

We're giving castle life a whirl. Galahad isn't thrilled about staying on, but Gwynn's elation is over the top. So is her subsequent hissy fit when I insist we continue to room together. Believe it or not, I was a wild child once. "Gwynnie, we have vital secrets to share." Actually it's my duty to safeguard her from the lads, both family and staff, giving Gorgeous Gwynn the naughty eye.

Living in our croft never worried me. Had's chivalry ranks up there with the saints—possibly higher depending on the saint. My concern lies with Mort who suddenly announced he'd changed his surname to Sinclair-Stewart. "I want to be part of the family," he said like we'd applaud. I envision Snake Oil Mort with fangs poised to sink into my granddaughter. Well, not while I draw breath.

Anyway, you understand my concern when Mort drags his chair next to Gwynn. You see, we received an invite to watch R.A. and Lance fence, so we're sitting in the castle's marble-walled gymnasium. Gwynn and Had flank my red velvet throne with matching footstool to accommodate my dang stubby pins. Raven kneads my lap in anticipation. I'm here for entertainment, but ever vigilant of operation Nab the Black-Hearted Tree Poisoner.

Over in the fencing arena that takes up a mere fraction of the gym's square footage, Gavin helps the fencers into their gear. Morgan, with Aidan panting close by, sips tea instead of her usual cocktail. Makes a body wonder.

"R.A. you have an unfair advantage," Lance says. "My head is pounding."

"I didn't pour champagne down your throat, laddie."

"Aye, the temptress was comelier." Lance takes his place opposite R.A. on the *piste*.

Mort leans close to Gwynn's ear. "The laird's the first fencer. See, he's the one with his right side toward Gavin who's judging the bout."

Gavin yells *en garde,* makes sure the fencers are ready then calls *allez.*

"That means play in French." Mort explains the obvious as his arm slips around the back of Gwynn's chair.

"I've never seen a fencing match, but they look yummy in those outfits," Gwynn comments.

"I started fencing when I was twelve," Mort brags. "I can explain it to you."

With his sword arm outstretched, R.A. lunges at Lance's chest—and they're off. Lance parries by deflecting the laird's saber followed by a quick thrust. Raven stiffens then flies off my lap barking like crazy at the fencers. Gavin calls *halte* and gives me a hands-on-hips dirty look.

"Sorry, but my dog's a pacifist."

"Then don't bring..." Gavin starts to scold me, glances at the puppy compromised on his watch and stops.

Had calmly says, "Raven, let's go for a walk." My Scottie tears over the marble floor to dance at his feet. As he leaves, I wonder what's going on with tight-lipped Galahad. Does he feel left out, or is he still miffed about me keeping secrets? I must speak to him, but for now Gavin draws our attention as he repositions the fencers.

R.A. says, "Let's annul that beginning." With exaggerated flourish, Gavin resets the clock and reorders the bout's beginning. R.A. lunges at Lance making an immediate hit.

Mort leans forward, his arm on the back of Gwynn's chair presses against her. "Most bouts are five hits within six minutes."

She leans away from his touch. "What if they don't stab the other guy five times?"

"Then the fencer with the most hits is the winner." Mort toys his thumb back and forth on Gwynn's shoulder. She flinches and he stops.

"What if they tie?" she asks.

Mort leans in close. "Since they're fighting with sabers, a deciding hit is fought."

Gwynn squirms free of Mort's advances just as Gavin issues a time warning then calls *halte.* Before long the fencers are at it again prancing and lunging and thrusting so fast and furious a body can barely keep up.

"The laird is winning," Mort says as he dangles his hand over Gwynn's shoulder.

Just then R.A. disarms Lance and again Gavin calls *halte.*

Gwynn does too, grabbing Mort's wandering fingers and throwing his arm off her.

Mort covers his embarrassment by saying, "That was an invalid play."

"It sure was," Gwynn snaps. Touché Gwynnie.

Mort shrinks away, but not as far as you'd expect for the abuse he's taken. I want to thump him, but it isn't my fight. Yet.

R.A. and Lance resume fencing where they were halted and the laird gets in another hit. Mort leans in on Gwynn and whispers, "Now they'll change ends because R.A. scored half his points. They only do that when fighting with sabers."

I turn and say, "Young man, could you find Gwynn and me some nuts? Our blood sugar is low."

Mort looks as if I asked him to smell my armpit. He starts to object then thinks better of it. "I won't be a minute," he says almost politely and leaves.

Gwynn squeezes my arm in appreciation, but her attention remains on the match. Lance scores a hit and Morgan cheers. Despite his hangover, Lance is making R.A. work to keep the lead. Their prancing resembles a staged ballet. Do they work as well together in their business lives? It appears Lance holds his laird and employer in high esteem, but who knows what petty jealousies might cause a body to poison trees. Nonetheless, the bout continues with the usual *attack, parry, riposte,* and *counter-riposte.*

Returning, Mort thrusts a jar of nuts at me just as R.A. makes his last hit and Gavin declares him the winner. The fencers pull their masks off and shake hands without a scrap of animosity. "Great," Mort complains, "I missed the best part."

While the men remove their gear, Morgan points across the room. "Mort those are the Stewart clan treasures." Mort swaggers to the display on the far side of the hall. He fingers the bronze oak leaves on the clan shield and caresses the jeweled sword with the lust of an adulterer.

"Ahem." Gavin nods toward the boy. R.A. turns then hurries his way.

Mort grabs the jeweled sword's hilt in both hands, tears it off the wall. He spins around cutting circles in the air then proclaims it, "Cool."

R.A. yells, "Mort," and the name echoes off the marble walls. Artie quickens his stride and retrieves the elaborately jeweled Claymore from Mort. With one heck of an edge to his voice, he says, "This sword is reserved for the laird of Camelon,"

"Then let's duel for it." Mort grabs a four-foot weapon from the wall, swinging it so R.A. is forced to protect himself. Swords clang together.

"There's no need to fight for the Stewart sword. She'll be yours unless I have a son."

Mort bristles. "Unless you have a son? In that case, I'd better fight for it now." He thrusts his sword forward and laughs when R.A. jumps back.

The laird regains composure, but his jaw tightens. Mort jabs at him and R.A. says, "Listen, we shouldn't fight with these priceless antiques. How about we fence."

Agitated, Morgan steps from one spiked heel to the other. "He's right, Mort."

"No, I'm fighting for my birthright. We'll do it with the Stewart family weapons." Mort swings his sword and R.A. catches it with his blade. They lock hilts and breathe in each other's face. Mort grins.

I figure Artie can overpower the smaller man, but it soon becomes apparent Mort can hold his own with the heavy weapon. He shoves R.A. back and walks a semi-circle around him. Although fatigued from fencing, the laird takes a stance and lunges forward. He's decided to settle it Mort's way, but the kid effortlessly flips Artie's sword up. Mort looks to Gwynn for approval. The laird takes advantage of the break in Mort's focus and swings. It barely fazes the boy, but something in R.A. visibly snaps. He counters Mort's attack with a fury gaining the upper hand slashing through the younger man's sleeve.

Mort grabs his arm drawing back a bloodstained hand, wipes it on his shirt and laughs. "Good one."

Mort circles R.A. and lunges. Their blades clash and slide up to the hilts, but Mort easily pushes Artie back. Smirking, he struts around the flagging laird like a bandy rooster. "Give it up, old man," Mort chides, and I want to slap him into next year.

Gavin's jaws clinch, yet he remains planted at Lance's side near the piste.

Panting R.A. drops the tip of his sword to the floor. Thinking the laird is a goner, Mort turns to the onlookers, but R.A. hefts his weighty sword high over his right shoulder. Mort jumps to attention and swings. The momentum of the turn allows his blade to strike hard against the ancient sword. A sickening crack screams off the marble walls, and the upper half of the laird's blade flies through the air.

Just like that, we're in one of those slow-motion Einstein relativity moments that actually happens at warp speed. We watch the fragment arc up and fly toward us, but nobody moves. At the last second, my whole being shoots sideways. My hands clap together capturing the blade within inches of Gwynn's sternum.

"Holy crap," Gwynn yells as she scoots her chair back turning unbelieving eyes on me. Shoot, I'm as shocked as she is and hang frozen over the arm of my throne, until she gasps, "Grandma Merle, you're bleeding."

R.A. places the remainder of his sword on the floor and runs toward us. "Hey," Mort calls after him, "aren't you going to concede the fight?" Gavin takes a step toward the boy, but Lance stops him.

The laird turns slowly like he's counting to ten. "Mort, I'll give up the Stewart clan sword and holdings over my dead body."

Mort laughs. "Okay, man, don't get bent."

R.A. motions for Lance to confiscate his broken sword, as the ever-alert Gavin heads our way. Artie kneels, pries the blade fragment from my bleeding hands and carefully gives it to Gavin.

"I won," Mort calls as Morgan steers him toward the door. "I have witnesses."

"Shut it," Morgan says. "Get your stupid arse back to my chambers." Her glare slices through him. Mort follows his mom out the door, but not with his tail between his legs.

Even though my cuts are superficial, Artie makes a fuss propping me on a chaise in the solarium with a view of the elaborate grounds and fountain. Trembling, Gwynnie adjusts the pillows on her chaise. The kid is pretty shaken.

R.A. drops to his knees beside us. "Nana, Gwynn, please forgive me. I don't know who's the bigger fool, Mort or I. One or both of you could have been killed."

"The good news is," I whisper, "Morgan knows her sidekick is out of control." I touch Artie's hand. "Preserving the blood on your sword tip might be a good idea."

"Already bagged and tagged." He nails me with that sly sideways smile he's had since birth. "I'll speak to Mort and Morgan. This incident was unacceptable."

Robbie Rose's wife, Bridget, trots in holding a tray brimming with enough iced cakes to ruin our dinner three days standing. She pours tea, stirs in half a bowl of sugar saying, "The Scottish cure for shock." The young woman almost curtsies, turns and leaves.

Gwynn grabs my arm. "Grandma that was a kick-butt catch."

"Any time, my girl." With bandaged hand I pat her arm.

"So" she says, "they're proving Mort really is R.A.'s son with his blood sample?" Gwynn has the makings of a superb sleuth. She sips her tea and adds, "Grandma, Igraine's ghost made that blade head right for me. I couldn't move."

"Oh sweetie, I'm sure as heck going to figure out a logical explanation for all this. Care to be Watson to my Holmes, old girl?" What else can I do? There's no keeping secrets from a canny MacLaren.

Mrs. Rose   22

I've spoken to Priscilla Rose, cook and housekeeper extraordinaire, several times, but it's time for a sit down. "Gwynnie," I say, "how about we see if Mrs. Rose sniffed out any gossip pertinent to nabbing tree poisoners?"

We navigate the servant's staircase to the castle's lowest level. Other than daylight windows up high, the biggest part of the kitchen's grey stone walls are underground. Camelon's ancestors knew ecologically sound ways to keep the cooks from suffering heatstroke during the summer months, yet insulate against the cold in the winter.

Gwynn steps across the flagstone floor. "What a wonderful place." Walking past long wooden tables we see huge bowls of rising dough, heaps of chopped veggies and fresh pastries. Bundles of dried herbs and wild flowers hanging from beams mingle into the best aroma in the galaxy.

Bridget grins a welcome. "Mammy, look who's here." Bridget is married to Robert Rose, Priscilla's son, yet calls Pris, Mammy.

Priscilla sidles toward us with an open heart. "It's yerself and good timen. You'll stay for a cuppa and Bridget's scones."

"Absolutely." Gwynn and I say in unison then recite, "we read each other's minds."

"Fey like me an Bridget, not that she'll admit it. Don't abide the old ways," Pris explains. "Sit while I brew up." She points to a time-scarred table then grabs a fat Brown Betty teapot. Tea preparation can't be rushed in these parts—you don't plop a teabag in water, zap it in the microwave and serve it with a box of cookies. No, we're talking serious tea ritual. The good news is, Mrs. Rose can talk while she works.

"Heard anything juicy, Pris?"

"Nothen 'cept Morgan's Aidan staying over, with Mort right there." Priscilla pours fresh spring water in the kettle and sets it to boil.

"What do you know about Aidan Hunter?"

"The laird likes him well enough, but I say he's getten too big for his *breekes*." Priscilla scoops loose tea into a teaball and sets it aside. "Don't know his place, that one. Plenty of our mothers was in service. But that Aidan prances round the castle like he don't come from common folk."

"Well, you might say the same for me, Priscilla."

"Oh no, you bettered yourself—became a doctor." She turns to Gwynn. "An a frightful good one I can tell you that. Saved my Robbie during that measles epidemic."

Gwynn looks at me. "You'll have to tell me about Grandma back in those days."

Wanting the conversation moving in the right direction, I say, "Maybe Aidan is trying to better himself."

"There's betteren a body, then there's betteren. And that Aidan don't care who he hurts ta do it. My Robbie were up for the field manager job, but Aidan saw he got his leg crushed. Now the laird's got Robbie doen office work. Big strappen man like himself sitten at a desk. Us Roses were none too pleased the laird gave Robert's job ta Aidan."

A body must take Priscilla's reports with a pound or three of salt. Her take on Aidan doesn't sound like the bashful guy I met. "That's quite an accusation, Pris. You sure Aidan instigated Robbie's accident?"

She bristles. "I'll tell you this much, after Aidan settled into that manager job he started acten all uppity. Comen round dinen with the laird. Taken our Morgan ta fancy affairs. Why, it ain't proper."

Priscilla stomps back to the cooker then carries the kettle to the sink. She heats the ceramic teapot by swishing steaming water in it then pours it out. Trundling back, she places the teaball in the teapot, pours in hot water, puts the lid on and covers the pot with a crocheted cozy— a kind of sweater the teapot wears while the tea steeps.

"I'd like you to keep an eye out, Pris. Report anything suspicious."

She brightens. "Anything for you, Dr. Bruce." She retrieves a tray with clotted cream, elderberry jam and scones hidden from my grasp under a tea towel.

"What can you tell me about Lance La Lac besides him remaining married, but having nothing to do with Lady Elaine or Galahad? He seems to get on well with Artie."

Pris shakes her head. "He does at that, but if there truly is a sex disease, he caught it. Canna keep away from the lassies. Mostly rich ones, married or not."

"This may be off the subject," Gwynn says, "but does Morgan ever visit her cousin, Had's mother, Lady Elaine?"

"Ever now and agin. Lady Elaine be a strange bird—rearen her boy in a monastery. Now there's a thing," Priscilla says accusingly. "If she knew you was comen ta Scotland then Galahad knew, too."

"No, Had couldn't have known," Gwynn says. "He acted so surprised, almost angry, when Grandma Merle's identity was revealed at the party."

"I know they're cousins, but why does Morgan visit Lady Elaine?" I ask. "The way Morgan lusts after Lance, I'd think those women would be enemies."

"Likely feeden Lady Elaine lies to get her to divorce Lance. How's Elaine ta know what's goen on? Never leaves that convent."

"What do you think of Morgan's son, Mort?"

"Now there's a strutten fool, if the Lord ever seen one." Gwynn laughs and Priscilla passes the basket. We don't hesitate to dive into scones with clotted cream and elderberry jam. "Heard the laird's puten Mort on at Logres. Afore long there ain't gonna be a job for my Jamie—an himself needen work. Seems the laird's forgotten us Roses."

"Don't you think that, you're family. The laird can see Mort has custard for brains."

Pris pours tea. "Mort lied about comen out from San Francisco. Tells us he skis near his university, Colorado State. That'd be where you live, in them Rocky Mountains."

I slap the table. "His slip about the sun shining three hundred days of the year—that's a Colorado claim." Ye ole light bulb brightens. "Morgan could have been in touch with Mort all along. If Mort spied on me at CSU then she was in touch with him all along. Yes, that could be how Morgan knew to set up the dead blackbird curse."

On that note, Robbie Rose thumps into the food prep area. "Bridget, where's me pills?" Bridget dashes off and Robbie notices Gwynn and me. "Sorry, Dr. Bruce. Have a temper with this infernal pain. Guess Mam told you Aidan Hunter dropped that log on me ta take me job. I'd like ta drop sommen on him."

"Now Robert Earl Rose, you take that mouth outta here," Prisilla scolds. "Have yerself a lie down." We hear Robbie thump up the backstairs. "He canna get over the loss," Pris says. "They were to buy their own flat. Instead, they're liven in servant's quarters while Aidan Hunter shacks up with Morgan in the main castle." She lowers her voice. "The worst of it—there ain't been any *bairns*."

"I'm sure they want a child," Gwynn commiserates.

I wonder if Robbie's complaint is truly founded, or if he just needs someone to blame. I understand his resentment. Nonetheless, we have two new suspects. Robbie if he's irritated with the laird, and Aidan if he truly is power hungry. But how would poisoning the Celtic trees and plants afford revenge for either of these guys? What importance would the ancient Celtic trees have to a couple foresters? See what I mean about those illusive motives?

I continue my interrogation. "How long has Morgan been here at Camelon?"

"Since June, shortly afore the laird found the Oaks poisoned. Them two facts stuck in me head. Morgan's up to no good, but the laird turns a blind eye. Wish she'd go back ta her Edinburgh flat." Pris tears a huge hunk off her scone and butters it furiously.

"It doesn't make sense for Morgan or Mort to poison the Stewart Celtic trees," I say. "That could very well affect the family finances."

"There is that," Pris concedes.

Priscilla looks at Gwynn then back to me, so I nod my permission for her to reveal a confidence. "Morgan's contacted her dead mother for donkey's years. Ain't a body safe round Igraine." Priscilla Rose reaches over and takes Gwynn's hand in hers. "Lass, you ain't from these parts. Thon Sinclairs have powers. An now Igraine's cursed you."

"But Had and Lady Elaine are Sinclairs, too," Gwynn says. "They seem all right."

Priscilla leans forward. "Ever one of them Sinclairs can conjure."

"Couldn't they use their abilities for good?" I ask. "After all, the Sinclairs are related to the Roslyn Chapel St. Claires. Galahad seems to be a good soul."

"He's a quire one, that Galahad Sinclair. Comes down here, eats his morning stir-about and leaves. When I heard he used Sinclair in place of La Lac, I couldn't bring meself ta trust him. An that Gavin Sinclair with the gash down his cheek, bodyguarden the laird." She harrumphs. "Thon Sinclairs never got over loosen Camelon to the Stewarts ages back. Likely schemen right now ta take it back."

I slather another scone with jam and cream to help swallow her accusations. I must admit, however, Had's reticent nature does make a body curious. Then again, I'm questioning everyone. "So, Pris, you think there's mischief at Camelon?"

"Aye, me gut says so, both alive an deed. I'm afeard for your Gwynnie bein cursed at the séance then near kilt by that blade."

"We'll be more vigilant." Aiming to get Gwynn away from Priscilla's superstitions, I say, "Thanks for the lovely tea, Pris. We'd best check Raven—pregnant by that Randy Sandy Lad. If you need us, you know where we live." As we climb the stairs, I whisper, "Think I'll tell DCI Armstrong about Mort attending CSU in case that means anything."

"Strange, and stranger" Gwynn agrees.

I whisper, "I don't trust Mort. How about we sweep our room for bugging devices."

"You know this how?"

I hesitate, but figure in for a pound, in for a ton. "The Laird General and I met on my one and only military special ops mission. I learned a few spying techniques back then."

Gwynn gasps. "Grandma Merle, you are the most interesting person I've ever met."

It's a real 'ah shucks' moment.

Relationships

After days of rain, it's finally a bright chilly morning, but since Artie has taken to chatting with Gwynn and me after breakfast, my cockles are toasty warm.

"I've been studying," Gwynnie exudes. "I knew some of this, but now I get why saving the old growth trees, the rain forests, the Celtic trees and all the plants on earth is super important. First of all, and this is so cool, the Greek word 'photosynthesis' means 'put together with light'. That's because plants use the sun's energy to convert water and carbon dioxide into glucose producing food. And when glucose forms in the tree's leaves the by-product is the oxygen that the whole world breathes."

Artie knows she's showing off, but says enthusiastically, "All correct and proper."

"Just imagine how magical it must have seemed for the ancient people that didn't know any of this scientific stuff," she muses. "No wonder the Old Ones thought trees and plants were sacred—watching everything die then green up in the spring."

I'm about to add something when Had rushes in. He releases Raven and Sandy Lad, and says, "The poisoned Broom site down by the ponds is enlarged. It looks fresh." R.A. throws his napkin on the table and matches Had's stride out the door.

Gwynn runs after the men while I hand the dogs over to Bridget. By the time I pant onto the scene, Had and R.A. are testing the poison while Gwynn takes photos. "It seems the poisoners slipped back," R.A. says. "For all we know, Aidan may have interrupted them the other day. These Broom plants are tall enough to hide a full-grown man."

As an aside I whisper, "Artie, when DCI Armstrong comes with DNA results, we should show him this enlarged Broom poisoning." Suddenly there's a roaring in my ears and a murky grey eddy spins me down into the suffocating darkness of the Otherworld.

A gust of icy wind blows just as Igraine pushes a faceless hooded monk toward me. "Be done with your Celtic beliefs," he growls.

"My scientific research has nothing to do with philosophical dogma," I argue.

"Aren't you just the smart one? Embrace the truth or die."

It's hard to breathe, but I'm more irritated than afraid. "I venerate the sacredness of a divine creation. The Celts held similar tenets."

His face is a dark vortex. "So you admit to worshipping the ancient religion?"

I don't like where this is going, but continue. "It's just that everyone has the right to believe as they choose."

From the shadows, Igraine scoffs, "She's hopeless." I open my mouth to argue further, but unexpectedly spin up and away from her and the menacing monk.

Artie holds me in his arms. "Nana. Nana. Come back."

"Don't rush her," Had says. "She'll come to."

I open my eyes, shade them from the brilliant sunlight and shakily report. "The poisonings aren't a bias against the timber trade. They stem from religious prejudice. But what's that to do with poisoning trees and plants?" Whether activated by revenge, insanity or greed, motives are slippery little fiends.

Artie shows no comprehension, so as she helps me sit, Gwynnie explains. "Grandma Merle's vision showed her the reason behind the Celtic tree poisonings."

Galahad groans. "Don't tell me you take these visions seriously?"

R.A. studies my face. "Nana, I remember trusting your visions as a child. I still do, but how do we convince Scotland Yard?"

I sit up straighter. "Can't. They'll think I'm a fruitcake."

"They wouldn't be the only skeptic." Had stalks away.

"Gwynn, tell Had I need a word with him." She dashes ahead while Artie helps me to the castle.

Inside, Galahad leads me toward Camelon's library. "You want to see me Dr. Bruce-MacLaren?" No expression crosses his mug.

"Alright, Had, cut the horse pucky. I think the world of you, but you've barely spoken to me since we arrived. You spend more time with the dogs than Gwynn and me."

He doesn't speak, but I'm very good at waiting. Finally he says, "I reckoned we were a family of sorts until you revealed you were someone else entirely."

"Had, you got to know one particular side of my multi-faceted personality, and seemed to like it. So how do I regain your trust?"

He clasps his hands. "Trust? With an absent father and a mother rarely available, Father Joseph was my trusted friend—until you, Gwynn and I were thrown together. When you revealed you raised R.A., I felt betrayed."

I grab Had into a hug. "Let's head home to Koad Croft real soon."

Abruptly the door opens. Gwynnie turns her alabaster fright toward me. "Are you in trouble? That guy from the airport is asking for you."

"It's DCI Armstrong from Scotland Yard," Bridget declares. "Your gran's famous."

"Yes, an international heroine." He shakes my hand rather lovingly.

R.A. joins us then suggests we show Armstrong the poisoned Broom site. As we walk along, Galahad speaks to Armstrong. "Was it wise for Mrs. MacLaren and R.A. to announce the Celtic tree poisonings to the media? The culprit, or copycats, might double their efforts to wipe out the Celtic trees so important to our culture."

You see, R.A. with his media connection and me with terrorist-nabbing notoriety, explained the systematic poisoning of the Celtic plants and trees to Scotland's public. We asked their assistance tracking down the culprit. The interview went viral when the Prince of Wales, with whom I have a nodding acquaintance, put in a good word. Well, where else did you think the impeccably dressed men took me when I left Gwynn to fare for herself in London?

"I wouldn't worry, Galahad, copycats and other issues were addressed before we set up our tip line," Armstrong reassured.

"Another thing, Chief," Gwynn says, "Besides being a swordsman, Mort belongs to a group that holds mock battles with medieval spears and axes. He showed me his black knight costume and sorta lives in a fantasy world. Is he dangerous?"

"We can look into that," Armstrong adds.

Halfway down the path, Gwynn asks, "What'd you really come here for, Chief?"

When the laird nods his okay, Armstrong says, "Mort Hamilton is your son."

Artie draws breath. "I thought so—just wanted proof."

"Also," Armstrong says, "the other blood on the broken sword. It has the markers of a not-so-distant cousin. Do you know the identity, sir?"

"What other blood?" R.A. is as confused as I am.

"On the blade. The female blood. Whom did that belong to?"

Realization hits that the blood was mine. R.A. gasps. "Nana, the Laird General had to have been aware of our relationship all along. That old devil."

If you can't follow this family's thorny family tree, Artie means I'm part Stewart. My knees buckle, he grabs me and we hug like the long-lost cousins we evidently are.

†ELDER (Sambucus nigra) RUIS†
November 25–December 23

This month is incredibly complex and one of my favorites. You see, the Elder tree represents the cycle of life found in nature. It reminds a body to unite with the flow of the life force rather than fight to control destiny. Some view the Elder as the fairy tree and accept its gift of protective qualities. The ancients recognized the tree's connection to death and rebirth when they carved the tree's wood into hearse-driver's whip handles then turned around and made protective crosses to hang in their cow barns. Nonetheless, before they cut an Elder they asked permission from the spirit of the tree—the Elder Mother. Having asked, they then fashioned everything from piper's canters to ornamental furnishings. What interests me the most are the incredibly diverse medicinal qualities of everything from the roots, bark and leaves to the flowers and berries. What a tree!

Gwynn, Had and I finished packing the Rover around midnight. We'll get a good night's sleep then return to Koad Croft after breakfast. Camelon's amenities aside, we're missing our cozy life nestled in the woods. Escaping the Sinclair-Stewart family intrigues will be a bonus.

At one a.m. Mrs. Rose barges into our room. "Dr. Bruce. Dr. Bruce." Gwynn and I pop up like a couple pieces of toast. Priscilla's urgency has me out of bed and throwing on my robe. "Thon nuns found Lady Elaine dead, but claim she never kilt herself." Pris thrusts a phone at me.

I press the speaker button so all will hear, then say, "This is Merle MacLaren."

Abruptly Mother Superior speaks. "Dr. Bruce-MacLaren you must be the one to tell Galahad. The laird will fetch Lance. Those preposterous constables say Lady Elaine committed suicide. You must arrive before they destroy evidence."

"What evidence?" I ask.

"That would be for you to say. They don't know our lady, so aren't looking for a...a murderer. Midnight chimes rang just as I saw our little rowboat in the moonlight. Thought it had come untied from the boathouse, so Brother Ushtey towed it in. And there was Lady Elaine laid out rather creatively. You'll see."

"Keep them from contaminating the sight. What should I tell Galahad?"

"That his mother is dead under suspicious circumstances—but hurry. I'll prevent the police from disturbing her as long as I can."

"What makes you think I can..." The line goes dead without so much as a Godspeed.

From the doorway, Had asks, "What's all the commotion?" Gwynn bursts into tears.

There is no way to break the tragedy gently. "Oh Galahad," I say, "your mother has died." He barely makes it to a chair before collapsing. Bridget enters with a tray of sweet tea that Pris forces down Had. I rub his wrists, but he simply shakes and stares.

Realizing time is of the essence Gwynn pulls herself together, dresses and takes Had in hand. Before long I'm behind the Rover's wheel and Gwynnie settles Had into the backseat. Gavin heaves Raven's crate in beside our luggage saying, "R.A. will follow with Lance." I pull the driver's seat forward as far as it will go, adjust the mirrors and take off toward St. Clair's.

Galahad allows Gwynn to cradle him in her arms. "Oh, our poor boy," Gwynn croons. "Turn up the heat, Grandma Merle. He's shaking really bad."

"Wrap him in that car rug. Had, you're in shock, you've got to stay with us."

"Feels like swimming in—sorry I..." he trails off.

"Tell me about your mother," Gwynn urges.

"Mum's dead," he says thickly. "But she can't be."

"Who would want to hurt your mother?"

"A saint—never harmed..." Had's answers are nearly incoherent, but Gwynn keeps him babbling.

A sort of hypnotic state allows me to focus on the road with hedgerows flying past both sides. I gain a modicum of relief knowing we'll return Galahad to the croft although thwarted by this caldron of grief. Cursing the scheming mind behind this, I question if Elaine's death is connected to the tree poisonings. But where does the murder of an innocent spiritual recluse figure in? Some floozy desperate to marry Lance? And how far behind us are Lance and Artie, anyway?

I'm racing down a road only wide enough for a car and a half—praying we're not the half. Suddenly, a black sportscar with no headlights, flies at us out of the Underworld. Before I can blink, I've taken a hefty chunk out of Old McDonald's hedgerow and stalled the engine. Thanking heaven, I rest my head on the steering wheel.

From the backseat Had says, "Morgan."

"You think it was Morgan?" Gwynn asks, but he doesn't respond. Fortunately, the Rover starts and we arrive at the convent in speed-demon time. "Act normal Had," Gwynn coaches. "They're going to like, ask you questions."

"Don't say like," he giggles then buries his face in his hands. "Sorry . . . sorry."

I shake my head. Gwynn hauls him out of the backseat as a nun bobs down the path with a torch. Without a word she leads us to the boathouse. A young constable tries to block our way. "This is a crime scene."

"My mum," Had says and pushes past the policewoman. Gwynn and I follow. Mother Superior motions us to a rowboat docked in the slip. Nothing can take the edge off what we see.

Lady Elaine's blue lips are twisted grotesquely. Her pale blue glassy eyes stare heavenward. She's laid out in a white rowboat on a blue blanket dressed in her white robe. Strangely, her gold locks hidden in life, halo her head. Chalky white hands with bluish fingertips cross over her chest holding a sprig of bluebells. The colors are unnaturally vivid, a sign of my own shock. The current rocks Elaine's boat. We flinch.

Galahad drops to his knees. Tears stream down his cheeks. He reaches toward his mother's corpse. "Mum, what have they done?"

Gwynn strokes Had's hair and he leans into her. "I know, I know," Gwynn says, and she does. How much of Gwynn's own mother's death is she's reliving? Although my parents died in their late eighties, I felt orphaned. How much more poignant it must be to lose a parent so young. I lean over to encircle both kids in my arms.

"Detective Inspector McGregor," Mother Superior interrupts, "this is Dr. Bruce-MacLaren, the monastery's private detective." I nod as if I know what the heck she's up to, but McGregor's too surprised to notice me glance at her not-so-innocent face.

"Unofficial detective," I say. "My granddaughter and I are helping research some local tree and plant poisonings. Mother Superior found one sight up the hill there." I point then turn back to Elaine. "If this is connected, it appears to have gotten personal. Lady Elaine was poisoned, wouldn't you say, Detective Inspector McGregor?"

"Most likely, from the blue fingertips." He trails off realizing he's said too much.

The two overhead bulbs cast crazy shadows, so I borrow his torch and lean over the corpse. Elaine is a perfect study in blue and white—too perfect. "She looks posed. See how the stems of these flowers are sticking out between her fingers? Possibly tucked in after her hands were crossed."

McGregor bends closer. "Campbell, get a picture of this before we lift the boat out of the water."

"Where are the oars?" I ask.

"There weren't any in her boat when Brother Ushtey found her,"

Mother Superior says. "That's all our oars there on the wall."

"So how did she row to the middle of the loch?" R.A. asks. I spin around surprised to see him. "D.I. McGregor, I'm R.A. Stewart—Lady Elaine's cousin. There appears to be several flaws in your suicide theory." McGregor shrinks.

Turning to me, Artie motions to Lance and shakes his head. I point toward Had to let Artie know both father and son are despondent. Lance gazes blankly at Had, the son he barely knows, on the dock near Elaine, the wife he barely knew. Lance wavers and R.A. helps him stumble to a bench. Did he love Elaine after all?

The procurator fiscal whose job is similar to a coroner, appears from who knows where. "Looks like we treat this one as a suspicious death, Detective Inspector. We'll know more when we identify the poison."

Mother Superior nods her approval. "Lady Elaine was devout," she insists as if that solves the matter.

McGregor knows the nuns consider suicide a mortal sin. To cover his butt he asks, "Where would the lady get hold of poison?"

"I can answer that," I say, and even Had looks up. "Someone planted hemlock outside Lady Elaine's door. I warned her it was poisonous. Gwynn, you took a picture with your phone, didn't you?" She nods.

"So if Elaine posed herself then somehow got her boat in the middle of the loch without oars, we could say she had the poison to do this," R.A. sums up. McGregor squirms.

"Mum wouldn't have done this to me." Had's voice catches in sobs.

I crouch beside my boy. "Galahad, you know where the Almighty resides." He touches his heart. "Rely on that strength to see you through. And you have family."

"Thank you...Gran." It's the first time he's called me that, and the endearment wets my eyes with the tears that hadn't surfaced until now.

Father Joseph's pitiful groan jerks us around. The elderly abbot clutches his chest as he views Elaine's morbid figure. "My spiritual daughter," he whispers.

Transformed, Had hurries to Father Joseph. Gwynn joins him and together they seat the ancient near Lance who simply stares. Galahad speaks to the old man in hushed tones, as do the officials who must ask questions in this unspeakable moment.

R.A. walks to the end of the boathouse dock. I follow and we stand staring out over the loch. I want to tell him Morgan may have forced us off the road, but stop short. Artie looks at the night sky. "Look, a falling star . . . an angel come to collect Elaine."

A fireball streaks toward us. Urgently, I pull him back up the dock. The glowing orb screams our way with the whining of an artillery shell. It plunges into the loch with an energy wave and impact so intense it knocks us over. The loch sizzles as shock waves ripple the water violently. The rowboats smack together and surge forward hitting the dock. Elaine's head rolls to one side and stares directly at Had.

After an age or five, the repercussions slow. From the water's surface, dead-eyed fish stare at us accusingly. Regaining a sense of authority, McGregor asks if anyone is hurt. We decide we're drenched and bruised, but not seriously injured.

Galahad announces, "It's Divine Intervention." The way everyone nods in agreement you'd think the tortured woman's soul was elevated to sainthood.

I won't go that far, but you have to admit a murder and a meteor strike in the same location on the same night is statistically off the charts.

The Mastership

laine's murder assaults my thoughts the moment I wake. It takes a second to realize Gwynn and I are catching four winks in a convent cell. I should rejoice over the dim shadow of light this time of year, but my tired soul rebels. I shove Gwynnie's elbow out of my rib—our narrow bed obviously penance for a body a lot holier than mine.

She looks around the austere room—a tiny window, a bed, a shelf and three pegs on the wall. "How's Had?"

"Don't know, he's with Father Joseph." Throwing on yesterday's clothes, I hike to Artie on the bench where Elaine and Had sat in early October. He gazes out over the mist-covered loch to the craggy escarpment on the far shore. "Glorious day," I say softly.

R.A. attempts a smile as he moves so I can sit. "Nature should be ashamed putting on such a lovely face the day after a murder." He sighs. "Mother Superior will allow me to recover the meteor." The fog swirls as Artie points to the spot where the space rock entered the loch. "Proper alloy, or not, I'm going to forge a sword from Elaine's gift to replace my broken treasure." A man of action would find something physical to do while grieving. Standing, we walk through wet rusty leaves. Artie says, "Holy Vessel and St. Clair's were always a refuge for me. Until last night."

Overcome by the ghastly memory, I pull my hood up to ward off the chill. "Mind if we discuss what these poisonings have to do with our family?"

"You're not suggesting Elaine's death is tied to the tree poisonings, are you? There's a huge difference between eco-terrorism and murdering my cousin."

"Are you sure?" I ask. "Any discontent in the Logres ranks, or at home?"

"My employees are family," he insists. "They share in the timber proceeds."

"Robbie told me that the Rose family despises Aidan Hunter for causing his accident—solely to get the managerial position Robbie was up for."

"I created a position and kept Robert on after he lost his leg. Aidan Hunter was the best replacement. I haven't heard any complaints."

We stop to watch geese fly low over the water. "Trust me," I say. "The Roses hatred for Aidan runs deep. Also, Pris wants you to hire Jamie Rose. And she believes your Sinclair cousins, Gavin and Had, are traitors aiming to reclaim Camelon."

R.A. shakes his head. "Mrs. Rose has quite the imagination. Jamie is set on making a go of it with his band, and the Sinclair claim to the Camelon Estate is ancient history."

Thinking it best to change the subject, I ask, "Does Morgan date Lance? She doesn't seem set on Aidan as her steady beau."

He laughs. "Lance detests my sister, especially now that she pulled Mort out of her pointy hat. Lance keeps an eye on her for me. You know Morgan, she enjoys scheming."

"Enough to poison the Celtic trees, or Lady Elaine? Morgan has quite a crush on Lance. He is . . . was Elaine's legal husband."

"Morgan admired Elaine. Visited her weekly these last months— good for the both of them. You know, such opposites. For all her pessimism, Morgan cherishes the earth. She's an herbalist. Believes plants have sacred mystical properties, especially the Celtic trees. The ecological cycle of life is a religion for her."

We walk to the boathouse. Artie gestures toward several monks working at the end of the dock. "Waste not. They'll use the meteor-strike fish for fertilizer."

My stomach growls like a mama bear. "I'd best visit the convent for breakfast. Say, did Elaine leave the nuns a legacy? It could be motive."

"She did, and Nana you have a suspicious mind. Go now, I'll join you in a minute."

After an uphill trek, I step into St. Clair's big oak-beamed common room. Seated with the nuns, Gwynn nibbles a chunk of bread she's soaked in porridge so thin even Oliver Twist wouldn't ask for more. "Oh there you are," she whispers.

Mother Superior saws a slice off a dry days-old loaf, looks longingly at a tiny dab of butter and passes them both to me. I push them back. "I need to eat my hazelnuts. Just tea please." I dump nuts from my pocket onto the wooden slab of a table, polished to a sheen. One of the sisters pours hot water over used tealeaves and places the pot in front of me.

She hands me a chipped teacup with mismatched saucer leading me to assume they are in financial straits. Why didn't Elaine, or even Artie, provide for them? Staying out of their business I say, "I hear Morgan visited Lady Elaine regularly."

Mother Superior nods. "Yes, because of Lady Elaine's fasting Morgan was under the impression we took Elaine's money then starved her."

"What will you do for finances now?"

"Elaine taught us to be frugal. Your laird's purchase of the meteor should last us a good long while." No mention of Elaine's legacy.

I munch hazelnuts and wait. When the woman offers nothing more, I ask, "Did Lady Elaine have any other visitors?"

"A nun called Sister Mary Faye from an Edinburgh convent came twice. Sister Bernadette checked her in and out yesterday. Also a month ago." Finally a clue.

"Well now, the police will want to question that nun. I'll call my friend at Scotland Yard. He needs to get involved in this investigation."

"Oh, we wouldn't want to bother the Yard." She states this emphatically then busies herself with cleaning up. Why object to Scotland Yard delving into the convent's affairs?

R.A. appears in the doorway. "Nana's right, Mother. We'd best call in DCI Armstrong." Artie draws closer and pulls out his wallet. "This is all I have at the moment. I'll send more after I research the fair market value of Lady Elaine's meteor." Mother Superior doesn't question the windfall. "The divers should arrive in a couple days," he continues. "For now, I need to collect Lance and head to Logres." He kisses the crown of Gwynn's, and my head then hurries off.

"Our laird is a generous man," Mother Superior says.

I smile in agreement. "Gwynn. Say your goodbyes. We need to take Galahad home."

"I thought he was home," Mother Superior snaps then softens. "Of course, you mean his temporary home."

"Yes, for all of us." Why does our claim on Had have her hot under the habit? Motherly attachment?

Gwynn stands. "Thank you for your hospitality." She leads me to the door with one of her 'let's get the holy heck out of here' looks.

We walk downhill to the monastery past black-faced sheep grazing even in late November. I've yet to speak with Father Joseph, so guide Gwynn to his cell. Raven meets us in the alcove, dances on her back feet then takes us to Father Joseph and Had.

We enter in time to witness the old gentleman sitting in bed holding a trembling hand over hollow-eyed Had kneeling before him. Father puffs out the words as if each breath is a chore. "The Golden Bowl line of masters must endlessly endure. I passed the Mastership to Lady Elaine. Now you must become our spiritual leader, Galahad."

"If you say so, Father." I'd be objecting, but not Had.

Father Joseph breathes out softly. "Galahad, I won't always be with you."

Had grabs the old man's hand. "Father, you can't leave me, too."

"None of that," the ancient says, "have strength. I reckoned you'd learn from your mother who was to be our next spiritual master." Had squeezes his lips together to staunch his grief. Turning to me, Father J. takes on a faraway look. "I initiated you many years ago. Still sitting in Golden Bowl meditation daily?"

"Yes, I try for three hours."

Seeming to make a decision, Father says, "Merle Lynn, come here." The kids register amazement at my being summoned so informally. "Galahad, I refer you to your adopted gran for the more profound teachings." I move a low stool to my spiritual teacher's bedside. He rests a feather-light hand on my head. "Daughter, I transfer the guidance of Galahad's spiritual journey to you. Teach him the intricacies of our philosophy, so he may reach the highest levels." A bolt of energy ignites my skull.

I'm overcome but finally say, "Are you sure I'm the right person?"

"Who better than you?" I was afraid he'd say that.

"What's going on?" Gwynnie asks. "I'm completely in the dark here."

The old abbot waves a trembling finger my way. Like a kid reciting for my venerated tutor, I explain. "Father Joseph just passed the Mastership to Had. And I'm to help explain the complex Golden Bowl meditative philosophy which is connected to the hierarchy of the Celtic Tree of Life. You recall my description of the levels of consciousness rising up to the top where the Old Unoriginated One resides?"

"Yes," Gwynn says, "the coolest name ever for a higher power."

Father J. smiles and I continue. "Well, those levels, or regions, are accessible in your very own golden bowl." I cup my hand over the top of my head. "Like I've said, the Tree of Life is a diagram of that internal journey."

"Intense," Gwynn declares.

"Yes, and the ability doesn't happen overnight. The purpose of sitting in Golden Bowl meditation is for the practitioner, through diligent hours of concentrated meditation, to travel upward from region to region. Eventually like the drop merging with the ocean, the meditator joins the Creator."

"Has anyone actually spoken to the Old Originated One?"

"Diligent meditators have."

I look to Father J. to see if my explanation meets his approval. He adds, "The presence of a spiritual master is essential . . . to guide the initiate on their inner journey."

The door opens and Brother Ushtey rushes in. "Excuse me, Father, but we need your signature." Without reading it, the old abbot signs an invoice. Ushtey glares at Gwynn and me. "Don't tax Father Joseph. You can see he's ill."

"I called them here," Father J. assures. The intruder stomps out, but closes the door softly. "Ushtey can be overly protective." And is obviously in charge of finances. Did he get caught stealing? Is that why Lady Elaine is dead?

I've no time to ponder as Gwynn pleads, "What if I want to meditate too?"

Father turns his full attention to Gwynnie as if he's scanning her psyche. "One day you will be a Golden Bowl initiate, but . . ." He lays a hand on his chest and breathes hard. "But you must first satisfy your intellect. Study the Golden Bowl philosophy and when the time is right, your spiritual teacher will be there."

Gwynn is more than a bit downcast, but says, "I look forward to it."

Father Joseph appears done in, so I ask, "May we take Had home?" I purposely repeat the phrasing I used with Mother Superior to gauge his reaction.

"Most certainly. After all you are distant cousins through the Stewart clan." He pauses. "The General swore me to silence, but he's long dead."

Galahad turns to me. "And just when I've begun calling you, Gran."

"And you better keep calling me, Gran." I smile at my sweet boy, but wonder how is it that tree, plant and human poisonings precede our every move? And what on God's leafy earth could it all mean?

The Storm

26

Gwynn drives us home from the monastery as a storm creeps over the foothills with an ambitious rumble. I'm sitting up front, but keep an eye on Had in the backseat. He wipes tears then scrutinizes his hand as if the waterworks are new to him.

I remain silent until we reach Koad Croft wondering what is the acceptable time limit to speak of murder. After we dash in out of the rain, build a fire and brew tea, I ask, "Had, do you have any clue who poisoned your mother?"

A muscle in his jaw jerks. "Certainly not."

I don't give up. "Does even a small incident of envy from one of the nuns come to mind? Did any of the monks resent Father Joseph passing the Mastership to Lady Elaine?"

"Everyone loved Mum."

"Even ex-con Ushtey—who's a real douche?" Gwynn snaps.

"Must you speak so crudely, Gwynn?" he growls.

"Excuse me, Laird Perfect." Gwynn starts sniffing. "Sorry, Had. Listen, don't hold the pain in, it'll make you do crazy stuff—like I did after Mama died."

As it turns out, they aren't sniffles of remorse. Before long Gwynn's in the throws of a full-blown head cold. I believe in consuming live-food enzymes—those little substances that heal on a cellular level. Since I get fresh fruit and salads down Gwynn, I haven't pressed the issue until now. "You know why you're sick don't you Gwynn?"

"This stupid Scottish weather, rains all the time." She stares at Had like it's his fault.

"No sweetie, it was the rich Camelon food. Your body is like a computer, garbage in-garbage out. Here, drink this carrot juice." Gwynn offers a weak salute as thunder knocks torrential rain from the clouds.

Raven runs to her crate carrying Had's wool cap. The kids let it pass since they're used to her kleptomania. Once the little dog claims a treasure, she takes very good care of it. Had stokes the fire then sits at our little square dining table staring at Lady Elaine's bank statement. Big finance to take his mind off mourning?

While I stew veggies Gwynn moves to the table beside Had. "Has Lance asked how you're doing? He seemed pretty upset about your mom's death."

Galahad's blonde features flush as he answers in clipped tones. "My birth father could care a pip about me."

Gwynn nods. "I know that one." My kids' eyes lock as they find common ground in their abandonment issues. She holds Had's clenched fist. He doesn't draw away.

I allow a poignant moment, but don't want him dwelling in loathing. "Had, to give you a research project for your dissertation, Father Joseph arranged for you to work at Logres. Then R.A. asked you to trace the poisoned trees—all before I got to Scotland."

"Yes, the first was a circle of old growth Oaks dating back to Druid days located on the Camelon Estate. Saving them is looking good— their roots are deep. R.A's private woods are registered with the Scottish Heritage Society. Preserving them is that valuable to Scotland. The second group were Holly trees at Logres inner solarium garden. Their discovery prompted R.A.'s suspicions of a vendetta against Logres."

Gwynn winces as a lightning bolt strikes so close you can't count one-hundred-one. Thunder shakes our thatch. Raven howls and streaks over to me. "What a watchdog," I croon. Truth is my body hair stands on end, but I'm not going to let the storm gods know. I mentally sink my roots deep and speak from a place of strength. "I don't want to think Lady Elaine's poisoning has anything to do with the tree poisonings, but we need to prove they aren't connected. For now, we'll postulate that they aren't."

Had gives me a pained look. "Please do." He hurries a bucket under a thatch leak.

As I lay steaming bowls on the table, the trees outside our rain-streaked windows bend under the raging gale. Surreptitiously Raven moves to her place by Gwynn as if I'm not aware of their eating arrangement. Had says grace and I say, "Eat your stew, Gwynn."

Thunder shakes the firmament as if to emphasize it has the upper hand. The adolescent looks heavenward. "I hear you, Grandpa Angus."

Had tastes the stew then insists, "Logres has had threatening warnings from radical eco-terrorists. These poisonings appear the work of groups promoting the false premise that Logres is destroying the woods.

Truth is, Logres protects the natural forests."

"Wouldn't it be against the eco-groups principles to poison the trees?" Gwynnie asks. "I think some demented person has it in for the old Celtic ways and I don't like it." Look at Gwynn supporting her ancestral roots.

"I'm sure they feel justified," I sigh. "You know what they say about arguing with a crazy mind." My last word is a screech as a limb smacks the thatched roof—proving nothing about my courage.

Looking miserable, Gwynn sneezes and wipes her nose. I brew up the nastiest tasting tea you'll ever encounter—goldenseal and echinacea, but it kicks the poop out of a cold. After forcing the concoction down Gwynnie I tuck her in bed.

Inevitably we lose our electricity, so Had stokes the fire and lights two lanterns. I burrow under an afghan in the understuffed chair. Nature's kettledrum rolls a cadence over the hills. The evening's conversation has proven Had's willingness to talk, so I ask, "Who do you report to at Logres when you call in? Who has access to our daily itinerary?"

"I inform Ms. McKay in the front office. She passes our location on."

I let him sit with that fact then ask, "R.A. hasn't kept the tree poisonings from everyone?"

"Gran, when Father Joseph received your request concerning the tree research,' Had says, "he discussed the tree poisonings. The monks may have overheard." Storm gusts chatter the windowpanes with a piercing determination as he thinks. "Father must have discussed it with Mum because she was concerned about our living arrangements." I'll bet she was.

We're jolted by a humongous crash and a scream from Gwynn's room. Raven scampers to Gwynn with Had and I close behind. Our lantern illuminates a massive tree limb jutting through the thatched roof. A drenched Gwynn sits in her very own loch as rainwater pours into the sick girl's bed. She crawls weeping into my arms.

"Do what you can here, Had." I lead the sobbing wet girl to the fireplace where I strip her naked. Raven licks Gwynn's feet and legs while I rub her down with a towel.

"Where should I put this..." Had halts mid-sentence staring at the shivering woman-child. Gwynn stares back as I throw a quilt off the sofa bed to her. She takes a few seconds longer than necessary to wrap it around her nude body.

Before Had embarrasses himself further I say, "Never mind, we're all family." Nonetheless, I do wonder if he's ever seen a girl in the buff.

He ducks behind the soggy mattress and drags it out into the storm, leaving me to body-slam the door closed.

Gwynn lets out a shuttering sob. "Grandma, I'm trying really hard, but Igraine has it out for me." She sinks into a puddle on the hearth.

"I'll never let Igraine's ghost harm you." I'm beating myself for telling Gwynn it was Igraine's taunting voice at the séance. I help Gwynnie into dry clothes then open the sofa bed. As I rock her like a two-year-old, she grabs my tartan against a chilling blast. Had struggles through the door avoiding Gwynn's gaze then begins mopping up.

"Grandma, you're all I have," Gwynn chokes. "Mama is gone. Dad and Cyndi don't want me." We lay our tired souls down and I stroke Gwynn's hair while singing. *"Let us go/ To the Braes of Balquhidder/ Where the blae-berries grow/ 'Mang the bonnie Highland heather."* Holding Raven, the girl drifts off to the Scottish tune and rhythmic rain plunking in pots.

Having dealt with leaks, Had transfers Gwynn's clothes to my closet then sits the lantern near his financial printout. He turns to me. "Gran do you have money you need invested?"

"Not a cent." I kick myself for letting him know I'm broke. Surely he hasn't squandered Lady Elaine's money. Had frowns at his calculations making me wonder if we should expect a burly loan shark pounding on our door some night. I'd hate to have to tackle another hoodlum.

I wake with the sun to find Had lying next to Gwynn who has me cliff-hanging off the bed. Prying my paralyzed hand from hers, I slip to the damp floor, turn around and see my adopted kids' noggins touching. All at once a dawning ray accentuates Had's sandy-blond hair against Gwynn's red-gold tresses fanned out like a beautiful plant branching toward the light. I'm keenly aware neither of them will flourish until spiritual sap enters their core. Like it or not, I've been volunteered to lead them to this miracle. The sunbeam causes both kids to open their eyes and smile at me so sweetly, tears escape. Sometimes the Old Unoriginated One doesn't play fair.

Mother Love

27

I didn't plan to snoop. Just happen to be peering through a hole some ancestor with a devious mind positioned in the concealed passage behind Mort and Morgan's chambers. Admit it, you'd be curious, too.

Gwynn, Had and I are back at Camelon until Artie's crew rethatches Koad Croft. This time we lassies have Had sleeping in our dressing room. "Grandma Merle and I won't feel safe without you close," Gwynn argued. Truth is, we don't want him grieving alone, so it's been family time to encourage conversation. We're big on jigsaw puzzles, and Gwynnie's teaching us high-stakes poker with buttons borrowed from Priscilla's sewing tin. So far, Had's chatting and I'm the button champ.

Right now, I'm captivated by the view of Mort and Morgan that my strategic paneling hole permits. Morgan's back is toward me, but she gestures for emphasis. "If we play it right, this castle estate can be ours . . . yours."

The young man slaps the chair's arm. "All ours, Mother."

"About that—could you call me, Morgan? We may want to project an image other than mother and son."

"Okay, I mean a woman as young as you."

"You do understand."

I don't. After all the kid is newly united with his biological family. He's already been forced, for propriety's sake, to call his father, Uncle. Now he can't even call Morgan, Mother. Talk about screwy.

"Anything you want, Morgan." The kid either idolizes his birth mother, or is in this for the glitz. "What's next?" he asks. "How do I break into the family business?"

"Don't appear too eager," Morgan answers. "After that sword fight fiasco, we need to play R.A. very carefully."

"I said I was sorry," he pouts then changes his tone. "This'll give me and you time to get better acquainted. There's a lot I want to talk about.

About twenty-one years' worth." He sounds desperate.

"The best way to get to know someone—take them shopping," she sidesteps. Morgan doesn't want a son, she wants a playmate. Mort looks dejected, so she asks, "What kind of car would you like?"

Mort propels forward. "Are you serious?"

"You're moving up in the world. You have to look the part. And clothes, too—they really do make the man."

I can picture the scene, mother and son bonding over a new shirt. Morgan's maternal juices are really flowing. But then it's been proven a person's maturity level stalls at the age they began using drugs, or alcohol. That would make Morgan about thirteen.

"When do we go?"

"Right after I coerce R.A. into handing over the cash." Mort flops back. "Don't worry," she says, "I'll get it." You can almost hear Morgan's conniving gears shifting.

Choking on what Morgan's dishing out, I stand motionless. I've now witnessed three generations of dysfunction in this clan. Lady Igraine infected Morgan with her narcissistic insanity. Without a strong desire to change, how can Morgan not pass the dysfunction to Mort? This family tree is a travesty of poisoned roots.

This is not to say I wear a halo. I experimented a bit, but soon determined an alternate reality was not for me. I chose a clear mind to juggle marriage, attend medical school and participate in meaningful activities. Picture me pregnant, chanting myself hoarse in the peace marches. Of course, real life slapped me in the face. I'd had a close bond with my unborn son and when he didn't live, a part of my soul died with him. Shortly after, I made a solemn covenant with the Almighty to devote my life to spiritual growth and helping humankind. That's when I became an army doctor, did a tour where I met Laird General Stewart, became Artie's surrogate mom, and you know the rest.

With such a distorted reality, I wonder if Morgan told Mort he's the byproduct of drug-induced trickery. That'd knock a guy back a couple miles. Which leads me to wonder why he lied about coming here from San Francisco, not Colorado? And how did Mort's adoptive parents die? I need DCI Armstrong to profile Mort. How many Scotland Yard favors does a body earn for saving a plane full of people?

Back in Morgan's chambers, I see Mort shifts uncomfortably. "Hey, Morgan, if you could have anything, what would it be?"

Without hesitation Morgan spreads her arms. "I want to be queen of Camelon and Logres. And Lance La Lac will marry me and you'll find some nice girl. Not too nice."

"Wonder what it'd be like to date Gwynn?"

Morgan snorts, "You need to get over her. She's Nanny Dumpling's step-whatever."

"Step-granddaughter," he offers. "Which means they aren't blood relatives."

"Yeah, but the old hag would be hanging around. She's trouble."

"Nothing we can't handle," Mort brags.

"That old lady's not what she seems. She's a magician, a wizard. Has visions. Watch yourself around her."

"I'll keep an eye out." Mort seems to half believe her and moves on. "I need to ask something serious." She nods and flings her hand up indicating the sky's the limit. "Well," he starts. "Do you actually like me?"

"What do you mean? You got everything you ever wanted growing up."

"Well, you've only told me you loved me twice."

"But who's counting?" She throws her arms around him, but after a nano-second pushes him away. "Listen, I'm too tired to take you shopping today."

"I could drive you." He's scrounging for scraps.

"Och, I need a lie-down. You go. You'll be fine." Morgan heads toward the bedroom. She twirls around and says, "Good talk, poppet." As her door closes Mort heaves a throw pillow across the room smashing a vase. Morgan yells, "You alright?"

He mutters. "Just bloody well fine." Mort turns toward my peephole with the biggest brownest loneliest eyes I've seen since I walked in on three-year-old Morgan in the clutches of her insane mother.

As I step away, I know fate's given me a chance to change the course of events. The Sinclair-Stewart family tree needs shaping up, and my loppers are at the ready.

Searching

28

The sleet circling Camelon looks pretty grizzly, but Gwynn declares, "I can't stand another day cooped up in this castle." I'm fed up myself, but try to put a good face on it when Galahad saves the day.

"The weather still prevents the completion of Koad Croft's rethatching, but you ladies could accompany me to Edinburgh. Perhaps you could purchase a Christmas gift for R.A. It can't be terribly expensive since the authorities froze Mum's and my joint account. They're investigating whether I killed her for the funds I always had access to."

"That's totally ignorant," Gwynn exclaims.

"They find it suspicious that Mum instructed me to invest large sums these past months."

"Have you told DCI Armstrong about these accusations?" I ask.

"Afraid he's the one who questioned my intent." Well, horse pucky.

Despite yet another snag in life's fabric, we dress in our tartan woolens and pile into the Rover. The roads are crusty ice crystals, so we have no trouble making it to the highway. After weeks at the estate, entering Edinburgh's fast-paced atmosphere feels like synchronized insanity.

We survive and meet R.A. just outside Logres' employee entrance. He's talking to a herd of lumberjacks who appear to pass Gwynn's inspection and vice-versa. The loggers disperse, but instead of following his men, forestry manager Aidan Hunter follows us inside. Although a tall man, R.A. must look up at the gigantic Aidan. "We'd like a bit of an archery competition during the holidays," the laird says. "Bet you can show us a thing or two."

"Oh yes, Aidan," Gwynn says. "Will you teach me how to shoot a bow and arrow?"

"Morgan hasn't actually invited me," Aidan admits.

"She took it for granted you'd join the family," R.A assures.

"I'll be there." Aidan smirks in a self-satisfied way then leaves.

At the elevator Lance La Lac joins our entourage. "Nice to see you ladies." He kisses our hands hovering longer over Gwynn's. "Watch the gap into the lift," he tells me, but puts an arm around Gwynn to assist her inside. R.A. steps in after Had.

I'm not the gorgeous gal I used to be, but still recognize Lance's flirtations. When Had escorts Gwynn to the back of the elevator it's apparent he doesn't approve of his birth father's attentions. After all, Lady Elaine, Lance's recently murdered estranged wife, is still on ice in the police morgue.

As the glass-sided lift rises, we look down onto a courtyard in the middle of the building. It is beautifully landscaped with paths spoking off a central fountain. "You can see all the Celtic trees and plants from here," Had tells Gwynn.

"Nice. What melted the snow around those bushy trees over there?"

R.A. and Lance block my view of the poisoned Elder trees. We reverse the lift and rush into the courtyard. Artie looks up at Logres' windowed walls surrounding us. "Lance, check who accessed this area on the CCTV."

I start to ask who knew Gwynn, Had and I were coming to Logres, but feel dizzy.

I swirl into a dungeon where ghostly shadows sing of tortured souls. Through the haze I see a dark cathedral. A monk-like specter points to the portrait of a brown-skinned Madonna. "Bow to the mother of the true messiah." His sweeping gesture floods the intricately-carved black-stone cathedral with candlelight.

"Why, it's beautiful," I confess. "But this shows me nothing of the philosophy taught here. How does your faith warrant poisoning the Celtic trees?"

The monk whirls around me in anger. "All false beliefs must be destroyed."

"You can't see the historical importance of Celtic lore in today's society?"

He reaches for me, but protective Celtic limbs pull me from danger. As I rise from the underworld they speak, "Stay clear of that one's deadly grip."

I drop into freefall and awaken on a hard cold bench. As I struggle upright, I pronounce, "The trees know who the poisoner is."

Gwynnie sits beside me. "Yes, trees do talk to each other."

An irritated Artie raises his voice. "Can't the two of you visit another day?" My brain unscrambles enough to recognize that Mort and Morgan have materialized while I gathered clues in the underworld.

"Strange," Gwynn accuses, "you two showing up the day we find more poisoned trees."

"No stranger than you and Nanny Goodwitch discovering them," Morgan snaps.

Gwynn rises up fierce and graceful. "Don't mock my grandmother."

R.A. intervenes before we have a serious mêlée, bribes Morgan with cash then ushers them out. "I've never seen anyone stand up to Morgan the way you do, Gwynn. Even I don't have your brass." He gives Gwynn a very long hug.

I regain my senses. "Did your security camera reveal who poisoned the Elders?"

Artie sighs. "Evidently they stopped working early this morning."

"The culprit is familiar with electronic equipment."

Gwynn smiles. "Grandma, a lot of people are."

I stand saying, "We'd best get to our Christmas shopping."

"Do you think you should leave so soon?" Artie asks.

"Stop fussing. You make me feel like an old boot." As we amble toward the front doors Artie looks at Gwynn who shrugs, but tells him she'll keep an eye on me.

To heck with that nonsense, as the doors close I say. "Alright Gwynn, just in case a fortuitous time to track Sister Mary Faye accidentally appeared, I printed a list of Edinburgh's convents. We need to interview this nun that visited Lady Elaine."

Gwynn whines, "We aren't going shopping?"

"Only after we find that nun. I saw an ancient carved church in my vision. If we locate it, we may find Sister Mary Faye."

We visit all of Edinburgh's convent addresses where I inquire after the illusive nun then ask to see their sanctuary. Alas, we come up empty. Sister Mary Faye doesn't reside in Edinburgh. Nor do I find the black-stone cathedral.

Disgusted, Gwynn sighs. "All this investigation and we didn't learn a thing."

"Oh yes, we did, Gwynnie. Out there, we've got a Sister Mary Fake."

Koad Croft, sporting a newly thatched roof, greets the kids and me with an old-fashioned *cead mile failte*, a hundred thousand welcomes. In short order Princess Raven claims the under-stuffed chair to shamelessly warm her pregnant belly by the peat and pine fire. Her attendants, however, must reshuffle and return to old routines.

Still, everyday life has an underlying uneasiness since Lady Elaine's tragic death. Had prefers to not mention the murder and confines his grieving to late night sobs. During the day he throws himself into winterizing chores. He's installed storm windows, changed the Rover's antifreeze and chopped enough wood to see us through an Artic winter.

On temperate days, Had takes Gwynnie and me tramping in the woods to gather dormant plant and tree roots for scientific comparisons. Soon Old Hag Winter will dig in her claws, but who minds when there are so few daylight hours? Determined not to hibernate I'm testing plant samples in my rudimentary chemistry lab, but at times it bores the pudding out of me. Gwynn, usually happy executing botany illustrations, yawns. Suddenly, tires crunching on gravel send her to the window. "R.A.'s here," she squeals and runs out to help carry bags of provisions.

Artie's arrival is a sunbeam from parting clouds. He enters saying, "The lads did a right good thatch." The dang tears stinging my eyes lead him to add, "You were needing company."

Even bereaved Had steps up to stow groceries. "I must apologize for not coming into work," the young man says, "however, I've not neglected Logres." Galahad hands R.A. a Logres financial report. "You may want to consider the strategy I've outlined to return Logres to solvency." R.A. studies it and nods. When I ask if the company's in trouble, Had merely says, "Possibly." Sometimes I could just spit.

Changing the subject Artie asks how we stay busy. I don't want to reveal we've spent days creating herbal soaps for the Camelon Christmas bash that's creeping closer. Fortunately, Gwynn pulls him to our work table to show him where I test Celtic plants. "You are welcome to use the Logres lab," he offers. I tell him the research is not far enough along when he notices Gwynn's art work. "Whose superb drawings are these?" She points to herself. "Gwynn," he exclaims, "you never cease to amaze me."

As if he wants to draw attention away from Gwynn, Had interjects. "Father Joseph made Gran my mentor. We study the Golden Bowl books he provides and she fields our questions."

Sounding genuinely interested, Artie says, "I'd like to hear some of that."

"I'll start," Gwynn declares. "How did the Golden Bowl meditation get all the way from the Holy Land to Holy Vessel's remote Scottish location?"

"I can answer that," Had offers. "Legend has it that while incarcerated in the Holy Land, a heavenly light lifted Joseph of Arimathea to freedom. He then traveled to what is now France, then to Great Britain concealing the Holy Grail. Most stories end there, but we believe Joseph of Arimathea founded our Holy Vessel monastery bringing with him the Golden Bowl teachings."

"I get it, Golden Bowl, Holy Vessel, Holy Grail." Gwynn exclaims. "All the same."

"Yes," I say, "it was often dangerous for the early disciples to reveal truths, so had to speak in code to protect themselves and their teachings from non-believers. Hence, the use of several names to describe both the physical and mystical Golden Bowl. Over the years, each of Holy Vessel's successors took Joseph of Arimathea's name, right up to our present Father Joseph."

Gwynn studies Had. "Just so you know, dear Galahad, when you become Holy Vessel's abbot, I am not calling you Father Joseph." Since this is the first smile that's crossed our boy's face since Elaine's death, I call for tea with chocolate biscuits.

"Other than collecting tree samples," R.A. asks, "do you get out much?"

"Well yesterday it rained enough dogs and cats to open a kennel," I begin, "but it was Gwynn's day to email her dad so Had took us to the library."

"The friends I message are so immature," Gwynn complains. "They don't seem to want to grow up. They could do so much more, even with their meager advantages."

R.A. turns to her. "You got it in one, Gwynn." I think she's still grinning. I sure am. Standing, he goes over to a long tube propped by the door. "What would you think of going fly fishing with me, Gwynn? I brought a couple rods."

"You'll have to teach me." She dashes to change her duds and calls out. "It's gotta be catch and release. No fried fish allowed here."

As the two of them drive off, Had asks, "Why does R.A. want to spend time with her?"

"She's the daughter he never had." Thinking Galahad feels left out, I ask him to help prepare stew. He lays the veggies on the counter in an orderly line. "You're very organized," I say.

"As opposed to Gwynn whose system is based on chaos theory?" We have a good laugh and take turns telling silly jokes while chopping veggies for the casserole.

Galahad turns petulant waiting for Gwynn and Artie's return. Baked aromas whet our appetites, our stomachs win out and my thoughts meander. "One element shines bright, Had. The Celtic tree and plant murderer seems connected to you and me. But who?"

"Foliage murderer?"

"Yes, I consider the blatant destruction of plant life, murder. It's been scientifically proven that plants have feelings. While attached to polygraph machines they respond to tests that reveal sensory perception. That includes humans encouraging them to grow." He groans, so I add, "Skeptics can look that up."

Instead of challenging me, he cleans his bowl and walks to the window. "Where could they have gotten to? They've been gone for hours."

"She's safe with Artie," I assure. Nonetheless, he puts on his coat and walks up the road leaving me to switch to detective mode.

Strong tea sharpens my wits, but every time I'm zeroing in on a culprit something makes me veer in another direction. I mean, why shouldn't I suspect the nuns? Mother Superior seems cagey. And who is this Sister Mary Faye that visited Lady Elaine? Are Elaine's and the Celtic tree poisonings connected? Is someone biased against the old traditions? Or against me attempting to find merit in the ancient plants? If it's not Morgan, what about angry Robbie Rose, discreet Gavin Sinclair, love-struck Aidan Hunter, playboy Lance La Lac, bastard Mort Sinclair-Stewart, or just about any of the Logres employees. Ahh, I have a newfound respect for investigators. It feels as if I'm walking a labyrinth weaving in and out of possibilities, never quite reaching the central truth.

Galahad slams though the doorway with an armload of wood, drops it noisily onto the hearth and goes about stoking the fire to a blaze. I don't bother asking if he's seen R.A. and Gwynn. Two hours later her giggles announce their return. As Artie shoves the door open, Had snaps. "Where have you been so long? We had to eat without you."

Gwynn blushes to the roots of her tousled hair, but R.A. attempts to smooth Had's worries. "Don't know how I did it, but I got us lost in the woods."

Recovering her composure, Gwynn says, "I can now cast without getting my line caught in the bushes. Not that it helped much. R.A. is the Fisher King Extraordinaire."

Artie drapes his arm across her shoulders and she dips her head shyly. He's so good for her.

†BIRCH (Betala pendula/alba) BETH†
December 24–January 20

Now here's an interesting tree. Since Birch groves were some of the first trees to flourish after the Ice Age, the tree was named Beth, meaning inception. Accordingly, the Birch tree represents new beginnings and change, making it very appropriate to usher in the Christmas and New Year season. Consequently, you can bet life-altering initiations were held this time of year. A sacred wood, Birch is also believed to have cleansing and shielding qualities. If you've read your Celtic lore, you may already know that folks often carried a wand or twig from this tree to ward off such malevolence as the evil eye. Yikes.

ꞕoliday Cheer

30

Once again, a long-awaited event materializes forcing a body to wrap that last gift, don the perfect ensemble and pack enough underwear for a stay. We drive onto the Camelon estate from the wooded side. Nearing the castle on the knoll, a mist swirls obscuring the turrets.

Gwynnie trembles. "Is that ghost breath wafting around the chimneys? Hope it's not Igraine's spirit." I shiver and not just from the biting wind as we step out of the car. Elaine's murder along with the tree poisonings trigger an unspoken foreboding.

Artie opens Camelon's carved oak doors and booms, "Happy Christmas. Happy Christmas." Despite his warm intentions I feel uncomfortable for, wandering among my Camelon castle cousins, there could be a poisoner. Maybe I can determine who's responsible. Big maybe.

Gwynnie buries her face in Raven's fur, hikes up her ankle-length tartan skirt and hurries up the stone stairs. I follow wrapped in billowing tweeds while a kilted Galahad trails behind with the luggage—bless his wood-chopping muscles.

Walking through the doors we're transported into a warm wassail Christmas fantasy. R.A. kisses Gwynn and me then says, "Gavin, might you lend Galahad a hand?" Artie looks to me. "You're staying a good while?" I return a noncommittal smile.

Priscilla Rose sweeps her plump arm around the enormous Entrance Hall. "What would you be thinken' of this?" Artie's determination to override the winter gloom is evidenced by holly, ivy and mistletoe. Evergreen garlands with red bows wind up the stairs. A humongous Scots pine decorated in tartan ribbon guards a cornucopia of gifts, while a giant wreath graces the mantle over a blazing fire that would unnerve Smokey Bear.

"Holy holiday," Gwynn says. "Looks like Santa arrived."

"Aye, never seen such extravagance," Bridget Rose chides. "The laird's showing off for you Americans. It was them rebellious sixties what brought Christmas parties ta Scotland. Our Pauline keeps herself to herself, in her garden shop in Edinburgh on holidays."

Aidan Hunter speaks up. "Nothing wrong with celebrating Christmas if it's done with respect for the holy family."

Morgan links arms with her boyfriend. "Och Aidan, there are all sorts of faiths here."

Lance La Lac joins the banter. "Yes, some of us run to confession with the same story every week." Galahad shoots his birth father a dark look.

"Religion is such a bunch of bull," Mort declares. "Where do they get off telling you what to do? Christmas is just a commercialized winter solstice."

"Come now, there'll be no judging other's beliefs," R.A. stresses. Pris smiles, but Robbie and Bridget look at the elaborate décor with chagrin.

"Grandma says it's the spiritual meaning behind the ritual that matters," Gwynnie adds.

Robbie Rose resists. "Christmas should be a humble affair like Christ's birth."

"In that case, I'd best return the presents," Artie laughs.

"Here, none of that talk," Pris exclaims. She actually enjoys all the fuss, but puts up a front for her conservative family. Seems when Robert married Bridget, she converted the lot of them to varying degrees of fervor. "Nothing wrong with a bit of Celtic tradition," Pris announces.

"It looks like a fairy-world," Gwynn gushes, so R.A. twirls her like a dance partner. I love the way he's taken to her.

"Well," Pris demands, "get yerselves to the Great Room for the banquet."

Holiday tradition permits the Rose clan to join the upstairs family. Nonetheless, Pris with daughter in-laws, Bridget and Janet, serve the traditional turkey with chestnut dressing, roast potatoes and parsnips, brussels sprouts, carrots, peas, gravy, bread sauce and cranberry jelly.

We sit wherever we want at the beautifully arranged table—R.A. at the head and Mort at the tail. As I look for a seat, my nosey old self wonders why Gwynnie, seated next to Artie, can't stop giggling. And what are Had and his Sinclair cousin, Gavin, agreeing to when they shake hands? And why isn't Morgan who's flirting with both Lance and Aidan, not getting sloshed? Even better, what is uncouth Mort angling for when he asks Lance, "Why don't you marry my mother, now that you're free of Had's?" Which causes the usually calm Aidan to call him an *ijiot*. Meaning idiot. Fascinating.

Eavesdropping aside, I squeeze in next to the robust one-legged Robert Rose. "Don't suppose you remember much about me, Robbie."

"But I do, Dr. Bruce. You patched me and the laird up more times than I'd like to recall." He grins at the childhood memories.

"I hear you work in the office since you wrestled that tree. Do you like your desk job?"

"Truth is I miss the logging. No arguing I have the soft job—so soft it's demeaning." Robbie gives R.A. a sidelong scowl before tempering his emotions. "Guess my heart remains with the trees." He shoves turkey and potatoes in his mouth.

"Nothing like working in the middle of a forest, is there Robbie? Pure magic. I can be tied up in knots then calm right down with a walk in the woods—especially among the ancient trees that seem to speak. No wonder our ancestors perceived them to be immortal."

Robbie looks thoughtful. "This entire isle were forested. Them scientists what takes ice samples found higher oxygen levels from back then." He swallows a gravy-soaked morsel.

"They knew not to clear all the trees. No wonder our elders created a tree and plant related alphabet and calendar," I add. "They knew enough to revere growing things."

"Och, ain't that the truth of it? A fella needs his trees so's as not to go off balance."

"Yes, doctors are now prescribing nature walks to cure depression. You don't suppose that's what happened to this tree poisoner? Got off center from lack of flora? There aren't enough mystical Celtic trees to go around without killing them off to make some sort of statement."

"Couldn't say, Dr. Bruce. Just know we need ta save our woods and forests."

Realizing I may have encroached on his religious beliefs, I move to another subject. "Tell me, does your stump give you much trouble?"

"Fact is, some nights the phantom pain is gruesome. Mind you, I'm the lucky one watching the bairns grow up." He motions to the three rowdy cherubs sandwiched between Jamie and Janet. Not wanting to mention Robbie and Bridget's lack of offspring, I remark that logging is a dangerous occupation. "That it is." Robbie points to Aidan and raises his voice, "Especially if one of the team has visions of grandeur." Aidan flushes as red as his hair, clinches his jaw then wisely turns away while Morgan shoots Robert a withering look.

"Do you honestly think that gentle giant caused your accident?" I ask.

"No doubt. But here, it's Christmas, let's not dwell on the sore subjects," Robbie concedes.

Ever the performer, Jamie Rose jumps to his feet and toasts, "A Happy Christmas and long life to the finest laird what's ever lived."

"How about we pull our Christmas Crackers so we can wear our silly hats?" R.A. says. Cracker's are a fancy cylinder you pull apart to emit a wee bang and spill trinkets, riddles, candy and the obligatory party hats. Fun is had by one-and-all. Even I give my sleuthing, as well as my diet, a holiday.

After dinner we troop back to the gigantic Entrance Hall. Gwynn plops down with the kiddos around the Christmas tree. "Who's ready to open presents?" Artie teases. A cheer goes up and packages are passed out.

Our handmade herbal soaps, although widely applauded, don't compare to the laird's extravagant gifts. I now sport a gold Tree of Life pendant, but Gwynnie and Morgan win the prize with diamond earrings. Everyone down to Jamie and Janet's toddlers, sport woolen scarves and tams in their family tartan. Even the Scotties wear plaid jackets—Sandy Lad handsome in the laird's tartan and Raven's going cattywampus around her expanded belly. After the gift exchange R.A. stands with his arm around Gwynn's shoulders. "I've smiled so much my jaws hurt," Gwynnie exclaims. Artie kisses her full on the mouth.

Although hitting the eggnog pretty hard, a tipsy Jamie Rose sets up the camera to photograph Aidan Hunter with the Stewart, Sinclair, Rose and MacLaren clans in our plaids displaying our favorite gifts. Most endearing is my Artie, not with the numerous offerings showered on him, but the simple bar of soap from the kids and me. Call me an old softy, but after the loving gift exchange and family photos I'm convinced none of these folks murdered the Celtic trees, let alone Elaine.

My assurance dissipates as Mort complains that the poisonings should have stopped R.A. from spending money on the peasants. Then Morgan warns Gwynn to stop flirting with Lance, leading me to question if Morgan did have something to do with Elaine's death. And when Robert Rose snubs R.A., I question if Robbie is ticked enough to poison his laird's trees.

Of course, all families have skeletons in their closets, but I question which ones aren't staying put?

More Evidence

31

It's the week between Christmas and the New Year. Seeking warmth, I've joined Raven in her library retreat insulated from ceiling to floor with leather-bound books and inviting fireplace. Gwynn peeks in dressed in her winter parka. "R.A. is taking me to the lakes for a bit of ice fishing." She takes off like a kid chasing an ice cream truck.

Me? I reign a relentless sleuth scrutinizing the hodge-podge clan portrait my R.A. framed after Christmas. Other than Artie and Gwynn, I've come up with motive and-or opportunity for every adult. If I don't check my overactive mind, I'll invent a conspiracy involving the lot of them. Fortunately, DCI Ian Armstrong, who appeared this morning, walks in. He nods toward the family picture. "Who done it?"

"There's no solid motive, but Morgan's my pick from the Stewart, Sinclair and Rose clans."

"Follow the money," he says, and it being after eleven a.m., pours himself a single malt.

"But to bring Logres down means financial ruin for the entire extended family."

I'm on the verge of telling Ian what I've seen in visions, but am saved by Gavin dashing in. "Where's R.A.? We arranged to exercise the horses."

"He took Gwynn fishing down to the lakes." Gavin has turned fourteen shades of purple, so I know full well there's more to his upset than losing track of R.A.

"Tell his highness it's on him if the stallion throws me." Gavin retreats fierce and furtive.

Drink in hand, Ian sits next to me. "We traced Mort back to Colorado State University, where he took forestry classes. Very near you. Previously, he was dismissed from University California Berkley, stemming from poor marks in chemistry and involvement with an environmental group. They protested logging by setting fire to an ancient redwood."

"Sounds like Mort's twisted logic. Would he destroy the Celtic trees for the same reason? No wait, he wasn't in Scotland when the poisonings began."

"As a matter of fact, he was," Ian counters. "He lived in Morgan's Edinburgh flat before she unveiled him at the Halloween party. There's more. Morgan paid the adoptive parents to raise him. She financed Mort's education and visited every few years." Armstrong knocks back a dram of scotch and slams the jigger on the side table.

I try to ignore his gesture. "How did Mort's adoptive parents die?"

"They didn't. I spoke to the Hamiltons at their home in San Francisco. They weren't unhappy to learn Mort moved to Scotland. They argued when he dropped out of CSU. After that he stopped communicating. But I don't think Mort's our man. He's not clever enough."

"Unless he's following a mastermind—Morgan's brilliant." I study the detective chief inspector for some sign of agreement.

"So far they haven't done anything but spend the laird's money as fast as they drive."

"They're dang extortionists," I agree. "Have your guys tracked Sister Mary Faye?"

"We're widening the search, but she was likely angling for a contribution. That's all for now." Ian stands to leave, but I touch his sleeve.

"What's this about freezing Had's bank account? You don't suspect he killed his mother."

"She was poisoned with hemlock that he had access to, but we want him for insider trading with Lady Elaine's money."

"A lot of people had access to that plant, and Had has always handled his mom's finances. Just because he works at Logres doesn't mean he shared inside information with her."

Armstrong grimaces apologetically. "I must reiterate—follow the money."

Must I do everything myself?

(Morning Prayers 32

espite job-training trips to Logres, there's not been much father-son bonding between Had and Lance. Nonetheless, I find them together in Camelon's chapel reciting prayers up front with Aidan Hunter. Morgan sits perched on a back pew. Either she's found religion, or she's discovered where handsome men hang out at dawn.

I scoot in beside her and she whispers, "Does the Yard have a lead on Elaine's murderer?"

I motion her to follow me out of the chapel. "The Yard is investigating, but there's not much headway. Did Elaine ever mention a Sister Mary Faye? She visited a couple times."

"Probably soliciting. Elaine was much too generous to those greedy nuns."

"But you, Morgan? You loved your cousin?"

"As a matter of fact I did," she spits and then softens. "Elaine had a peaceful aura—calming. She was going to initiate me into Golden Bowl meditation once I got my life straight. What'll I do without her? Aidan invited me to this recitation. Certainly no replacement for Elaine."

"Any idea why someone wanted Lady Elaine dead?" I ask.

"None, but Armstrong damn well better find out. I've never given you reason to like me, Dr. Bruce, but I trust you to put the Yard on the right road. Not for revenge. Elaine deserves justice." Tears glisten in Morgan's coffee brown eyes. Should I buy the sob story? Morgan le Grinch suddenly growing a heart sets me to questioning all sorts of established givens. I want to ask if she poisoned her cousin to free Lance from a loveless marriage, but the woman covers her mouth and scurries down the hall heaving sobs. Holy stars, either Morgan deserves an Oscar nomination, or a reprieve from my suspect list.

I walk to the solarium where Gavin sits muttering the end of an Our Father. He jumps up and snaps to attention so fast I expect a salute.

"Sorry, Gavin, didn't mean to interrupt."

He stashes his beads. "Promised me mum I'd recite the rosary every-day. Hasn't helped."

I park it on a wicker sofa then pat Gavin's vacated spot. He sits stiffly in the opposite corner. "Forest temples give me a lot of comfort, Gavin. Have you tried talking to the Creator while you're out doing your rounds?"

Gavin studies me. His demeanor reveals a lot more than his poker face. "Mum wanted me to return to the Church." I raise an eyebrow and he adds, "The Church abandoned me."

"Because you're gay?"

He looks away, but his eyes slide back to mine. "R.A. warned nothing gets past you."

"Well, nothing but who murdered Lady Elaine and who's poisoning the Celtic trees."

He jumps on the subject change. "Let me know if I can assist your investigation. It helps to toss ideas around."

I sidestep his offer, but ask, "You've seen combat? Can't miss that scar down your cheek."

"Saw a bit of action. R.A. claims you did more than patch up soldiers —some covert mission with the Laird General?" He's trying for a shock attack.

"Yes, before I came to Camelon. How'd you get here?"

"Couldn't find work suited for a lad with PTSD. Since I'm family, R.A. hired me for security. Me da was Igraine's cousin. Mum was Jamaican. You knew that?"

I make a noncommittal nod. Continuing the ambush inquiry, I ask, "What's this I hear about the Sinclair's wanting to take Camelon back after all these years?"

"You Yanks are direct. Must be listening to the Rose clan. They're suspicious of anyone new." He forces a laugh. "I've only been here seven years."

"And it's R.A. that keeps you out here?"

Backed into the honesty corner Gavin nods. "R.A. doesn't return my ardor, but we're close. I'd take a bullet for him."

"Let's hope it doesn't come to that. How do you handle it when Artie has women here?"

He jerks as if poked in the eye. "I admit to jealousy." He bites off his words and feeds them to me in chunks. "You're suggesting I poisoned the Celtic trees out of spite?"

"Just searching for clues, Gavin." I try to read something in his steady amber eyes, but he's weathering my interrogation. "Suspect any of the gardeners?"

He shakes his head. "This case is too complex for any of the local lads. I can't reckon a motive." He's echoing my thoughts, but adds, "Best look to the Rose clan, they're an angry lot." He trails off as if he knows more, or is he averting suspicion?

What if Gavin and Had are plotting to take back Camelon? Bring Logres to its knees by forcing the laird to sell cheap? Had will inherit a pot-full of money that could finance such a plot. Holy Cow Pies, did Gavin murder Lady Elaine with the idea of sharing Had's millions? But Gavin loves R.A., he wouldn't take Camelon from him. Would he?

I stand. "Think I'll take my pregnant dog for a walk."

Since Gavin's responsible for her condition, he blanches. "She doing all right?"

"So far." I make to leave. "Gavin, I often say morning prayers in the Oak grove, my sylvan sanctuary." I don't specifically ask him to join me. Truth is I need to hang out with someone without a possible motive for murder.

The Round Table 33

After a bit of shopping, Gwynnie and I make it back to Logres to meet up with Had. In the lobby we're met by a young woman with hair as black as her business suit and sea-foam eyes as mystic as the sea. She grabs me by the underside of my arm and rushes me into the elevator saying, "Come along Gwynn. The laird held up the board meeting for both of you."

"We'd have been on time, had we known we were expected, Ms. Whomever." Gwynn replies.

"I'm Fiona Percival, Logres Lumber attorney. I can be rather brusque."

Gwynn touches Fiona's arm. "I get that. Had is teaching me social graces."

Stepping inside the lift, I can't bring myself to look at the poisoned Elder trees in the courtyard below. Abruptly the doors open and Mort steps in pulling at diamond-studded cuffs. "Well now," he says, "aren't I lucky riding up with three beautiful women?" The kid's so oily it's a wonder he doesn't slip on his own blather.

The elevator opens on the top floor and Fiona whisks Gwynn and me into the conference room. R.A. sits on the far side of a massive round table divided into thirteen sections representing the thirteen Celtic months. And round to signify the circle of life.

"This is new," Mort remarks. "Looks like big slices of pizza." His ineptitude degrades this magnificent work of art in various inlaid wooden hues and textures.

R.A. conveys with a sweep of his hand that the table honors our Celtic tree heritage. A large embossed gold vessel sits at the table's center. Is Artie an initiate of Golden Bowl meditation?

My unspoken query goes unnoticed as raised eyebrows and sharp inhales follow Mort. He could claim the chair between a couple gray-haired gentlemen, but instead plunges into the empty seat beside R.A. You can believe that straightens the board members' backs.

One older gent has the presence of mind to reprimand. "Young man, that section of the table with the whitest of woods is reserved for Logres' successor."

"Not to worry, Granddad, I am just that. Aren't I . . . Uncle?"

The vein throbbing on R.A.'s forehead speaks louder than his measured, "Mort, you must sit elsewhere. Aidan, relinquish your seat so we may resume business." Aidan stands abruptly, an irked Mort moves in beside Morgan and stiff backs relax.

R.A. stands. "I reckon you'll agree the new conference table is remarkable. An American benefactor, Mr. Leo MacLaren, authorized its creation by our local craftsmen." Gwynn looks to me for confirmation the laird is referring to her dad, but you could knock me over with a leaf. R.A. motions toward Gwynn. "This young woman's father, in appreciation for our hospitality toward his daughter and grandmother, donated this round table in her name. Ms. Gwynn Avera MacLaren, please honor us with a few words."

Gwynnie timidly rises. "Wow, I'm pretty speechless here. I had no idea Dad had anything like this in mind. But no group of people deserve it more than the Logres Lumber family of employees." Beaming, she looks around the circle and finishes with, "It's an honor to be part of this surprise." Everyone applauds except Morgan who silences Mort's clapping. As my girl sits, she whispers, "I'm afraid Leo misunderstood R.A.'s intentions toward me."

Before I can ask how that transpired, Artie's introducing me, so I stand. "And our latest stock holder—my nana, Dr. Bruce-MacLaren."

"Thank you for the introduction." I say and glance at the members. "But by this time I'm not exactly a new face. You'll remember me from the laird's Halloween party, or worse, featured in the tabloids. Trust me, if I could skydive with my Scottish terrier, I'd take it on the road." Laughter and applause follow, so I bow and sit while I'm ahead.

Artie shakes a finger at me and turns. "Most of you know my nephew, Mort Sinclair-Stewart. I'd appreciate for one of you department heads to offer him a position." Mort stands, waits for the applause and pulls a face when it doesn't come. Morgan tugs him back to his seat. The room remains embarrassingly silent, but R.A. intimidates with patience.

"If you're not afraid of hard work," Aidan finally says, "I'll train you for logging."

"Fine. I'm all for learning the business from the ground up." Is he intentionally alluding that Aidan resides on the lowest rung?

"Sign up with personnel before you leave today," R.A. says. "Join the crew at seven."

"In the morning?" Mort exclaims, causing a burst of laughter.

Aidan responds with a voice of authority. "Receive instructions then leave out at half past from the west gate." This could be what Mort needs.

R.A. looks across the table at Had. "Logres should return to solvency thanks to the five-step strategy proposed by Galahad Sinclair. So for our final piece of business, it is my pleasure to announce the Board's intention to promote him to Assistant Vice-President. That is if you'll accept the position, Had."

"What the?" Mort begins, but Morgan shushes him with a pointy elbow.

Remaining seated, Had addresses the Board. "This is unexpected." He gathers himself and continues. "So much so, I'd appreciate time to discuss the responsibilities with the laird and of course your Vice-President." He means his birth father, Lance, a situation stickier than tree sap.

R.A. covers the young man's hesitancy with his usual grace. "We appreciate your thoroughness in this decision. I will, however, attempt to sway you with the fact that we," he motions toward the senior members, "came to a majority vote."

Had turns pink. "I am grateful and will give your offer my utmost consideration."

Mort clinches his fists. Morgan had him convinced he'd inherit the company, yet here's pious Galahad being groomed to sit at the right hand of the laird of Logres. Yet, Mort not stomping out proves he won't go so far as to cut the purse strings attached to his unorthodox pedigree.

R.A. draws the meeting to a close then says, "I'd invite you to gaze at the golden bowl at the center of our round table." We turn expectantly toward the gorgeous vessel. Three seconds later the artifact wavers slightly and disappears.

"A hologram," Gwynnie proclaims. "How appropriate." Yes, symbolizing the illusiveness of Golden Bowl meditation.

R.A. smiles. "I'll close by sending you forth on your own quests."

I'm so pleased with today's wonders, I could just stick gold stars on everyone's foreheads. Well, almost everyone.

(Missing the (Target

Tonight is New Year's Eve. My plan to sleep this morning is thwarted by Raven who I'm guessing simply wants to hear her howls echo off the gymnasium walls. I tear down the castle stairs only to see Mort beating the tar out of Gwynn with a plastic sword—then bark as loud as the dog. "What the holy heck's going on?"

Gywnn ducks a blow while wielding a rubber knife. "Mort's teaching me to fight."

Raven lumbers over and grabs Mort's pant leg, so he flings her off. If anyone can induce a pacifist's rage, it's Mort. "Don't treat a pregnant dog like that," Gwynn yells.

Taking the advantage, Mort stabs Gwynn full on. She grabs her ribcage and bends over. "Lose your focus and you're dead meat," he chides. Sidling up beside Mort, I pull his shoulder back, sweep his foot and land him on his butt. My punch stops a millimeter short of his scowling face. "That's not fair," he accuses.

"Just demonstrating, or didn't I understand your teaching method?" My tone is glacial. Carrying cinderblock Raven, I lead Gwynn toward the door giving Mort the stink-eye.

"You gotta be tough if you want to win," he yells. Camelon's heir-apparent demonstrates his might by swinging his plastic sword through the air.

I cringe at the thought of him in R.A's seat. Out in the corridor I say, "Artie needs another kid. Can you imagine Mort inheriting Camelon?"

"What if the laird has a girl?" Gwynn asks.

"Women had the right to inherit and own property under Celtic law. If Artie doesn't agree, I wasn't much of a nanny."

Aidan Hunter rounds the corner and says derogatorily, "What's keeping Morgan from inheriting if R.A. believes in women's lib?" I'm about to say that since the Laird General didn't officially adopt Morgan, she isn't in line to inherit, but he strides away announcing. "Archery competition for everyone, but the kitchen womenfolk. Meet in the gym at one o'clock sharp." Dang, I thought Aidan was one of the good guys.

"Come on," I say, "we could use some fresh air." Gwynn and I throw on warm gear, tug a sweater over Raven's belly and head out.

Taking advantage of a mild wind at our back, we walk toward the foggy woods past the frosted mermaid fountain. "Bet those ladies are cold," Gwynn laughs.

"Indeed. Do you want to make Birch tree wands to usher in the New Year? Legend has it birchwood assures protection in new endeavors, like actually catching a poisoner."

"I might need it for Aidan's archery boot camp," Gwynn decides.

As one o'clock rolls round, we meet in the gym. Aidan lines us up on the eighteen-meter line, shows us how to use our short bows then satisfied, moves us to the twenty-five-meter line. At both distances he betters us by hitting the bullseye every time.

Morgan hangs on her boyfriend. "He's brilliant."

Grabbing her shoulders, he turns Morgan to face us. "The countess and I have an announcement." Jerking away from his grip, Morgan's nostrils flare, but Aidan grins. "I've asked this beautiful Madonna to marry me." Morgan steps away from Aidan.

Silence reverberates until R.A. says, "We look forward to her decision. Don't we?"

Our round of embarrassed applause and Morgan's dark glances knock the bravado out of Aidan. "Best line up for another round," he mumbles.

"You're kinda cheating using that compound bow," Gwynn accuses Mort. He's not a Robin Hood, but scoring pretty high. "They don't take nearly the strength as ours."

"Jealous?" he reproaches.

"I didn't expect to do as well as trained archers," she states. Indeed, DCI Armstrong, Had and Gavin, Robbie and Jamie, Lance and Artie, prove to be above average while Gwynn, Morgan and I are all over the place. Gwynn laughs with delight when she hits the target most anywhere. With my trusty lockpick and a snooping agenda in mind, I make sure my shots go shy of the coveted mark.

Aidan steps up then misses the bullseye for the first time today. "Sin," I yell, and his eyes widen as if I've damned him. "Surely," I explain, "you've heard that archery term. To *sin* simply means missing what you aimed for. The word was adopted as a theological term for obvious reasons."

"Forgive me Father, for I have sinned like crazy today," Gwynn sings. Laughter for her self-deprecating humor ripples along the line.

Recognizing the perfect time to escape, I miss the target and feign exhaustion. "Think I need a lie down."

"Not until you hit the bullseye," Aidan demands.

I walk up to the line, gain a serene state of mind, shoot a bullseye then hand Aidan my bow. Gwynn's chiming laughter follows my clue-seeking retreat.

When the laird was a child, we explored the castle's dark hidden passageways. Some say they were installed so the servants could skirt the main quarters, but I think the original laird was a sneaky devil. As am I. Squeezing uninvited into Morgan's, therefore Mort and Aidan's chambers, is a thrill.

A book titled *Britain's Poisonous Plants* sure makes the hair on my neck stand at attention. Not that anyone marked the poison hemlock page. However, nothing toxic among Morgan's potted plants and a shelf displaying a crystal ball, pentagram, tarot cards and other occult articles don't prove anyone's guilt—or innocence.

Juicy paraphernalia on Morgan's nightstand announce extracurricular addictions. In contrast, on Aidan's side of the bed there's a Bible and passages scribbled on notecards. Why are Morgan and Aidan together, other than giving him reason to run to confession?

Mort's bedroom is a real testament to his fantasy world from dragon posters to a wicked sword and daggers of graduating size lining the dresser top. A cardboard Stewart family crest hangs over a plastic crown inscribed *King Mort of Camelon*. But a medieval preoccupation doesn't point to a tree poisoner.

Riding the service elevator to the third floor, I enter Gavin's room. I don't get to use my lockpick—other than a saber, the guy doesn't own a thing. I'm talking sparse. What does this groundskeeper-bodyguard spend his money on? Wait. Here's a book on estate management. Not that he and Had are in cahoots, but does Gavin Sinclair have his eyes on Camelon like Priscilla warned?

Across the hall in Had's room, the exact estate management book rests on his desk, which doesn't prove a darn thing. In his emotionally fragile state, I can't take a chance of him interpreting it as an accusation. I cannot lose his trust.

Although ridiculously tempting, I don't go through DCI Armstrong's room. Figure he's done something clever like stick a single hair on his briefcase flap. These Bond types know all the tricks, so I creep down to the servant's quarters.

I hear Priscilla Rose and daughter-in-laws Bridget and Janet, gabbing away over a hot cooker while the children play. Nipping up a few steps into Robert and Bridget's wee chambers, everything looks normal except a nursery that holds the couple's junk as if the hope of a baby lies buried beneath the debris. His grudge against Aidan and R.A. could be significant if Robert lost his ability to procreate along with his leg. Enough so, he'd poison the Celtic trees? My stars, here's that same estate management book. Surely, I'm not reading the clues correctly.

Confused, my initial exuberance for sleuthing wanes and it's back to the secret passageway. I enter Lance's chambers—nothing sparse here. Sleek modern décor tastefully intertwines with every expensive techno-toy known to man. Either Lance has majored in investing, or moonlighting as a gigolo pays darn good. Checking for evidence I find Lance also has the estate management book. Surely Lance, who by all accounts is kin, wouldn't mastermind a Camelon takeover by poisoning the trees.

Covering all the bases, I scurry out and cross the yard to Jamie and Janet Rose's croft with a few ewes and coos. When he's not playing gigs, Jamie also farms a plot, hence bags of fertilizer piled in their unlocked shed. Anyone could swipe a few. Or Jamie could use them to cause havoc, but the clues remain bereft of motive.

Inside their refreshingly cluttered cottage, it takes but a few minutes to realize this branch of the Rose's bush does not own estate management materials. Despite Janet and Jamie's identity stamped everywhere, a tsunami of regretful memories wash me off my feet. I stumble to a chair. You see, I lived in this cottage with my Scottish husband eons ago—the one Morgan seduced and married. Destiny didn't write a similar family into my life story. I didn't get to raise my baby boy with the heart defect. But just look at the children Spirit gave me.

And there you have it, possible evidence of an estate takeover, but no proof of tree poisoners out the kazoo. Nonetheless, I have an inkling I saw an important clue. Archery participants disperse as I reenter Camelon, so I follow Artie into his study. "Who won the competition?"

"Your man, Armstrong. Aidan likely would have, if Morgan hadn't axed him."

"Yes, that was uncomfortable to watch. Say Artie, what do you know about Gavin, Had, Robert and Lance studying estate management?"

"Och, that's the assignment for our next roundtable discussion.

If you have any suggestions for cutting costs, be sure to let us know." His eyes narrow. "You've gone sleuthing haven't you, Nana?"

Talk about missing the target.

Ḟogmanay Omen  35

After serving a light evening buffet, Priscilla Rose produces birch-twig brooms for the extended family ordering us to sweep then sprinkle our rooms with water from one of Scotland's holy wells.

Mort rolls his eyes. "What's the point?"

"Tis' Hogmanay, boy," Mrs. Rose explains. "You must clear away anythun unsavory afore we see the New Year in. Makes it clean for the first-footer."

"What's a first-footer?" Gwynn asks.

Pris turns on me. "Haven't you taught this child anything?"

"In old Scottish tradition," I quickly explain, "the first person to cross the threshold after midnight is the first-footer—always a dark handsome Scotsman."

"Och, don't forget thay most important piece," Priscilla scolds. "He carries coal, black buns, salt, whiskey, even money so there be warmth, food, and wealth o'plenty in the New Year."

"Sounds charming," Gwynn sighs. Artie nods approvingly.

"Off with you then." In charge, Mrs. Rose is loving every minute. "Get yerselves back tae the Great Hall for singing in the New Year no later than eleven."

Scowling Robert mutters, "More superstition," but knowing better than to defy his mother, sets off with Bridget to sweep their quarters. Not having any of it, Aidan Hunter lays his broom down and leaves while Mort makes like a witch flying up the grey stone staircase.

"Himself is trouble, that one is," Pris says. Morgan smiles and follows her son.

Gwynn and I, blotto from lack of sleep, hoof it upstairs. You see, Raven had her puppies in the wee hours of the morning. I taught Gwynnie how to play puppy midwife to two black females, two brindle males, and one wheaten already named Sandy Lass after the litter's sire.

Isn't it grand?

Gwynn looks up from her birch broom sweeping. "It's the Scottish tradition to leave nothing unsaid before the New Year. So I want to thank you for rescuing me and turning my life into a virtual fairytale." I hug her figuring pure love needs no comment.

We sprinkle holy water, grab a quick nap then dress for the evening's festivities. Determined to watch for guilt-ridden tree-poisoners, I follow Gwynn holding the hem of her gown as we descend the stairs into the three-story Great Hall. Jamie Rose's lively Celtic music echoes off the massive stone walls while Hogmanay banquet aromas entice. The extended family meander through another of Priscilla's contributions—a fireplace emitting a haze of 'evil-clearing' cedar boughs.

R.A. kisses our cheeks then spins Gwynn feasting on the demure elegance of her emerald gown—a nod to her dad's approval of the company she's keeping. "You're stunning this evening," Artie declares and Gwynn blushes. She may be seventeen, but my Gwynnie has matured at light-speed. She should be thirty by next week.

"Here lass, taste ol' Priscilla's eggnog," Mrs. Rose bids. "There's a bite tae it." Gwynn looks to me and I nod consent.

Had, who acts a stranger whenever we visit Camelon, sidles up and gives us awkward hugs. "The Rose women have outdone themselves. Shall we sample their vegetable stew and black buns, Gran?"

"Ask me twice." He escorts me to the decadent table festooned with fresh holly, crystal goblets, silver candelabras and mounds of food. It's the obvious focal point for starving men and plump grannies who might overhear something pertinent.

Aidan walks up to Robbie. "Shall there be a truce between us, Robert Rose? I'd not want hard feelings seeing as how I'm sure to marry Morgan."

"A fellow wouldn't be a good Scotsman if they refused to forgive on Hogmanay Eve," Robert replies stiffly.

"What's tae become of this family if that preachy Aidan Hunter joins us?" Bridget Rose whispers. "Claims we aren't none of us in the true kirk. And look who himself idolizes—Morgan le Fey."

"Maybe he plans to convert her," I suggest. Bridget laughs at the prospect then rejoins Robert, both avoiding Aidan—not difficult in this gigantic room. The Roses don't like Aidan, but just like him, they seem intolerant of anyone different.

And what's up with Gavin handing Had an envelope? "This should cover my commitment before the midnight bells ring, cousin." Paying one's debts is another Hogmanay tradition, but those Sinclair cousins are up to something. Making them tree poisoners? Never.

Their secrecy torments my meddlesome mind, but I have no time to speculate. Gwynn needs saving from Mort the Wart who's trying to drag her to the dance floor. Seems he wouldn't know a brushoff if it swept him to the North Sea.

I scurry up behind him. "What's up, Mort?"

The slimeball jumps away from Gwynn so fast, he bumps into Lance dressed to the nines plus nine. When I'm Queen of the World I'll pass a law against men that handsome. No wonder Gwynn swoons over him, Lance La Lac even makes me paw the earth.

"I brought you ladies champagne."

"Fancy Lancy, what part of teetotaler don't you understand?"

"Not even at Hogmanay? I promise I won't tell."

"But I would know. Besides, Gwynn's had Pricilla's eggnog. We're high on joy."

Morgan, a definite suspect of something, appears. She slips her arm through Lance's, seizes a glass of bubbly, downs it then looks at Gwynn. "I'm not a prude."

Gwynn smirks. "That would possibly sting if I valued your opinion, Countess."

Lance laughs. "Miss MacLaren, how'd you get so feisty?"

"Who cares," Morgan snarls. Why she prefers a playboy to the more stable Aidan puzzles me. She's captured Aidan's heart, but appears willing to throw him over for the more handsome, suave and filthy rich Lance La Lac. Okay, maybe I do get it.

While I ponder Morgan's love-life, R.A. strolls up. "Care to dance, Gwynn?"

"Well, sure, but nobody else is."

"And a shame that is with Jamie's band playing." Artie maneuvers Gwynn to the center of the room. Jamie who's too laid-back to take on tree poisoning, deftly leads his band into a slow haunting melody. Talking subsides as everyone watches R.A. glide Gwynn around the stone floor like silk over polished marble—Gwynn in green satin, and Artie in red tartan Stewart regalia. If pride is sinful, I'm in for it.

I'm about to well-up as the Camelon Village church bells begin ringing in the New Year. Artie plants a big ol' smackaroo right on Gwynn's lips causing a cheer to echo off the hall's beamed ceiling. Twirling his dance partner the laird cries. "Good New Year."

We dash to the entrance hall windows and join in singing *Auld*

Lang Syne. A Hogmanay bonfire reveals the village folk circling the front garden, their kiddos busily choosing gifts left by the laird. Fireworks scream into the air. The moment the pyrotechnics end there's a knock on the door.

"The first-footer," Pricilla announces. She swings the double doors wide for Lance, weighted down by a basket of treats.

"Good favor be on this home," he shouts.

Just as Lance moves to step in, Mort rounds the doorframe first. We gape at the scoundrel. "What?" he asks. "I fit the dark handsome Scotsman criteria."

"You've cursed our year entirely," Pris cries. "Crossing the threshold empty-handed."

R.A. growls. "Get yourself gone, before I mop the floor with you, boy."

Mort slinks to the edge of the room, but the damage is done. The Camelon residents, both inside and out of the castle, melt away with a thick foreboding pressing their hearts. Call it superstition, but they're not the only ones convinced Mort's *faux pas* set the stage for a tragic year.

†ROWAN (Sorbus aucuparia) LUIS†

January 21–February 17

The Rowan is the perfect tree to represent the yearly emergence from a long hard winter. Just imagine how running across a Rowan tree, with the promise of scarlet-berried glory, could delight a body that's seen nothing but gray skies for months on end. It's easy to understand why this tree was considered to have magical properties. As a matter of fact, sprigs of Rowan, believed to protect from evil fairies, or get this—psychic attack—were hung over the front door, the cowshed, and even the baby's cradle. But let's not stop there. The liquid from soaked rowanberries was sprinkled around any area needing protection because the 'sacred' red berries were connected to the cycle of life, death, and renewal. Sounds like pretty powerful stuff.

Life Forces

A couple weeks ago, Had, Gwynn and I returned to our wee cottage. Now we're racing to Holy Vessel Monastery after my heart-stopping premonition to rush to Father Joseph's side. He hasn't been well, but as we arrive his pale transparency tells me everything. Did you know a photograph of a near-death person appears out of focus as if their life force were fading away? Well, I don't need a photograph to predict he has only a few hours at most.

"May I have time alone with Father?" Galahad asks apologetically. As Gwynn and I leave, we hear Had say he's been meditating a full three hours daily since his mastership ritual. Well, I'm impressed.

Before trekking over to the convent, we look in on Raven and her little brood snuggled together in a basket near a meager fire. Gwynn gazes at Mama Raven. "I had a good mother, but Had's mum died only a couple months ago, and now..."

I motion toward the pups. "Yet the cycle of life goes on." We step out for a breath of stinging cold air. It smells of life. Glorious life.

The day appears unusually bright for January. Every frozen twig and stem sparkles in the morning light and reflects off St. Clair's stone exterior. The grounds are extensive for such a small order, its big old buildings speaking of a more prosperous age. "This place doesn't look so scary in the daytime, but people keep dying," Gwynn muses.

The hut on the banks of the loch where Lady Elaine spent her last days draws my attention. Sheep lift their heads in greeting, but the pastoral peace doesn't fool me. Nothing can erase the morbid memory of Elaine's posed corpse. "There's unfinished business here. They can't bury Lady Elaine in consecrated ground until her case is closed."

"I don't understand religious rules, they vary so," Gwynn says.

Never one to pass a chance, I wisdomize. "My true expertise is studying similarities in world religions. I've discovered amazing theological crossovers then wondered why the heck religious tolerance isn't more prevalent. Personally I believe if it weren't for all the nuances, the world would be practicing the same philosophy. After all, Spirit remains constant, no matter how you worship."

We're walking down the knoll with the rise to the convent ahead of us. "Grandma Merle, your ideas could start another holy war."

"Or put an end to all wars," I counter. "But that kind of peace probably only exists on heavenly realms."

"Where the Tree of Life grows?" Steeped in the sacred, this place brings out queries. And Gwynn's asking for a synopsis of Celtic metaphysics. Luckily, I'm up to it.

"The tree symbolizes immortality in nearly every culture. As you know, our ancestors resided under huge trees that outlived everyone. Those giant branches seemed to reach into the cosmos and the roots down to the earth's center. They appeared to be divine as well as immortal."

Gwynn sighs. "It musta been magical living out in nature."

I don't stoop to mention her abhorrence to the wilderness merely months ago, but Celtic philosophy has piqued Gwynn's interest so I relent. "Imagine being attuned to the life cycles—birth, life, death, the phases of the sun, moon and stars and the changing of seasons—with the trees as conduit to Spirit. The ancients knew the trees weren't the Source of life. They realized the Creator resides within all that exists and likely attempted to communicate with Spirit."

Gwynn's eyes widen. "Have you done it? Talked to the Old Unoriginated One?"

"If I did, Gwynnie, it would be too sacred to share."

"You're like really mystical once a person gets to know you, Grandma Merle."

Tuckered out from the jaunt up the slippery cobbled path, I sneak us in the convent's side door. These high ceilings echo every footstep. It makes a body want to shout just for kicks. I'm sure to go to hell if I do, so I keep my trap shut.

I head to Mother Superior's office savoring the thought of the old lady's tea. I open her door, but Mother S. ushers us back into the hallway. "I found something for your investigation." She's abrupt, almost abrasive. I admire her a lot.

The three of us, perfectly stair-stepped in height, trot through gray stone corridors to the main entrance registry book. She runs the place by strict rules insisting everyone sign in and out. No dawdling in the gardens around here. Overcome by guilt, I sign us in.

174

"Sister Bernadette, this is the lady I said would come." Evidently Mother S. predicted my unplanned visit. "Show her the entry the day Lady Elaine died." She turns to Gwynn. "In the month of Elder, that's late November on the modern calendar." Gwynnie knows this, but nods politely. Holy Vessel and St. Clair's use the Celtic calendar which explains Had's awareness, yet he considers the tree symbolism superstition.

Sister B. points a boney finger to a scrawling script in the month of Elder.

Sister Merry Fey of Edinburgh entering 3:24pm . . . Visiting Lady Elaine La Lac.

Sister Merry Fey leaving 5:36pm. What did she do for more than two hours? The fact that Lady Elaine never used La Lac as a surname, doesn't escape me. Nor does the nun's name. Not spelled Mary Faye, as assumed, but Merry Fey. Meaning something like the jolly foreseer, or cheerful bearer of death. You choose.

Handled properly, this Sister *Merry Fey* visiting Lady Elaine *La Lac*, could be the lapse in judgment that proves premeditated murder. Did the killer think she was being clever? Ego gets them every time. Well, it gets all of us, doesn't it?

"I prayed for your speedy return," Mother S. says.

"Good thing Grandma Merle's transceiver works," Gwynn chides.

Mother Superior and I exchange knowing smiles. Having the fey can be a good thing. We both possess the second sight and used our 'gift from God', as Mother S. calls it, back when Lady Elaine needed a midwife. And, yes, I helped Had into this world, but there's no need to go blabbing that around.

I say we need the page for Scotland Yard, but Mother S. flashes a look of disapproval, pulls a wicked letter-opener from her habit and cuts it from the book. When she doesn't relinquish the evidence, I say, "I'll let DCI Armstrong know you're keeping it safe. By the way, which one of you actually saw this Sister Merry Fey?"

Mother S. nods to the wheelchair-bound Sister Bernadette, who expounds. "That nun were a tall woman. Herself hid awful well in that big wimple, but her hands were bronzed." Smart cookie, this one. "Youngish," Sister B. adds, "between twenty and forty." Well, that won't hold up in court, so I pray for a fingerprint match.

I turn to Mother S. "Now that you've had time to think, can you reckon who'd want to harm Lady Elaine? If soliciting for their convent, Elaine would be worth more alive."

Instead of answering, Mother S. says. "You need to return to Father

Joseph. He's giving the boy his last instructions." She dashes off in a black and white streak and I have the feeling she didn't disclose everything. I bet she won't go to hell for it either.

As we start to go, Sister B. says, "Excuse me for saying, but the nun was that proud. Fancy shoes with buckles—allowed only at progressive convents." She blushes then hands me a drawing of the shoes from under the registry.

"May I keep this?" Sister B. nods. I'm about to break into a jig, but speak calmly. Far be it for me to scare off an eyewitness. "Remember anything else?"

Sister Bernadette looks at her hands. "We don't wear nail varnish." With the eye of an artist, she points to Gwynn's sweater, "A paler pink shade." She pauses then says, "When Sister Merry Fey came with that plant, I reckon she planted it for Lady Elaine."

"And it resembled Queen Ann's lace?"

"Yes, but it weren't, now were it?" Sister B. has a pained look on her face.

"No, Sister, and there was nothing you could have done."

"Do you want the page from Sister Merry Fey's first visit in the month of Ivy?" Why didn't she give it to Mother Superior? The razor sharp nun cuts the page out, encases it in a manila envelope she just happens to have handy.

Holding evidence of Elaine's murderer in my hand, I tell her she's been an enormous help as I sign us out. On the way to Father Joseph, I tell Gwynnie to check the Rowan trees for poison. Rowan protects against psychic attack, so I might need a twig in lieu of my next vision with Igraine. Look at me acting like it's bound to happen.

Gwynn dashes across the meadow while I propel downhill—a hedgehog on a treadmill—my mind working as fast as my feet. Why is Mother Superior acting suspicious, surely not to cover her holy behind. Dang, I could find suspects in heaven.

Could Sister Merry Fey, most likely an imposter, have committed murder—the mortal sin of all mortal sins? Why else use Lance's last name? None of my thoughts weave into a complete tapestry—and why contemplate this rather than Father Joseph? After all, it would be an honor to see such a great man leave for the heavenly planes.

The upslope to the monastery doors has this hedgehog huffing while Gwynn, barely panting, joins me. Youth, you've got to love it. "The Rowans are fine. Here's some twigs." I smile a thank you. We link arms and go in to Father J.'s bedside.

Had holds Father Joseph's withered hand. Brother Ushtey hovers nearby. Father J. turns his head to the monk. "You may leave."

Ushtey is none too pleased, but notices a glass on the bedside table. "Who brought your milk, Father? They know that's for me to do."

The ancient man grimaces in pain, but manages to say, "Your friend." The brother places a napkin over the glass and carries it out. Once the door closes, Father J. directs his cobweb-whisper to Galahad. "Ecclesiastes 12: 6 and 7."

Without opening a Bible, Had turns his mental pages and recites: "Remember Him before the silver cord is cut . . . and the golden bowl is broken . . . Then the dust shall return to the earth as it was; and the spirit shall return to God who gave it."

I nod to let Father Joseph know I've deciphered his double meaning. Not only does this make reference to breaking the silver cord of life, Father J. means for me to help Had fully understand our Golden Bowl's meditating apparatus—the vibrant pineal and pituitary glands. Very esoteric stuff.

With a barely audible voice, Father Joseph rasps, "Passed mastership to Elaine. Now depending on you, Galahad." He falls silent except for his breath scraping through his chest. With his last strength the old man lays a hand on Had's head and transfers such a jolt of energy the young man jerks upright. Allowing a painful spasm to pass, Father Joseph's finger wavers toward me. "Your gran knows . . . where to find Holy Grail."

Had leans forward. "Father, won't you tell me?"

"Knock . . . it shall . . . be opened." Father Joseph manages to say as his soul slips from his tired tortured body.

Galahad's head falls to Father Joseph's chest. He wails so long and hard, Brother Ushtey scurries in to pull the boy away. "Hold your horses," I growl. "There's no time limit on grief." With a twisted glance at Father, Ushtey leaves without closing the door.

Raven slips in and heads straight to Had, keeping vigil with her muzzle on his foot. How do dogs know what's appropriate when humans can't figure it out?

Slings and Arrows 37

So as not to inconvenience anyone, Father Joseph has his grave waiting. And yes, highly attuned spiritual people can predict when they're going to die. Within hours of his passing, we attend his requested unassuming funeral. As the monks lower the coffin into the ground, I feel they are burying a lot more than an old man's bones.

The future of Golden Bowl meditation is now Galahad's duty. And the zinger. Me mentoring Had when I've spent half a lifetime concealing my secret Golden Bowl meditation vows—not discussing their deeper philosophical nuances.

Back home these concerns dissipate as I pull up to the cottage and R.A. steps out the front door. "Hey kids, Artie's here." Had, Gwynn and Raven emerge from a pile of tartan blankets. They smile, and if you think dogs can't smile you haven't met a happy Scottie.

R.A. somehow manages to tuck a wriggling Raven under his arm, grab the puppy crate and give Had a condolence hug. "Our spiritual leader's funeral," Artie says, "was over before I was informed. I thought a hearty meal might warm our bellies if not our hearts." Inside a pot of stew simmers on the cooker while soda bread cools on the counter. We're limp from grief, but even Had eats.

"You just drove over here to fix us dinner?" Gwynn has a way of getting straight to the point when the rest of us civilized folk sit around hoping for the facts.

R.A. pauses. "I do have a bit of bad news. I sent Robert looking for you and he found poison under the Rowan trees by your gate."

I shake my head. "Somehow, the poisoner knew we'd left. Are they taunting us?" The Rowans are the seventh cluster of Celtic trees conveniently located so Had, Gwynn and I would discover them. "You say Robbie drove out here?"

"Yes, I had a truck fitted for his disability. It allows him to do a bit of field work." R.A. turns to Galahad. "I rang up DCI Armstrong, but thought you'd want to be the first to inspect the poisoned area. Hope it's not too soon."

"I need to stay busy," Had assures.

"So R.A.," Gwynn says, "if you're staying over you can sleep in my bed." She turns thirteen shades of scarlet. "I mean I'll sleep with Grandma Merle. Not that . . . okay, I'll shut up now." Artie chuckles. Even Had grins.

Turns out we all hit the sack early. A terrifying 'Igraine' nightmare wakes me. To show her who's boss I head out to the Rowans. The creaking door brings Artie to my side. "Why put yourself through these visions, Nana?" Not voicing that his long-dead mother is haunting me, I sit in the poisoned area and close my eyes. Just like that, I'm whirling, swirling to the Underworld.

"*Can't stay away?*" *Igraine scoffs then with a wave of her hand illuminates the cathedral I've begun to expect.*

"*What is your ultimate plan, Igraine?*"

She cackles. "*Anguish, agony and angst for the Stewart clan.*"

"*Because old Laird General Stewart tricked you into marrying him?*"

"*For sending my dear husband to his death,*" *she shrieks.*

I fight to remain standing as a strong gust blows. "*Why torment me?*"

"*You're the conduit—receptive enough to send my message. The Stewart's must perish for the sins of their father.*"

As if infernos open, I'm thrown in a billowing fire-cloud up to consciousness.

As Artie helps me back inside, I say, "You Stewarts are in danger."

"Don't worry, Nana, I have Lance, Robert, Aidan and Gavin keeping watch."

"But what if . . ." I fall into a troubled sleep and awaken to stumble toward breakfast aromas. Artie mans the kitchen like a Priscilla Rose student—scones, porridge, toast and beans, all going at once. He pours me strong Scottish tea with one hand, and feeds Raven a buttered scone with the other. "Where are the kids?"

"Surveying the damage to the Rowan trees. They should have been back by now."

Raven jerks her head around, drops her scone and stands barking frantically. Had kicks the door open, my granddaughter in his arms. "Someone shot an arrow through Gwynn's side. It came out of the woods."

Fright grips my being. The fletching end of an arrow protrudes from Gwynn's right side while the point is well through her back. Blood stains her pink jacket.

Exhausted, Had carries Gwynn to the sofa flinching as she shrieks, "Grandma, Igraine finally got me."

"No, you're not a Stewart." Before Artie can ask about the Igraine comment, I urge him to break the ends off the arrow. "She'll bleed out if we pull it through." Stifling a cry with every jostle, Gwynn squeezes my hand. Clinching his jaw, Artie makes quick work of it. Gwynn's pulse is thin and thready. There could be internal bleeding. I cut her jacket away from the oozing wounds.

As I work, my mind plays a wartime infirmary rerun. Moaning soldiers line a stiflingly hot tent. Who do I treat first—the worst wounded, or the young men who have a better chance of making it? Claustrophobic hyperventilation grips me. I want to abandon my post, but there's no escape.

"Gran . . . Gran . . ." Had's urgency pulls me back.

"Make it stop hurting," Gwynn begs through chattering teeth.

Artie snatches the receiver off our landline phone and dials 999. "Laird R.A. Stewart here. We have a young woman with an arrow shot through her side."

Gwynn's glazed irises start to roll back. "She's passed out." Artie hands me the phone, "Dr. Merle Bruce-MacLaren speaking." I give them the medical lowdown then hand the receiver to Had. "They need directions to meet us halfway. We'll not let them wander around trying to find the croft."

The guys carry Gwynn to the Rover's backseat. Scooting in, I'm surprised to see my tears drop on her face. Please God save my Gwynnie. She's just got to pull through.

Had slides behind the wheel. Artie jumps in saying, "Gavin's bringing Bridget to get Raven and the pups. DCI Armstrong has already been informed and will meet us at hospital." Bad news travels at warp speed.

"How could this happen?" I ask.

It's a rhetorical question, but Had answers. "I moved just as she was hit. The arrow may have been aimed at me."

"This wasn't a hunter's arrow?" I ask.

"No hunting allowed," Artie says. My forests are wildlife reserves."

"A poacher?"

Galahad shakes his head. "There wasn't any game near us."

Meeting up with the ambulance, I climb in beside a paramedic that resembles a young James Bond. As he hooks up the I.V., I automatically start to help. More war horror escapes my mental archives—boys on both sides of the Red Cross ambulance dying in route. "My responsibility," I mutter.

James frowns. "Excuse me?"

"I saw a lot of punctures in the Army, but never an arrow piercing." I'm convinced of my sanity by the ability to speak an intelligible sentence.

Gwynnie cries out as we hit a bump. "How did this happen?" the paramedic asks.

"Someone shot at Gwynn and her friend, Galahad."

"Did this Galahad do it? A lover's quarrel?"

"They aren't involved that way. He likely saved her life." What about Had makes people suspicious?

At the hospital they whisk my Gwynnie into surgery. Artie goes for strong sweet tea, leaving me bereft. I'm at the admitting desk forced to answer a gazillion questions—me barely in present time attempting to remember when Gwynn got her last tetanus shot.

Signing on the guardianship line, I realize I need to contact her dad. How do you tell a parent their kid's been shot? Suddenly the war zone doesn't seem so ominous. I decide my stepson shouldn't be bothered until the surgery results are in, so walk into the waiting room that's done up in plastic wood and plastic leather. I detest plastic. It pollutes our oceans and poisons our food. Well, I have to lash out at something.

Then there's Had, nabbed for questioning by DCI Armstrong—how'd he get here so soon? "Your Galahad," he says, "is tangled in another unseemly incident." Armstrong is suspicious by nature, which is advantageous when he's on your side. Instead, he has a tyrannosaurus-sized bone to pick with my Had.

Moving beside his chair, I place my hand on Had's shoulder. "Ian Armstrong, in case you haven't been informed, our Gwynnie is in surgery with a life-threatening injury. We lost Father Joseph yesterday and Lady Elaine was murdered two months ago. My boy isn't obligated to answer another one of your accusatory questions."

He turns to Galahad. "In my personal capacity, I'm here to advise you to contact an attorney. You're to be charged with insider trading on behalf of your late mother."

Walking in with our tea R.A. bristles. "Now see here, Armstrong."

While Had sits calmly, I grab Ian's lapel. He easily unhands me. "Dr. Bruce-MacLaren, you are too close to this situation to have an unbiased opinion."

"I don't hold opinions about my children," I state. "I hold convictions."

"Be that as it may," Armstrong says, "Scotland Yard deals in hard evidence, and we've gathered enough against Galahad to prosecute. Will you testify in his defense?"

"Of course, and since we're sharing information, both Mother Superior and I have pages from St. Claire's registry that may help in Elaine's murder investigation."

Instead of patting me on the back, he says, "You tampered with evidence? Now you have gone too far."

"Kick us while we're down, Ian. You won't have another chance." Ashamed I let him get to me, I walk away swearing I'm going to exonerate my boy, catch Lady Elaine's murderer as well as the tree poisoner, not to mention track down who shot my Gwynnie.

I look up. "Angus, if you have any clout up there, now's the time to use it."

Light Seekers

ave you ever stood vigil over a loved one devoid of spark, strung up to machines like some science project? As I wait for Gwynnie to gain consciousness, horrid scenarios swirl down my mind gutters. Fretting challenges my undying faith as I bargain with the Almighty to swap this old lump of a crone for Gwynn's young life. St. Peter can enter that offense in his megawomper computer—I'll deal with him later.

Despite the mental ping-pong, I pray fervently knowing Gwynn's fate is written in Heaven's book, not mine. Why are we allowed the free-will to get so attached that compassion slices our hearts to bits?

I stubbornly reject Artie's pleas to leave the nursing to the hospital staff. "Priscilla Rose," he attempts to cajole, "supplied a fresh Rowan twig to hang over the lass's bed." He places the charm overtop the blinking machines. "Now that our Gwynn is duly protected from evil fairies and psychic attack, you can come home to Camelon. Bridget Rose is spoiling Raven and the puppies something fearful. We'll have Scotties as wide as they are long if you don't oversee their diet." I shake my head. "Nana," he scolds, "I'll be terribly miffed if..." And on and on.

I'm not budging until my Gwynnie finds her way back. Artie and Had take turns delivering crumpets and company for days on end. Well, five.

As if he has eons to spare, Artie holds Gwynn's hand and tells her tales from his childhood. "There was the time Robert Rose and I stuffed ourselves into the dumbwaiter—that's a wee elevator for food trays. Gravity smashed us boys to the kitchen with such force the doors flew open throwing me into a tray of meringue pies. Nana said no football for a month, but she went soft when I wrote her an apology poem."

"I didn't."

"Afraid you did, old love."

Between Artie's reminiscing and Priscilla's cooking, I gain the strength for Had's hospital visits. "How can you just sit there, Galahad?" I rebuke. "Gwynnie's been shot by some crazed archer, your mother was murdered and DCI Armstrong pressed charges for your purchasing Logres stock when you knew it was plummeting."

"There's no reason to worry, Gran. I prayed for the Old Unoriginated One to heal Gwynn, find Mum's poisoner and prove my innocence."

Either Had is the most naïve person on earth, or he truly has a hotline to heaven. He must be a spiritual master after all. Makes me feel under-qualified to guide this young man on a spiritual quest. Nonetheless, I am doing my best 'wise old sage' imitation.

Galahad leans forward. "That day by the loch, Mum told me to value your advice."

"Elaine recognized me?"

"Seems so. If the Logres attorney weren't wasting my time on the upcoming trial, I could pull Logres Lumber through this financial slump. Then again, I feel like searching for Father Joseph's Golden Bowl."

"It's your treasure to seek, but as destiny would have it, you must decipher the finer points. Be a spiritual seeker in every aspect of your life, but stay grounded." I lead him closer to Gwynnie's bedside. "It's time to give the patient her healing light session. Lay your hands on the soles of her feet."

He hesitates. "You think it's a viable therapy?"

"As your mentor, I recommend you remain open to new possibilities. Visualize healing light flowing through your hands into Gwynn."

Touching her ankles, he says, "Reading Father Joseph's books, I've come to realize he and Mum taught the main tenets of Golden Bowl philosophy while they raised me."

"Joseph and Elaine certainly emitted the glow of sainthood. Empowered by Golden Bowl's precept 'do no harm' they ate no animal products which in turn purified their body temples. Their lifestyle helped them reach ultimate spiritual levels."

"Why didn't they elucidate the finer points to me sooner?"

"Father said he wanted you to come to the spiritual path on your own," I explain. "Seeking is an integral part of the quest."

"He said that? Then I must share that Gavin and I are planning an archaeological expedition. As you know, legend claims my templar ancestors buried the Golden Bowl, the Holy Grail at Rosslyn Chapel. We've gained permission and purchased equipment."

So they aren't planning a Camelon takeover after all. However, after what Father J. revealed to Galahad, I didn't expect the young man to go down this track. But I won't dissuade his change of direction. "Had, there's more to this spiritual journey than digging up an artifact. You're not planning to excavate Rosslyn Chapel, are you?"

"We plan to use GPR, Ground Penetrating Radar, using pulse high-frequency electromagnetic energy to locate buried objects. But I want you both there."

"Concentrate on the light flowing into her. Enough talk for now."

Gwynn's eyes flutter open. "Gwynnie," I cry, "you're back. Where were you?"

"In the light with Mama. Need me to help find the Grail?"

"When you're able," Had says, "we'll take up lodging at the Rosslyn gatekeeper's house." The three of us grin like a goony-bird family.

"I wanta go home." Her head lifts, but falls back to the pillow.

Gwynn's doctor walks in. I ask if she'll release Gwynn into my care, but she replies, "Tests will determine that. I could use a bit of room."

Had and I step into the hall. He wipes his eyes with thumb and forefinger—the big marshmallow. "I'll hold off on the Grail quest until our family's reunited."

"The here and now is the only time we actually own."

He brightens. "In that case, I'll fetch the chapel's floor plans."

I realize Galahad is a divine gift despite his running into the world to find what is within all of us to discover. Then no one is promised an easy time of it. Knowing when to keep my trap shut makes for a good mentor, even if it means walking Had's convoluted labyrinth until his spiritual light switches on.

†ASH (Fraxinus excelsior) NUIN†
February 18–March 17

In Celtic cosmology, the Ash is known as the World Tree, or Tree of Life. You know the one with its roots in the ancient Underworld, its trunk in present day Earth, and branches reaching toward a future on a Heavenly plane. This Tree of Life, Ash tree, connects these three realms of existence. Don't you just wonder how this particular tree got to be so important? Not only do these majestic trees protect against charms and enchantments, but its seedpod bundles, or ash-keys, are reputed to open the door to the Universe. I mean of all the trees out there, the Ash is recognized as the microcosm and macrocosm, reflecting Heaven and Earth. Holy stars.

Had's Day in Court

39

I hate going to court, especially when the procedures are foreign and I might add, intimidating. A British courtroom puts a body in the mind of a coliseum the way the audience sits up there in the balcony staring down on the pulpit-like witness stand. Not that it seems to bother R.A. and Mother Superior, nor me as I give my 'Galahad Sinclair' character reference.

"And besides," I continue in a much bolder voice, "I distinctly heard Galahad tell Lady Elaine he could not discuss Logres Lumber business." I state this just as instructed by Had's savvy Logres attorney, Fiona Perceval. DCI Armstrong frowns as I walk back to my seat, so I shame him with a head shake.

In retaliation the Crown releases its lion on my boy. "Did you, Mr. Sinclair, in fact purchase Logres Lumber Ltd. stock for your mother, Lady Elaine, while researching Laird Stewart's poisoned trees knowing full well that those poisonings would cause the Logres stock to plummet?"

"Yes, but the poisoned trees . . ."

"Just answer the question," the prosecutor roars.

"Yes," Had says without malice.

"That wasn't so hard, was it Mr. Sinclair?"

Good thing British attorneys disguise themselves in George Washington wigs. If I recognize him outside the courtroom, I might have to hurt him. Okay, I can dream.

The Crown stops abusing the imperturbable Had, so now Ms. Perceval can get down to Galahad's alibi, which I pray to heaven he has. Fiona gazes at a file then begins. "Mr. Sinclair, did you purchase Logres stock for your mother before, as well as after, you were employed by Laird R.A. Stewart at Logres Lumber Ltd?"

"I did."

"Of your own volition?"

"No, by Mum's request."

Fiona glances at the magistrate to make sure he's listening. "Why didn't Lady Elaine make these purchases herself?"

"Because my mother lived as an anchorite, a nun-like recluse, her entire adult life. She never left St. Claire's convent, nor did she use communication devices."

"If Lady Elaine was so cut off from the world what made her want to invest in Logres Lumber stock to begin with?"

"Her cousin, Morgan Sinclair-Stewart, was a frequent visitor. She requested Mum invest heavily in Logres stock to help save the Camelon Estate. It seems the five-hundred-year-old castle needs major repairs. Consequently, Mum instructed I invest in the family business, Logres Lumber Ltd."

"Did you at any time communicate to Lady Elaine," Fiona turns toward the audience, "the media's overreaction regarding tree poisonings on Laird R.A. Stewart's property?"

"No. She was aware of the Ivy poisoning at the convent, but not the media's reaction."

Ms. Perceval turns toward the magistrate. "My Lord, I request to submit new evidence pertinent to this case, in the form of Lady Elaine's Last Will and Testament."

The crowd sits up straighter. DCI Armstrong turns to give me the evil eye. Submitting the will should have happened beforehand, so the rigmarole takes an age. What's in the dang thing? The suspense is unbearable—likely what Fiona planned. Finally, she turns back to Had, pauses then asks, "Mr. Sinclair, what exactly did Lady Elaine have you do with the stocks you bought in her name?"

"Actually, I didn't purchase them in her name. She had me purchase them in Laird R.A. Stewart's name." Artie jerks and stares wide-eyed.

The courtroom lets out one collective gasp. DCI Armstrong's nostrils flare as he glares at me. I shrug, but can't keep the wide, vindicated grin off my face.

Fiona's not done. She walks over, picks up Elaine's will, looks at it a second then reads. "And I bequeath all Logres Lumber Ltd. stock purchased in Rex Arthur Stewart's name, to the aforementioned, in the hope that he shall use it to retain the Camelon Castle family estate, in the event it is required for such."

Ms. Perceval turns sideways so she addresses both Had and the magistrate. "In other words, Mr. Sinclair, you didn't profit from your mother's purchase of Logres stock?"

"Quite the opposite," Had says.

Well that brings the house down. There's loud exclaiming and lots of gavel hammering. DCI Armstrong looks a bit more contrite, but we still have to wait for the magistrate's decision.

He may have the most impressive long curly wig of the bunch, but I'm worried while his honor deliberates. I pat my sweaty upper lip with a hanky since despite Had's innocent demeanor, he's technically guilty of insider trading. Anyway, you can imagine my relief as the magistrate does not commit Had to a full-blown trial. Instead my boy is severely reprimanded, but free of any charges.

I rest my case.

As Above, So Below  40

With Gwynn out of the hospital and Had's court case over, our wee family is finally off in search of Galahad's Holy Grail. Cold rain pelts the windscreen as Galahad drives Gwynn, me and Raven toward Rosslyn Chapel. Not far behind, Gavin follows in a van full of equipment so expensive I'm surprised it doesn't run on champagne. Damp green pastures and wee crofts roll past—pristine in a bygone time-warp sort of way.

"Had," I say, "a true Grail quest is the search for one's divine nature."

"Right you are, Gran. Right you are." He agrees benignly and I intend to needle him into a bit of soul searching, but he turns abruptly at Roslin Village waking Gwynn.

"Holy potholes," Gwynn cries. "Guess we'll see if my stitches hold." On the mend, she uses the back of my seat to pull herself upright. Had reaches to pat her hand. All this sibling nicey-nice is disconcerting. They haven't squabbled since Gwynn's close call and not just because she assured DCI Armstrong Had didn't shoot that arrow.

We pull in at the Cock and Clair for some pub food. Their St. Clair-Sinclair coat of arms featuring a rooster and motto 'Commit thy work to God' graces the entry along with a rose-garlanded St. Claire statue. Whether alehouse or chapel, the ages roll back. I love these dim history-worn establishments with low wooden beams and scarred tables.

Our eyes adjust to see Lance La Lac with sea-green eyed, Fiona Perceval on the far side. Had weaves through the crowd like a retriever and demands, "What are you doing with him?" So the blood in his veins is humanoid after all.

By the time Gwynn, Gavin and I make our way over, Fiona is red in the face. "And even if we were traveling together, you have no right to object."

Thoroughly rebuffed, Had turns toward the bar. I grab his arm. "Order the usual."

Lance leaps into action pulling out chairs, but I don't get my back caressed like Gwynn. "I do hope you have recovered," he coos. Flirting for some men encompasses their entire female communication skillset. I do suspect, however, that like R.A. some of Lance's behavior stems from old-fashioned chivalry.

"You guys being here isn't a coincidence, is it?" That's my girl, straight to the point.

"Interest in the Grail," Fiona replies, "inspired me to explore my spiritual side."

The usually quiet Gavin, adds, "Same for me."

Gwynn turns to Lance. "What about you?"

He laughs. "No remote possibility there's more to me than the tabloids report?"

"Since when?" Gwynn asks.

"Gwynn Avera," I admonish, "apologize this minute." Don't tell, but I secretly enjoy Gwynnie getting a rise out of this notorious womanizer.

"I deserved that," Lance admits. "Truth is, Had influenced several of us to seek the esoteric. I thought he would be pleased to see me."

"Not when you show up with his girlfriend," Gwynn chides.

"I'm not," Fiona says defensively, "involved with anyone at the moment."

A contrite Had sets orange squashes in front of Gwynn and me, tea for Gavin and himself. He pulls a chair in beside Fiona and gives his best sad puppy impression. "Forgive me, Fi." She lays a hand on his arm. They've called a truce.

"It must be gratifying," Lance ventures, "to have your day in court behind you."

"The less said on that subject, the better," Had snaps. No truce on that front.

Changing the subject, Gwynn gushes, "Isn't it grand Had and Gav put this venture together?" Since when has Gwynnie become such a diplomat? She carries the conversation over lunch and we climb back into the Land Rover. Raven wriggles from tail to neck. She's been like this since Gwynn's recovery. "Had," Gwynnie says, "I know you can sense your ancestors in Rosslyn Chapel, which is pretty occult for a scientist, but could you talk to Igraine's spirit? Tell her to back off?"

"See for yourself," he says. "I don't believe in the supernatural, but I've felt entities at the chapel since I was a lad. Roslin Glen seems to be in its own vortex."

We follow Gavin's equipment van down the lane. Rosslyn Chapel and the gatekeeper's cottage that Had arranged for us to bunk in, aren't far off. "Look over there," Gwynn squeals, "a graveyard to explore." Outside the stone-enclosed cemetery, a crazy quilt of fields intersperse with woods for miles. Gavin drives on ahead, but I grab Had's attention. "Ash trees—just there. We need twigs."

We roll to a stop just as the heavens open both faucets. I struggle into an oversized rain poncho and resemble a walking puptent as Had and I lean into the storm. We tromp through a glistening green meadow to the grove. I snap off a wee limb as Raven, defying orders, runs over. "Back to the car with you." On cue, my little black Scottie draws a perfect zig-zag in the wet grass. Had and I bring up the rear. Okay, I bring up the rear.

Towel drying my soggy doggie is such a chore, I'm grateful that Bridget Rose, attached to Raven's pups, only hesitantly grants puppy-visitation rights.

"We've not discovered a poisoned Ash grove this month," Had reminds us. "The tree poisoner may have waited for us to reunite."

"The nightmare may be over," I say, but don't feel it in my bones.

The storm suddenly picks up force as Galahad punches his mobile phone. "DCI Armstrong, Had Sinclair here. Gran and Gwynn are with me at Rosslyn Chapel...she's much better, but listen, the land belongs to my St. Clair kin and there were no Ash poisonings while Gwynn was in unconscious...it's likely we'll discover poisoned Ash trees . . . yes, ring when you clear your schedule."

"No hard feelings between you and Armstrong?" I ask.

"Until this poisoner desists," Had says politely, "we need the strong-arm of the law. This fellow is determined to poison every plant and tree in the Celtic calendar."

"The poisoner could be a woman," Gwynn insists. "Don't forget Sister Merry Fey. She may have poisoned the Ivy and possibly your mother."

A steady rain cloaks the countryside in misty pastels. Had says, "I've other concerns, too. As well as prepping me for the trial, Fiona explained Logres' inner workings. I assumed more responsibility. Now that Lance, Fiona and soon R.A. are following me on this quest, I fear Logres could lose cohesion. Then there's Mort making quite a show over my position being his right."

"You be careful," I warn. "Mort is a couple puppies short of a dog pound."

"Now that I'm in charge of Holy Vessel, I may be wasting Fiona and R.A.'s time. I'll not remain at Logres if the Grail leads me to a higher calling."

"You are so naïve," Gwynn admonishes. "The laird gave you Mort's coveted round table seat. Then you spent all those late nights with Fi. Don't you see she's crazy about you? Think of the cute babies you'd make."

"Now, there's a solid argument," Had laughs. And that's that. He turns on the wipers and points the Rover down the hill to Rosslyn Chapel.

"Gavin and Lance are rooming with us," I state without much enthusiasm.

"Great," Gwynn complains, "my prospects keep getting better and better. A monk wanna-be, a gay guy, and a world-famous playboy."

"Didn't know you were seeking a mate," Had remarks.

"Don't be a pudding head. I'm female and my pulse has recovered nicely. You better believe I'm looking for Prince Perfect. Here, attach this Tree of Life Ash twig to your jacket." Had threads the stem though a buttonhole like a dutiful squire. "Angels hang out in the golden boughs," Gwynn adds.

Ever armed with my podium, I step up. "As Above, So Below. The Tree of Life is the physical manifestation, or macrocosm to the more subtle microcosmic reflection of the heavenly levels."

"So why wear an Ash twig?" Had asks.

Rosslyn, the majestic stone chapel lies just ahead, so I answer as succinctly as possible. "Spirit's laws supersede nature's any day of the week. Knowing you're protected by the Old Unoriginated One is always better than relying on an amulet."

"Then why am I searching for the Holy Grail?" he asks.

"Oh, I know this one," Gwynn says. "You gotta' go through the golden bowl, or golden boughs to reach the highest levels. I went there when I was unconscious. Hey, we're here. Wow, this place is like a giant gingerbread church. Look at all those spires, and pointy windows. Now, Had, don't ruin it for me, I want to sense the spirits myself. Come on Grandma Merle."

How Gwynn skips from Celtic cosmology to scolding her adopted brother in one breath, is beyond me. And what journeys did she take in that coma? We need to talk.

Ḧeads

41

Gwynn links her arm through mine hitching me up sideways which I don't mind as long as I'm near my girl. Had strides over and we trudge up the hill to Rosslyn Chapel—Gwynn holding her side and me my aging dignity.

"I'm so excited I'm buzzing," Gwynn exclaims. "Can't wait to feel the spirits."

"Hope you're not disappointed," Had says ending the conversation until we step over the threshold to silent centuries past.

"Holy art eruption," Gwynn gasps. "They didn't know when to quit, did they?"

Frankly, I concur. If it weren't for the stained-glass hues tempering the intensity, the profusely sculpted chapel would overwhelm the soul. Intricately carved stone buttresses, window jambs and lintels all scream for attention. "Look Gwynn, that magnificent spiraling giant is the Prentice Pillar." We walk over and caress the stone. "This beautifully carved column cost the artist his life. The master mason was overcome with jealousy and smashed his apprentice's head for creating it in his absence."

"Holy extreme. Bet the carving impressed the pants off the priests though."

"Gwynn, remember where you are." Had scolds, but has trouble keeping a straight face. Are some of his ridged edges smoothing?

"Grandma Merle believes the Old Unoriginated One has a sense of humor."

"He'd have to with the two of you." Yes, a teasing Galahad.

Gwynn ignores the mock affront and slowly spins. "Look at all these carved creatures—a griffon, an elephant, a dragon, a unicorn—even angels, stars, and flowers. And look at all the Green Men with their leafy faces."

"There are over one hundred foliate heads," Had informs. "In that corner he is but a young lad, but your green man ages as you turn clockwise."

Gwynn follows the carvings around the building. "Very cool." She floats down the aisle absorbing the crafted details with a touch here, a sigh there.

My Scottish husband and I visited Rosslyn Chapel a lifetime ago. We were very much in love before he succumbed to Morgan—dang her hide. Infuriating how misery crowds out the good times if you don't rip its wretched head off. Forcing a thought change, I say, "Gwynnie, do you sense anything otherworldly?"

She spreads her hands, scanning the atmosphere. "I feel kind of tingly on the crown of my head. Spirits must be near." Gwynn stops and stares at a row of heads carved into a buttress. "Are these decapitated guys your ancestors, Had?"

"Probably legendary characters," I answer. "The Celts venerated the human head. A severed head was considered powerful as if it held the person's essence. They thought the human head contained the spirit's source and preserved the heads of friends and even enemies they respected. In many cases, they displayed them on a stake as a warning."

She grimaces. "Gross."

The chapel door opens, giving us a start. Sunlight outlines Gavin in the doorway. "Here you are. We need to unload and settle into the gatehouse."

"Now you've ruined it," Gwynn complains. "I was starting to feel some spirit vibes."

"Suit yourself," Gavin says and looks at Had. "Cousin?"

The guys leave and Gwynn turns to me. "Want to know what I experienced in that coma?" I nod and she says, "There was this beautiful music and light. I think I was in the golden boughs of the Tree of Life. With Mama."

"No wonder you didn't want to return."

"But she told me to. Oh, and Mama wanted to thank you for the linen hankies."

I grab a pew and sit down. "Avera passed away before I gave them to her."

Gwynn sits beside me. "Wowwie zowwie, now I know my time with her was for real. But I kind of want to cherish it for myself. It felt . . . sacred."

"Certainly. You didn't see your Grandpa Angus, did you?"

"No, he had a date with an angel." She laughs and the stone walls echo her joy.

I tilt my head heavenward. "Must I clip your wings, Angus?"

Gwynn and I hug just as Lance and Fiona step in. The attorney uses her cross-examination voice. "Where should we be looking for this grail?"

Looking straight at Lance, Gwynn answers. "You have to be worthy."

"I'm not the shallow man I used to be. I've found a spiritual resolve." Lance may deserve what she's dishing, but if I may steal from Shakespeare, *Methinks the lady doth protest too much*. Lance stares at Gwynn. "The grail is here. I can feel it." Fiona and Lance leave before Gwynn's daggers blind the poor man.

"Hey," I say, "it's the last day of Ash and no poisoning."

"How about we look over by that cemetery?" she suggests.

Walking over, a mist swirls round the gravestones—not thick, but disconcerting. "Look," I say, "some of Had's St. Clair and Sinclair clan members."

Her eyes widen. "Is Igraine buried here? She was born a Sinclair."

"Suicide kept Igraine from being buried in consecrated ground. The Laird General spread her ashes in Camelon's flower garden. He loved her despite everything."

We meander through the headstones so old the names and dates are worn away. Makes a body realize that once we leave this earth, all trace eventually dissolves with the ages. Few mortals leave indelible imprints. We work for perfection on earth when it can only be obtained in heaven. But don't the higher planes sound glorious? No taxes or dirty dishes. Poisoners need not apply.

A breeze clears the mist. "Gwynnie look, wilting Ash trees. You really are honing your psychic abilities in this place—this vortex." Then before she can reprimand, I sit near the poison and my head goes foggy.

In an Underworld cemetery from hell, Igraine's hardboiled eyes bore through me.

"Can't grasp what's in front of you, Dr. Bruce?" the specter hisses.

"The poisoner is someone I know?"

"Of course. You trust too easily." Her fetid breath repels.

"Did they murder Lady Elaine? Are they hiding in a dark cathedral?"

"Wrong and wrong."

I try to hang on, but begin rising back to consciousness. On hard ground with my head tilted skyward, Gwynn wipes the mist from my face. She says, "We have to follow our destiny to reach those higher levels, don't we Grandma."

I smile at my granddaughter. "You learned a lot in that coma, didn't you?"

"Enough to spin your little ol' Celtic head."

Is it the atmosphere, or does Gwynn gaze through eyes as old as Rosslyn's? It's clear she visited a level of consciousness that matured her beyond all understanding.

†ALDER (Alnus glutinosa) FEARN†

March 18–April 14

The Alder represents stability and soundness. The wood—look for it near lochs, rivers and streams—is so hard and waterproof that the Celts used it for milk buckets, warrior's shields and underwater structures. It's not too surprising the month of Alder symbolizes building on a strong foundation. There's a good bit of Celtic lore about this fellow named Bran the Blessed who had the power to enter the Underworld and prophesy to the ancestors. One day Bran carried a sacred Alder branch into the Battle of the Trees—where trees actually marched—and he came out unscathed. Since Bran means 'raven' it links the bird to the Alder tree. In fact raven-shaped ritual pipes, or whistles were often fashioned from this wood. Like Bran, the raven is said to demonstrate guidance due to its alert, and intelligent air. Don't you think my Raven lives up to her name?

Lady Moon

42

Whenever I'm homesick I gravitate to the moon for comfort. You see, no matter where you are in the world if you gaze at that familiar face, it will transport you home. Okay, I admit I'm a closet romantic. That's why I crept out with Raven tonight.

There's a flutter and a full moon lights a bird in flight. Picture a crow spreading the tips of its wing feathers—like fingers reaching to the sky. My old dad loved blackbirds, as do I. My folks christened me, Merle, meaning blackbird—middle name Lynn. They freed me from gender restraints prevalent at the time, encouraging my dreams of saving lives in far-off lands. I left the farm, got an education and ended up traveling to some of those foreign shores. That's how this big old moon and I became so well acquainted.

"Hey there, Lady Moon," I say, "why do you suppose I'm standing in the Alder trees watching the river crash over boulders down into this pool? Shouldn't I be back at Koad Croft living a quiet life with my kids?"

Out of the dark I hear, "Good question, Nana."

I spin around. "Holy stars, Rex Arthur, I thought you weren't coming until Sunday."

Artie gives me a grizzly bear hug. "Came to steal you and Gwynn away if I can. It seems the lads aren't having much luck finding their grail."

"Well, they haven't finished viewing the underground vaults with their equipment."

"Yes, tomorrow we'll complete that task," he says.

"Good, I want to go home and complete some Celtic tree research."

"Sure you won't use Logres' facilities? I'd certainly feel better with you and Gwynn closer." Artie offers me a supportive arm and we walk down the narrow path.

"No, I need the quiet woods. Galahad will help me set up shop. Speaking of shop, who's minding yours?"

"Mort."

I stop short. "You must be kidding."

R.A. hesitates. "Let's see how he does."

A chill wind blows as we continue down a rough path. "You're a trusting soul, Artie. Both by allowing business to falter and placing Mort at the helm."

"Either that, or a fool, Nana. The tree poisoner is now positioned to snap up stock. That way, the Yard can nab him." He laughs uncomfortably, but adds, "I've got Robert Rose and Aidan Hunter watching Logres and Camelon, and therefore Mort."

We walk on. "Sure you can trust them?"

"With my life, Nana. Now stop fretting, and consider a holiday. So the culprit won't notice a change in my routine, Gavin and I are taking our annual holiday trip to Aaran Isle. Thought you and Gwynn might join us. I never have enough time with you ladies. Och, what's that light over there?"

I squint at the Alder thicket across the stream. "It's either the fairy folk, or someone up to no good."

I scoop up Raven and hoist the little chunk into Artie's arms then use stepping stones to wade through the icy *burn*. On the bank, Artie leans near my ear. "You stay put, Nana. I'll sneak closer."

I give him a swat. "We'll sneak together."

The dew-slick groundcover slows our urgency toward the light. Artie sidles near the Alder grove. I come up beside him to see a black-robed monk-like individual working through the trees. Raven twists her head free and barks. The culprit hesitates, extinguishes the light and darts away.

"Who goes there?" Artie calls, shoves Raven at me and goes after the guy.

A dark hood masks his identity, but my flashlight beam catches him in the eye. Artie gains ground, flies through the air, tackles one leg, rolls sideways to throw the cad off balance and loses his grip. The monk kicks backwards catching Artie in the side of his head then dashes off. Like an idiot I scream. Bet the culprit recognized us anyway. Clutching Raven, I tramp through tangled Alders toward Artie. The familiar overdose of fertilizer sears my nostrils and the swirling underworld sucks me unconscious.

Black cathedral walls loom revealing a shrouded Bible on an altar. Reverently, a dark monk lifts a black silken cloth then somehow he's behind me. He pulls me by the scruff of the neck and holds me over some underlined verses from Isaiah.

'He shall cut down the trees, and Logres with its glory shall fall. There shall come forth a dark shoot out of the stem of Camelon, and a branch shall grow out of his roots.'

"That's not accurate," I reproach.

"It is prophesied." *Announcing this, he throws me into a wormhole.*

Awakening on stony ground. Gwynnie smooths my face with a cool hand and Had helps me sit upright. Where'd my kids come from? I mutter, "Where's Artie?"

"With Gavin. He regained consciousness," Galahad assures.

I turn my head. "Raven?"

"Gavin is bandaging her feet," Gwynn says. "They aren't burnt too bad. She fetched us like a real rescue dog. Can you stand? We need to get you out of this poison."

"Alder trees protect warriors," I proclaim with false bravado.

Had hoists me to my feet. "The month of Fearn begins."

I gaze at my unresponsive legs. Had nearly drags me to the open meadow. "The poisoner was dressed like a monk."

"A seriously deranged one," Gwynn adds.

"Why does he need to destroy the trees?" I ask this, but only the monk poisoning the Alders knows the answer—the same monk from my vision? I struggle to understand the reworded Bible verse, but give in to exhaustion.

Galahad lifts me into his arms and my head tilts back. Lady Moon sees me safely back to our little gatehouse cottage.

Passages

43

Before dawn everyone headed for Rosslyn Chapel leaving me to catch four of my forty winks. Suddenly, Artie rushes in with rain tracks running down his bruised face. "Oh, Artie, that monk kicked you really hard last night."

"Never mind. We've found a passageway under the chapel. Appears to lead into a cave of some sort."

Raven pads over wagging everything behind her ears then does a ballerina twirl on bandaged paws. The laird cradles her under one arm. "Fetch your coat, Nana. We've tunnels to explore."

My adrenalin kicks in and we're off. Storm clouds off the Pentland hills cloak the countryside. Our wipers throw rain a smidgen faster than it falls. "You know why God invented rainy days, don't you Artie?"

"Why's that, Nana?"

"So humans would snuggle down with a book and a hot cuppa."

"Sorry, but the Holy Grail would be the find of the century." He has a point.

A short drive later, we trot up Rosslyn Chapel's path so fast I'm bushed once we rush inside. Our crew is down a set of worn stone stairs in a small underground room. Gwynn and Fiona sit on a low table drinking thermos-bottle tea while Had, Gavin and Lance busy themselves removing hand-hone blocks from the cellar wall.

Seeing me, Galahad shines a flashlight into the hole. Broken stone carvings line a passageway that's half manmade, half natural cave. "Oh, where does it lead?" I query.

Gavin answers testily. "We'll know in a minute." He's been curt since hearing Artie invited Gwynn and me on the vacation he and R.A. take annually.

The guys clear an opening that allows Had to squeeze through. He holds his lantern high to better see the crude pictographs featuring trees and plants—Celtic calendar flora. I'm so jazzed I want to dive in, but give him a moment to soak in the past. "It's a portal into history," Had's voice echoes. "No soul has stood here for ages."

"Mind if we join you?" Gavin snaps.

"Not at all. You must feel the antiquity." We scramble through the narrow opening. An excited Raven follows. Sweeping his lantern, Galahad leads us into ever-darker depths. The further we go, the fewer traces of manmade masonry line the walls. The cave weeps ground water in places, but overall, it's pretty dry. "Look," Had says. "A partially hidden room." Without hesitation our team relays stone out of the wall. I'd help, but don't want to break their concentration.

In an attempt to catch a first glimpse, Gwynnie clambers inside. Lance says, "Let this be what I think it is." He follows Fiona, Artie, Had and Gavin through the opening.

So much for age-before-gorgeous. At last I see the intricately carved antiquities strewn over the cavern floor as if hurriedly concealed. "Look Gwynnie, figurines of trees and plants with their Ogham names etched underneath."

"It's the lost carvings." Lance points out icons expertly carved from marble, alabaster and onyx. "Most probably the sculptures that disappeared from Rosslyn Chapel in 1650," he says. "You know, to wipe out any vestiges of the Roman church. The priests likely saved these priceless artifacts from being confiscated or destroyed."

Artie puts his arm around Gwynn's shoulders. A reverent hush fills the room until we hear, "Arr arr," scrape, scrape, coming from the corridor.

Gwynn sticks her head through the opening. "Raven's found a ginormous bone."

I shine my beam on my dog's archeological find. "Gracious, that's a human femur."

"Leave it," Gwynn orders. "Show us where you found it." Our proud little dog prances down the passageway, flattens to the floor and shimmies through a hole. Gwynn shines a light inside Raven's doggie door. She shrieks, "Dead people."

"If you enlarge that opening, I'll squeeze in and take pictures," Fiona offers.

They set to work, so Gwynn and I slip off down the corridor. My beam catches a tunnel off to the right. Gwynn ducks to get through, but I walk upright and exclaim, "Holy stars, it's some kind of sanctuary." In the middle of the room, I run my hand over a stone slab of a table. There's no dust on the objects that appear to have been laid out recently. "Gwynn, I don't like this. Go get Had." She hesitates then dashes off.

In short order, Had and Gwynn stumble through the opening. "What is it, Gran?"

"Human heads burnished with gold." I shine my beam on the cups fashioned from upturned skulls. Each goblet rests on a metal stand. "They are museum pieces, but look, modern-day candles with wax drippings, crusts of bread and vessels that smell of wine."

"We'll have to document this site," Had says.

"Galahad, don't you see? The sacred skull may have represented the esoteric pathways of higher consciousness for these people. These artifacts could be an outward representation of what we seek in Golden Bowl meditation."

"Indeed," Had says. "Record this." Without further investigation he scurries off.

"He's so caught up in his archeological find, he can't hear the truth, Grandma."

"Give him space, Gywnn." I'm about to say more when we hear loud voices.

"You cannot betray me," someone shouts.

"But you killed my spiritual father," the second voice argues. Scuffling then a cry echoes through the cavern.

Gwynn and I rush to the corridor. A light reveals a passage and we dash to the opening. "Who's there?"

By some odd chance, Had answers, "Stay back." So we hurry inside. He's peering down. The smell of blood enters my nostrils.

My flashlight beam slides up the body of a black-robed monk. His head lays sideways from a twisted corpse. Gwynn moans and backs away. Artie and the others arrive with Raven bucking to escape from Fiona. "A man has been murdered," I warn.

Gavin holds a lantern over the body. "Call the cops."

"How did he get down here?" Artie asks.

"Another entrance?" I suggest. Proving my point Raven escapes, runs a little way up the tunnel and drags a monk's robe toward us. "Must be the killer's," I deduce.

Galahad shines a beam directly on the dead man's face. "Look Gran."

I gasp and immediately feel guilty for not having liked him. "Dear Lord," I say, "it's Brother Ushtey."

Reconciliation 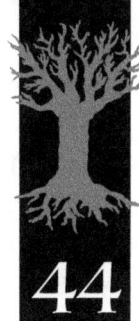 44

Our Rosslyn Chapel archeological find is smack in the middle of a murder investigation, so the grail search is either on hold or abandoned. Artie, Fiona and Gavin headed off a while ago and it's jiggety jig for the rest of us. A deflated Galahad left in the Land Rover with Raven guarding a mountain of equipment and a hill of luggage. Don't judge, we didn't know how long we'd be grail hunting.

Now there are times when I as mentor, need to nudge my student's destiny a wee bit. I refer to the fissure between Had and Lance. That opportunity arises when Lance offers to drive Gwynn and me back to Koad Croft in his vintage Bentley.

I'm not making excuses for Lance—Had certainly has reasons to resent his birth father. However, if damaged emotions are not dealt with, they seem to become entities in and of themselves. No matter how painful, it's human nature to cling to the familiar. It takes courage to change.

Anyway, this scheming granny invites Lance into the cottage for tea. Koad Croft is freezing, but emotes pleasant memories. Galahad sets the fire blazing, I whip up a batch of scones and Gwynn chats with Lance. "It's good to be home," she sighs.

Lance looks around our simple abode. "You're happy in this wee croft house?"

"It's not how much you own that brings happiness," Had says caustically.

Grabbing the tray, I hurry to the sitting room motioning for everyone to partake of tea and scones. "True," I agree. "A huge amount of love fits in this tiny cottage."

"Not that you've had much experience in that area," Had murmurs.

The kid is stirring the caldron, so I take the lead. "All right, it's time you guys talked. This wedge between you has gone far enough. Father Joseph's dying wish was for the two of you to work through your differences." That was blackmail, but their chastened faces show I've struck a note. Nothing happens, so I prod. "What's eating you, Had."

Galahad crosses his arms. "Why did you abandon Mum and me?"

Lance looks around the circle. "I would need to tell the story from the beginning."

Had scoffs. "This should be good."

"It is," I agree. "I was there for part of it. I saw your mother's mental anguish."

"Why were you there?" Gwynn asks.

I pause deciding how much to reveal. "I occasionally doctored at the convent." Had shakes his head like I'm some kind of wonder. I simply say, "Tell the story, Lance."

Lance clears his throat. "Galahad, your mother and I met at school. As adolescents we loved as only sweet first-love can. We felt our devotion was so strong it would defeat all our family issues. We were wrong. Our parents helped turn our story into a tragedy."

"Because they forced you to marry when you got Mum pregnant?"

Lance's jaw tightens, but says. "They didn't force me, I begged to marry Elaine." Wisely he takes a bite of scone and sip of tea to let that fact sink in before he says, "After the quiet wedding, and despite our parents' economic differences, Elaine and I were full of hope." Lance bites his lower lip. "Through poor management Grandpater left my family the La Lac manor house, but no maintenance money. We lost everything. Alas, I held no title, land or wealth. Elaine was her parents' only child and would control the Sinclair Estates one day. They didn't want me in the equation. Although we wed, they separated us for the remainder of her pregnancy—and after."

"How awful," Gwynn gasps.

Lance takes a ragged breath. "Elaine believed her parents when they told her I didn't want you, Galahad." Lance closes his eyes. Had stares into his teacup, but shows no emotion while his father regains composure. "My parents were no better, telling me Elaine chose to stay away. I suspect the Sinclairs paid my folks to keep me out of their daughter's life."

Tearful, Lance continues. "Eventually, I rode my horse across the Pentland hills only to be turned away at the Sinclair's gates. I hid outside those walls and stole in after dark." Lance studies Had's stoic face and sees only mistrust. "You have to remember I was only sixteen. When I found you in the nursery, I held you against my heart. When you began to cry, Elaine ran in, but her parents held her back. I was arrested for attempted kidnapping of my own child." Lance looks Had straight in the eyes. "Your grandparents gave Elaine the choice of living in public shame with no husband, or joining the Order of St. Claire."

I lean forward. "This is all true, Had. Your Sinclair grandmother confided her excuses to me." The young man doesn't respond.

"Shortly after that," Lance says, "I was told Elaine was going to take holy vows."

"She never did," Had snaps. "She didn't give up waiting for you."

Lance hangs his head. "No, it was me that gave up. I nearly took my life—my heart was so bruised. Instead of committing a mortal sin, I vowed to never love again—to be cavalier. I took women's hearts and then walked away. I have a trophy chest full of hearts, but I've only ever loved Elaine."

"You didn't see Mum when you could." Had steps to the fireplace and jabs a log.

"By the time I could, I'd gotten caught up in liquor and ladies. R.A. saved me—gave me a job, responsibility, a surrogate family."

Had whirls toward Lance. "What about us? Did you ever think we might need you?"

"When I'd sorted my life out so much time had passed. Elaine blamed me. There didn't seem to be any love there. I know I should have tried harder. I was weak...didn't have the courage to work it out . . . create a family life. Elaine was right, it was my fault."

Galahad plunges into the understuffed chair. Lance goes over and kneels before Had. On the adjacent sofa, Gwynn and I sit with Raven between us, her ears laid back. Lance looks pleadingly into Had's eyes. "I know it is too little, too late, but I ask your forgiveness." Lance bows his head to the arm of the chair. We hear soft weeping.

It feels like eons pass before Had raises a hand and priest-like places it on his father's shoulder. Lance doesn't look up, but when his sobs subside, he leans forward embracing his stiff son. Had pats Lance on the back indicating an end to so public a display. Lance doesn't let go and Had's rigidness eventually relaxes. As they pull apart Lance says, "We have a lot of work to do. I don't expect an apology to absolve me."

Had looks embarrassed and a bit chastised. "I'll try. Father Joseph wanted it."

I go over and embrace both men. Gwynn follows suit. "Good work," she pronounces.

"Okay, who's starving?" I prompt. Someone has to cheer this lot.

"Son," Lance says, "we owe Dr. Bruce a home cooked meal."

He leads his boy to the kitchen. Before long Lance is posing questions about Had's life—how it led to an interest in forestry. Evening passes and Lance ends up bunking with his heretofore estranged son.

I'm snug between flannel sheets, when I hear Gwynn on the phone. "Leo . . . Dad, can you talk a second? . . . No, everything's fine. Listen, I know I probably don't deserve it, but could I video-chat with you and my little brother sometime? . . . Saturday's perfect."

Sometimes life is flat-out grand.

Last evening Lance asked who might have had the audacity to shoot an arrow at Gwynn—the one possibly meant for Had. Before long we planned a morning search of the forest for evidence. It's barely dawn now, but we're psyched and hurry to the grove to determine the arrow's trajectory.

The sun that filters through the thick barren woods illuminating snow-patched undergrowth could lull a body into believing nothing sinister happened here. But Captain Merle on reconnaissance is not deceived by singing birds, nor the sweet smell of decaying leaves with tiny green fronds pushing skyward. "Alright, Gwynnie, tell them what you remember."

She colors slightly. "Well, I was helping Had gather poisoned Rowan samples. I looked into the woods and saw something with teardrop shaped eyes staring right at me." She points to a stand of thick bushes.

The guys pull doubtful faces, but I command, "This is serious. Cover as much ground as you can."

We begin our arduous task with enthusiasm. Raven assists by flushing out sparrows then putting squirrels and forest Brownies in their place. Before long I don't find sifting through prickly thicket a lark. "Raven," I joke, "I'm coming back as a pampered Scottie." Time slows to a plod with every grieving muscle. We soldier-on long after the dog has sense enough to head for a cozy hearth through her wee door.

Eventually, and much to my relief, Lance announces we're past the distance an arrow could have traveled with any accuracy. Weary, we trudge to the cottage where Raven greets us with a yowling yawn. Feeling a bit dejected, we mortals wash up in silence. I rub lotion on my hands, Gwynn repairs her nails and Had rustles up breakfast.

Borrowing my hand cream, Lance asks, "Who do you suspect shot that arrow?"

Too tired for deep reflection, I say, "Like the tree poisonings, someone from Camelon or Logres."

Gwynn lays her nailfile down. "Everyone, except Morgan, did good in the Christmas archery competition."

I accept a plate of baked beans on toast from Lance, but complain, "We've hit another impasse. There's an intertwining knot ensnarling our every move."

"Yes," Lance agrees. "Scotland Yard discovered that an entity called Dark Cathedral of Truth has been snapping up Logres stock—possibly working toward a takeover."

"Hopefully, Mum's stock will save the day," Had says.

Gwynn groans. "Trouble is, R.A. sold stock to keep Logres afloat. He no longer holds a majority vote." Well, horse pucky. And since when does Artie confide in Gwynn?

As if Raven knows we need a diversion, she grabs Gwynn's nailfile and runs like a sprite to her crate—the Raven Haven. "You bandit," Gwynn yells, "give that back."

I clap my hands. "Fetch, Raven." Proudly, she returns, but she doesn't hold a nailfile in her mouth. She holds a tan glove—an archery glove with three teardrop-shaped knuckle inserts that look like eyes. I'm pretty sure my dog is smiling.

†WILLOW (Salix spp.) SAILLE†
April 15–May 12

There's a great Celtic Creation myth that goes like this: Two scarlet sea-serpent eggs contained the Sun and Earth. These two eggs were hidden in the boughs of the Willow tree where they hatched bringing forth all earthly life. The symbolism in this story connects the Willow to the lifecycle—from birth to death. Willow trees are found near rivers, streams or other water sources. Since the moon affects the tides, wouldn't you know it signifies the feminine lunar rhythms. Willow is considered a tree of enchantment and intuition, and from the time of antiquity was used to make magical wands. What interests me is the Willow's medicinal quality to treat headache, fever, and a number of other ailments. As a matter of fact, its bark is one of the main ingredients in painkillers such as aspirin. Naturally, I welcomed it in my curative formula.

Arran Isle

Artie whisked Gavin, Gwynn, Raven and me to Arron Isle off Scotland's southwestern coast—the most clement island ever plunked smack dab in the heart of the North Atlantic Gulf Stream. Aaran Isle is a miniature Scotland with its southern rolling hills and meadows, northern rugged mountains, and sweet glens all surrounded by ragged shores and seascapes. That my dear friend, means we're basking in sunshine while the rest of Great Britain mopes around in a cold mist.

Not to complain about a free vacation, but too much spare time stresses me when my tree research stands idle back at the cottage. It's just that Artie insisted we encroach on his and Gavin's annual trip, but now spends most of his day playing blacksmith. He's forging a sword, *drawing* it as the term goes, out of the meteor that streaked into the loch after Lady Elaine died.

Gwynn and I are regularly left with Gavin whose hospitality is laced with derisive jibes. It seems this jaunt to the laird's little whitewashed cottage has become Gavin's yearly reward for selfless loyalty. "Gwynn," he reproaches, "why don't you and your gran go pick leaves, or whatever it is you do?"

After three weeks, I've run out of nice. "Holy stars, Gavin, go watch R.A. forge his sword. You're not protecting your invaded territory by harassing us."

"R.A. won't let me watch. Claims drawing a sword out of a meteor is a tedious project. You think I enjoy being ignored?"

"Grow up, Gav," Gwynn says. "R.A. doesn't spend time with us either."

"He talks to you women all evening. Won't even speak to me."

I sigh. "He's waiting for you to stop playing victim."

Obviously angry and frustrated, Gavin grabs his jacket. "I'm going out. Don't dare sample the jam Mrs. Rose sent explicitly for R.A." He slams the door behind him.

"What should we do, Grandma?"

"I'm heading back to Koad Croft. Want to tackle that work we put on hold?"

Gwynn crosses her arms. "No way."

I demure. "Alright. I won't force you."

"Have you forgotten we're celebrating my eighteenth birthday today?"

"May Day," I say. "Mother Earth and you evolve from the maiden aspect into the fullness of young womanhood. I'm no longer your legal guardian."

"R.A. can watch over me."

I don't like it, but Artie is a good father figure, so I concede. Besides, this could be a safer place for her since a crazed archer may still nurture murder in his heart. "Gwynnie, do you realize I'm terrified of losing you?"

"You old silly, you could never lose me. Give it a week, you'll be happy I've grown up." She hugs me and I hold on.

Artie steps in the door. "Here now, what's this?"

"Grandma Merle is suffering separation anxiety and she hasn't even left yet."

"And where do you think you're going, Nana?"

"Koad Croft," I snap. His huffs raise my hackles. "You may not think my work is important, but you should respect what it means to me, Rex Arthur."

"I do. This is my feeling deserted. Forgive me, old love?" He pulls a mock sad face.

Gwynn says we both have abandonment issues then adds, "Grandma Merle is taking my not wanting to go pretty hard."

R.A. stares at Gwynn. "You want to stay with Gavin and me?"

"If I may." She smiles sweeter than honeysuckle before getting down to business. "What with that darn hollow Koad Croft is in, we'll have to get satellite connection even if it only works a short time each day."

"With Had living out at Koad Croft," R.A. says, "it'll be a business expense."

"Now he tells us." Gwynn's laugh is fairy chimes. Who am I to douse the kid's joy?

Tonight we held one heck of a blowout birthday for Gwynn. Juxtaposed with the Arran Isle May Day celebration, it's a ruckus event. A bittersweet farewell for me.

Morning brings a sleepy farewell from Gwynn. Artie drives Raven and me to a misty-sea ferry crossing with Had waiting on Scotland's western shore. Raven wriggles into his lap with a hundred thousand doggie kisses.

More than curious how Mort is running Logres, I ask, "You been busy at Logres?"

"No. Mort felt threatened by Lance and me monitoring his Logres managing skills, so Da and I went to Holy Vessel. Da's keen eye for how each monk would function best, helped get the monastery operating smoothly.

"Did Lance take to such a tranquil life?"

Had laughs. "I believe he was quite relieved to return to his more worldly life."

"And you? Putting the grail search on hold?"

"As horrid as Ushtey's death was, it saved me from making a huge mistake." He touches his forehead. "Father Joseph meant the Golden Bowl was within."

"You must have needed to search the outer world one last time. How did you see the light?"

"As you can well imagine. By seeing the heavenly glow and hearing the ringing radiance in my own Golden Bowl." I'm so proud of the young man, I could bust. He looks a bit shame-faced. "Gwynn easily reckoned the Golden Bowl was not external."

"My granddaughter's a smart cookie."

"I'm going to miss her. Should we have left her? R.A. is . . . awfully fond of her."

"Gwynn's safe with him. Besides she's of age, I had no choice."

"She has a mind of her own, that one."

We drive through drizzle and fog. Raven stands alert sensing we are drawing near Koad Croft. Had suddenly brakes then backs the Rover. "Look," he says, "those Willows by the *burn*. They've been poisoned." We walk toward the gurgling stream.

I sit beside the poisoned area. "Don't try to stop me, Galahad. I need this."

I whirl down to a filmy gray figure stepping out of the gloom.

"Why," I ask, *"are Holy Vessel people dying? First Lady Elaine then Father Joseph, now Brother Ushtey. Is it an attempt to shut down the monastery?"*

"Mere payment for my underlings." So she does have collaborators.

Igraine's laugh is a screech that stabs my brain as I spin up.

Galahad helps me to the Rover and drives us home. Raven checks

Gwynn's room then looks at me accusingly. "She wanted to stay." I'm explaining Gwynn's absence to my dog, but I also keep expecting my girl to step out and warm me with her laughter.

Of course, we'll soon have the capability to see her on the computer screen. But truth be told, I loathe the adjustment. I've rather enjoyed reexperiencing the twentieth century with nothing but a landline, a radio-cd player, a fridge and cooker.

The door opens and Had walks in with a microwave. Change is pulsating ever closer.

Bending the Law

I've plunged into the understuffed watching Raven run her doggie dustmop of a beard along the buildup on the coffee table. You step away five minutes and dirt happens, giving credence to my archeological theory. "Galahad, ever wonder why civilizations build on top of the previous era's site? House dust. Give it a hundred years and you're buried in the stuff."

"There are ancient rooms and alleys below Edinburgh, built on volcanic rock."

I'm out of my chair. "That's it, there must be a pitch-black cathedral down there."

Instead of scoffing, Had does an on-line search. "Say we find it. What then?"

"Second sight doesn't come with instructions, only impressions." Had didn't grow up knowing there are dimensions within dimensions in this universe. "Lines blur and we cross over—whether we want to or not."

I'm about to ask him to drop me off in the city, but he says, "Let's go now." You have no idea how glad I am he said that.

So here we are in an Old Edinburgh underground room. If time can be measured by sore feet, you'd know we've been investigating for hours. I run my hand over the ancient brick that arches up cathedral-like. Had says, "Similar to the others, this space never functioned as a sanctuary." He's bored rigid and I'd curse if I were one notch less a lady.

"I'm beginning to wonder if that black cathedral is under Edinburgh after all."

Galahad picks up Raven and leads me toward the Land Rover. "How about using my company computer to search for Camelon and Logres property owners in Edinburgh?"

"Don't you get the gold star for the day."

Two hours, six cups of tea and a tin of shortbread later, we've made considerable headway. Turns out R.A. owns the Logres Lumber Ltd. block, Morgan a swanky townhome, Gavin a ground-floor flat the size of Raven's crate, Aidan a warehouse and surprisingly, the Roses, a gardening supply store run by daughter, Pauline Rose.

"Galahad, how do we determine what's under these folk's establishments?"

He swivels in his chair. "Let's use the ground penetrating radar."

"Son, you get any smarter I'm going to have to retire. I'll use my lock-picking kit. After all, we're attempting to catch a poisoner-cum-murderer. Who would prosecute an old lady acting on a vision, if we accomplished that?"

Evidently spoiling for adventure, Had says, "The laird did hire me to track the poison. Who's to say it's not located in a Logres employee's cellar?"

"Had, your confessor is going to have you on your knees for weeks." He breaks into a conspiratorial smile.

While he pulls the gear together, I call Arran Isle. One ring and Gwynnie answers. "Where are you? I've been trying to call."

She doesn't need to know I'm guilty as hades dragging Galahad the Pure into a criminal act. "Turned my phone off. Had and I are busy with research. How are you?"

"R.A. took me for a drive around the island. It was simply glorious. But Gavin feels left out. He's leaving on the morning ferry."

Had scoops up Raven and we enter the elevator. "Do you think you should stay alone with Artie? People might talk."

"Grandma, you're so old fashioned. Gotta go. Love you." She hangs up.

I stare at the phone. Since when does Gwynn describe scenery as simply glorious? The lift stops at the main lobby. Had unlocks a workroom, turns on his GPR gizmo and begins checking for anomalies under the marble floor.

"We need to do Gavin's apartment. He's coming home in the morning."

After two cups of coffee, four sandwiches and three dog biscuits to keep Raven and our innards from growling, we haven't found a dang thing. Artie's block, Gavin's flat, and Morgan's townhome are built on volcanic bedrock. "Shall we call it a night, Gran?"

"I won't sleep until this is done. And who would suspect us in the wee hours of the morning?" If not for street lighting it'd be pitch dark. "Let's go to the Rose's shop and Aidan's warehouse before dawn."

We drive to *The Rose Garden*. A cellar door leads to a basement revealing a stack of the same type of fertilizer that in concentrated quantities poisoned my trees. Drat, where there's a Rose, there's fertilizer. Robbie has access to Logres' fertilizer and Jamie has a shed full. How would I face Priscilla if I frame her family for the Celtic Tree Caper?

Had stabs a bag of fertilizer with his pin knife and drops a sample in a clear plastic pouch. "It's circumstantial evidence, Gran." He runs the GPR over the exposed basement area. You guessed it—no sinister hidden black cathedral to be found. But the fertilizer has me worried and I leave the scene downhearted.

We climb into the Rover. "Want to do Aidan's warehouse?"

"Drive on chauffer." Raven paws my arm for attention. Ah, for the simplicity of a dog's life. Yet my crafty canine did discover that monk's robe and the archery glove.

The warehouse district in medieval Old Town has original narrow streets and passageways as opposed to New Town that was designed in 1767. The concept of 'old' being decidedly different than back in the colonies. Makes me feel positively adolescent.

My partner in crime turns off the Rover's headlamps before we pull up next to Aidan's centuries-old stone building. Even with the lockpicks I carry for emergencies, it takes a while to open Aidan's two deadbolts. What's he got stashed? Using flashlights, we work our way around moldering machines. After forever, Had's GPR doohickey reveals the ground is not bedrock, but nothing suspicious. To my relief, he packs the gear.

We haven't checked a big walled-off room that juts out into the main warehouse. The door won't budge, so I begin picking the lock. Unexpectedly, Aidan's angry voice booms, "Who's there?" Dang it, must be a sound sleeper, but he's awake now.

Loaded down with equipment, yet grabbing my hand, Had runs toward the door. As I hightail it with my accomplice, an earsplitting gun blast echoes through the warehouse. I grab my burning thigh, stumble out the door and haul myself into the Rover. Had spins gravel and gets us the heck on the road.

Galahad reaches under the seat and digs out a first aid kit. I rip my pant leg then wrap gauze tightly around the bullet's entry and exit holes in my upper leg. It didn't hit bone or artery, but the wound is a screaming agony. "I thought guns were illegal in this country," I complain loudly.

"They are, Gran, but so is breaking and entering."

He would bring that up.

†HAWThORN (Cratregus spp.) hUAThE†
May 13–June 9

This tree is full of surprises. Besides being associated with spring celebrations, the Hawthorn is the legendary guardian figure that bloomed after being felled, symbolizing the defeat of winter. As nature's sentry, the thorns of this hedge-tree provide protection around Oak and Ash trees. And imagine this, they guard the portal to the fairy realm. As if that weren't enough, Hawthorn is also the custodian of celestial fire associated with metalsmiths and higher powers of consciousness. Consequently, it possesses a strong connection to the Holy Grail, divine secrets and immortality. But there's more. The Hawthorn also rules over the hearts of lovers while strengthening the physical heart with its medicinal berries. You've got to love it.

Deception

I regularly see Gwynn out on Arron Isle on our phone chats. You wouldn't believe how good she looks, her face has even filled out. R.A.'s off working on his sword, so when she does call we gossip like a couple of magpies.

Today I see Artie on the screen for the first time since I left. "What on earth is wrong, Artie? You look like warmed-over porridge." Sunken, bloodshot eyes stare at me out of a whitewashed face accented by blue-blistered lips.

Gwynn gives Artie her 'I told you so' look. He leans back in his chair as if to distance himself. "It's just a touch of flu." When I ask for symptoms, he recites, "Weakness, dry mouth, swollen tongue and queasy stomach."

I mentally flip through medical archives for the ailment. "Have you seen a doctor?"

"He called Doc Buchan, but wouldn't stop work on his sword." Gwynn looks accusingly at R.A. "And all he'll eat is toast with Priscilla's jam."

"Is your project about done? If not . . ."

With Gwynn's help, he hefts a humongous weapon. "It took longer than expected, but you know Duncan, the blacksmith. He helped me complete the sword." Artie pauses then adds, "He held a ceremony last evening for . . ." Something like embarrassment crosses my boy's face.

"We wanted to tell you," Gwynn begins, but Artie's eyes plead with her to stop.

They're keeping secrets, but he stares with such intense troubled exhaustion, my doctor persona takes over. "Listen, you are seriously ill. You may have inhaled poisonous gases in the smelting process." Artie's haggard face glows with sweat as he nods assent. I turn my attention to Gwynn. "Take him to the ER. Let me know what they say."

"You got it. Talk later."

Holy stars, here I am hiding a gunshot wound and going nowhere until I retire my sword cane. You should see what it takes to haul my dumpling out of the understuffed. But Gwynn won't mind playing nursemaid to her adopted father.

More than a twinge of guilt grips me. You see, I hadn't realized how much energy Gwynnie took until she wasn't around. I've been able to test every piece of bark, root, leaf, twig, berry and pod from the thirteen Celtic trees and plants. Now to adjust the formula combining the thirteen extracts—so rewarding. It'll be a while before Gwynnie calls, so I toddle to the cooker, make myself a cup of tea then settle on the sofa with an entire package of chocolate biscuits.

Looking distraught, Had dashes in. "Gran, not to alarm you, but R.A. and Gwynn aren't answering their mobiles. I must speak to the laird immediately."

"Gwynn took Artie to the ER. He's pretty sick. Why?"

"I've just been informed that Mort canceled Logres' regular customer orders. He's opened all new accounts at discounted prices."

My phone rings and I suck in breath. "Artie refused treatment?. . . Insisted you fly him to Camelon?. . . Good, Dr. Buchan . . . Of course . . . Had's here, we'll drive over."

"I'd best contact Da, Robert and Aidan," Galahad decides.

"Yes, oust Mort the Moron." While Had rallies the Logres troops, I fight the pain in my thigh and quick-smart gathered necessities for me and Raven.

We're off, but it seems an age before Had pulls onto the castle's main drive and starts to unload. I limp up Camelon's stairs and Bridget Rose meets me. "We carried a bed to the sitting room for the laird when we seen himself couldn't make the stairs."

She hurries me along. I'm trying to keep up, but the leg demon has its teeth in me. "Where's Gwynn?"

Noticing my cane Bridget slows. "Her Lady got Dr. Buchan here ta check the laird ."

"Why are you calling Gwynn, Her Lady?" Before Bridget can answer, I round the door into the sickroom. Artie's so pale his eyes look burnt into his skull. I read Artie's medical chart thankful the doc is 'old school' enough to use paper and pen. "Dr. Buchan has you on an anti-toxin. So it is some sort of poison." I look up and come to the realization that Gwynn is sitting on the bed next to Artie. With a defiant stare she kisses him. My brain cells don't want to acknowledge the awkward moment, but hear myself ask, "What's going on here?"

Artie speaks in a gravelly whisper. "Nana, the straight truth is, Gwynn became my wife at that ceremony yesterday." When I don't reply, he adds, "Blacksmiths still perform marriages in places like Arran Isle." Like that explains the bomb he just dropped.

I clutch the footboard, let out a derisive snort. "But she's too young."

"Old enough to fall in love and get pregnant," Gwynn says.

"Pregnant? Artie, you'd do such a thing?" Angry tears blur the scene. Shattered, I turn and gimp out as fast as my leg allows.

Gwynn calls after me, "We love each other." I hesitate, but forge ahead purposely causing the pain in my leg to scream almost as loud as the voices in my head.

Galahad stands in the foyer with Raven under his arm. "Gran, what's wrong?"

"Artie and Gwynn. She's pregnant. They're married. I can't stay."

"I did attempt to convey their closeness to you," Galahad says.

A body could scrutinize their entire biography to prove that if a particular event had not happened, i.e. me leaving Gwynn on Aaron Isle, then the next would not have taken place—all the way to infinity. This mess is on me. Did Leo know they were together? Is that why he provided that pricey round table?

While my emotions run the gambit from disbelief, to remorse, to outrage, I climb into the Rover. Had places Raven and my gear inside. "You sure you want to leave like this?"

I nod then finally speak once we're on the highway. "When I was a kid, a gigantic age-old Cottonwood tree grew in the middle of our pasture. The cattle had rubbed its bark to a beautiful sheen. I loved that tree and hugged it as often as I could. One night a bolt of lightening split it in half. I felt as if a malevolent power had torn asunder my family tree. Half of that mighty tree survived, but I never hugged it again."

"Is that why you're crying?"

"My leg hurts like the devil." I rub my bullet wound, but Had knows as well as I do, it's my children's deception that's left a gaping hole.

Today's Scotch mist suits my mood as my blame for Artie and Gwynn's subterfuge lingers. If envy is green, then guilt is a murky-purple that clashes with everything in a body's emotional wardrobe—a garment you hold onto because it cost you dearly.

Fed up with my mopey demeanor, Had lands me with a firm reprimand. "For someone so observant, you should have perceived how affectionate they were toward one another."

"I guess I wanted it to only be a warm father-daughter bond." Why was I blind to what was in front of me?

Interrupting my thoughts, Had says, "I spoke to Gwynn when I was at the castle documenting the poisoned Hawthorns that Robert found. The ones you wouldn't go see. It seems she informed her father about the marriage and pregnancy. R.A. says Leo was very supportive."

"Yes, Leo would be thrilled to have Gwynn marry into a prominent family." I want to stay mad, so Had having talked to Gwynn and Artie, feels like a betrayal. But I'm too nosey to stay out of their business. "How did Dr. Buchan know which antitoxin to administer?"

"Elementary my dear Gran. Out on Aaron Isle, R.A. ate toast with Mrs. Rose's elderberry jam—the concoction she makes exclusively for the laird. Poisoned berries had somehow been mixed among the others. Mrs. Rose is devastated."

"Has Artie recovered?"

"No, but against doctor's orders he's returned to work." Great, now I can add not helping Artie to my guilt list. I'm ashamed of not forgiving him, well both of them.

"Gran, if I can work on pardoning Lance, surely you can excuse the children you love." Had leaves me to ponder—well, stew in my own juice, as my old granny put it.

After stewing myself wrinkly, I take responsibility for my misconceptions and realize my kids have a right to their own lives. To make amends I call Camelon hoping to speak to Artie. Bridget says he's not available, so I ask for Gwynn. Nervous energy has me pacing in front of the fireplace. Getting by without my cane, I've a free hand to poke the logs that don't need poking.

Bridget says, "Telephone for you, Lady Gwynn. It's your grandmother."

After a pause, Gwynn says, "Well, give it to me."

Heart beating, I gaze out at the dense fog. "Hello? You there Gwynn?"

"You know I am...Merle." Her tone could peel paint off a Plymouth.

"You aren't calling me Grandma anymore?"

"I don't know if I have a grandmother."

"Okay, I deserved that, but I called to apologize." No response, so I say, "I shouldn't have acted like that." I pace over to the coffee table and pick up my teacup.

Gwynn doesn't give me a break. "So I'm supposed to forget you walked out on R.A. and me, for what? Me being eighteen and him forty?"

I spit my sip of cold tea in the sink. "That's a seriously wide age difference. I thought you saw Artie more as a father. I had no idea you were lovers." I resume pacing.

"You just think we're still your kids," Gwynn snaps.

"Yes, and I always will. It's just that I felt betrayed and deceived when you came home married and having started a family." I walk over and put the kettle on the cooker then toss a teabag really hard into my cup.

Gwynn sounds perturbed. "We wanted to get to know each other better and figured you'd prevent that if you knew what was going on. Then had to rush things when I got pregnant." With hot water in my cup, I frantically dip the teabag in and out.

"Were you talking about marriage before the baby?" I sip the tea I've gotten so strong it's bitter.

"R.A. and I fell in love the moment we met at the Halloween party and then snuck around to be together." Attempting to drizzle honey in my cup, I drop in a whole glob. She continues. "Of course, he's back working all hours—trying to save Logres. And someone sabotaged the sawmill. And nobody's caught the Celtic tree poisoner."

The tea's so strong and sweet, I set it down. "What's this about sabotage?"

"Robbie said the big saw is damaged, but says he doesn't care. He's such an angry guy, he makes me wonder."

"Well, whoever's attempting a Logres takeover, has upped their game. But you know Had is investigating the tree poisonings as well as running Holy Vessel." I take a swig of bitter, oversweet tea as penance for my part in this debacle. "I'm working on the tree and plant formulas. It's quite a job." Gwynn snaps that's not her fault. But listen, when you make amends, you're not to expect an apology from the other guy. "I'm saying I miss you, Gwynnie. But falling in love and . . . well, destiny happens."

"It sure does. But how did Igraine know I'd marry R.A. way back at the Halloween séance? She warned me about claiming Camelon. Now I'm lady of the castle."

"Oh sweetie, that old sack of bones didn't predict your destiny. Morgan was jealous. Only the Old Unoriginated One can predict your future. And look at you, you're going to be a mother." I walk back to the window—the fog is lifting.

"And you're going to be a great-grandmother. How do you feel about that?"

I haven't given it any thought, so I say brightly, "I'm excited, how about you?" I take another gulp of bittersweet.

"Not so much. I'm sick all the time, unlike Bridget, three months along and glowing."

"Bridget's going to have a baby? Robbie must be ecstatic."

"Hard to tell with him, but Pris figures Bridget mothering our puppies did it." Gwynn ends on a sour note. "Everyone's ecstatic about her pregnancy."

Interesting how normal the bittersweet is beginning to taste. Suddenly I snap to attention. "Gwynnie, your morning sickness should be getting better."

"Well, it isn't. I throw up everything, even my special drink." I ask what drink and she says, "Lots of herbs that Morgan taught Mort how to make. He cares how I'm feeling." She lets out a wee sob. I pour my tea down the drain. I've had enough of that mistake.

"Listen, I'll come and stay a while." I fill the kettle and set it back on the cooker. Sometimes when you mess things up, you have to start completely over.

"I don't know, I'm still mad at you."

Determined to check on Gwynn, I say, "You can be mad as long as you like. Had will drop me off tomorrow morning on his way to Logres."

"Bridget," Gwynn says, "make up my grandmother's room. She's invited herself." Gwynn's still smarmy, but her tone isn't peeling paint.

My girl hangs up just as I say, "See you soon." I pour hot water in my cup, carefully dip the bag then add a bit of honey. I've got to get it right this time.

†OAK (Quercus robur) DUIR†

June 10–July 7

Meet the royal Oak—King of Trees. Like many an eminent ruler, this tree symbolizes understanding, change and sacrifice as the sun begins its cycle back into darkness. I know you'll be duly impressed if you make an effort to visit a strong mature Oak. It takes three or more adults, holding hands, to properly span (hug) a gargantuan Oak's trunk. Do this and you will grasp why the words en*durance*, *du*ration and even the word *door* stem from the ancient Duir, meaning solidity and protection. Likewise, the Druids in Celtic history acquired their name from this tree. Try to imagine those ancient priests carving a circle, symbolizing the cycle of life—Duir representing the soul, or *Eye of God*—on their most sacred tree during a summer solstice ceremony. Sounds like a profound experience.

ῃealing ῦrees

50

A pallor hangs over Camelon despite greening foliage enlivening the grounds. You see, Gwynn lost her baby last evening. My granddaughter, weak and wan, lies on a sofa in the library. While Raven licks the tears from her face, I say softly, "Gwynnie, let's go visit the healing trees."

As we step into the corridor, the atmosphere sizzles. Aidan, Gavin and an exhausted Artie stand with DCI Armstrong. They've assembled Mort, Morgan and the Rose clan.

"Yes," Armstrong barks, "you are all alleged suspects."

Pricilla cries, "You dare question our loyalty to the laird or the trees what provide for us? Look to thon newcomers—Gavin, Aidan and Mort."

"Hear now," Gavin shouts.

Robbie limps forward. "I've given my leg for the laird, does he want my arm, too?" It's a complete nervous breakdown of trust tearing the family asunder.

"Did Granny Gumshoe call the cops?" Mort growls.

I did, but reply evenly, "Mort, you prepared Gwynn's tea."

Armstrong scans the group. "We've yet to prove who shot Lady Gwynn or poisoned the laird's jam. Did one of you poison the Celtic trees? Indeed, did Morgan's herb tea bring on the lady's miscarriage?" Beside me, Gwynn goes limp.

Without trepidation Morgan admits to putting hellebore root in Gwynn's tea. "It was for depression. I didn't realize the herb could cause abortion."

"Morgan le Fey," I shout, "since when do you not know every contraindication of every medicinal herb on record?" My words echo off the castle walls and into the next county. Okay, not very pious, but then I'm just a fallible tutor.

"Ian," Morgan says, "Gwynn was devastated when Dr. Bruce ostracized her for marrying my brother. I had to give her something strong."

I step closer to Morgan. "You're not going to shift the blame to me."

"Mine was an honest mistake. I didn't mean to poison Gwynn's fetus."

Gwynn flies into a fury. "I know my pregnancy wasn't far along, but to minimize my loss is unforgiveable. We'll let the police determine if the poisoning was on purpose."

"Listen," R.A. says, "we're not pressing charges."

Confused and angry, Gwynn exclaims, "We're not?"

Too much the businessman for the delicate situation, he replies. "Gwynn, I'm sorry you lost your baby, but publicity is the last thing Logres needs."

"Our baby's dead and all you worry about is publicity?" She stumbles back. "Who are you, anyway?"

With an attempt to save the laird from his *fax pas*, Armstrong adds, "Most likely intent could not be proven." Gwynnie looks from one man to the other. Her face dissolves from contemptuous, to horrified realization.

As much I'd like to give him a talking to, but not knowing if Artie can repair the fissure he's created with his grieving wife, I usher my granddaughter out the door. The shock is too raw, so we walk into the old-growth forest in silence absorbing the therapeutic vitality of nature's perfume.

Along the path, the trees form an arch like a cathedral. "Before churches and temples, there was this sylvan sanctuary. A body can feel the Old Unoriginated One's presence."

Gwynn lays her hand on her empty belly. "Baby never had time to connect with a higher power."

"She's in loving hands, sweetie. When babies' souls come to earth, they stay connected to the upper realms quite a while after they're born."

A flurry of birds swoop down then back up to the trees on the opposite side. Unable to abide newcomers, a different species flies to the other side. Why can't worldly beings embrace each other's variances —accepting blue wings instead of grey? I'll bet our souls are all the same hue. Well, maybe not poisoners.

In silence, we follow the path to a circle of Hawthorn trees that loop around a ring of Ash trees. They in turn, open to three giant Oaks fused together over time. Gwynn whispers, "This is a magical vibrating place."

A red squirrel runs down the tree. Raven lunges toward the wee sentry who gives us a good scolding then scurries. Why do some foist themselves on folks? Territory and ownership—our culprit wants Camelon and Logres, possibly even the Holy Vessel estate that now belongs to Artie and Galahad. Ponder that one.

"Sit between the roots and hear the music of the spheres. The trees hum their healing energy." We remain there for some timeless time before we saunter back.

Armstrong meets us. "Dr. Merle." He calls me that now. "Everything above board with the Oaks?" I nod. "Even though the perpetrator has poisoned all thirteen trees. I question if they will begin again with the Oaks? Have your visions provided any clues?"

"Don't mock, Chief." Gwynn says. "We've just felt the tree's healing power."

He pulls a face, so I scold. "Don't denounce what you don't understand, young man." The fifty-something detective chief inspector actually smiles.

Hand on tummy, Gwynn heads off for a lie down, saying, "Chief, catch this guy."

He leans toward me in confidence. "The main DNA on that archery glove Raven found is indeterminant, but it's most certainly from Camelon. The fingerprints on St. Clair's roster were smeared and the DNA was inconclusive. There's DNA from nearly every monk at Holy Vessel on the robe your little mystery dog found in Rosslyn's tunnel and as suspected, Brother Ushtey's blood spatter. Regrettably, Father Joseph's milk glass did reveal poison, but no fingerprints. And we're no closer to finding the tree poisoner."

"Should I stand guard over the three Oaks?"

Ian lays a hand on my arm. "Your helping is my concern, Dr. Merle. It's more than coincidental that you were on flight 713. You may have been the one targeted. Anyone want to prevent you from arriving?"

"Morgan must have known I was coming. Why do you think I was targeted?"

He looks concerned. "Turns out the fellow you apprehended on flight 713 was part of a small group of radicalized students in Denver. The FBI had been surveilling them and caught Mort on tape, entering and exiting their run-down rental. We're not saying Mort joined them, but while in Colorado, he had at least one contact."

"You think he may have arranged for my plane to be targeted?"

"There's no proof at this point, but why else contact them?" Armstrong poses.

"But Mort didn't even know me. And where's the motive?"

Armstrong can't supply an answer, so it's back to the healing trees for another dose of tranquility.

Lunch with Lance

y frail Gwynnie sequestered herself in the North Tower—yes, Igraine's old chambers—more despondent than I've seen her since her mother died. Artie visited, but when she turned away, shut himself in his office. She lies there staring at the clouds passing the arrow-slot windows.

I'm not going to watch another mistress of Camelon lose touch with reality. Since she won't speak more than five words, I try a little shock therapy. "The final word from Scotland Yard is that Artie's poisoning was premeditated."

"But who did it?" Gwynn's voice is flat, but at least I sparked a response.

I park my bum on her bed. "Don't know. Priscilla showed me a magazine article from a few years back. It mentions her preparing the jam delicacy for her beloved laird."

"So it could be anybody."

"Those with access to the kitchen. Yet, our castle family believes it was accidental."

There's a rap on the door. It opens and of all people, Lance La Lac enters in all his manly glory. It's not just the black curly hair, swarthy complexion and muscled physic that sends a dame dizzy—the guy emotes an undefinable charisma. "Mademoiselles, I've come to save you from abject ennui."

"Is it fatal?" Gwynn asks.

"Boredom has cut down many a fine woman." Something about Lance's tantalizing Celtic-French accent makes a body want to believe every word he utters.

"What's the cure?" I ask.

"Lunch at Gopal's, our finest Indian restaurant."

"No," Gwynn argues. "I'd ruin it for everyone."

Lance breaks into an irresistible smile. "I'm visualizing summer pink." He swaggers to Gwynn's armoire. "Come my ginger-haired beauty, I must see you in this frock."

"Okay, Mr. Playboy," she says, "get out, so I can clean up."

Having waved his magic wand, in less than two hours Lance is driving us over the green hills toward Edinburgh in his plush Bentley with blue velvet seats, embroidered in gold for heaven's sake. Everything about Lance is over-the-top, but somehow this man makes it work. We willingly soak in the sorcerer's panacea.

"See the leaves on the hedge, Lady Gwynn? Darkness fades and life is in full bloom."

"I get the message."

"Then we will have a lovely day." Lance turns his head. "Comfortable, Dr. Bruce?"

"Our family name is MacLaren," Gwynn fires back.

"Yes, Dr. Bruce-MacLaren and Lady Gwynn MacLaren-Stewart. With that settled, we must clear the air between us. If there are apologies left unspoken, now is the time for them." Silence ensues, so he says, "Dear ladies, I admit how right you were about me—womanizer, carouser and despicable father. But I have spent these past weeks celibate and in search of an ultimate truth. What do you think of me now, Gwynn Avera?"

"What does your God think of you? Have you squared it with Him?"

"Galahad claims atonement lies in the present. Remaining chaste unless true love comes my way, I stay busy with a number of character flaws." He ends on a laugh.

Lance informs us it's our turn, so Gwynn and I apologize for our former estrangement. She reaches back and squeezes my hand.

"Now that we are all friends," he says, "let's have music." Lance turns on the stereo and insists we sing along. By the time we reach Edinburgh, we're a slaphappy crew.

You've got to admire a man who pries a recluse out into the world, urges forgiveness then utilizes music therapy to lift the spirits.

Having arrived, we park and take an elevator underground. Intoxicating spice-filled aromas tease our senses as the lift doors open into an intimate cavern with candlelit tables. The hostess, in a gold-trimmed sari, takes us past a wall of arched niches holding elaborate floral arrangements, to a corner table with crystal, china and linen.

Seated, we look at our menus. "I'm familiar with Northern Indian food," I confess. "I lived there and married a very nice Sikh. What vegan dishes do you recommend?"

"See Lance, my grandmother drops these juicy tidbits," Gwynn exclaims, "like we don't want to hear the whole exotic tale."

"Another time. Lance, will you order for us?" He does—in Urdu, the showoff.

While we wait, he whispers, "Can you ladies keep a secret? Of course, you can." He leans in. "Not that I was tempted, but Morgan asked if there was hope for the two of us."

Loving the gossip, Gwynn asks, "What'd you say?"

Lance lowers his voice. "That we'll always be friends. But then Morgan confided she planned to marry Aidan right away."

"Why so sudden?" Gwynn asks. "Unless she's pregnant."

At this critical moment the waiter interrupts. I'd send him packing but for his basket of breads. As he leaves, I say, "Pregnancy would explain Morgan not drinking."

"She's still getting high," Gwynn assures us. "I recognize the dilated pupils."

Lance joins the speculation. "R.A. discounts the fact that the Laird General didn't adopt Morgan, so she may believe a legitimate child could inherit Camelon."

Gwynn bristles. "And she saw to it R.A. lost his heir. Our baby."

"Or Mort did. Or they're working together," I add.

We're in such rapt conversation that we don't notice a woman walk up to our table. "Lance, darling," she coos, "I should be furious, but here you are with your grandmother and this charming young lady."

"Teddy," he says, "let me introduce Dr. Bruce-MacLaren and her granddaughter Lady Gwynn. This is Theodora Sterling. Her husband is a colleague of mine."

Nostrils flaring, Teddy turns to Gwynn. "He doesn't know the meaning of fidelity."

"It doesn't sound like you have room to judge," Gwynn chides. With a huff, Teddy strides across the room to order a drink at the bar.

"A ghost from my past," Lance explains. "I'll have to hide in a monastery to keep from straying from my spiritual path."

The mood changes as a gentleman decked out in Indian attire, complete with a turban and peacock feather, serves our food opening every covered dish with practiced flourish. "Mr. Lance, just as you ordered, coconut milk in place of the cow."

"Perfect Gopal. I'm sure it will be superb as always."

"Thank you, sahib." He bows out, bringing back fond memories of India's decorum.

Lance describes each dish then fills Gwynn's plate. "I must know what you think."

I'll have to remember his tactic. Gwynn is actually eating after picking at her food for weeks. Then again, this is insanely tasty. "I had no idea there was such exotic food so near Camelon," Gwynn enthuses.

"In that case," Lance says, "I insist you explore your newly adopted country."

"I would if I had someone to show me around," Gwynn pouts. "R.A. is too busy saving Logres. Besides, I'm also swimming in unfamiliar waters at Camelon."

"Allow me to emphasize," Lance says, "that you need to take your place as chatelaine of Camelon, before Morgan claims it."

A blush of anger creeps up Gwynn's neck. "Let her try. I'm not taken in by R.A.'s half-sister. R.A. doesn't comprehend how the castle is run. He seems oblivious to the fact that Morgan can be a real . . . female canine."

Lance roars with laughter, "Now that's the Gwynn I remember." Seemingly unaware of the other patrons, he grabs her hand. With a clear view to Teddy, I see her knock back enough scotch to float the British armada. Lance continues, "Mrs. Rose could use help running an efficient castle. She could tutor you. Own your place by making yourself indispensable."

We're interrupted as Gopal serves cardamom flavored rice pudding and chai tea. Lance feeds Gwynn her first bite of pudding. Scientists really should study this guy. His charm could single-handedly put the antidepressant companies out of business.

"Camelon needs a sense of solidarity not only in management," Lance says, "but by you reclaiming your husband." Gwynn starts to object. "No, listen to my logic. If you achieve that, Morgan cannot displace you. The future of Camelon depends on you." Aha, just as Igraine predicted.

Gwynn sits stock-still. "I need guidance—to become indispensable."

"Glean the depths of your grandmother and Mrs. Rose's experience."

"And you?" she asks.

"If necessary, even me." He agrees with a smile that's broken many a heart. "So ladies with our plan formulated, I must return you to the castle for I have business to attend to."

"Thank you, Lance." I'm sure he realizes I'm speaking of the miracle he just worked.

"Yes, thank you," Gwynn adds. "Grandma Merle, do you need to wash up before we head home?" I'm impressed. She usually just asks if I have to pee.

As we enter the powder room a thoroughly soused Teddy staggers toward Gwynn. "Lance," she slurs, "is always wonderful til he moves ta his next conquest." The older woman slaps Gwynn on the cheek.

I grab Teddy's arm pinning it against her back then leveraging her to her knees. "Are you going to play nice?" There's no comment. "Gwynnie," I say, "have the maître de call a taxi for this amorous alcoholic."

"Gladly." Gwynn flounces out.

"Sorry, Theodora, that was my mama bear reaction." Regret causes me to lay a hand on Teddy's head sending her spiritual energy. She looks at me a bit wide-eyed and I help her stand. "I'm sure you know drinking yourself into the grave will not bring your lover back. A bright, attractive woman like you, can accomplish so much on your own."

Teddy nods. "I'm sure you would be right." It's a gratifying end to a lovely lunch.

L ance's recommendation that Gwynn embrace her position at Camelon has been nutrition for her soul. "Gwynnie," I explained, "a chatelaine, or lady of the castle, is responsible for running her household. You inspect the staff's work, keep an eye on numerous domestic matters, and oversee entertaining guests." Under Priscilla Rose's competent tutelage Gwynn is learning to run Camelon like a pro.

I stand beside my Gwynnie in Artie's castle office to confirm her success. Still looking puny from jam-poisoning, R.A. sits at his ornate mahogany desk.

"Gwynn," he says, "you've impressed me with your organizational skills."

"So how about rewarding me with a play day? Just the two of us?"

"Well now," the Knave of Naive says in his administrative voice, "I must tend to Logres or you won't have a castle to manage. Time off is out of the question."

In her defense I admonish. "Artie, can't you . . ."

"Never mind," Gwynn says and walks out closing the door with an almost imperceptible click. Her silent despair lingers.

I lean over his desk. "Rex Arthur, Gwynn is your wife, not one of your employees. Avoiding your shared pain has driven a wedge between you."

Lance enters the double doors and sits down. R.A. immediately turns his attention to him. "Lance, our clients are responding to my refilling orders personally. I need you to postpone your sabbatical until I've cleared up Mort's mess."

Lance squares his jaw. "If I must, but then I'm off on my meditation retreat."

"Brilliant. We can finish these calls together. And Lance, it would help if you'd take Gwynn for some fresh sea air whenever you can fit her into your schedule."

Lance's eyebrows pinch together, holding his thoughts in place. "I'd rather not." An oblivious Artie glares until Lance acquiesces. "Well, if you truly need me."

Having handled that little hiccup, Artie takes a phone call—not noticing Lance flash him one last pleading look as he walks out. I'm not done here and sit down.

Artie raises his voice. "Mort can simply learn to like hard labor . . . All right, Aidan, bring him here while I pacify the clients he alienated." He firmly punches the off button.

"You sure you want Mort here?" I ask.

"What better place to keep him out of trouble?"

"Prison?"

"I'm trying to prevent that. Will my adolescent idiocy never stop haunting me?"

"Young people are often subjected to life-changing decisions at a time their frontal lobes haven't fully developed."

He laughs. "Leave it to you to site a biological excuse for having behaved like the biggest fool in Scotland. Now, what can I do for you?"

"Your Logres lab tech is testing my Celtic tree curatives on volunteers from Logres—not only the topical ointments, but also the oral formula." Artie's computer screen gains his attention. "And, fobbing Gwynn off to Lance is a huge mistake."

His nostrils flare and he begins typing. "What's the oral formula again?"

"*Old Crone Tree Sap.* Be the first sap on your block to use Tree Sap."

"Uh huh."

I slap my palm on his desk. "Rex Arthur." He looks up. "Not to diminish your Logres issues, but you do have a young bride in mourning over something you didn't chastise Morgan for causing. Can't you find an hour to take Gwynnie on that drive?"

"She'll be in good hands with Lance. She's simply young and needy."

I lean over his desk. "Artie, we all search for our perfect someone. And when we think we've found them, we discover they come with twenty-seven faults. You must learn patience and respect."

"Wise words, Nana, but I have an entire extended family to support. If I don't undo this muddle . . ." His head drops.

"Are your shoulders broad enough to handle this?"

"They have to be." He turns back to work.

I leave feeling wretched for suggesting we reveal the tree poisonings to the media last December—the disclosure that began this financial slump. Unless Armstrong's geeks trace the holder of the company snapping up Logres stock, this mistake is on me.

It's been weeks without Artie and Gwynnie reconciling. I head to Gwynn's chambers that nightly leaves Artie in bed alone. Igraine's eerie presence prompts me to carry my cane concealing an impressively sharp sword—to what, battle a ghost?

My granddaughter is out with Lance, again, so Raven helps me sniff around Gwynn's room. I hear tires crunch up the drive, go to the window and peer down. Lance helps Gwynn out of his red sportscar. She caresses his cheek. He looks toward the castle, dashes around his car and drives away. Gwynn watches then dances up Camelon's front steps. I plant myself firmly on her bed.

"Oh hi, Grandma." Gwynn twirls herself onto the dressing table bench. "I had the most marvelous day." She removes an earring.

"Gwynn Avera, why are you tormenting Lance? You're a married woman. Or have you forgotten that part in this dream you're living?"

My speaking to her mirrored reflection seems to embolden her. "Believe me, spending time with Lance is not torment."

"Gwynn." The disappointment in my voice turns her toward me.

"We're in love, Grandma. Totally and completely. Not like what I had with R.A."

"Had?" I speak through the despair constricting my throat. "Your love for Artie doesn't matter?"

Her defiance melts as she moves to the bed. Raven, who is beyond judgment, nestles between us. "Well, I honestly love R.A. But Lance, I mean, wow. I'm floating on some plane I've never experienced before."

"Gwynn, a state of euphoria is always enhanced when there's an element of danger. It's an artificial high and it's going to fade. This affair will wound Artie so very deeply."

"Grandma, you don't understand."

"No? Sweetie, I made every relationship mistake in the book. Why do you think your Grandpa Angus was my fifth husband? Believe me, I've earned the right to advise."

She purses her lips then says, "So stop lecturing and tell me what to do."

This calls for brutal honesty. "First of all, any analyst would tell you that R.A. and Lance are father figures. Your dad practically abandoned you and now you're with men his age. You can't replace your negligent father with these escapades."

"That's just gross. Lance and I are in love."

"Did losing the baby and Artie's inattentiveness make you feel empty?"

"There's a lot of hollowness," she sobs. "What fills this awful space?"

I swear, humans should come with instructions. "The Old Unoriginated One's love already fills what we perceive to be the heart's empty spaces. A body's acceptance and experience of Spirit, is how you feel whole. Knowing this, a body has a sharable love. Without that awareness, you can only offer an incomplete person to your mate."

Gwynn abruptly pulls away. My deserter dog moves with her. "But," my granddaughter argues, "if both people are half full, don't they complete one another?"

"Two lost individuals don't make a whole. Self-realized folks make a strong union."

"So what do I do? Run off to a convent?"

"A body can find Spirit wherever they are, but maybe you do need a retreat."

"I can't take a chance of losing Lance." She pounds a pillow and Raven jumps down. "Besides, Lance wants to live a more spiritual life, too."

"He does that by seducing his best friend's wife?"

"Lance isn't celibate like Had," she shouts.

I don't ask the obvious. "Then you must tell Artie. And how do you think Had would handle you running off with his dad?"

She spreads her arms and falls back on the bed, a wounded bird. "You sure know how to ruin a perfect day, Grandma Merle."

"Perfect?"

"Oh, leave me alone."

I do. Alone with the hole in her soul.

I'd like to return to Koad Croft, but Camelon is an overflowing caldron threatening the fire that feeds it. Lance and Gwynn continue disappearing heaven knows where. Artie remains sequestered in his office while Mort insists he would save Logres if he only had a corner office. The Roses, miffed that the upstairs folk thought they intentionally poisoned Artie, remain surly. Oh yes, seeing as how Morgan announced her pregnancy, she and Aidan are asking R.A. for a wad of money as they plan a highfalutin wedding.

And me, you may ask? Well, I find myself peering through a peephole in the passageway behind Artie's office accidentally overhearing Mort laying on copious amounts of manure. "Listen R.A., you need to send Lance packing. He had his chance to marry into this family, but turned my mother down."

"Lance would never have an affair with my wife, destroying our lifelong friendship."

"I can use my new surveillance equipment," Mort insists. "You'll wonder otherwise. And you can't hire someone—they'd sell the messy details to the tabloids."

"That's too underhanded. I'll speak to Lance in private."

Mort leans over Artie's desk. "Don't be naïve. You think he'll admit to hooking up with Gwynn? Lose everything?"

Artie ponders the implications. "What's your plan?"

"You pretend to go to . . . say France. You resurface just as we catch them in the act."

"I don't know."

"Then picture the headlines with pics featuring the laird's wife and his best friend in a lusty embrace. You and Logres would be ruined . . . along with the rest of the family."

Oh, the family reference clincher. Artie rubs his jaw. "When would you arrange it?"

"What's wrong with tonight? I'll plant surveillance devices in their rooms. I'll tell them you went to Paris to meet with a prospective customer."

"All right, let's be done with it."

No matter how much I disapprove of her philandering, I've got to warn Gwynn—out with Lance again. I hurry to my room, but now it appears her mobile phone is turned off. The way I'm pacing, you'd think I was the guilty party. Raven gives me a worried look, so I snap her leash on and make my way to the healing Oaks. Not convinced the culprit is satisfied with poisoning the complete Celtic calendar's worth of trees and plants, I decide on a stakeout. "Despite Armstrong's cautions, I've got to do this alone." Raven cocks her head. "No, you couldn't be surreptitious if our lives depended on it."

Having filled a duffle and dug out a sleeping bag, I'm ready for the night's reconnaissance. I join the family for the usual late supper. As planned, Mort announces R.A. took an unexpected flight to France.

I can't warn Gwynn over dinner, so I try to waylay her. "Grandma Merle, what part of leave-me-alone don't you understand?" She follows Lance out the front doors.

Knowing it will be a long night, I mean to lie down but a few minutes. Hours later, I wake with an urgency that brings me to my feet. I grab my sword cane and take the well-worn stairs up to the gallery overlooking the Great Hall. Is it the height or this situation that's got me woozy?

Rounding the corner that opens to Gwynn's North Tower chambers, I hear her speak. "R.A. where did . . . I thought you were . . . oh, dear God." She's standing half-clothed just inside her door. Artie turns, slams past me with a mixture of rage and despair on his face. The man betrayed staggers down the stairs.

Lance in underpants yells, "R.A. wait. Nothing happened." The fool stands in the doorway wrapping a pink polka-dot sarong around his middle.

Mort appears from a closet at the end of the hall. "Got it all," he laughs. Guess he thought R.A. would stick around for the uncut version.

I shake the business end of my cane at him. "Move it or I swear I'll damage you permanently." Mort's nostrils flare and the bully charges with his head down. I turn sideways and he skims past. I can almost hear the crowd yell Ole'. Furious, he charges back. I step dangerously close to the guardrail then grab the back of his t-shirt reeling him in before he does a Humpty Dumpty. Yanking free, he turns. I hold my cane horizontally. "You want more?"

Mort rubs his ankle. "Not now, I'm hurt." He takes his sorry backside down the stairs without a limp. Quick healer.

Just outside her bedroom door, Lance stares into Gwynn's ghost face. "For heaven's sake," I scold, "get dressed." Gwynn scurries inside.

I turn to Lance. "Dismantle Mort's surveillance equipment." He obeys, turns the key in the keyhole and hands it to me. "Now leave Camelon." Lance grabs his cloths then slinks away without a word.

I turn to my granddaughter. "We'll find Artie, so you can make a full confession."

Her eyes widen. "Oh, what have I done?"

"You mistook lust for love."

"Yes, real love wouldn't feel so . . . wrong."

We find Artie slumped in a chair, staring into an unlit fireplace. Gwynn lowers herself to the edge of the chair opposite his.

He looks at me with the eyes of a shattered soul. I want to hold him and make it all better. Instead, I say, "Rex Arthur, Gwynn needs to talk about losing the baby and feeling abandoned. You are going to hear her out. Then you are going to tell her how you feel. Oh yes, and divulge what's going on at Logres. No more secrets." I leave them, shutting the door behind me.

Although I'm eager to escape the drama, my heart isn't in my planned Oak tree surveillance. Nonetheless, I grab the packed duffle and sleeping bag. Raven runs to my side. "You go find Priscilla and your babies." I can't take the little scamp with me. At the last moment I snatch up my purse and sword cane then sneak out the back.

It's a clear night and the moon is high. Slipping though the Hawthorn thicket past the Ash trees that ring the Oaks, I drop my gear by a huge gnarly root. I embrace a mere fraction of the trunk, its bark rough against my cheek. Leaning back, I rap on the giant tree three times. "Please, I need your wisdom. My children have tied themselves into one heck of a knot. Can you help untangle them?"

A dark form rounds the ancient Oaks. "No one can help you tree worshipers."

Holy stars, the black-clad monk is real. The attack comes and I throw my arm up—blocking late. A sparking pain plunges me into darkness.

†ḢOLLY (ilex aquifolium) ᚷINNE†

July 8–August 4

If you get a chance to tour Scotland, and I certainly hope you do, you will find Holly in hedgerows, woodlands, and on hillsides. Most folks don't know that Holly with its many-pointed leaves and red berries isn't merely holiday décor, but recognized as a symbol of good fortune and health. Holly, in Celtic mythology, is the evergreen counterpart of the deciduous Oak. The King Oak rules the light, or waxing portion of the year while the Chieftain Holly rules during the dark, waning season. And get this, when Holly is planted as protective borders, the prickly foliage repels evil spirits attempting to pass through. Consequently, adorning a body's home with Holly defends against mischievous fairies. Finally something to keep the little blighters in line.

Dark Awakening

My eyes open to dungeon dimness. Sitting up, a jolt pierces my brain. Gotta cracked-egg head—crusty blood and a lump back there. Blinking away the pain, I see votive candles on an altar in an apse—the domed semi-circular end of a cathedral which always faces east. Should I recognize this? Try to stand—world goes catawampus. Probably suffering from concussion.

I know I'm Merle MacLaren. My husband, Angus, is deceased. This isn't a vision. Flash on a black-clad monk. "Anybody here?" Echoes needle my skull. It's a big place, underground? Struggle to my feet and edge toward the altar. Light a tall candle off a votive. Light another. Good news, flickering candles mean ventilation.

Candlestick in hand, I slowly light candles in niches along the wall all the way to the back. Gradually they illuminate a medieval church with crisscrossed vaulted ceilings. Oh, dizzy. Don't look up. Slowly make my way to the hefty door in the back wall. Locked.

"I need to use the loo." Loo? I follow a sound to a corner closet. There's a hole in the floor with a raging underground river down there. The highlight—toilet paper for which I give thanks. Upper thigh hurts, as does my head. Am I in danger? Dumb question.

For fear I'll run out of candles, I return to the front extinguishing those I lit along the wall. Here's my cane—the one with a sword inside. Could I actually use it to save myself? My eyes raise toward heaven. "Better send an angel, Angus, I'm in one heck of a jam." Jam. Something about poisoned jam. And poisoned trees—no, it's gone. Here's my duffle bag. Oh good, a flashlight, my blue jacket and shortbread, homemade by who? Pounding head, mud for brains. I lie down. Drift off wondering why I've been granny-napped.

Must have slept. Weak sunlight, as out of reach as heaven, announces morning from a tiny east window maybe a story and a half above the altar. Better take Raven out. Where's my Scottie? Probably with Gwynn.

Gwynn? Holy time travel, I'm in Scotland with Gwynn . . . and Had . . . and Artie and all the rest at Camelon. And the Celtic tree poisoner. Was that the black-robed monk that hit me on the head.

This must be the dark church from my Igraine visions. I walk to the altar where an easel supports a portrait of a divine Morgan with child—with halos over their heads.

I pick up a slim hand-lettered book, *Testament of God's Return*. It opens to: *The woman was made Queen of all Earth, through her union with God on Earth, and the conception of the Holy Child.* Morgan with delusions of grandeur?

"Better send a band of angels, Angus. I'm in worse trouble than I thought."

I walk up the center aisle to a stack of bottled water that appeared overnight. Dang, I missed my tormentor. Here's a note. *Drink one bottle every hour to baptize your soul.* So some nutter abducted me, carried me to an ancient underground church and now wants me to take a water fast. "Angus, you best make that twelve bands of angels. The ones with flaming swords."

Setting up a campsite on the front pew, I pray forgiveness for whatever I did to deserve this. It must have pushed some loon over the edge. What if it isn't Mort and Morgan? Maybe Gavin Sinclair is still angry that Gwynn and I ruined his vacation with Artie. Could Aidan Hunter be upset I accused Morgan for Gwynn's miscarriage? Or maybe Robbie Rose blames me for Armstrong's accusations about the poisoned jam? Which of them is the tree poisoner—or the monastery murderer?

I must follow this maniac's instructions to survive, so drink a bottle of water while shuffling along the church's circumference. Trailing my fingers on the antique brick feels disturbingly similar to the underground rooms Had and I toured in Edinburgh. What must my Camelon family think of my absence? Has DCI Armstrong sent out the bloodhounds?

I nap and wake to the evening *gloaming*, the dim light before dark. By candlelight I reread the *Testament* ravings, trying to make sense of my confinement. Get this: *One must fast until a cockroach looks good to eat then deny yourself even that pleasure.* I toast Morgan with water. "To you, dear deluded soul and the boy you spawned."

After the soundest of sleep, another day of feeling faint begins. Finding a heap of treasure piled by the heavy oak door, I hope for food—not that I've experienced any cockroach cravings. But no, besides an insultingly large sweat suit there's blankets and count them, two cots. Will I get a roommate?

Since I know my abductor provides simple supplies, I decide to celebrate by lighting the candles along the walls. I've only just slumped on my front pew when I hear voices. The door scrapes open. Adrenalin jolts me upright to meet my captor.

"Dr. Bruce," a male voice says. "I see you lit the cathedral for us." Aidan Hunter walks in with Morgan on his arm.

"No, Aidan. Not you."

He sets a picnic basket on the back pew. "How do you like your cathedral, Morgan? Quite a find, wouldn't you say?"

"Aidan, get real. Is this your idea of a wedding venue?" Turning to me, Morgan admonishes, "Dr. Bruce, they've got the whole country searching for you. Scotland Yard set up a tip line and it even went viral—like you were some kind of celebrity."

When she questions Aidan, he explains, "The good doctor is going to deliver our child. That is, once you've accepted the true religion."

An incredulous Morgan attempts a laugh. "What are you going on about?"

"Here, my Madonna, take Dr. Bruce her lunch."

"What? You said this was my surprise."

One and one add up to two cots and a roommate. Aidan Hunter abducted me and is about to imprison his fiancé. "Morgan," I warn, "there's more to Aidan than we knew."

"Take the food hamper to the doctor," he encourages. "I'll snuff the candles."

He slips Morgan's handbag off her arm replacing it with the basket. She snickers as if Aidan is playing a practical joke and walks to me. As she nears the altar her eyes widen and remain nailed to the Madonna with child painting. "Is that supposed to be me?"

Aidan turns to Morgan as he extinguishes candles with bare fingers. "You don't realize it, but our son is destined to save the world from all corrupt religions."

Morgan turns from the portrait to look at me. "What's going on?"

I watch Aidan. "It seems your boyfriend has discovered mankind's true religion, and you, Morgan, are its Madonna."

"Excavating this cathedral," Aidan announces, "buying up Logres stock after poisoning the Celtic trees, dealing with disloyal Ushtey who swore to take over the monastery—I did it all to present our true religion to the world."

Aidan's a psychopath. The man is behind all this mayhem. Remaining calm I say, "Aidan, I never guessed you were responsible for poisoning the Celtic trees."

"The tree worshipers were to be taught a lesson, weren't they, Dr. Bruce?"

"And Ushtey's beheading?" I inquire.

"It had to be done. Ushtey the traitor wouldn't poison Father Joseph. I had to do in the old bloke meself."

"What?" Morgan cries. "You did what?"

Hoping Morgan will have the sense to escape, I bait Aidan. "Surely you had help. Was it Mort?"

A derisive bark echoes off the walls. "Himself thinks he's to inherit Camelon." Aidan motions toward Morgan. "The King of Earth is about to be born."

Morgan takes a couple steps toward him. "What the hell are you talking about?"

"Watch your mouth, this is a scared place." Aidan's malicious alter ego has emerged.

"You didn't poison R.A, did you?" Morgan presses. "Or Elaine?"

"Never. Once he's read the manifesto, the laird will join us. Dr. Bruce, you explain it to her." Aidan rounds the back pew, picks up Morgan's handbag and backs to the door.

"Morgan," I yell urgently, "he's leaving you."

Aidan opens the door saying, "See she drinks the water."

"She needs food for the baby," I shout in my best authoritative voice.

A confounded Morgan runs up the aisle, but not fast enough. With precision, Aidan slams the door and slides the lock. I sit stunned wrapping my mind around Aidan as killer, tree poisoner, abductor and religious fanatic—a powerful deranged giant of a jailer. As Morgan pounds on the church door, a pall of hopelessness deflates me. If this madman imprisons the woman he claims to love, no, the Madonna he professes to adore, how little must I mean to him?

Comrade in Captivity  55

organ's frantic screams bounce off the dark cathedral's vaulted ceiling. Her demeanor changes from exasperation to disillusionment. She gives the door one last slap then says, "You're the genius, Dr. Bruce, how do we get out?"

Ignoring what might have been a compliment, I ask, "Are we in Edinburgh?"

"Yes, under Aidan's filthy old warehouse. He's got a sort of flat up there. We're down a long flight of winding stairs. How'd you get mixed up in this?"

"Let's eat, my taste buds have all but shriveled from fasting." As we tuck into cheese and pickle sandwiches, I explain. "From what he said, Aidan poisoned the trees in an attempt to prove his religion's superiority over what he perceives to be nature worshipers. My adoration for the Celtic flora must have turned him against me."

"I can't believe my sweet Aidan beheaded a monk and poisoned Father Joseph."

"Brother Ushtey was presumably placed as an informant, but was killed when he failed to take Father J.'s place at the monastery. Psychopaths are good at deception, but when they lash out, merely rationalize their behavior and feel no remorse."

"Psychopath," she repeats as if trying to grasp its implications. "Does Aidan think he can convert me down here?"

"It seems so." I eat a bite then ask, "Did Aidan tell you about his childhood? I'm wondering how this fanaticism formed."

"In the Laird General's day, Aidan and Ushtey were childhood friends. Their families lived out on Camelon crofts. Their fathers provided hay for our livestock and firewood for the castle in exchange for housing."

"I didn't know the crofters, just remember their cottages being left derelict."

"Camelon's central heating was paid for by emptying stables and crofts. The boys' fathers never found work—ended up beating their families then dying of the drink."

"Hence, the battered boys became the abusers. What became of their mothers?"

"Ushtey's mother took to the streets while Aidan's took in laundry. A devout Roman Catholic, Mrs. Hunter insisted Aidan and his sisters attend mass every morning and twice on Sunday. They hid in the chapel when his da was on a tear."

"So Aidan equates church to a safe haven. He has created his own refuge by mimicking his mother's religious devotion. Why didn't you tell Armstrong that Aidan held a grudge against Camelon?"

"And put my fiancé in his crosshairs when I was sure Aidan was innocent?" Morgan looks forlorn. "How could I have been so gullible?"

"Aidan appeared a stabilizing force for you and at Logres. But what better revenge than to insinuate himself into the Sinclair-Stewart family then slowly take over Camelon and Logres? Psychopaths usually aren't loyal, yet Aidan turned his adoration toward you. But why lock you up?"

"He caught me getting high...again. He's adamantly against alcohol and drugs." Morgan looks at her belly. "I can't allow Aidan to raise this little guy. A legitimate male heir—if we marry." Morgan rummages in the food hamper looking up expectantly at this wizened old crone. "So how do we get out?"

No plan here, but I want to keep my comrade-in-captivity calm. "Before we discuss our escape," I hedge, "bring me up to date on Artie and Gwynn. And Lance."

"That's right, you don't know what became of the love triangle. Long story short, Lance ran off to a French monastery while Gwynn moved to St. Clair's—something about cleansing their souls. Very medieval."

"And Artie? And Had? And my Raven?"

"Not to worry, Bridget's obsessed with dogs and has your mutt. Galahad's running Logres. And in an inane gesture of forgiveness for his wife's lover, R.A. went out searching for Lance."

"Yes, Artie always did have a heart bigger than his brain. He knew I was missing?"

"R.A. thought you abandoned him because he hadn't done right by Gwynn. Armstrong said you hadn't left the country. As I said, your disappearance went viral. Even the Prince of Wales asked us to look for you. You know him?"

I shrug, but desperately want to brag about having tea with the prince at the palace. Those well-dressed men in London, didn't exactly take me to Scotland Yard, now did they? Yanking me from visualizing tea and crumpets, Morgan asks, "Why are the men I love either unavailable, or totally mad?"

"Life is complicated. I've observed that people draw unresolved issues into their lives over and again, until some cosmic lesson is learned." I don't add that she's drawn this negativity into her life by being her spiteful, unstable self. Instead, I watch her spill tears. "You need a nice lie down. Let's set up your cot near the water closet."

"There's a loo? Lead me to it."

"Don't get your hopes up, Morgan. Aidan's true religion has returned us to biblical times in more ways than one.

Confidences

56

Day seven of my abduction. Following his daily schedule, Aidan thumps down the stairs. Morgan and I stand at the back of the church ready to put a plan in action. I hide behind the door as it opens inward. Morgan pulls her sweater up revealing a bare belly.

Up close Aidan's as big as a defensive lineman. I dash forward and sidekick his knee. Aidan grunts, drops the food basket and stumbles into Morgan who wraps her arms tightly around his neck. I dash in and punch his kidney. He bats me off like a parasite then yanks Morgan off his neck and swings her onto a pew. I run for the open door, but he throws me sprawling on the cold stone floor. Marching over, he slaps his beloved Morgan so hard the sound echoes off the vaulted ceiling.

"How dare you," she shouts, but shrinks from his fiery glare. A thin line of blood runs down her chin.

I speak firmly. "Aidan, the baby." His nostrils flare, but he backs away.

Aidan throws a crazed look at me then one of dark disgust toward Morgan. "Heretics." He stomps out.

Defeated, we retreat to our cots falling into troubled sleep. The dawn illuminates a mark I scratch on the wall indicating my eighth day of imprisonment. Our failure to overpower Aidan has thrown Morgan into deep despair. Me, the great heroine, assure myself I'd definitely escape if it weren't for Aidan harming Morgan and the unborn child—their responsibility my albatross.

We take our daily exercise along the brick walls, chatting as we walk. "I've done it all wrong haven't I, Dr. Bruce? Hooking up with big broken Aidan. Trying to force R.A. to accept Mort as heir apparent. Always scheming, that's me."

I've gained trust by playing therapist, so say, "Attempting to control events was a natural response to your chaotic youth, Morgan."

"I enjoyed Mum's darkness. You warned me, Dr. Bruce, but Igraine's black arts seduced. Lady Elaine had power—an undercurrent of spiritual love that obliterated evil."

"But you didn't fully embrace her teachings—the Golden Bowl meditation."

"I wanted to hold onto the dark side. I'm such a cliché. That's why I had to hurt you those many years ago—so you'd leave Camelon. You were simply too good—too right."

"You didn't want me in Scotland when you sprung Mort on R.A. How did you know I planned to return?"

"Igraine told me in a vision then Elaine confirmed you planned to stay with Galahad in a Camelon croft testing the Celtic trees. I had Mort spy on you out there in Colorado. He got hold of your itinerary."

I snort. "So you're aware Mort was linked to the terrorist plot on my plane? Armstrong claims Mort likely coerced that would-be bomber."

"Are you sure?" She seems astounded. "But why? Mort didn't know you then."

I turn to her. "Could he have misconstrued your disdain, thinking you wanted me out of your life permanently?"

For a split second her expression spells pride then she surprises me. "I've passed Igraine's darkness to Mort, haven't I?"

I want to accuse her of overlooking glaring faults in Mort's and Aidan's demented minds. But by the time we've reached the north wall I feel hungry, so I tease, "Whatever should we have for dinner, Morgan?"

She brightens a bit. "I'll have a big bloody steak."

"And I'll have a huge salad." Fantasy food improves our predictable soggy sandwiches. So much so we're able to sleep soundly all night.

This morning we sit in our slice of sunshine drinking cold bitter tea soaked overnight. Who knew eternity was only nine days long? As the psycho Aidan comes to mind, the door opens. Joining him, Morgan clings to the lunatic's forearm. "Aidan, darling, Dr. Bruce has explained your religion to me. I'm ready to become a disciple."

Aidan removes her hands then goes to light several candles on the altar. He turns toward us. "You two, go kneel at the altar." Obeying, he lays a hand on my head. I instruct myself not to cringe. "Dr. Bruce, do you accept the deacon position in the True Church of God's Return?" I tell him I will. Aidan pulls me to my feet then kneels beside Morgan. Reaching into his pocket, he pulls out a ring and a handwritten ceremony. "Dr. Bruce, you will marry us, if Morgan can honestly submit."

"Morgan," I read, "do you promise to honor, obey and worship Aidan, the True God, until death do you part?"

Morgan agrees, he slips the ring on her finger then says, "I will honor my Madonna." I pronounce them husband and wife. Aidan has her sign the certificate and laughs. "We're bound together for all eternity. You will cooperate and accommodate me."

Morgan sneers. "Learned a lot of new words, haven't you my lord and master?"

Aidan starts to backhand her. I simply say, "The baby." He squeezes her face in his mighty hand then leaves with a bang. He's becoming more violent with each visit, but I attempt a semblance of normalcy. "Anyone for tea?"

After remaining silent while eating a dry honey bun, Morgan speaks. "Mort may have misunderstood my anger over Gwynn's pregnancy and added too much hellebore."

"If he was willing to kill a plane full of passengers to eliminate me, he may very well have caused your brother's baby to abort. Why does he feel he can kill with impunity?"

"From early childhood, I convinced Mort he was an uncrowned Scottish prince—superior to others. Did that turn him into a monster?" Agitated and hyper, Morgan abruptly walks down the center aisle then scurries back. "Dr. Bruce, Aidan went ballistic when R.A. made Galahad his right-hand man. Aidan insisted he was meant to become head of Logres, as well as Camelon. So I shot that arrow at Galahad. Your Gwynn stepped right into the line of fire. Good thing she pulled through," Morgan says brightly.

"But you could have killed my Gwynnie."

"It's a moot point now." She shrugs and twirls off down the aisle and into the loo. Holy fruitcake. Morgan has reverted to mania—a full-blown swing from doom to euphoria. She steps out of the loo caressing her tummy bump. "I'll get Aidan to trash this religious mumbo jumbo and take me to Bermuda." So this manic state of endless possibilities allows Morgan to overlook all sins and misdemeanors.

I step over to the makeshift kitchen. "Surely you won't leave Camelon not knowing who poisoned Artie?" I pour tea into the heavy ceramic cups that Aidan so generously allowed us. "R.A.'s poisoning was certainly premeditated."

"One of the Rose clan is responsible," Morgan snaps. "They made the jam didn't they? That Robbie Rose is one angry guy."

She's right about that, but I ask, "Why? The Rose family depends on their laird. On the other hand, Aidan wouldn't mind stepping into R.A.'s shoes."

"If Aidan poisoned R.A.," Morgan insists, "I'm definitely annulling our marriage."

I see no sign of jest so say, "Mort could have slipped poison berries into the jam."

"Next thing you'll be telling me Mort and Aidan killed sweet Elaine, but Aidan was with me the night she was murdered. We were at my Edinburgh flat making like rabbits."

Improvising, I say, "I believe Sister Merry Fey killed Lady Elaine, but at this point that nun is a phantom possibly driving a little black Jaguar. One exactly like yours."

"It wasn't me, if that's what you're insinuating. Mort used to drive around when Aidan stayed over. I remember giving him money for petrol that night." How about that for pertinent information? She sits then jumps up again. "That Lance, what a fool. I asked him to marry me back then. Oh, he gave me the nicest refusal—claimed he simply couldn't divorce Elaine. Poor Mort, he was so mortified for me."

"Did Mort prefer Lance over Aidan for a stepdad?"

"Almost as much as me. Mort told me to hold out for Lance, but I have needs that Aidan fills admirably."

So Mort had motive and opportunity. He was out that night and the Jaguar driver resembled Morgan. He could have stuck around making sure Elaine's body was found. Carefully, I say, "Could Mort have, through a sense of loyalty to you, eliminated Lady Elaine—freeing Lance to remarry?"

"Thought you said Sister Merry Fey killed Elaine."

Tiny factoids begin lining up. Sister Merry Fey was described as being about Morgan's, or Mort's, size—rather large hands with nail polish atypical of a nun. Was Mort masquerading in a habit and lady-shoes? "Morgan, what became of the black pumps with silver buckles you wore at Halloween?"

She strides to the altar then turns. "Somehow I stretched them out." She trails off into sullen silence, but Morgan is exceptionally bright. "Are you accusing me...or Mort?"

I'm thinking, 'If the shoe fits . . .', but say, "You both look a bit suspicious."

"I could get Aidan to be rid of you with your damned steel-trap of a mind."

"But you're a better person than that." I don't mention she shot Gwynn.

"You're right. Besides you're my best bet for escaping." Morgan's logic is like scatter-shot. Suddenly, she sprints up the aisle then across the back. Panting, she leans into one of the north wall arched niches. "I get hungry whenever I reach this spot."

An obscure possibility surfaces. I pick up one of the ceramic cups, throw it on the stone floor then choose a pointed fragment. Rummaging through our clothing, I tie Morgan's scarf over my nose, grip the broken pottery firmly and walk toward her.

She backs away. "What you doing, old woman?"

I turn toward the niche. "Maybe a lot. Go listen for Aidan while I make some noise."

"You breaking us out? We're underground." I scrape the mortar between the bricks with the ceramic fragment then use my cane to punch the brick. I change hands, but it isn't long before both arms ache. "I'm bored," Morgan offers.

Anger renews my strength. I scrape mortar until I've reached the brick's deepest edges then use my cane as a battering ram. I hit the loosened brick dead center making no headway and slam the cane a few inches to one side. Miracle of miracles, the brick pivots inward. A dim light and glorious Indian spices waft through the small opening.

I put my eye to the peephole as Morgan runs my way. "What can you see?"

I'm met by a lovely brown face. "No, no, no," it says. "You cannot be doing that. This is a first-class restaurant."

Just as I'd hoped. Aidan's dark cathedral, deep beneath his warehouse, shares a wall with Gopal's where Gwynn and I lunched with Lance.

Morgan pushes me aside and yells through the small opening. "Call for help. We're being held hostage, you idiot."

I nudge her away. "Is that you, Gopal? It's Dr. Bruce-MacLaren, Lance La Lac's friend. This pregnant lady and I are trapped down here. Could you call 999 for us?"

"Memsahib, you have gone missing for many days," he accuses.

"Yes, Gopal. Could you phone for help before our abductor returns?"

"Oh, yes, yes." He turns and announces, "I have found Dr. Bruce-MacLaren. I have found her and another lady trapped behind my restaurant wall."

Gopal disappears then a woman yells through the opening. "Move back in there." I pull Morgan well out of the way then hear the woman order. "Bash that wall in." Pounding commences. Before too awfully long the niche collapses inward with a crash of tumbling brick. A face appears through the billowing dust and Teddy—yes, the one I gave a healing jolt—sings out. "Have I made amends, Dr. Bruce-MacLaren?"

Whirlwind

57

Events rip ahead at tornadic speed. After scrambling through the rubble, a rescue team arrives to take our vitals. Teddy leans in close without a whiff of alcohol on her breath. "Gopal, alerted the media. I notified Scotland Yard's tip line. Your DCI is on the way. Meantime, I'll run interference." Our Teddy certainly wears sobriety well.

Morgan points to the camera crew. "I need..." She huddles deeper into her rescue blanket as she looks in a mirror Teddy pulls from her handbag. "I should wait for an exclusive interview—with the *Times*," she decides.

One of the media mob asks loudly if I had to eat bugs to survive. Pointing to the first hot meal I've had in eons, I hold up a hand. "Mr. Gopal and his staff are my saviors. I'll make a full statement after I've spoken to the authorities."

A constable pushes in front of the media telling them to leave, but Gopal intervenes. "No, no. They must have their story." He leads them to the gaping hole and elaborates, "I hear a voice and say, Dr. Bruce-MacLaren, you have gone missing a very long time. Then we break the wall." His version makes me smile and will be good for business.

Morgan is ingesting an entire chicken while I relish the best vegetable curry in the entire civilized world when DCI Armstrong steps off the elevator. "Secure the scene," he orders. Strobes flash as he strides over and gently takes my hand. "I thought we'd lost you." He helps me to a private table. "Who did this, Dr. Merle?"

I want to say Igraine, but that's just crazy talk. "Aidan Hunter. He admitted to poisoning the trees and killing Brother Ushtey and Father Joseph, but there's more."

Armstrong stops me and puts in a call. "Set the plan in motion." He turns to me. "When Morgan also went missing, we had an agent surveil Mr. Hunter. We inspected his warehouse, but didn't find his underground church you were held in." He frowns then says, "Do you think Morgan will help obtain his admission on tape?"

"She's vacillating. But listen Ian, I think we can prove Mort murdered Lady Elaine."

"Seriously? I'll interrogate him after we have Hunter in custody." Collecting a reluctant Morgan who's busy applying Teddy's makeup, Ian bundles us onto the lift. He uses the title gained from her last marriage. "Countess, you're off to hospital."

The shock of being thrust into civilization feels otherworldly. The honking, exhaust and hectic masses whirl round like a fantasy. At the hospital we're examined, jabbed, pronounced sound and given beds that feel like glory. Thanks to the media, my rescue has gone viral, so Armstrong proposes Morgan and I confront Aidan before he flees from Camelon. The best part—we get to wear wires and earwigs.

Morgan demands, "What makes you think I'll go along with this?"

I sit up even straighter. "Because you admitted to shooting that arrow meant for Galahad, but put Gwynn in the hospital." I look toward Armstrong's raised eyebrows.

If Morgan's glare could vaporize, I'd be a fatty spot on my bedsheet. "That's just hearsay." She glares at Armstrong. "The cops have no proof."

"Oh, but they do," I lie. "Scotland Yard found your DNA all over an archery glove we discovered near where you shot Gwynn."

Playing along, Ian says. "Dr. Merle, you shouldn't know that."

"Don't you know she's an old wizard? Besides Aidan forced me to shoot at Galahad. Gwynn just got in the way." As usual, Morgan adapts her story to remain on the winning team. "And Aidan made me go through an illegal marriage. I didn't even have a dress."

Suddenly Artie bursts in, hugs Morgan and me then shakes Ian's hand. "Thanks for contacting me. Lance won't be leaving that monastery. I cannot believe Aidan did this."

As if Morgan despised her lover all along, she wails, "Aidan beat me and made me follow his ludicrous religion." To avoid post-traumatic melancholy, I force my thoughts to Morgan spilling details of her harrowing plight. But when I'm told Had escorted Gwynn to Camelon, a nostalgic lump causes me to yearn for life at Koad Croft.

I get up, take Armstrong aside and say, "She's skewing the facts." He whispers he wants me to intervene if Morgan doesn't get Aidan's confession.

After being wired for sound, I don somebody's idea of old-lady clothes. Armstrong already left to set up spy gear, so Artie, Morgan and

I climb into a police helicopter. Trust me, soaring across the ethers in a goldfish bowl is not as thrilling as a body might imagine. The rotor raps a monotonous tattoo and I'm back in the war zone medevacking wounded soldiers. Why remember the young men and women that didn't make it when so many lived to tell their story? I cry out, "I did the best I could." Artie asks what I said. I blink the combat scenes into their compartmentalized closet and yell, "Good to be heading home." Must buck up for this entrapment.

Landing in Gavin's finely trimmed garden brings him running. Artie helps Morgan and me out of the whirlybird. Raven runs up and I receive the licking of a lifetime. Gavin hugs his laird. "So, you're back." Only Gavin can emote gratitude and accusation all in one breath. "You canna fathom how it's been with Aidan and Mort becoming pals."

I want Gavin to spill the whole pot of beans, but Artie says, "Let's settle in first." He shames everyone when it comes to patience. I try to be nice, but can only envision throwing Aidan in the dungeon and tossing the key down the privy hole.

Entrapment

limbing the castle stairs, I soak in the homey bliss of Camelon's every hand-hewn stone and oaken beam—all the way into the dining room. Having been alerted to our arrival, Priscilla stands watch over a lunch made in paradise. And me wanting to put a few pounds back where they belong. "My laird," Pris scolds, "yourself has been needed here." Artie accepts the chastisement by hugging her a good one. Embarrassed, Pris looks at me. "Dr. Bruce, we reckoned you was a goner—and you too, Morgan Le Fey."

"Good someone noticed me missing," Morgan pouts. Her demeanor changes as Aidan saunters in as if nothing untoward has transpired—so delusional he thinks we'll overlook our imprisonment? Morgan cries, "You saw our rescue online? Well, you have a lot to answer for, mister." Red blotches color Aidan's neck. "Word has it, you didn't miss a day of work trying to find me." He stammers in an attempt to follow her storyline, so Morgan slips her arm in his. "Come on you big lug, we need to talk." Aidan's jaw sets as Morgan escorts him to a prearranged room.

"That lad is in for it," Mrs. Rose predicts. She knows very well that Armstrong and his merry men are concealed in an eavesdropping room.

I can hear what they are recording through my earwig, beginning with Morgan's snooty voice. "What got into you? I only smoked a little weed." Her acting is superb.

"My Madonna will no' be poisoning our Messiah."

Morgan sticks to the entrapment. "Or what? You'll kill me like your pal, Ushtey?"

"Don't tempt me, Morgan." He lowers his voice, but for an old gal I hear impeccably. "I had to do in Ushtey for promising me the monastery then falling for Father Joseph's Golden Bowl nonsense. Elaine's death inspired me ta be rid of the old codger with Death Angel mushroom in his milk. Appropriate, don't you reckon?"

Morgan moans. "Father Joseph was good to Elaine."

Here in the dining room, R.A. and I nod and touch fingers to our earwigs. Priscilla crosses her arms under her ample bosom. "You two gonna share what's what?"

Figuring I'm the one to eat crow, I confess. "Morgan's getting proof, but you Roses were right about Aidan. You realized he had his eye on Camelon, Robbie accused him of wanting seniority at Logres and Bridget claimed he was a religious fanatic. Add beheading Brother Ushtey, poisoning the Celtic trees and Father Joseph then abducting Morgan and me—I'd say that about sizes up Aidan Hunter."

"My trusted friend is insane," Artie moans then looks around. "Is Gwynn safe? I thought she'd be down by now."

"Galahad is with her. Mort pesters Lady Gwynn somethin dreadful when herself is home from that convent. Robbie was gonna knock some sense inta Mort, but I stopped him on account of himself be'en . . . kin. You shoulda been caren for your lady."

Duly reprimanded, Artie stands. "I'm going to her. Can you handle this?"

"Yes," I say. "Keep your earwig in, we may need you." Artie, who finally got his priorities straight, hurries off. "Pris, I'm sorry I couldn't see through Aidan. I wanted to believe Morgan had found a stable man. Is my Gwynnie all right?"

"If it means wearen white robes and liven at that convent. After you went missing and the laird goes off, Lady Gwynn abandoned us entirely. The lass reckoned you left her for taken up with that devil, Lance."

Poor kid. I did get granny-napped at an inconvenient time.

nowing Morgan got what was needed out of Aidan, I plunk my napkin down. "Guess this means Mort is mine. Where is the scoundrel?"

"Himself would be in the gym playen with swords. Take care, he's a wily one."

"That he is, Pris, then I've been known to have a bit of vinegar myself." I lift my doggie who took up residence at my feet into Pricilla's arms and head toward the gym.

I'm not far down the corridor when a commotion has me turning around. Backed by three men, DCI Armstrong speaks with authority. "We heard your confession, Mr. Hunter. Best come peacefully."

Aidan bellows, "You think you can treat the Lord of All like a common criminal?"

As if he can sway the berserk, Armstrong reasons, "It was against the law to abduct Morgan and Dr. Bruce-MacLaren."

"I'm saven the world from ruin. You lock me up—false religion will reign."

"We're sure you meant well," Armstrong says and his men circle Aidan.

Priscilla peers from the dining room holding a growling Raven. "Aidan Hunter," Pris yells, "you caused that tree ta fall on my Robbie's leg."

The fiery-haired giant shouts. "He stood in the way of the Most High God."

Morgan approaches Aidan. "Shutting me in that dungeon could have hurt our baby."

"Cathedral." Aidan insists. "The Holy of Holies—to put an end to all nature worshippers and blasphemers. Do you ken nothing?"

Armstrong and his crew move on Aidan, so he grabs his pregnant Madonna. "You're hurting me," echoes to the timbers.

Mort sidles up beside me, smirking as if Aidan's antics are no more than a schoolyard tussle. "Aidan's really something, isn't he?" he brags.

Two of Ian's men dive for Aidan's legs. Morgan breaks from the melee as a third man shackles the huge man's arms, as slick as spit. Aidan lunges against his restraints. "Dr. Bruce," he bellows, "I expected a scholar to get the importance of the True Church."

"I can't disregard your poisoning the Celtic trees and Father Joseph. The Almighty made us stewards of the natural world. How can you destroy it and resort to murder?"

"You'll taste hellfire from my followers." Kicking, eyes blazing, Aidan is hauled through the foyer with him shouting, "Dr. Bruce, your bloody head will adorn my altar."

Holy stars, that image shakes a body's roots. Armstrong says, "Sorry about that." Then indicating Mort. "I'll be back." He joins his men out Camelon's heavy front doors.

Morgan pivots toward Mort. They hurry away and she exclaims, "My darling boy, whatever shall we do without Aidan?" There are a lot of nuts in her fruitcake.

I whisper to my wire. "Make sure you record this." My earwig gives me the silent treatment, so I pray for a higher protection and follow them into the gym. Mort's all black ensemble includes suit jacket, silk tee shirt, jeans and running shoes. He walks to the wall of impressive swords, spears and lances. He removes a spear.

"Playing Knights of Old?" I chide.

"This is no game." He rushes forward launching the spear directly at me. I avoid the spear's path and grab it midair. "Not bad," Mort allows, but backs toward the armaments.

Morgan glares at her son. "Stop harassing Dr. Bruce. She saved my life." Morgan's loyalty is all over the map.

"She wants to prevent our having Camelon." He looks at me. "This is over, granny."

"What's over, sonny?"

"You and my old man are dead. Camelon is mine."

"Ever heard of thou shalt not kill?"

Mort sneers. "Taking life is the most powerful thing a man can do."

"Murder is for cowards. Saving lives is what takes courage." I flip the spear then settle it pointing toward him. "Was Lady Elaine your first kill?"

"How'd you figure that?"

I try for incriminating facts. "You masqueraded as Sister Merry Fey, wore Morgan's silver buckled shoes and ran a Rover off the road after posing Elaine in the rowboat."

"What are you, a sorceress? People who know too much end up dead."

Morgan whimpers. "Mort, tell me you didn't kill my dear cousin."

Mort turns to her. "Elaine was screwing with your head. That fraud deserved to die."

"Are you going to coerce another terrorist to blow me up?" I ask.

"Why bother? You're no match in a sword fight." He's right, but the kid is spilling, so I play tough granny. Mort turns to the weapons wall then pauses. "What gave me away?" An enormous Claymore hisses as he slides it off its metal brackets. With tremendous strength, Mort swings the broadsword overhead.

Shaking in my sturdy shoes, I continue the reproach. "How about that botched job posing Lady Elaine's body in the rowboat? Those flowers in her hands? Just sloppy—the stems sticking out willy-nilly."

"You've got nothing." Mort balances his sword and looks at Morgan. "And you won't rat on me like you did Aidan."

Morgan sobs, "Did wanting Lance for a stepdad lead to you killing my Elaine?"

"I wanted you to have Lance, your heart's desire. Like you gave me any credit." Mort laughs sardonically. "But it's Aidan that understood my rightful position."

"Consequently, you manipulated the herbs in Gwynn's tea?" I ask.

"I wouldn't have poisoned your precious granddaughter," Mort shouts, "if R.A. had treated me like a son and heir. But no, Gwynn's kid was going to get it all. Aidan realized I was special when no one else did. My name, Mort, means Angel of Death."

"In his cult, maybe." Goading, I ask "You poisoned your father to take his place?"

"No, Dr. Bruce-MacLaren, MD, PhD, Smartass. But I thank whoever poisoned dear old dad's jelly. Now he's weak enough so I can take him in battle."

"You will do no such thing," Morgan screams and Mort simply snorts.

Reclaiming his attention, I say, "If you kill Artie you'll wind up in prison. Since Aidan married your mother, he would become Laird of Camelon. You're nothing but a pawn. Aidan told us you won't inherit. That honor goes to his baby."

Mort storms me with his sword. "Shut up, you old psychic."

Swinging my spear, I brace for the bout when the doors fly open. R.A. dashes in wielding his newly forged sword, a meteor transformed into gleaming protection.

Mort laughs, lays his Claymore on the floor and pulls a Browning Hi-Power from a shoulder holster concealed under his jacket. "Got you outgunned, Daddy. What caliber is that piece of garbage?"

R.A. holds his weapon skyward. "It's my Ex-caliber." He circles the boy. "Pick up your sword and fight like a man."

The Battle   60

Ceiling-high windows reveal a waning moon against a darkening sky as Mort shrugs out of his jacket then lays it and his holstered gun on the floor near Morgan. He squares his muscled shoulders and saunters back to his sword. Spear in hand, I scribe infinity signs in the air before pointing the business end at Mort. How did my escape from an underground prison merely hours ago lead to this?

"Nana, lay your weapon down," Artie insists. "This fight is between Mort and me." I step back, but don't relinquish my weapon. "I'm serious. Stay out of this," he orders.

The bastard son laughs, swings his Claymore into fighting position and holds his ground. With eyes locked on Mort, the laird steps forward wielding Excalibur.

Morgan stomps her foot. "Stop this. Stop it now."

Neither man breaks concentration. Gripping Excalibur in both hands, R.A. booms, "Leave us to it." A crazed gleam shines from Mort as he watches R.A. following his movements. There's a good ten feet between them until Mort charges swinging his weighty sword overhead.

"No," rings from the doorway. It's Gwynn. She starts to run onto the battleground, but Morgan grabs her. "Mort," Gwynn pleads, "leave R.A. alone."

Glancing her way, Mort scoffs. "Now you're worried about your husband."

Pointing my spear skyward, I hurry over and wrap my arms around Gwynn. She holds me close as we turn toward Artie. He has several inches on Mort, but not the younger man's strength and responsiveness.

R.A. and Mort's blades clash then slide to their hilts. Artie shoves the young man back and threads Excalibur through an opening that nearly unhands the Claymore. Mort falters, but regains his footing with primate agility. Rushing forward, Mort tosses his sword to his left hand cupping his right palm over the hilt. R.A.'s sword wavers and Mort whirls nicking the laird's arm. Artie reels as blood dyes his shirtsleeve.

"That poisoned jelly left you weak as a girl," Mort chides. "How about giving me Camelon for the price of your life?"

"Never," R.A. says, but for all his bravado the Laird of Camelon staggers.

Releasing Gwynn, I steady my spear then follow Mort from a distance. Artie attempts to lift Excalibur, falters and bends over breathless. With no sense of fairness, Mort swings his blade nicking Artie's other arm. Should I break my vow to do no harm and throw my spear?

"*Halte*," echoes off the walls as Gavin races in holding a saber.

Mort laughs. "This is no fencing match, Scarface."

Gavin's eyes meet his laird's weary face then like some crazed Celt the devout friend rushes into battle. The more experienced Mort turns aside gouging Gavin's arm as he flies past. Incensed, Gavin turns swinging his weapon while the gash in his forearm paints his saber's grip slick with blood.

"Why come here, Mort?" Gavin implores. "You've brought nothing but misery." Mort dances cat-like then charges. Stepping back, Gavin lunges at Mort only to stab open air, but the fervent bodyguard hisses, "You'll not have my laird."

R.A. steps into the fight. "Gav, I'm good now. Leave this to me."

Mort sneers at Gavin. "I'll have either Camelon or your laird's life."

Gavin lifts his weapon overhead and runs toward Mort. "Never." Taking advantage of Gavin's velocity, Mort plunges his Claymore deep into the loyal man's chest. Gavin's sabor clatters across the floor as he reels forward.

Gwynn screams while I step back barely able to accept the scene before me. Morgan cries out, "You've done it now." Then as if speaking to herself, "Your fate is sealed."

Artie dashes to the impaled Gavin, held upright on Mort's sword. As Gavin's beautiful mocha complexion fades to grey, he whispers, "My laird."

Disbelief, then grief, drops a shadow over R.A's face. "How could you? Have you no decency?"

"Decency?" Mort chides, "A man who impregnates his own sister has no right to speak of decency." Mort drags Gavin to the wall then unskewers him from his weapon. He wipes his blade and pales as his handkerchief goes crimson.

Is he vulnerable now? I try to reason. Could I do any better than Gavin if I try to take Mort down? Would Mort slay me to prove himself to Aidan. Or Igraine?

Galahad strides in giving the smirking Mort no heed. He hurries to his dead cousin, kneels then turns. "Mort, you must ask for forgiveness. Surely you believe in an afterlife, or like the Celts, another chance of life on earth. You won't want eternal punishment."

"Your pretty speech means nothing to a man with no soul, choir boy."

"Gavin's soul has left his body, but you remain alive, therefore you have a soul."

"I must be awfully powerful if I caused a so-called soul to scoot off to the afterlife." Mort looks toward R.A. "Aren't you proud of a son that wields the power of life and death?"

A dawning realization washes over R.A. "Mort, were you envious I admired Gavin more than you?" Artie points to Gwynn. "There's my heart."

Armstrong enters with one of his men, saying, "There's been trouble transferring Aidan. He's escaped." Mort crows with laughter. Armstrong sizes up the volatile situation—our stricken faces, Had kneeling over Gavin's corpse and Mort pointing his sword at Artie. Armstrong speaks in a practiced tone, "Put the sword down, son."

Mort's face darkens. "I'm not your son. I'm nobody's son."

"Here," R.A. says as he swings Excalibur off his shoulder. "End this and I'll be the first to lay my sword down." He bends, but doesn't release his weapon.

Conveying the resolve of a man with nothing to lose, Mort yells, "Not a chance." A flicker of a smile crosses the slayer's lips as he raises his Claymore. With renewed vigor Mort swings his sword overhead and steps toward Artie.

With his agent videoing the scene, Armstrong picks up Mort's holstered gun. Is he allowed to use it? "Unhand your weapon, Mort. We don't want more bloodshed."

Mort sneers, so I edge closer. Should I throw my spear? Armstrong signals an almost imperceptible 'no'. "Now Mort," he says, "what's the sense in this?"

Armstrong's man capturing his every move seems to bolster Mort. He turns to Morgan. "What do you think, Mother? It's all been for you. The terrorist bomb on the plane—now that took some planning. Poisoning Lady Elaine—sorry Had, it wasn't an easy death. Ridding

Gwynn of R.A.'s offspring, simple with that herb you provided—we couldn't let his heir live, could we? Those were all simple offerings so you could have what you wanted. Even joining Aidan's church to make you Mother of God and Queen of Camelon, was for you. But do you love me for all I've done?"

"How can you say that? I gave you everything out there in America. But to gain my love you commit murder?"

"Yes Mother, you daft cow." Mort snorts derisively. "And I've got one last thing to give you—Daddy's head on a plate." Mort swings his sword into fighting position and steps toward the laird. "A fight to the end, isn't that the honorable way?"

"Mort," I yell, "you are not the Angel of Death. Aidan's cult beliefs are imaginary."

"What's really real, Dr. Bruce? You thinking you can save R.A. from Igraine's curse? Well, witness his end."

"That's enough, Mort," Armstrong gruffly orders. "You'd best come with me."

"Not on my life." Mort shouts.

Gwynn shouts for R.A. to run, but the laird straightens holding Excalibur in front of his chest. "This evil must be irradicated by Old Law." Without a clue how to halt this feud, I pick up Gavin's saber and run into battle.

"End this, all of you," Armstrong begins, "you can't possibly believe . . ."

Mort lifts his Claymore overhead, wildly rushes forward then leaps through the air. In a frame-by-frame slow motion, Mort falls onto Excalibur while his own sword slams down on R.A.'s skull. In unison, father and son cry out.

Agony echoes off the high ceiling. Mort's Claymore clamors to the marble floor as the men separate. Weaving where he stands, blood cascades down Artie's face. As if suddenly molten, he releases Excalibur. The sword slides cruelly through Mort's chest as he crumbles to the floor.

I run to Artie, his eyes those of an injured child as he sinks to his knees and topples into my arms.

Out of the Woods

61

Y ou'd think a mother would run to her dead child oozing his dark red life over the white marble floor, but not Morgan. She and Gwynn dash over to me as I assess Artie's head-wound. Morgan wads a handful of her maternity blouse to staunch his blood. "Keep the pressure steady," I instruct.

Armstrong speaks on the phone. "Yes, the medical team. Every second counts." He presses another button. "Any word on tracing Aidan Hunter? Well, keep me informed."

Raven's toenails click across the marble floor. She paws Artie's hand then gently bumps his arm with her muzzle. I motion for Pris and Bridget standing in the doorway carrying folded laundry. "Your laird is seriously injured. Tear that sheet into bandages." The pregnant Bridget holds her hand over her mouth, so I hand Raven to her. "Lock the dogs up Bridget and inform Robbie we'll be at Edinburgh Surgical Hospital."

The split in my unconscious boy's head stops my breath, but not my hands educated in the art of saving lives. Morgan and Gwynn steady his skull while I apply a dressing. Together we perform like an experienced surgical team.

Ever the one to recall omens, Pris declares, "It were that Mort barging ahead of the first-footer at Hogmanay what caused this grief." Superstition alone couldn't produce this mound of anguish, yet Mort did seem to foreshadow disaster.

Helicopter rotors send me to my feet. "This soldier is ready for evac." Gwynn holds me back as a flurry of paramedics, capable and strong, take Artie. In a swirl, Morgan and I strip off surveillance wires and with Gwynn, let Armstrong drive us hurling through countryside then city streets for an inordinate stretch of Einstein's relativity.

At the hospital I'm told Artie will likely be in surgery for hours. "Let me in there," I say. Gwynnie shakes her head and I fall quiet wondering at her strong reserve.

Armstrong commandeers the ICU waiting room then steps to the far side to take a call. "How can Hunter have disappeared so completely?" Still on the phone, Ian speaks to us. "Aidan has an online church called the True Church of God's Return with over five hundred disciples." He adds, "Put our best people on it." He hangs up.

"This church thing came as a surprise," Morgan says. "Aidan called me his Madonna, but I thought that was like calling me, babe."

Armstrong's brows knit. "Did you meet any of his cult? I'm sure they helped him escape custody."

"We didn't exactly move in the same circles. I thought he was a loner. You could write a book about what my fiancé kept from me." Grabbing the thought, Morgan chirps happily, "Not a half bad idea."

Galahad, having seen to affairs at Camelon, walks in and immediately kisses Gwynn's and my cheeks. This from a young man I thought incapable of *exudiance*. Okay, not a word, but it should be. "How is he, sis?" Sis? You leave the kids five minutes and they sprout into grownups.

Gwynn motions toward Morgan. "Sit," Morgan dramatizes, "this is a long tale."

Robert Rose rounds the doorway red-eyed and distraught. I hurry over and guide him to an empty corner. "Artie's wound is critical. I can't even guess what his odds are."

Robbie grabs my arm. "He canna die, Dr. Bruce." He rushes convulsively to a waste can and vomits. I get a tissue to wipe Robbie's face. "Don't fuss. Don't ken what came over me."

"It's shock, Robbie. Rest a minute." He does, but soon declares himself fit.

Galahad steps over. "Robert, we'll be needing you to rally the troops at Camelon." Happy to be given a job, Robbie claims his women-folk would be needen direction. I doubt that very much, but congratulate Had's move.

After an age, the surgeon enters. "Lady Gwynn," she says, "your husband survived surgery, but the next twenty-four hours are critical. He is far from out of the woods."

"Out of the woods," I repeat.

"So we simply wait?" Morgan spits.

"You could pray," she adds flatly then leaves.

Morgan grabs hold of Armstrong. "This is all Aidan's fault. You need to find him." He takes Morgan aside to discuss the nationwide manhunt.

Alone with Gwynn and Had, I whisper. "Out of the woods—my Celtic tree formula. The test trials on the Logres foresters have been very promising. It's nearly a cure-all. Taken orally it heals and strengthens. Galahad, you can retrieve the tonic from the lab."

Hope flashes in Gwynn's eyes. "How can we give it to R.A. here?"

"Who would object," Had asks, "to the laird's priest administering consecrated wine?" So Project Holy Tonic is set in motion. Galahad visits wearing a cleric's collar to administer the consecrated Celtic formula. Had's collar may be a sham, but our fervent prayers over Artie are nearly tangible.

Critically injured Rex Arthur is the root that nourishes our family tree—the trunk around which the rest of us revolve, yet sluggish time passes. If furrowed foreheads don't mark us as the worried-waiting then our spirits do. Between spending time with Artie, bolstering Gwynn and listening to Morgan's ramblings, we feed on gifts of grapes. Never underestimate the power of grapes in a crisis. I'm jockeying for the last sprig when the doctor walks into our appropriated domain.

"Ladies, sir, I have good news and bad."

Gwynn jumps up. "Give us the bad news first."

She hesitates but continues. "The blow the laird sustained formed a subdermal hematoma, between the brain and the outer membrane. It's pressing on the brain in an inoperable location. He may not . . . he probably won't recover."

Our group-inhale sucks the air right out of the room. Looking for a fragment of reassurance, Morgan snaps, "So what do you consider the good news, doc?"

"The tube we inserted allowed enough drainage that the laird is fully conscious."

Gwynn dashes to the door then stops. "I can see him?"

Morgan starts to follow, but I hold her back swallowing hard before speaking in my doctor's voice. "Give it to us straight, Doctor. How long does he have?"

"Hard to say—a week, maybe two."

"Can we take him home? He'll want to be at Camelon."

She looks at Had and Morgan then back at me. "I wouldn't refuse a dying man's wish, but I must hear it from him. I'd best join Lady Gwynn." As heaven's tears wash across the hospital windows, the surgeon leaves to do a doctor's hardest job.

Morgan starts to follow, but nearly collides with an aide who says, "There's a call at the nurses station. A Robert Rose asking for Dr. Bruce."

Following her down the hallway, I say, "He must have lost my mobile number." Picking up the receiver I say, "Robbie, your laird is conscious. His prognosis isn't good, but we're going to move him to Camelon."

"Thanks for letting me know where everyone will be, Dr. Bruce."

"Holy stars, Aidan is that you?"

Aidan laughs. "Yer a dead woman, Dr. Bruce. I've got disciples."

"So I've heard. I could come see. Where do you hold services?"

"No you meddling hag. You must die." The line goes dead.

Back in the waiting room, I fess up. "I thought I was talking to Robbie and spilled the whole barrel." When Had says he needs to take me to safety, I object. "Just a berry-picking minute, I go where Artie goes."

My tears well up, but aren't allowed to fall as the surgeon walks back in. "Your laird wants to return home."

Had and I go to R.A's bedside. Tubes and blinking lights blur. My jaw clamps the grief down to that place where emotions hide. "How's my little warrior?"

"Must get things . . . in order." That's my Artie, taking care of business. Not me, I'm royally ticked his destiny dealt him the raw one. R.A.'s eyes focus on Had. "A favor, Galahad? Throw Excalibur back . . . in the loch...belongs to Lady Elaine."

"Your sword is being held as evidence."

"When you can . . . I should never have taken it."

"Oh Artie," I say. "You didn't cause this."

He smiles knowingly. "My fate...written before birth."

I lower my wet face to the bedsheet then feel his fingers attempt to stroke my old grey head. Rex Arthur—Laird, no King of Camelon, comforting me while he lies dying.

Circle of Life

62

Before dawn Armstrong's team, Had, Gwynnie and I unload and carry equipment in St. Clair's back entrance. By the time all's in place, daylight streams through the stained-glass windows. Galahad, Gwynn and I climb into the Rover then circle round outside the walled-in monastery and convent grounds. We pull in behind Jamie Rose easing Camelon's Rolls Royce up to Holy Vessel's ornate wrought iron gates.

Only the Rose clan, Morgan, Gwynn, Had and I will be allowed in for the private burial. Gwynn holds Artie's urn while Gavin and Lady Elaine's urns rest at my feet. Morgan has yet to decide where Mort's ashes will land. Not here, that's a given.

A monk swings the gates wide for us then closes them to representatives of the press wielding high-powered lenses. They seem eager to report on the burial purposely-leaked by Armstrong in hopes of luring Aidan Hunter out of hiding. As Jamie helps Bridget and Morgan—both pregnant, out of the Rolls, cameras whir into action. Breaking the silence a reporter inquires, "There hasn't been a public notice, who's to be buried?"

Robert Rose lumbers toward the gates. "You media folk, show some respect." Robbie shakes a fist at the paparazzi and walks back. The sky begins to weep, so other than me in an appalling yellow slicker, we huddle under hoods and bumbershoots.

"Why you only now buryen Lady Elaine after all these months?" Bridget asks.

Although her question is a bit impertinent, Had explains. "Since Mort confessed to Mum's poisoning there's no question of suicide. We can now lay her to rest in the monastery's consecrated ground."

White robed monks and nuns circle us and Mother Superior leads us to the St. Clair-Sinclair family plot. Had lowers his mother's urn into the soil. A monk fills the grave and Morgan hands him a white lily to place on the little mound. Mother S. says a few words of praise for Lady Elaine, not taking a chance, even in death, of prideful pomposity.

Galahad, lovingly addresses his mother. "I cannot see how this terrible end was part of your fate, Mum, but I'll leave that discussion for when we meet. I'm sure you are pleased I have family and embraced teaching Golden Bowl meditation." He lays white roses on the dark soil. A few steps away, Had places Gavin's urn in the ground speaking the kindest of words. Gavin, who left his invested earnings to the Camelon estate, apparently won't be accused of pride. As Galahad bends, the sword Excalibur protrudes from his black overcoat.

Mother Superior leads us to the Stewart ancestral plot where the Laird General Stewart's body lies. After her suicide, the General scattered Igraine's ashes in Camelon's flower garden, those many years ago. Priscilla gives me a significant look, likely remembering entirely too well the drama Artie's parents shared.

Morgan stands near her stepfather's grave with dark disgust, so I turn her toward the freshly dug hole. Gwynn lowers Artie's simple urn, that doesn't begin to portray the extraordinary man it represents, into the ground. The rain pelts the loose soil in front of his granite tombstone already in place. Under my Artie's full name, it reads:

HERE LIES ARTHUR
OUR ONCE AND FUTURE KING

The officiating monk drones his impression of the laird's consequential life. Mere words seem an insipid way to celebrate a person's existence. At the very least, this man deserves fireworks and marching bands. Instead, from the monastery portico, a bagpipe skirls a mournful dirge. Ever the proper one, Artie would approve.

Tearful, Robbie helps his pregnant wife lay white carnations on the grave. Jamie does the same for Pris and Morgan. Gwynn, Had and I lay red roses among the white flowers then continue to stand in silence.

Galahad is the first to turn. "Shall we convene to the loch?" As lightning flashes with thunder on its heals, the monks and nuns head for shelter and refreshments in St. Clare's. The heavy rain thrums its own dirge as we walk the distance to the boathouse dock where Lady Elaine's poisoning was marked by a screaming meteor. A mist hangs over the loch, but nearby, Elaine's tiny thatched meditation hut remains visible.

Galahad lifts R.A.'s sword and says, "Take me up," flips the blade over and says, "Throw me back." With this, Excalibur arcs high into the air illuminated by lightening as the sword enters the loch's depths. The thunder's rumbling roar spreads the news down the escarpment on the loch's far side.

Our group scurries under the boathouse shelter where we stop to give our pregnant mothers a breather. From here we will trudge up the incline to a promised brunch in St. Clair's. We've not gotten two steps when an explosion blasts a giant hole in the far side of the surrounding stone wall. Rocks and debris thud to the ground allowing seven black-clad invaders entrance. They fan out and run toward us.

Dashing from the bushes, Armstrong bellows to his men, "Nab the big bloke."

Robbie opens the boathouse door. "Bridget, Morgan, Lady Gwynn, be getten yourselves inside. Mum, you too." Ready for a fight, Pris falters, but Robbie scoots her through the doorway. "Be keepen the women safe."

A couple of thugs advance and grab my arms. Had punches one with an impressive undercut and Armstrong slugs another while I kick shins and stomp insteps. Armstrong's agents take on three imposing brutes as Aidan's all too familiar voice shouts, "Rick," while pointing at Had, "finish that one off." Rick dashes up to Galahad, looks directly into his mystical eyes then back off. Had turns to assist Robbie and Jamie, flung aside despite fighting Aidan with all their might. Aidan grabs me, but I drop into a crouch repeating the Golden Bowl protection prayer. Amazingly, Aidan can't get a grip on my wet slicker.

Aidan, Rick and two others lope toward the hole in the wall, scramble over stones then disappear through the opening. We hear a revved motor then gravel thrown by retreating tires. "Catch them up," Armstrong orders. A couple of agents run for their vehicle.

Jamie opens the boathouse door and the formidable Priscilla Rose dashes out fuming. "Leave me at 'em." Gwynn hurries to my side as Morgan and Bridget lumber out.

As the remaining three invaders are cuffed, Robbie, adrenalin still pumping, confronts the captives. "Who are you daft gits?"

The men call out, Smith, Larson and Kielian as if answering role call. The one named Larson says, "We be devotees of the True Church of God's Return."

Robbie shouts as they're led off, "You sods are to become devotees of His Majesty's True Penitentiary."

After trudging uphill for a promised brunch, we wait in St. Clair's dining hall speculating whether Aidan has been nabbed. Gwynn leaves to help out in the convent infirmary while Morgan complains about Aidan not asking after her. Losing patience, Priscilla Rose seethes. "Morgan le Fey, yer asken ta be thumped up aside yer head."

Armstrong receives a call and tells us that Aidan disappeared on the A803. "His disciples probably drove Aidan's car up into a lorry. What's worse, a reporter's long-range lens filmed our botched seizure. Her video has gone viral. Aidan Hunter is getting the notoriety he craves."

I ask Armstrong if his people traced Aidan's internet church. "Everything is routed and encrypted," Ian says. "I'm assured they're close, but still working on it."

"Then put me, his favorite cheese, in the trap," I suggest.

Armstrong looks toward my adopted family. "Dr. Merle, you don't realize what a heroic celebrity you have become. Your kin, all of Great Britain and the Prince of Wales are very fond of you. If anything were to go awry you'd be..."

"Full of holes like Swiss cheese," Robbie finishes.

An amused groan breaks the tension, but Bridget's moans grow. She stands and embryonic fluid splashes to the stone floor. A contraction causes Bridget to cry out then again two and a half minutes later. Priscilla and I jump into action. "Mother Superior," I yell, "we have need of the birthing chair."

Robbie phones an ambulance, but looks to us pleadingly. "No fear," Pris assures, "Dr. Bruce and Mother Superior birthed Galahad here. An look at himself, a big strapen man."

"You ladies brought me into the world?" Had exclaims.

"Details later. Right now, Bridget's having a baby."

"Babies," Bridget hollers. "We was wanten ta surprise Mammy . . . it's twins."

And I didn't think I'd be able to smile today.

†ᕼAZEL (Corylus avellana) COLL†

August 5–September 1

What a year it's been. And here we are back to the lovely month of Hazel. I sense I'll need to utilize nearly all the characteristics the Hazel tree symbolizes. All of this month's wisdom, spiritual awareness, intuitive knowledge and negotiation skills may be necessary to complete my task ahead. So far my daily handful of Hazelnuts have kept my wits sharp . . . most of the time. If only I could bring about a modicum of serenity for my extended family. Not that I expect World Peace, but I'd sure like to be considered a wise old counselor.

Transformations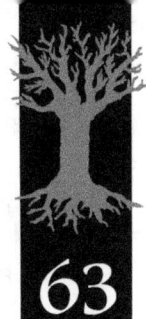

63

L ast month somehow compressed time, squeezing a tremendous number of events between its folds. My prison break then Aidan's capture and escape, juxtaposed with Mort, Gavin and Artie's traumatic sword fight—well it's been a weighty worry. Even so, Bridget and Robert's twins brought a glimpse of gold back to Camelon.

Turning the page to the month of Hazel finds Gwynn and me tirelessly setting up our Celtic Tree Test Clinic in St. Clair's infirmary. We haven't had a good sit-down until now—and me with a gazilla-womperload of meddlesome questions.

Gwynn and I sit on a convent bench in the sunshine as we celebrate with chocolate biscuits and tea, our one-year anniversary living in Scotland. With Galahad overseeing Holy Vessel, the eats are now plentiful and divine. Clouds bubble up promising an afternoon shower. Black-faced sheep dot the lush noll between the monastery and convent. Fruit trees bow reverently with abundant offerings—the Almighty's artistry.

I smile at my granddaughter in a sheep's wool robe woven by the humble monks. A Golden Bowl initiate, Gwynn now helps teach Had's meditation sessions. I know, I'm shocked too. "Gwynn, you've changed so it feels more like a decade has passed."

"It's just that I got a shock-course in adulthood," she says. "Your tough love and connection to Camelon made my world blossom. I lived a fairy tale life, even married Laird Charming. When he stopped communicating, I searched for a deeper love and lost my way—falling for Lance and hurting R.A. Instead of repairing our marriage, he left. And I assumed you abandoned me, too, Grandma Merle. Not knowing where you were, or why you disappeared—every minute was an agonizing age." Her voice cracks. "I had no baby, no husband and no grandma. I thought I'd lost everything precious to me."

I want to hold my Gwynnie, but she's no longer the teen I knew. Her adolescent demeanor has changed into serene Lady Gwynn.

Wanting to reach this unrecognizable woman, I ask, "How did you survive?"

"Grandma, you pretty much ordered me to get in touch with my spiritual self and for once, I listened." This new Gwynn smiles reservedly. "I'm learning to connect with the Old Unoriginated One. Golden Bowl meditation is healing my soul." I squeeze her hand and she says, "Hope returned the day you and R.A. came back to Camelon . . . until the sword fight." She pauses for a quiet moment. "Nothing will ever be the same."

"The worst storms produce the strongest branches on a body's Tree of Life. And look, Gwynn, your *Plant to Save Our Planet* reforestation project has really taken off."

"We've only begun, yet a hundred and thirty-seven trees have been planted. Spirit created our trees and plants to provide oxygen to sustain humankind. Watching a living thing grow...well, life is very sacred to me now."

"Yes," I agree, "dominion over nature comes with great responsibility. We should never take Mother Nature for granted. Or take advantage. I missed life's blessings in that underground church."

"It's hard to believe Aidan kidnapped you and Morgan."

I decide she's resilient enough so say, "I haven't told you, but Morgan admitted she shot you. But that arrow was meant for Had. Armstrong let Morgan off the hook in exchange for Aidan's confession. We didn't bank on his followers grabbing him."

"Holy nutzoid. Is Morgan deranged too?" Okay, this is my old Gwynnie.

"Morgan feels little remorse for her attempt on Galahad's life and injuring you."

"Well, I can't be totally mad at Morgan. Talking to Mama while unconscious, was profound. Awareness of an afterlife made me aim higher." I tell her that's a very noble attitude, but then she reroutes the conversation. "The procurator fiscal declared Mort took his own life by jumping on R.A.'s sword, but what happened after the inquest?"

"Outside the courthouse, you can imagine how Morgan attracted swarms of reporters. One nervy journalist asked if she was worried her baby would become a suicidal killer like Mort or deranged like Aidan?"

"What'd she say?" Who knew ratting on Morgan would restore Gwynn's and my rapport?

"Well," I continue with gossip gusto, "Morgan patted her belly, glared at the cameras and said, 'My beautiful baby boy is the innocent one here.' Of course, the media loved talking about Aidan's baby . . . completely forgot about Mort."

"Smart woman."

"Yes, and yesterday Morgan signed a book deal for the whole sorted Aidan Hunter story. She may be pregnant, but no longer barefoot."

With that the clouds let loose huge fat drops and we hightail it inside. Not to worry, I grabbed the chocolate biscuits.

†BRAMBLE (R. fruicosus) MUIN†
September 2–September 29

I wandered the stalls at this year's Harvest Festival, but without Had and Gwynnie at my side it held little charm. Of course, the Rose's were there—Bridget and Priscilla winning their annual pastry and jam awards and Jamie playing with his Celtic rock band. The twins slept through most of it while Janet and Jamie's little Rosebuds enjoyed it all. You may remember this month of Muin manifests predictions. Since I experience prophecies erratically, I declined to read palms, leaving that to the clairvoyants. Muin 'tis also, the season to speak anything a body has harbored all year. With my unrestrained mouth, I think I've got that covered.

Aidan Hunter remains a big part of my karmic conundrum. DCI Armstrong just walked in my lab to give me an update on my nemesis. "Step in my office, Ian, I'll be right with you." Since Had accomplished miracles here at Logres, there's funding for my Celtic tree research. I turn to my science tech who helped set up the equipment, perform laboratory tests and record our observations on the Celtic tree curative experiments. "Annette, we need a double batch of formula this week. You might want to call Starr and Stith to help." She nods her approval and I join Armstrong.

"Close the door, Dr. Merle, this is for your ears only." Intrigued, I quickly follow orders and sit at my desk. He leans forward. "Our agents infiltrated the homicidal Mr. Hunter's commune. His disciple called Rick, has turned informant. Turns out Hunter's disciples smuggle handguns to support his nonprofit organization. We're holding out to connect Hunter directly to the gun trafficking. We know where he's hiding, but haven't incarcerated him as yet."

"Don't hesitate to use me as an enticement."

Worry furrows his brow. "That's problematic. You've become a bit of a heroine to us Scots."

Touched he included himself in Clan Admiration, I say, "But I caused Aidan to lose face. He needs to prove he's all powerful."

"Aye, but we have him for Father Joseph's murder. Hunter admitted to administering the Death Angel mushroom and the old abbot's exhumed remains contained enough amanitin and phalloidin toxins, to down a Highland cow. Anyone who claims to receive heavenly instructions to kill, yet insists he's sane is dangerous."

"Is my family safe from this perfectly rational psychopath? You know we never discovered who poisoned Artie."

"We're watching your Camelon castle kin."

"Okay," I concede, "I'll accept how things stand." To lighten the mood, I opt for a bit of tittle-tattle. "Have you heard the delicious gossip about Lance over in France?" Armstrong perks up. "It seems Lance and a young novice he lured from a convent, moved to Britany so their child, when it's born, can grow up near his La Lac kin."

"Fatherhood might tame Mr. La Lac." Being privy to our family dynamics, Ian asks, "How does it stand between Galahad and Fiona Percival? She'd be good for the lad."

"Once Had abandoned the grail quest, Fiona never asked about the inner pursuit of Golden Bowl meditation. They grew apart. Anyway, he has loads of responsibilities at Holy Vessel and Logres. Life must go on despite juggling the hard emotional matters."

"With Lady Gwynn away from Camelon indefinitely, who's managing the estate?"

"The Roses. I've been named Camelon's Clan Chief for now, as well as physician to the premature, Bonnie and Ronnie and a very pregnant Morgan. Then there's my work here. These roots, berries, leaves and barks have given up potent secrets held by the ancient Celts. In addition, I'm in 'proving ground' heaven at Holy Vessel and St. Clair's—the perfect closed community to monitor monks and nuns with varying disorders. But I always have time to help snare Aidan Hunter."

"You perfect your cure-all, Dr. Merle. I'll keep hunting the Hunter."

Armstrong departs leaving me eager for Monday Mash Day—you know, turnips, tatties and mushy peas. I turn to my lab techs. "Annette, I'm headed down to the cafeteria." "You ladies lock up when you break for lunch."

I nip into the lift, but part way down the doors open and a disheveled Robert Rose, reeking of scotch, stands frozen. "You getting on Robbie?"

He steps in and as the doors close, pushes the stop button. "Dr. Bruce, I deserve to lose my place at Logres and Camelon, but I were so bitter, I couldna think straight." The apparently broken man covers his eyes and slides down. Thankfully I meditate cross-legged, so am able to join him. "The laird," he chokes out, "I as much as killed him. And after himself given me a job when I lost me leg. Now Lady Gwynn payen for the care of our *bairns* what come too early. Och, poor little twins, but I canna live with the guilt."

"I'm sorry, Robbie, I'm not following this. What exactly did you do?"

He swallows hard. "I poisoned your Artie, Dr. Bruce. That were me what sneaked them poison berries in the jam. I were eaten with envy when the laird gave Aidan Hunter my promotion an let him live in the main castle. Me in the servant's quarters with no leg, thinken I could never make a *bairn* because of that prat. I didna know my laird would fall so ill, nor have to fight Mort, now did I? I canna live with this eaten me." He claws the front of his shirt.

My thoughts go to his wife and twins. I wait for the man to stop wailing before saying, "Robbie, give me time, but tell no one what you admitted, you hear?" We struggle to our feet and ride the elevator to the lobby in silence. The doors open to chaos. As I hurry off the lift, I see an uprooted Blackberry Bramble propped against the far wall. Hurriedly, Robbie plucks a handwritten note from one of the bushy branches.

DR. BRUCE YOU DARED DEFY THE TRUE CHURCH OF GOD'S RETURN SURRENDER OR PERISH

Moving closer, I realize the Bramble's roots reek of poison. I slither to the floor.

In an ebony underworld, Igraine meets me with a maniacal grin.

I yell, "What part did you play with this Aidan Hunter fiasco?"

Igraine's tattered cloak bellows as her anger meets mine. "I deployed Aidan to destroy the tainted blood on the Stewart family tree." She hoots like a demented night owl. "The General's line be near dead. And Aidan will get you yet."

"For revenge on the Laird General you dragged your own children, Morgan and Artie and your grandson, Mort, through hades. What about Lady Elaine's and Gavin's deaths by Mort's hand? They were from your Sinclair bloodline."

"Collateral damage." I can smell Igraine's rotting breath as she chides, "You never did appreciate evil sport."

I surge forward calling on the Old Unoriginated One to send this wicked entity to her rightful abode. Celestial music resounds along with a brilliant light I can barely abide. A melodious glow intensifies and fills the murky cavern.

Igraine backs away. "Stop this you old conjurer. Leave me to reign in peace."

"Peace is not your forte, Igraine." I watch my words reverberate through the rarified air. "You chose evil. Go be with your own kind." Before me, Igraine's remains dissolve. Only the resonating radiance of the cosmos rings true and clear.

With a whoosh I'm back on the physical plane. "Let her rest a bit," Robbie urges.

"No," I say, "Igraine is vanquished, I'll be fine." Robbie frowns, but you and I know I'm more than fine.

Camelon's Old Law Council

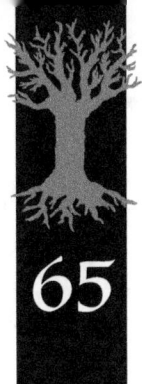

65

lected to preside over Robert Rose's case, I sit at our laird's big mahogany desk with Raven at my feet. The council members present consist of Morgan and Galahad. Gwynn, with St. Clair's obligations, appears on a computer screen. Facing us, Robbie and Jamie sit next to Priscilla and Bridget cradling the wee twins.

I begin recording the preceedings. Since we couldn't locate a gavel, I hammer Pris's meat tenderizer on a stump. "Let the Old Law Council that has met since ancient times begin. I issue the charge of weakening our laird, Rex Arthur Stewart through poisoning. Robert, how do you plead?"

Robbie stands and looks at me with resignation. "Entirely guilty." Bridget gasps.

I nod and say, "DCI Armstrong generously provided a video of Laird R.A. Stewart's last battle as evidence." I replay Artie and Mort's sword fight all the way to Mort rushing forward followed by his death cry and R.A.'s agony. I stop the video there. Robbie Rose widens his stance to remain upright.

I announce we'll hear from the members of the council beginning with Morgan Sinclair-Stewart, the laird's half-sister. With a determined look, Morgan speaks. "I guessed Robert Rose added those poison berries to the jam. I believe he should be punished to the full extent of Scottish law." A low murmur rises from the Roses.

I turn to Galahad who clears his throat. "It's my belief that Robert Rose knew the severe weakening of his laird through poisoning was wrong in God's eyes. I find him guilty and recommend he be turned over to the authorities."

"Oh Lord," Bridget gasps. Pris pulls her daughter-in-law's hand to her heart with a look that conveys a plead for leniency.

"Robert Rose, we've heard from two of the committee members and received guilty votes." The accused looks almost relieved until Bridget begins to weep. "I now give Lady Gwynn MacLaren-Stewart, the laird's wife the floor."

Robbie turns to the computer screen and Gwynn stares at the man that poisoned her husband. "I believe we can agree R.A. chose to stay in the battle although he was weakened. However, I feel the blame for spurring this tragedy on falls heavily on Mort who took the coward's way out with suicide. Because of that, I see no sense in tearing another family apart by incarcerating Robert. I say he's not guilty on the grounds of temporary insanity and suggest he work off his debt."

All eyes are on me as I pause then say, "Since I was elected head of this council, I not only have the final vote, but the final say in this matter. Before I give my verdict, I'd like to hear from the accused. What say you, Robert Rose?"

He looks at his feet then back to me. "Madame, I never intended to kill my laird who I loved and always will. I'd say I'm sorry, but them words won't undo anythung."

"Does anyone else wish to speak?"

"I do," booms out behind me as Aidan Hunter steps from behind the wall tapestry. He pushes my chair forward pinning me to the desk. Still standing, Robbie bellows, "Leave her, you have no business with this clan."

"I am a member through Morgan le Fey who carries my child. My blood."

Galahad calmly asks, "What do you need, Aidan?"

"I'll be needen Dr. Bruce ta pay for insulten the True Church of God's Return."

"Pay? How?" I croak.

The pregnant Morgan struggles to her feet. "Haven't you hurt this family enough? You poison our trees in an attempt to take over Logres and Camelon. And that's not to mention imprisoning me and Dr. Bruce, who you now intend to do what?"

Aidan wraps his massive hands around my neck. As he tightens his grip, a snarling Raven dashes from under the desk and clamps vice-like jaws on Aidan's leg. "Oof, get your mongrel off." Evidently taking offence to the pedigree slur, my terrier holds fast.

At an advantage, I swing my interlaced fists overhead delivering a smashing blow to Aidan's nose feeling bone and cartilage collapse. He cries out releasing his grip. Galahad dashes in from the left, Robbie scoots over the desk and Jamie takes up the right flank. Together they knock Aidan to the floor with a mighty thud. And me wanting to whoop my nemesis worse than anything.

Bridget shifts baby Bonnie to Priscilla, tugs the strap off her diaper bag and throws it to Jamie. The tenacious Raven releases her mouthful as Jamie ties the culprit's wrists, yanks a bellpull rope off the wall then trusses Aidan up like a carcass ready for the spit.

DCI Armstrong with a couple of his men slam through the French doors. "Sorry Dr. Merle, we were in the shrubbery securing Hunter's armed forces." Aidan struggles. "Not that you seem to be needing our assistance."

"Release the God of All," Aidan rants.

"Would you be admitting everything?" Ian inquires. "It's just that any deal to be had is being offered your followers outside."

"Lock me up. My son will save us from the false religions."

"We'll see about that," Morgan shouts as Armstrong's agents take over.

"Sir," Robbie Rose interjects, "could you be moven this garbage out? We have a council meeting ta finish."

They haul Aidan out while my extended family regain their seats. I take a drink of water and massage my neck. "Well now, that took care of a wee piece of business. Shall we proceed with ours? Does anyone want to add anything?"

Bridget stands. "I plead mercy for my husband and father of these *bairns*." She reaches over to Bonnie and Ronnie who slept through the entire fracas. "I promise himself will serve you right."

"He will at that," Jamie snickers. "We've strong women in our clan."

"That's enough, Jamie." To keep from smiling, I clear my throat. "Robert Rose and all assembled, we've received two guilty votes." Pris sends me a cut-your-heart-out-look. "And one not-guilty vote." Robbie rubs his sweaty palms on his trousers. "It's my belief that to be rid of evil, our beloved laird was willing to forfeit himself. Just as he did in everything, he sacrificed for the family he loves." I make a sweeping motion that includes the Rose clan. "How can we now, in all faith and love for our laird tear that apart? I decree that Robert pay his debt to his laird through dedicated service."

You can imagine the elation.

†IVY (Ḣedera helix) GORṪ†

September 30–October 27

It's fitting we've spiraled back to the month of Ivy, which to my mind is the most spiritual of all plants. Since being 'called' to Scotland, I've felt led in an Ivy-like fashion coiling in and around forming a Celtic knot so complex I've not always been certain of my path. Fortunately, the month of Ivy imbues motivation and survival instincts that permeate a body with earthly, as well as divine energy needed to face life's challenges. And I must say, there are times I get tangled in Ivy's tendrils spinning from the outer to the inner realms. Nonetheless I'm confident that by trusting Spirit to guide my winding route, I'm sure to eventually reach the highest of heavenly planes.

The Beginning 66

Galahad drives through one of those misty iridescent October bronze-scapes. We're taking DCI Armstrong to St. Clair's infirmary where my Celtic tree trials continue. Ian turns to me in the backseat. "Congratulations on being knighted, Dame Merle. The Crown recognized not only your service, but that you've captured Great Britain's heart. I personally want to thank you for your investigative perception."

"I knew I'd get you to thank me for being a nosey old dame."

"You wouldn't be taking my words out of context? I expect better from an honorary Scotland Yard detective." We laugh and he turns back to Galahad.

Raven snuggles up. I stroke her head then allow my eyes to close. Of course, I can't help but hear Had ask, "Are you close to an Aidan Hunter conviction? I fear he'll be sent to a high security psychiatric unit for diminished responsibility. He does believe Morgan's baby is the living son of God."

Okay, Morgan Le Fey newsflash: After giving birth to Caledonia Arthur, Morgan and her infamous baby made the tabloid pages promoting her what looked like matching silver space suits. Although her line of baby apparel has made it no further than the diaper pail, I do trust Morgan will somehow rise above the stink with her tell-all book.

My thoughts return to Armstrong. "We have Mr. Hunter on tape confessing to abduction, beheading and poisoning, yet the man claims he'll be acquitted." Ian seems to be responding from a far-off place.

Falling into meditation I don't descend, but ascend this time—my soul rising up and up to the top of the Tree of Life.

The Golden Boughs dim in comparison to the radiant alabaster throne and the Old Unoriginated One's brilliant face. "You look upon the Light without difficulty," the Old One says.

"It certainly beats the Underworld."

The ancient smiles. "That piece of your destiny is complete. The departed Igraine shall remain in her realm." The Old One leans forward. "You deserve a boon after fulfilling that onus duty."

I gaze into holy eyes. "May I stay with you?"

"Not yet." I feel a hand on my head. "You must return to reap your reward." A flood of bright energy flows around and through me with a surge of renewal.

I start to thank the Old Unoriginated One, but I'm spinning back into Had's car on terra firma. Shifting to the physical plane proves difficult, but I must accept Spirit's will. As I slowly open my eyes, gratitude and adoration for the Divine permeates my every cell. Knowing there's a job at hand, I rub my face briskly. Galahad pulls up near the convent's back door. I hand Raven to Armstrong and we dash inside.

Sister Bernadette wheels toward us. Having blossomed after alerting us to the Sister Merry Fey masquerade, the nun is now my Celtic trial administrator. However, she brushes off the praise Gwynn and I heap on her—any hint of pride shunned like the wrong end of a skunk around here. Sister B. puts a finger to her lips before allowing us in the infirmary. "Lady Gwynn has begun the meditation session."

No longer a quirky teenager, Gwynn is one of St. Clair's white-robed inhabitants standing in front of patients in wheelchairs and loungers. Raven wiggles free seeing her chance to greet the meditators. My granddaughter nods our way and continues, "Our story began in ancient times when Golden Bowl meditation was transmitted to humankind. Over the centuries fewer people followed this practice. Fortunately, select Masters remained adept in Golden Bowl meditation—the true Holy Grail."

A young monk asks, "What do you mean, the true Holy Grail?

Galahad steps in front of the group. "We've all heard of the physical Holy Grail reportedly brought north by Joseph of Arimathea. Along with it, he carried the secret philosophy of Golden Bowl meditation. This teaching imparts the method to activate one's Golden Bowl—the mystical Holy Grail—to ultimately connect with the Divine."

"Sounds arduous," the monk complains.

"The path is narrow and few will follow, to paraphrase Matthew 7:14," Galahad intones. "However, with meditation we have a better chance of rising to higher levels. As you know, our own Father Joseph passed the Golden Bowl teachings to my mum, Lady Elaine. She was unable to share it with us, so Father Joseph passed the mastership to me asking my gran, initiated into Golden Bowl meditation decades ago, to assist me. We are fortunate to have Dr. Merle as spiritual leader, as well as healer."

That's my Galahad, humble as ever.

"You may close your eyes," Had continues. "Focus your attention on the center of your forehead. Begin repeating your silent chant. Gently bring the concentration back when it strays. You may, or may not, experience a ringing illumination filling your cranium, your skull. A radiance in that area means you have activated your Golden Bowl, your Holy Grail. Don't try to force it, eventually you will see the light."

Raven's doggie sensors tell her we're on the move as Gwynn walks our way. I scoop up the pooch and usher Gwynn and Armstrong through the infirmary past rows of hospital beds. At the very back we enter a private room. My patient, the top of his head still bandaged, sits propped against pillows. I hand Raven over. "We brought you a visitor and I don't mean this bundle of trouble." Raven licks his face then flops over.

Armstrong steps up to the bed. "How are you?"

Rex Arthur speaks slowly and deliberately, but enunciates each word. "They tell me I'm not the man I was."

"I would expect not," Armstrong says. "On the other hand, it seems Dame Merle's restorative has kept you above ground."

The men laugh, but Gwynn tears up. "Grandma Merle's Celtic tree formula saved R.A. when the surgeons gave up."

Embarrassed by the show of emotion, Armstrong clears his throat. "R.A., are you up to discussing the Robert Rose case?"

"Yes, poor dear Robbie." Artie says. "But our ruse worked."

"It did," Ian agrees. "Sequestering you here at St. Clair's, burying an empty urn and allowing the press to speculate your demise was a brilliant move."

"But, I did remain near death...could have ended in that urn."

I pat his arm. "Even during that mock funeral, it was touch and go."

"Until we increased the Celtic tree dosage," Gwynn adds.

"I wasn't sure the mock death," Ian says, "would lead to a confession."

"It's just that Aidan and Mort admitted to everything but poisoning R.A.," Gwynn explains. "We figured someone else at Camelon poisoned the jam."

"I hope Robbie has forgiven us," I say. "The guy nearly lost his mind thinking he'd led to Artie's death. It was tough watching him and the Rose clan mourning."

R.A. nods. "Their visit convinced them I was alive. And now we're sure our Camelon family is safe.

Ian steps closer. "You're satisfied with the terms laid out by your Old Law Council? You want no police involvement?"

"Nana, Gwynn and I thought it best not to . . . press charges," Artie says.

"That is if you agree with our ancient laws, Chief," Gwynn adds.

Armstrong chuckles at Gwynn's use of that nickname. "You did the right thing, however unorthodox. Robert Rose is diligently working off his debt. But when are you going to resurface, R.A.? The public still thinks you're dead."

My patient pulls a serious face. "Not sure. The walking is coming along. But this brain injury, there is so much to relearn."

Gwynn smiles. "We're working on that together."

I put a finger to Artie's pulse. "How are your studies coming?"

He sighs. "It's confusing, Nana. Time is a difficult notion . . . the movement of the earth around the sun and all that. But what is time out in space where there is no day or night?"

I shake my head. "That's debatable. I'm of the school that time is an illusion . . . until the morning alarm goes off. How about not concerning yourself with the hard questions for a while? As long as you sleep at night and awake with the dawning light your brain is functioning normally." I shine a penlight in each eye. "You're doing fine."

"Good. Now if I could grasp money."

We all laugh, and Armstrong muses, "Money is a difficult concept, especially if you don't have much."

"But everyone needs money," Artie insists. He reaches over and takes Gwynn's hand. "Babies are expensive."

Gwynn gasps. "R.A., we agreed not to tell just yet."

"Did I tell?"

Armstrong laughs. "Cats out of the bag, old man."

Gwynn lays a hand on her tummy. "We're only two and a half months along." Raven cocks her head sideways. "You smart girl. Raven knows doesn't she, Grandma?"

"I wouldn't doubt it. But Gwynn, two and a half months ago . . . "

"Yes." Gwynn blushes. "Our baby was conceived when we . . . reunited at Camelon."

R.A. pats Gwynn's belly. "To think we made a baby is . . . is incredible."

Filled with pride and elation, I gaze at Gwynn and Artie. Speaking to the Old Unoriginated One up in heaven's Golden Boughs dazed me more than a wee bit. I couldn't imagine a bonus over and above ending the poisoned roots and watching the Celtic tree formula restore Artie. But now I realize my holy reward is the continuation of my family tree. Igraine's revenge could have ended my clan, but as Divine providence would have it, it's just the beginning.

Acknowledgements

My thanks go to those who helped make this book possible.

Love and thanks to my family—sister Sheryl my unfailing cheerleader, daughter Annette for her confidence and superb formatting, daughter Leah for her years of assurance. For brother, sis-in-law, aunts, nieces, nephews, the greats and all the rest of the family that applauded my efforts—even those that spurred me on by questioning if I would indeed complete the task.

Massive love and gratitude to the greatest of friends, author Cory La Bianca, tireless manuscript assessor and superb copy editor. My other greatest friend, author and artist Elena Willets whose support and de-wrinkling app saved the day on my bookcover watercolor painting. And my longest-known greatest friend editor Cindy Taylor, for her no-bars-held critique that helped tighten and polish *Golden Boughs and Poisoned Roots*.

Huge appreciation to friend and author Sandi Ault who taught me the rudimentary methods of writing fiction and assured me from the start that I could write.

Enormous thanks to the Fall River Writers critique group for their constant wise counsel, inspiration and encouragement—Cory La Bianca, Gary Miller, Steve Mitchell, Karin Edwards, Anna Oberg, Vic Anderson, Julie Harvey, Hiedi Tryon, Nina Kunze, Lisa Hutchins, Wendye Sykes, Lin Smith, Brian Mack, Sandy Ewing, Dennis Brown and those passing through.

Vast appreciation for Robin Shukle and Liz Mrofka at What If? Publishing, in Loveland Colorado, for their expertise, warmth and patience with, what I call my MS brain.

Profoundly and most of all, gratitude to my husband Rick, for his unending love, great humor, support and belief in any project I endeavor, not to mention the best vegan chef one could envision.

About the Author

Sandra Patterson-Slaydon was destined to write *Golden Boughs & Poisoned Roots*.

The characters and story line—loosely derived from the Arthurian epic tale—were fostered out of her love of all themes Scottish, Irish and Celtic. Firmly rooted in her life experiences, including teaching English Composition at Colorado State University, owning a Celtic shop in Estes Park Colorado, combined with degrees in physiology, philosophy and natural medicine, *Golden Boughs and Poisoned Roots* is the melody of her heart.

The cover of *Golden Boughs & Poisoned Roots* is Sandra's latest work. At a young age, Sandra painted for Hallmark Cards in Kansas City then put herself through university as an illustrator and drafter for engineering companies. She has shown her watercolors in galleries in New York City, across the US and abroad.

After decades living in various cities, Sandra, with husband Rick, returned to her Kansas hometown to be near family.

Discussion Questions for *Golden Boughs & Poisoned Roots*:

1. Were you acquainted enough with the 'King Arthur' story to recognize that this novel loosely follows that saga's plot? Did being less familiar alter your enjoyment of the book?

2. How was a portrait of contemporary Scotland revealed through traditions, beliefs, language or food?

3. In what way were you entertained, educated or inspired?

4. Share a quote that was profound, amusing, illuminating or disturbing to you.

5. Did the author do a good job creating distinct and complex characters?

6. Were you left with unanswered questions? If the author were here, what would you ask her?

7. Did the novel have a satisfying ending? Were there implications for the character's future?

8. Did the various nemesis have redeeming traits or were they totally evil?

9. What did you think of Merle's bond with her late husband, Angus MacLaren?

10. What events portrayed Merle's greatest sorrows and joys? Did they surprise or touch you?

11. How great a role did guiding Gwynn and Had's development help in Merle's own growth?

Author's Note

Spinning the *Golden Boughs & Poisoned Roots* saga brought me hours (okay years) of pleasure and insight into an ancestral people and culture with which I share blood. Throughout my research into Celtic history, it became apparent how elusive the lore and philosophy that shape this ancient civilization varied over the ages. Unexpectedly, I discovered the Celtic calendar's monthly dates and even the plants and trees attributed to each, differed from text to text and country to country. Fortunately, my muse chose the calendar and plants that best entwined the story's Arthurian cast and plot. Since this is a completely authentic work of fiction, I want my readers to note that Golden Bowl meditation is NOT a lost ancient practice, but a blend of meditative disciplines for the purpose of this novel. I beg that you bear with any mistakes caused by what I call, my MS Brain, disability and the many artistic liberties I took to bring this novel to life.

Note to Reader

I do hope you enjoyed *Golden Boughs & Poisoned Roots*.
It would benefit and honor me greatly if you would leave a review
of this novel on Amazon.com or your chosen platform.